By C. E. Murphy

The Queen's Bastard
The Pretender's Crown

THE WALKER PAPERS
Urban Shaman
Thunderbird Falls
Coyote Dreams

THE NEGOTIATOR TRILOGY
Heart of Stone
House of Cards

WITH MERCEDES LACKEY AND TANITH LEE
Winter Moon

The Queen's Bastard

The Queen's Bastard

C. E. MURPHY

BALLANTINE BOOKS • NEW YORK

The Queen's Bastard is a work of fiction. Names, characters, places, and incidents are the products of the author's imagination or are used fictitiously. Any resemblance to actual events, locales, or persons, living or dead, is entirely coincidental.

A Del Rey Books Trade Paperback Original

Published in the United States by Del Rey Books, an imprint of The Random House Publishing Group, a division of Random House, Inc., New York.

DEL REY is a registered trademark and the Del Rey colophon is a trademark of Random House, Inc.

LIBRARY OF CONGRESS CATALOGING-IN-PUBLICATION DATA
Murphy, C. E. (Catie E.)
    The queen's bastard / C. E. Murphy.
        p. cm.
    "A Del Rey Books trade paperback original"—T.p. verso.
    ISBN-13: 978-0-345-49464-1 (pbk.)
    1. Illegitimate children—Fiction.   2. Kings and rulers—
Fiction.   3. Magic—Fiction.   3. Imaginary places—
Fiction.   I. Title.
    PS3613.U726Q84 2008
    813'.6—dc22   2007043848

Printed in the United States of America

www.delreybooks.com

9 8 7 6 5

Book design by Mary A. Wirth

The Queen's Bastard is for the Rocky Mountain Fiction Writers.

The RMFW and their fantastic Colorado Gold writers' conference provided me with the impetus I needed to pursue my dream of publication. I literally wouldn't be where I am today without the RMFW, and I can't thank you all enough.

The Queen's Bastard

Prologue

SANDALIA DE PHILIP DE COSTA
12 OCTOBER 1561 † *Lanyarch, north of Aulun*

She wears a sheepskin against the wind that shrieks around cathedral walls. The skin is soft and smells surprisingly good, and its creamy warmth seems a more fitting nod to wedding colours than the tartan blues and yellowed whites that the man at her side wears. Her gown beneath the sheepskin is sturdy, not fashionable; it has been made for travel. Indeed, she's come from the ship to the carriage and thence to this lonely, wind-whipped cathedral with no time to arrange herself as suits her station. She was told it would be thus, and if she feels disappointment, she's put it away in the name of duty.

Her hair is still damp and tangled from the wind that beats grey stone into submission and whips grey clouds into hungry, gaping scars across the sky. Rain clatters against stained glass until Mary, Mother of Christ, weeps with it. No shard of sunlight streams through to bring joy to her tears. It's said that rain on a wedding day is good luck, though that seems contrived; certainly no one claims sunshine is ill luck.

Voices murmur beneath the violent rain, echoing within bleak stone walls. They're critical, sympathetic, disdainful, sorrowful, curious, and above all without respect.

It is not done to whisper and comment during the marriage of one royal to another. After, yes, and before most certainly, but as a priest's sonorous tones ring through the dismal cathedral there should be silence. Respect. Awe. Even when the wedding is done in haste, and with none of the pomp that might be expected, it should be an occasion for solemnity, not gossip. In time, those who chatter and mock will come to regret their loose tongues, for it will be made clear to them why their lands are forfeit; why their children are made involuntary guests; why a handful of heads roll and feet kick in the depths of serene dark forests.

But that is in time, and not a thought to be entertained on a wedding day.

Sandalia, aged fourteen years, sister to the prince of Essandia and soon to be queen of oppressed Lanyarch, lifts a warm brown gaze to the bishop who bestows her husband's name upon her, and smiles.

They're done together, the marriage and the crowning. Rough Lanyarchan rubes clamour to make oaths to the aging king and his fresh bride. He's old, too old, for a girl of her age, though he isn't yet feeble. What he *is*, is too wedded to his faith. He's taken no wife until Sandalia, and that's done only under pressure from Rodrigo, Essandia's ruling prince and Sandalia's brother. Aulun, the sister country to Lanyarch's south, chokes under the Reformation Church's hold, and Ecumenic Lanyarch suffers for it. Should Charles, last of the house of Stewart, pass without an heir, there will be no stopping the Red Bitch in Aulun from sweeping over Lanyarch and bending it to her rule.

Rodrigo, as in love with his faith as Charles but far more pragmatic, will not allow that to happen. Sandalia remembers his apology as they stood on an Essandian dock, in the moments before she climbed aboard a tall ship to sail north and meet her fate. In memory, he takes her hands in his, studying her with sad eyes. Rodrigo is twice her age, handsome and fit in the prime of his life, and he doesn't like sending a young sister away as a piece on a playing field. He murmurs words of sorrow, words that hang in Sandalia's mind even now, for all that she's tried to forget them. She is a princess of Essandia, and did not, does not, will not, need the prince's apologies: she is young, but she knows her duty, and would do anything for her brother besides.

So now, with the weight of a queen's crown on her head, she turns from the man who crowned her and holds the hand of the one she's wed, and speaks in a clear strong voice and in a language that is not her own. People will admire her mastery of the Aulunian tongue now, and later say her speech held wisdom and charm beyond her years.

"I stand before you now a queen, and beside my husband as protector of our faith. Lanyarch is like my child to me, and I will not see it fall beneath Reformation rule. I will be mother to this brave northern country and mother to its heir, standing beside my lord until God finds it fit to help us all shake off the law that has been so cruelly brought down upon us. I have received the blessing of our beloved church, but now I beg of you to share your own blessings of hearth and home with me. I come from a warm country far to the south. Let me now know the warmth that is Lanyarch!"

All the voices that had babbled in contempt now rise in a furor, raw welcoming cheers and stamping feet, tartaned men sending ear-shattering whistles to drive back the sound of rain. They swear fealty, one after the other, while Charles stands at Sandalia's side, distant and polite. He doesn't see the masses before him; his gaze is cast to the glorious stained glass windows that tell of Christ's suffering. He thinks not of his country's future, but of his own part in the King of Heaven's tale.

Sandalia, her absent king at her side, rides the breadth and width of Lanyarch all through the winter, chapping her fine skin and accepting dark bread and ale as her nightly meals. She sleeps before the fire in common rooms and learns, poorly, to weave a tartan, but most of all she learns the laughter of the crude Lanyarchan people, and learns to share it.

In the springtime she retreats to the capital city of Agned, insisting she can hardly be expected to bear an heir when she and Charles spend their nights crowded into common rooms with little time to themselves. The people whistle and roar and share ribald winks, all of them more than half in love with the dusky princess from the south, and grant her privacy to tend to the serious business of making a child.

Fifteen months from their wedding date, Charles's story ends in a phlegm-filled fit of coughing, leaving his wife without the rounded belly she's promised her people. Rumour whispers Charles has gone to the grave as godly and pure as he came from the womb, no woman ever breached by his sword.

Sandalia, queen of Lanyarch, belovéd to her people and no longer protected by a husband whose claim to the throne is incontestable, gathers her skirts and flees her adopted northern land with the threat of the Titian Bitch at her back.

SANDALIA, QUEEN OF LANYARCH
17 October 1563 † *Gallin, northeast of Essandia*

She wears a sheepskin, not against biting wind, but to remind her deserted country that she has not forgotten it. The skin doesn't suit a silver-shot gown encrusted with pearls, nor the mildness of the Gallic day; the sky lies against the horizon as pale and calm as it does directly overhead, autumn's sunshine enough to make the day bright and delightful without blinding the youthful Lanyarchan queen.

She wears a sheepskin to remind the gathered throngs who call her name as she rides through Lutetian streets in a carriage behind six matched white horses that she does not come to their king merely a princess, but as a queen in her own right. A queen in exile, to be sure, but a queen loved by her people, and a queen whose faith supports her. She has forgone a crown; such an obvious symbol of power speaks of desperation, a crassness in announcing who she is. Sandalia needs not stoop so low.

But she wears the sheepskin, and no one who sees her on her wedding day will forget it.

She rides alone that day, and when the carriage stops before the cathedral entrance, it is her brother who steps forward to offer his hand. Rodrigo, who sent her north to Lanyarch as winter came on, and who made her a queen by doing so. He had not been there to see her crowned that day, and the softness in his eyes offered apology for that now, two years later, as she goes to make another match in the name of duty.

"A new fashion?" he murmurs as she steps down from the carriage. "Will you set Lutetia on its ear and have them wearing sheepskins before winter has set in?"

Sandalia's laughter, easy and bright, rolls through the autumn air and reaches the cathedral ahead of her. Behind her and to all sides, voices soar in approval of the young queen's mirth. It is a good sign, the people agree, that Sandalia goes happy to their king. That she's a princess of Essandia and not one of their own Gallic-born high ladies is forgiven today, on her wedding day, in face of her delight. Laughter is an omen of the things to come, and the people will forgive her anything for her joy.

"No," she answers beneath the roar, but smiles as she says it. "Though now that you've put the idea into my head, perhaps I'll make that my legacy. A new fashion for every season. I'll be even more frivolous than the Red Bitch."

Amusement quirks Rodrigo's mouth. "Be careful, Dalia. Such things legacies are made of."

Sandalia tosses her hair and laughs again. "I'm only a woman, dear brother. No one expects my legacy to be anything greater than sturdy heirs and fashionable clothes."

"So long as you provide the one, I can accept the other." Steel slips into Rodrigo's voice and Sandalia casts a coquettish glance at him.

"Do you doubt me in the bedroom, Rodrigo? Charles was old. Louis is not. There will be an heir." The same steel, as well-tempered if lighter in tang, comes into her own voice. "My son will be born within a year."

"May God's blessings be on you all." Rodrigo releases her at the doors, and she walks the aisle alone to face the man who will be her new husband.

He is slender and aesthete, blond hair loose in a manner that dictates fashion because of his rank, not his sense of style. That he dresses beautifully is through no deliberation of his own, heavy collar and broad padded shoulders lending him a gravitas that the youthful bloom of his cheeks doesn't support. He plucks at the collar discontentedly, actions of a man too unfamiliar with fashion to have it made to suit him, rather than the other way around.

Still, he makes a finer picture beside Sandalia than Charles had, the blue of his gaze sharp and strong. It is only Sandalia, standing at his side, who sees in her new prince what she also saw in the old: that the light in his eyes comes to life as he gazes piously on the windows depicting the lives and deeds of saints and disciples.

God save her, she cannot help but think, even as she speaks her vows. God save her from men whom God had saved. Is she to be damned by their presence all her life, wedded to those whose souls were already bound to a higher being? Even Rodrigo, now in his early thirties, seems too fond of God and not enough of flesh, though he, at least, dances in careful negotiations with the Aulunian queen, whose years are still tender enough to bear children, should she finally bow to a marriage bed. That's the hand Rodrigo wants, not for love, but for the Church: with an

Ecumenic king the heretical country might yet be brought back into the fold. If wedding Lorraine is the price, it is one Rodrigo is willing to pay.

Louis at least comes to the bridal chamber, more than Charles ever did.

When it was clear Charles would not come to bed, Sandalia told him through gritted teeth that there would be an heir to Lanyarch if it took her dying breath to make it so. He gazed at her without apparent comprehension, and agreed that there must be a child. Sandalia, innocent, betrayed, furious, turned her eyes from the king in search of a man who could be used and discarded.

She found better in the guise of a hazel-eyed man who wore the collar of a priest. He remained apart from her court, alluring for his remoteness. She warmed to him, seeing in his sharp features and collar a creature that could be used and kept: for all her faith in the Church, she had equal faith that it desired power on the throne, or behind it. Better by far to own a priest than be owned by one. He had long hands, beautifully shaped and soft, and the virgin queen ached with unfamiliar desire at the thought of his touch.

She was trembling on her hands and knees, his soft hands stroking and exploring her sex, when word came that Charles was dead.

And then she was a virgin no more, her priest's urgent weight behind her, pinning her with a desperation to couple that they both understood. For the rest of her life colour came to her cheeks when she thought of that night; of that week; of the hope to catch soon enough to call the child a king's. But her blood came, and with it the last chance of pretending a pregnancy that was her husband's. Sandalia fled Lanyarch, a failure as a woman and a queen, her priest and confessor and no-more lover at her side. She resigned herself to a convent with the memory of a few days' passion to warm her for the rest of her days, until Rodrigo came to her and spoke quietly of the young Gallic prince and his need for a wife.

Enough time had passed that it was clear there would be no Lanyarchan heir, save through Sandalia's claim to that throne. The Church declared her fit to be taken as Louis's bride, and when he makes a feeble, uncertain pass at her breast in the bedchambers, exasperation floods her and she unlaces his breeches and climbs atop him, more determined to be successfully bred than caring for decorum. She will not look to her priest in the days and weeks to come, though he remains at her side. Louis approves; it is well that Sandalia shows such faith, and her piousness makes him more eager to share a bed with her. They will make a godly child, he promises her, and she sets her teeth and keeps her gaze from her hazel-eyed priest.

Ten months later, his young wife pale with the first weeks of pregnancy, Louis rides east to lead a border skirmish against encroaching Reinnish troops, an ongoing dispute that goes back before Sandalia's memories.

A harried, misery-pelted courier rides back six weeks after that, just a few days ahead of the sledge that carries young Louis's body home to his devastated country.

Sandalia closes herself away when the cramping and bleeding begins, claiming shock and horror that no one doubts. She will see only her priest, whose soft hands she has not again allowed to touch her. The people whisper she commends Louis's soul to heaven so often she has no other words left to speak.

Behind locked doors, she claws her fingers in her man's throat and demands, raw-voiced and full of rage, that a child be found to replace the one her body rejects. It is too well known how far along she is, too long a recovery from a child lost to a new one made, to risk her priest's long slim body again. If she has regrets they are buried beneath the fury of orders given: a child must be found; a boy, born six months hence. Kill its parents, she says, and because the priest is no fool, he will vanish the same night he brings the child to her. She has given orders for his death; she trusts that his disappearance and that death are one and the same.

At seventeen, widowed twice, exiled queen of one country, young regent to a second, princess to a third, Sandalia de Costa will have her heir.

At any cost, she will have her heir.

1

BELINDA PRIMROSE
15 March 1565 † *Brittany, north of Gallin*

"It cannot be found out."

She knew the words as if they'd come down to her through the blood, in the first moments of awareness. There was darkness, red-tinged and warm, a battlefield of sound filling it: explosions and grumbles that came so steadily they were comforting rather than cause for alarm. There were voices, both low, but one more distant than the other. The first voice, closer, tickled through her to the very centre of her being, becoming a part of her that could never be cut away. It was that voice that carried fear into her, intense and sharp: "It cannot be found out."

In the first moments of cold, with the air screaming all around her, she heard the voice again, high and distorted. She grasped with tiny fingers at a blurred, weary face that retreated before her wide, tearless gaze. She was pressed against a different warmth, scratchy and soft and scented. She would come to know the scent as chypre, and associate it with safety for the rest of her life. She was enclosed in strong arms, the world shifting perspective dizzily as she was taken from the first, the last, glimpse she would have of her mother for twelve years.

Behind her, from the breadth of a man's chest, the less familiar voice echoed the words that seemed to define her, even at mere minutes of age: "It cannot be found out."

Then he spoke again with more clarity, the certainty and strength of love colouring his words with richness: "I know. It will not be found out, my lady. Have faith. I'll return by dawn, and by the ninth bell you must be dressed for court. You must be seen well, or their hearts will fail. Attend her." The last words were spoken to someone else, somewhere else; a murmur of reply in a deep voice came, and then the woman spoke again:

"Yes. Go. Go, Robert. And be seen with a woman in the small hours of the morning." Weariness is left behind by command. "There are too many who see you dance attendance on us already. We demand they find nothing of import. We shall be furious with you when we learn of your dalliances. Now go!"

A single image, burned into a newly made memory: slender shoulders, a proud straight spine. Linens clutched over milk-heavy breasts and wrinkling over a still-swollen belly, contracting with afterbirth labors. Thin grey eyes, a high forehead, and a proud chin, lifted in expectation.

Titian hair worn loose, bloody curls against translucent skin.

Enormous hands enveloped Belinda's head, turning her away from her mother, into the warmth of her father's body.

BELINDA PRIMROSE
8 February 1577 † *Aulun, isolated by the sea*

Memory, from what others said, did not stretch so far back.

The dream came often, sharp enough to take her breath on waking, but no one remembered the moment of her birth, not with clarity; not at all. It was only a dream, nothing more. Belinda crawled from her bed, pulling a duvet, down-filled and heavy, with her: the keep fires were long since banked for the night, the comparative heat of the winter day left behind. Her first steps were warm, onto a tapestry rug that told the story of hunting a white deer. The next steps were icy, nimbly taken on tiptoe before she scrambled into the velvet-cushioned window seat. The duvet hissed across unheated stone as she hauled it up.

Frost spread across the windows, spiked fingers growing up from the lead lining between the sheets of thin, undistorted glass. Belinda pressed a fingertip against the thickening frost, melting through to the cold glass below. Water beaded and spilled over the lead, a glistening black line picked out by the half-moon's light. She put her finger in her mouth and pulled the duvet farther up, hunching and squirming her shoulders until the warm comforter slid between her back and the chilly stone wall. Her breath fogged on the window, mixing with scattered clouds to obscure the moon for a few moments before winter proved stronger than one girl-child's exhalations and clarity crept back over the middle of the pane.

Memories she trusted more than the dreams reached back to her second Yule. The pageantry of Yule, she was told, was less than the Christ Mass whose date and name had been set aside by the Reformation Church as it schismed from the Ecumenists. Still, call it Yule or Christ Mass, gifts were exchanged in the shortest day of the year, just as they had been for what seemed to Belinda to be uncountable centuries past.

The first remembered gift from her rarely seen, beloved papa: a tiny dagger, sharp for all that she was not yet two years of age. Had her nurse—a dour-faced, dull woman with a grim sense of propri- ety and little in the way of imagination—not been so shocked, so very determined to remove the toy from her determined grip, Belinda thought she might not remember it at all. As it was, she carried it even now: a soft length of string, clipped from a chemise, held it around her waist. The tiny dagger and its soft leather sheath made an impression against her spine when she leaned harder against the wall. By day it was tucked against skin, held tight by corsets and layers of fabric, inaccessible but reassuring. The blade had dulled with time, leaving it barely more dangerous than a butter knife. Yet, without it, Belinda felt naked. Vulnerable.

There were dancing shoes the next Yule. Now, more than nine years later, she still remembered the tangy flat taste of disappointment in the back of her throat, although she smiled and put the shoes on her toddler feet and danced with the tall, brown-eyed man called Lord Drake by the others, and Papa by herself. Standing on his feet, she learned the steps to the dances of the Old Measures: the Quadran Pavan and the Tinternell were her favourites, for the fun of saying their names more than the dances themselves. At her third birthday her nurse dressed her in the costume of a grown-up lady, rich cream that brought out highlights in her brown hair, and with farthingaled skirts that allowed her small size to manage the weight of the dress without stumbling. That night she danced each of the eight Old Measures with Lord Drake, solemn and determined to do her papa proud.

And the back of her mind repeated: *it cannot be found out.*

Those were the words Papa had whispered to her that morning, when he gave her the second blade of her short life. A rapier, he called it, weighted and sized for a child, but only young gentlemen learned fencing. "So," he told her, with the air of a conspirator, "we must be secret, and never let Nurse know. You have learned your dances with great patience," he teased, "and this is your reward, my girl. The grace learned on the dance floor stands anyone, man or girl, well in the art of fencing."

Belinda threw herself into her dance lessons with an enthusiasm entirely unexpected by the long-nosed man who tutored her.

By the time she was five she understood she was spoilt; within a year, she understood why. Her real father was dead in a war, and Rosemary, her mother, had lived only long enough to bear the child her husband had gotten on her before joining him in the next world. Robert, Lord Drake, was the only relative Belinda had, and

properly he was uncle, not papa. He called her Primrose, in remembrance of the sister who had died, and those who thought of
it at all admired his fortitude in taking on the child's well-being.
Drake was a favourite of Lorraine the queen, and her jealousies
would fain to include even a girl of Belinda's tender years.

Belinda listened hard, and understood the words not said: she
was a forgotten child, her birth parents of no particular import, her
adopted papa's nobility a gift from a fond queen. It was enough to
make a good marriage of, if she were charming and healthy
enough to bear strong children. Robert was easy with money, but
his visits were rare, and bittersweet. He had little time for her, and
so her drive to accomplish all the things he might expect of her
filled her hours, in hopes of making him proud.

That the things he expected were unusual for a girl-child passed
by Belinda without note; the only other children she knew were
the sons and daughters of the serving class, and they, of course,
would be expected to learn and do different things. So Belinda
learned reading and developed a fair hand at writing; studied history and politics, and when her nurse objected, the old woman
found herself left with a pension to see her to the end of her days
and no more girl-child to meddle with. Released from that stifling
watch, Belinda became adept at horseback riding and swordplay,
and learned to stay out of the way when Robert visited with other
nobles, understanding she would be called for when and if she
were necessary.

She never was.

Colour rushed along Belinda's jaw, crawling upward until her
cheekbones felt scarred from the heat. Her reflection, faint in the
frosty window, darkened perceptibly. She pressed her forehead
against the glass, listening hard for a hiss, like water striking hot
metal. Ice melted against her skin, silent, a bead trailing down between her closed eyes. It tickled, pushing the blush back down
with an itch. Belinda relaxed her jaw, keeping her eyes closed, de-

termined not to rub the tiny blot of water away. It slid down her nose, the itch subsiding, and she let out a puff of air. Frost steamed, melted, and crystallized again under her breath.

Clear memory was a curse, when the memories were of waiting for the call that never came. In summer of her ninth year it was Robert's honour—and burden—to host the queen's court for a month. The estate was in a flutter; Robert came early, barking orders and clapping his hands together, suddenly master to a house that had drifted along in quietude without him. He carried Belinda around on his shoulders, deliberately unaware that she was too old and too big for such behavior. Giddy with happiness, she was blind to exchanged glances among the servants. For a blissful week, she rode out every day with her papa, hunting and bringing back boar and deer to dress the tables with for the queen's visit. She pleaded, cautiously, for a new dress, and got two. The evening before Lorraine's arrival, Robert came to Belinda's room and knelt, taking her hands as he smiled at her.

"I will call for you, do you understand? When it's time for you to be presented to the queen, I'll come for you, my dear. Until then, it's best if you stay out of sight. Will you do that for me?"

Belinda, dressed in one of her new gowns, tightened her fingers around Robert's and nodded eagerly. "Of course, Papa. I can wait."

For thirty mornings, Belinda dressed with care, choosing one of her two new gowns or the very best of the older ones, and stood by the door, fidgeting and breathless with hope. At noon and night she ate the same rich meals that the courtiers in the dining hall below ate, but dined alone in her room, meals carried up from the kitchen by the servants, and waited with all the reserve she could muster. At sunfall each evening, she undressed as carefully as she'd dressed, and retreated to her bed, strands of coldness wrapped around her heart and tempered with hope for the next dawn.

At the end of thirty days, the queen and her court rode away again, Robert with them. Belinda knelt in the window of her room, fingers pressed against the thin glass.

Robert did not look back.

Belinda began, that morning, the game of stillness.

It was a game of nonexistence, of not being there. The rules, as Belinda laid them out in her mind, were simple: she would be stronger than the events around her. A biting fly might land on her skin; she would learn to ignore the tickle of its feet as it walked across her throat. If it bit, she would learn to hold inside the flinch of pain and the slap of motion to dislodge it. A scratch earned in a fencing bout would no longer pull a gasp or paling cheeks from her; a burn from the embers might raise a blister, but not a cry.

The rules were easier in thought than action.

In the beginning there were more failures than successes. Belinda taught herself to use the memory of Robert's shoulders in the soft gold sunlight of morning as a cloak, wrapping it around herself. She made it into armour, hardening the memory of being left behind into a layer of protectiveness between her skin and the invading entities.

The tiny dagger, held against the small of her back, began as an irritation, and became the test itself. Days turned into weeks, and the stiffened brocade of her dresses changed from pressing the hilt of the dagger uncomfortably into her spine to something she no longer noticed, and finally felt undressed without. She sharpened the little blade, and drew it carefully against her palm, waiting days for each last cut to heal, until she could part the skin without tears.

Then she began with fire.

When Robert returned at Yuletide, nothing could touch her unless she allowed it to. She had grown, taller and more slender, beginning to leave a child's shape behind even at the youthful age of nine. The cloak of memory grew with her, pinning tightly against her skin, constricting and safe. Robert's gaze upon her was sharp and appraising, even approving. She thought, in between moments, that he could see the wrap of memory that clung to her. Challenged, she strengthened it, lending it her indifference in the form of an uplifted chin and a cool hazel gaze.

Robert's smile grew warmer.

Once rooted in her bones, the game of stillness spilled out of her. The near-perfect memory that both blessed and dogged her wouldn't let her forget the moment when the stillness became larger than she was. She was dressed unfashionably, though the brown velvet was expensive enough to almost forgive the colour; Belinda didn't care. The depth of the fabric made her hair rich and soft-looking, especially against the gold net snood that kept loose curls from falling into her eyes. The dress was a Yuletide gift, warmer than the two summer gowns. Extra length was nipped into the hem, a seamstress's silent expectation that Belinda would grow taller still before spring. For now, she curled her fingers into the velvet's weight, lifting it a few inches to allow her feet clearance from the petticoats and skirts. She clung to the shadows along the manor stairs, following the curve down into the great hall. It was cold, the new year a few hours from ringing in. Belinda's boots, lined with rabbit fur, flashed beneath the hem of her gown as she trotted down the steps.

Voices echoed upward from below. Belinda hesitated between torches, recognizing Robert's voice and uncertain if she was welcome to greet his evening's company. Footsteps echoed off the stone floors, coming closer. Robert's voice dropped in confidence, words becoming murmurs that rumbled in the small bones of Belinda's ears. She stood frozen with indecision, then knotted her fingers in her skirts and scurried back up the stairs, ducking into a shadowed doorway.

The choice was well-made. Speech became more easily understood as Robert and his guest mounted the stairs. Belinda caught her breath, leaning into the doorway, pulse leaping in her throat as she willed herself not to be seen. Her dagger, like a reminder, pressed neatly against her spine. Belinda's breath spilled out of her again, on the verge of silent laughter. The next breath was slow, calmness washing through her. Tranquility stretched taut, like a pulled bow, then snapped. In silence, it surrounded her, tucking her safely into the shadows. Belinda lifted her chin brazenly, a smile pulling at the corners of her mouth. She leaned forward from the doorway, confident in the darkness and eager to see the man in whom Robert confided.

They came around the head of the stairs shoulder to shoulder, heads inclined toward one another. Robert was the broader, his shoulders dwarfing those of the other man, who was narrow and thin-featured. Black hair, thick and oily under the torchlight, was swept back from his face, worn much longer than fashion dictated. Whoever he was, he could not belong to Lorraine's court: Robert's brown hair, clipped short with a hint of fringe to hide the hairline itself, was the style favoured by the Queen for her courtiers. The stranger's beard followed the line of his jaw, mustache neatly trimmed around a thin mouth; that, at least, was the popular look. He had a hawkish nose and deep-set eyes, black in the torchlight. His voice, low-pitched, was marked with an accent: Khazarian, from the sprawling empire beyond Echon's eastern borders. "—begun. The imperatrix is with child—"

Rumbled amusement from Robert: "That was quickly done."

"As it had to be," the dark man replied. "With the imperator's wars, that Irina has even a chance of childbearing is—"

"A blessing to us all," Robert said, tone lofty and sanctimonious. The dark man let go a staccato laugh that cut through the stillness surrounding Belinda. Her heart lurched, one too-strong beat, though her body never dreamed of betraying her with a flinch. Robert turned his gaze away from his dark companion, meeting Belinda's eyes through the shadow. She read no leap of recognition there, no sign that he had seen her, though her pulse fluttered alarm in her throat. Within a moment his gaze left hers again. He extended a hand, gesturing the dark man to precede him as he pushed open the door to his private rooms. Light and heat swept out, the fire inside testimony to the servants' knowledge that Robert would entertain tonight, although Belinda herself had not known.

The dark man inclined his head, thanking Robert for the gesture. The door closed behind them, leaving the hall dark and cold. Belinda remained where she was a few seconds longer, arms folded around herself to ward off the chill. Then shadow released her and she caught up her skirts, scurrying downstairs to tend to her original task of asking that more wood be brought up for her fire.

The door to her room opened late that night, cool air from the halls sweeping Robert and his companion in. The latter hung at the door, a scent of cloves washing on the air with his entrance. Belinda, buried beneath her duvet, came awake, her eyes still closed, her breathing still deep and easy. Familiar words raised goose bumps over her body, even beneath the warmth of blankets: "It cannot be found out, Robert. Not yet. It's still too early."

"I know, Dmitri." Robert's voice was a comforting murmur at the side of her bed. He put a hand against her forehead, brushing tangled curls away. Belinda followed her impulse, stirring, sighing a little, and turned her head. Robert's voice warmed with a smile. "Sleep, child. Forget. The time has not yet come for you to know such things." The words were intoxicating, heavy with compulsion: Belinda, trusting impulse a second time, kept her learned stillness about her, not resisting. A surge, like the sound of water suddenly bursting through a waterwheel, pushed into her mind, and, like water again, spread through her, trickling down her spine and into her fingers and toes. She could almost see it, behind closed eyelids, faintly golden and glimmering: a concept just beyond her understanding.

Sleep comes hard on the heels of that near-understanding, exhaustion waving through her so quickly she doesn't hear the door close again. Doesn't hear, most certainly, Robert's sigh beyond that threshold, or Dmitri's short sound of dismay. "She's female. What did you expect? Power and ambition are built into the females."

"I expected more time." Robert exhales another sigh, then gestures down the hall. "Another cup of wine? She's young. Too young to show such talent."

"They mature quickly. Faster than we're accustomed to." Dmitri falls into step beside the Aulunian lord, neither raising his voice above a murmur. "And they die young. It may affect the development of their skills."

"Still, she's yet to see her tenth summer, and if I hadn't looked straight at her . . ."

"You'd have known. The air was charged with her hiding. Or have you become too inured to it already? Does power only quiver your skin when it's an unfamiliar taste?" A mocking smile curves Dmitri's mouth as he bows before the door to Robert's chambers, inviting the other man to enter before him. Robert's expression sours, but he goes ahead.

"Perhaps I'd have known. Still, it's sooner than we anticipated, and ambition in women is not well looked upon here. You know that as well as I."

"Can you control her?"

Robert gives the black-haired man a flat look as he pours wine, then sits before the hearth's glowing embers. "Neither of us would be here if we were incapable of controlling one child. Our queen chooses her standard-bearers more carefully than that. She'll remember nothing, nor have any urge to try again. She'll be the creature we need her to be, and never question me."

Humour plays upon Dmitri's lips a second time. "I meant no disrespect." That's a fob, intended to soothe waters without being believed. Robert accepts it for what it is, and half a beat later Dmitri says, "You're certain. You're certain of her loyalty? Why?"

Robert snorts. "Because they always are, Dmitri. Faithful to the queen. It's as much part of them as it is of us."

"But they don't normally show such promise so young," Dmitri murmurs. "Watch her, Robert. Be cautious."

"Heed your own advice. Return to Khazan. Watch Irina."

"Mm." Dmitri lowers his head over his glass of wine. "In time. Let Feodor crow over her pregnancy first. Irina wants me gone until they're well settled. There are things to be done in Essandia. Rodrigo needs a mistress. Even an illegitimate claimant for his throne is better than none. His sister's son is too far out of our control. I want a stronger hand there."

"And what of Seolfor?"

"Unchanged. Biding time. We have enough of it."

Robert nods, swirling wine without slopping it. "Well enough, then. Keep me apprised of Essandia, and get back to Khazan when you can. If you're successful with Rodrigo, I'll call Seolfor to be the guiding hand there."

Dmitri stands, draining his wine. "I will." He sets the glass aside, ponderous action, then turns back to the broad-shouldered lord by the fire. "Is three enough, Robert?"

"It always has been." Robert keeps his eyes on the fire. "And if it isn't, you can be glad you're not the queen's favourite, and that you won't be the one to answer for failure."

Belinda woke with a clear memory.

She knew in her belly that she wasn't meant to, and that Robert's peculiar actions had somehow failed in their purpose. She remembered shadow gathering around her; she remembered Dmitri, and the snippets of conversation she'd overheard.

What she could not remember was *how* she had hidden in the

shadows. How the stillness escaped from her and surrounded her; how she had stood all but in plain sight and gone almost unseen. Over the next three years, she practised and tried to bring that stillness out again.

She failed.

Irina, imperatrix of Khazar, gave birth to a daughter, Ivanova, four months after Dmitri visited with Robert. The whole of Echon sent gifts and congratulations to its eastern neighbor; Lorraine sent Robert himself to bear Aulun's presents. For the child, a baby rattle made of eggshell and gold; a rabbit-fur cloak, trimmed in royal ermine; and for Irina, the sister queen on the Khazarian throne, a gown of the latest Aulunian fashion, littered with jewels and nearly as elegant as Lorraine herself wore. Belinda asked, without real hope, to journey across the sea, north and east, with Robert, to see Khazar's capital city of Khazan and help bear Aulun's gifts to the new mother and child.

When Robert denied her with a fond, patronizing smile, she curtsied and slipped away again. He would be gone for three months, perhaps longer. It was time in which Belinda studied.

Unable to re-create what memory told her she could do, she learned to hide in plain sight more conventionally. She learned to dress conservatively; she learned to sew servants' garments, so she might slip in and out among Robert's guests without announcing herself. He returned, and noticed, his contemplation of her thoughtful and interested, but he said nothing. Belinda took silence as tacit permission, and continued. She learned to be unremarkable, if not wholly invisible, and slowly gained confidence in an ability to hide in shadows, if not disappear into them entirely.

Even now, her forehead numbing against the cold pane of glass, Belinda reached for the ability that had enveloped her just one time, three years earlier. The duvet around her shoulders held her safe in its warmth; the glass held her safe from the plummet to the earth, but shadows would not enfold her in their safety.

You are waiting, a voice inside her whispered, and she knew it to be true. Waiting for a sticking point, for a moment of culmination that would explain the solitary, focused studies of her almost twelve years of life. It felt like standing on a knife's edge, fathomless depths below her and impatience prodding her on. There was purpose there somewhere; Robert would not otherwise have troubled himself with the cost of her eclectic education.

Lately she had realised that girls were not taught the things she had been taught; they did not study the blade, or learn politics and history. Rather, their days were filled with learning embroidery and managing households. Belinda had learned those things, too, but her math went beyond the numbers to balance the manor books, and her languages, written and spoken both, were numerous. Robert had purpose in educating her. Belinda only waited to learn what it was.

Lamplight glittered on the road beyond the manor walls. Belinda blinked twice, hardly realizing her eyes had been open, then knelt up to peer through a windowpane unstained by fog from her breath.

Light flashed again, then spread out more broadly as a distant corner was rounded and Robert's carriage, black against shallow snow and starlight, came into view. Protected lanterns, glassed-over and swinging wildly, made streaks of brilliance to Belinda's dazzled eyes as the carriage came pell-mell for the gate, horses' breath steaming in clouds as they galloped.

Belinda slid from her window, throwing her duvet off as she ran for the door. "The gate! The gate! Papa is coming! Open the gate!" Alarmed and startled voices, rough with sleep, took up her cry. Belinda, clutching a pair of fur-lined slippers in one hand, raced down the steps to the great hall behind Marshall, the thick-bodied manservant who tended to Robert when he visited his country estate. Heedless of the icy ground outside, Marshall flung open the broad manor doors and ran through slush, his booming voice rousing the stablehands from their roost. Belinda, more prudent, hopped and shoved her feet into slippers as she reached the main floor, then ran past Marshall through the courtyard.

It was she who scrambled up to the heavy gates and pulled the pins that kept them locked at night, and she who put her feet through the iron bars and rode the swing of the gate as it opened. She waved through the bars, then climbed higher on the gate, standing on the cross-bars halfway up. Her fingers and cheeks were numb with cold where she pressed against the iron, hanging on with one hand and waving with the other. Her breath came in short, hard gasps, heart hammering inside her with an excitement that bordered on pain. The air she drank down was no longer bitter with cold, but burning with hope. For the moment, Belinda forgot stillness, and prayed.

Robert, lit by the frantically swinging carriage lamps, leaned out a window, laughing and waving in return. "Pack!" he bellowed over the carriage's rattle and the horses' hooves. "Take yourself off the gate, and pack, girl!"

Belinda touched Robert's outstretched fingers as the carriage thundered by, the coachman calling out to the horses as he reined them in. The touch was hard enough to be painful, her cold fingers aching with the impact, but Belinda savored it, drinking in the ache the same way she relished the hard hammering of her heart. Maybe the night's dream of her birth had been a portent, a harbinger of coming change. Perhaps that was what had driven her from her bed in time to see Robert's impetuous midnight arrival.

Robert swung out of the coach before it stopped moving, his ground-eating strides bringing him to her before she could jump down from the gate. He swept her off the iron bars, disregarding her size, and spun her around before setting her on her feet again. "You've grown," he said approvingly. "Now go on, Belinda. Pack your things. We leave the moment the horses are changed."

Belinda gaped. "Tonight?"

"Tonight. There is a man at court whose business is yours, and the need is urgent."

Ice slid through Belinda's insides. Stillness overtook her even more quickly than the ice, and her gaze remained steady on Robert's face, her hazel eyes expressionless. "Papa?"

"Your wardrobe, Primrose. Come, quickly now. I've no time to tarry. I'll tell you what you need to know in the carriage."

"Of course, Papa." Belinda curtsied, an instinctive thing, and stepped around him. Wind picked up, sending freezing shards through her sleeping gown, and her feet took her back into the manor heedless of the turmoil in her belly and mind. Her maid-servant, Margaret, met her at the head of the stairs, hands twisted in her skirts with excitement.

"A husband, my lady, think of it," she whispered, herding Belinda down the hall. "Do you think he'll be young and handsome, or old and rich?"

"I'm sure Papa will have made the best match for me," Belinda replied, as reflexive as her curtsey earlier had been. She was very nearly twelve, the legal age for marriage, though young. She hadn't expected it so soon: adopted daughter or not, Robert was not yet old, and a marriage might yet be made for him. Heirs of his blood might still be possible, though Lorraine's favouritism showed no signs of waning, and the queen had flown into tempers before when her courtiers made matches of their own. The man Robert had in mind for her would be without an heir himself, a child bride extending the years it might be possible to get one. If he was old enough, he might die before she caught, and his lands would become Robert's.

Belinda expected him, then, to be older. Not handsome, but wealthy, with any sons already dead in wars or foolish accidents. She allowed Margaret to dress her without awareness of what she wore. Her dagger caught in the folds of her chemise, pressing uncomfortably against her spine. Belinda straightened it before the stiff fabric of her corset was tightened around her. He would be minor nobility; a duke or an earl was beyond her scope.

"Your boots, my lady."

Belinda startled, looking down. Margaret knelt, waiting patiently for Belinda to respond and be done with the dressing process. "We'll want to bring makeup," the woman said as she slipped first one boot, then the other, onto Belinda's feet. "It'll run if we apply it so early, my lady, but you can't be seen at court without it."

"Yes, of course. I leave the details to you, Margaret. I know you won't embarrass me."

Margaret dimpled and ducked her head in a nod. "I won't, my lady. I'll have you packed within the hour. Lord Robert will be waiting for you downstairs now, I think."

"Yes, of course," Belinda repeated. "Thank you, Margaret." Skirts and petticoats gathered, she ran to the great hall, then to the kitchen, where Robert sat on a rough wooden table before the fire, gnawing a goose leg to the bone.

"Margaret says my things will be packed within the hour, Papa," she said from the door. Robert glanced up, gesturing with his meal. Belinda came in, smoothing her skirts as she sat on the table's bench, facing the fire. Robert twisted, propping a foot on the table.

"An hour. Worse than I'd hoped, better than I'd imagined. Keep that one, Primrose; she's efficient."

"Yes, Papa."

Robert split a grin, toothy in the darkness of his beard. It was longer than when she'd seen him last, coming to a full lengthy point and trimmed shorter along the line of his jaw. He stroked his hand over it, noting Belinda's critical gaze. "Does it suit, Daughter?"

"Yes, Papa," Belinda repeated. Robert's grin cracked through the beard again.

" 'Yes, Papa, but I would like to know about this man whose fate is entwined with mine,' is that what I hear you saying?"

Belinda swallowed. "I am sure you've made the best choice for me, Papa." She waited a few seconds, a fingertip tapping against the table, hard-won stillness at war with the opportunity Robert presented her. The latter won out: she blurted, "Yes, Papa!" and Robert threw his head back with a laugh.

"All right. All right, my Primrose, let me tell you of Rodney du Roz."

"Du Roz," Belinda echoed. "He's Gallic?"

Robert nodded. Belinda's eyebrows drew down. "Papa, an Ecumenic?" Gallic sympathies lay with Cordula, heart of the ostentatious Ecumenic Church in southern Echon. Aulun's break with Cordula was still fresh, and her people still wounded from it. Lorraine herself followed the Reformation, and her religious passion held Aulun in its sway. Belinda's faith was in the asture Reformatic God to whom Lorraine declared herself devoted. In all her hours of waiting and considering what she waited for, marrying outside the Church was a thought that had never risen.

"Is he . . . wealthy, Papa?" she asked cautiously. Religious differences could be put aside when profit was on the line, but Robert's status as viscount was a gift from Lorraine, and had little money to go with it. Belinda herself was pretty, with wide hazel eyes and soft brown hair that made her pale skin dramatic, but she hadn't the beauty that would make an unprofitable marriage worth considering, not to a man whose religious trappings were the opposite of hers.

"Merely a baron," Robert replied. "Landed, but not extravagantly. You, barring blood of my blood, are heir to more."

"Then—" Belinda traced a half-circle on the table's surface, thoughtful motion. "Then I am a good match for him," she said slowly. "With land and a title, if you should have no children of your own. And . . . with a father who has the queen's ear." She

looked up to see Robert's smile, so pleased that he hid it behind
another bite of goose.

"That's a clever lass." The smile faded into drawn-down eyebrows, making his expression unusually dark. "And this is how it
shall go, Primrose. Heed me well."

Belinda listened, her arms drawn around herself as if for
warmth, despite the heat of the kitchen fire turning her cheeks
pink. She listened, and learned what it was she had been waiting
for all her life.

BELINDA PRIMROSE
14 February 1577 † *Alunaer, Aulun; the Queen's Court*

He was younger than she expected.

Belinda stood at her father's elbow, studying du Roz across the
gathered court. In his twenties and thin-cheeked, he might be
handsome if his disposition were choleric, but standing in the
court, speaking with a courtier dressed far more expensively than
he, du Roz looked mild to Belinda's eyes. His hair, like his cheeks,
was thin; his hands, in motion as he spoke, were long and elegant.
There were worse matches to be made, if a glance could tell her
anything.

But it had not yet been made. The queen's approval came first,
and that could not be granted until Belinda had been presented to
her. Only after that would the nominal steps of courting be taken
and permission to wed asked of Lorraine.

Trumpets blared, half a dozen courtiers nearby flinching into
squared shoulders and sucked-in guts. Belinda smoothed a hand
over her skirts, watching du Roz. He straightened, but not in
startlement, and turned to the far end of the hall with calculated
smoothness. Belinda, guided by Robert's hand on her shoulder,
turned as well.

The doors swept open with a rush of warm wind that carried

the sound of the queen's footsteps down the length of the silent hall. Seconds passed before Belinda saw her clearly; the room from which Lorraine entered was dark, making her entrance all the more dramatic. From darkness into light; Belinda, despite her own excitement about being at court, could not help a rise of amusement at the deliberate pageantry behind the staged arrival. Then, fighting down laughter, she admonished herself for the thought that Her Majesty, queen of all Aulun, had to earn her, Belinda's, approval for how she manipulated her court. Belinda shifted forward a little to see beyond the barrel chest of the courtier beside her.

Titian hair fell loose, bloody curls against translucent skin. A crown, gold and understated, nestled among the curls. Lorraine bucked fashion—or, more likely, set it—with a gown of stiff brocade that pushed her breasts high and left her throat and shoulders exposed, sleeves set further out than fashion dictated, just at the curve of shoulder. Thin grey eyes, a high forehead, and a proud chin, lifted in expectation of received adoration.

Thunder pounded through Belinda's veins, narrowing her vision to pinpricks, until she saw no one but the queen. Motion of bodies nearby told her to curtsey deep and slow, as the men and women around her did, and she did, black gaze fixed on the floor. When she straightened again, Lorraine had moved beyond them, and Belinda could stare openly at the queen's fine, slender shoulders. Robert had not told her.

It must not be found out. Belinda closed her eyes, letting Robert's chuckle wash over her. "Beautiful, isn't she?" he murmured above her. "Fear not, Primrose. Very few, upon their first visit to court, are affected differently."

The very lowness of his voice itched through her, making it seem as though he spoke from much farther away. Through a distance of comforting grumbles, perhaps; through a barrier of red-tinged warmth so familiar it wrapped around the edges of her dreams. It seemed extraordinary that she had never quite known it before, not the way she knew it now. Her vaunted memory had not abandoned her, but neither had it offered the puzzle piece that she now recognized. Heat burned her cheeks, a thing so unusual that she had not yet learned to control it with the stillness. It was something to work on, as she'd worked on keeping her breathing steady and her presence unremarkable even when, as now, astonishment and curiosity sparked through her like the promise of a blaze. She knew. She *knew*. She had thought she'd understood when Robert had spoken of her fate, but now, in the press of courtiers and hangers-on among the queen's court, Belinda Primrose knew the heart of what had gone unsaid for all her short life, and wanted to fly with it.

"Then I will try not to be too embarrassed." Her reply was soft and clear, betraying nothing of excitement. Blackness had faded from her vision. All around her, the queen's attendants exchanged astounded whispers over Lorraine's daring gown. The women of the court clutched at their partlets and blouses as if they longed to rip them away at that very moment. The men looked as if they hoped the women would.

Belinda, in unconscious sympathy, pressed her hand against the embroidered partlet that covered her throat and chest, even curling her fingers against the fabric. Robert's touch stayed her and she nodded without argument, letting her hand fall again. Lorraine approached the throne, turning with an elegant swish of skirts to sit. The gathered court let out a collective breath, voices rising into low murmurs as, Lorraine's procession over, they began to fill the empty space in the middle down which the queen had walked. Robert put his hand on Belinda's elbow, guiding her through the crowd. Every step echoed through Belinda's heels and rattled into her bones. She curtsied as deeply as she could, her eyes lowered, when they reached the throne.

"My adopted daughter, Your Majesty. Belinda Primrose, the daughter of my late sister and her husband."

"Yes." Lorraine's voice held no remembered warmth; it was rich and cool and arrogant. She leaned forward a scant inch, examining Belinda as if she were a mote found on a piece of jewelry. "Born in Brittany and raised by your people at your Aulunian estates."

Robert inclined his head so far it was nearly a bow. "The lands so graciously provided by Your Majesty."

"What pretty courtesy you always remember to pay us, Robert." Faint mockery coloured Lorraine's voice. Belinda heard in the derision all lies of her heritage, and in her own mind, gave words to the truth: she was Belinda Primrose, natural daughter of Robert Drake and Lorraine Walter.

The queen's bastard.

She straightened as Lorraine spoke her name, stepped forward as the queen beckoned to her. Cool fingers took her chin, turning her face to the left and right. Belinda kept her eyes lowered, but satisfaction in Lorraine's voice made her dare to glance up. The queen's grey eyes showed no sign of recognition, no subtle acknowledgment, but neither, Belinda remembered with a shock, had Robert's, the night he looked through concealing shadow to see her. For an instant, Belinda held Lorraine's eyes, willing the stillness inside of her to betray nothing. Inside that moment of no exchange, certainty settled around Belinda's heart. Lorraine could never, and Belinda must never, confess. Belinda lowered her eyes again, lowered them so far that she sank into another deep curtsey, the only acknowledgment she could make. Lorraine clucked her tongue and once more drew Belinda to her feet.

"We are well pleased you have finally allowed us to see your adopted daughter, Robert. She is an attractive child and we are sure great use will be had of her." Lorraine's hand brushed down the bodice of Belinda's dress, and moved up again, touching the partlet that covered the girl's throat.

"We suggest you continue with this until the summer months," she murmured, bringing her mouth close to Belinda's ear. "We have a rash, and the lace irritates it, and so today we have chosen to go without modest coverings. Tomorrow the ladies of the court will be most distressed when having followed our lead makes them both chilled and unseemly. But in the spring, we think we shall flaunt our assets."

Lorraine flicked a brief, mischievous smile at Belinda, and sat back again. "Heed our words come May Day, girl." She made a dismissive gesture with one long-fingered hand, and Belinda murmured thanks as she backed away from the throne.

"My lady Primrose."

Belinda's spine stiffened, the tiny dagger making itself felt for a moment. She turned; Rodney du Roz stood a few feet away, head inclined politely, though his gaze was fixed on her through dark eyelashes, calculating and interested. "Forgive me." His words were marked with a Gallic accent, but carefully spoken. "Forgive me, my lady, but I overheard your introduction to Her Majesty, and thought I might make so bold as to present myself to you. Baron Rodney du Roz." He executed a small bow, arms folded to the front and back of him.

Belinda allowed herself a smile and dipped a curtsey exactly as deep as du Roz's bow. "My lord Baron. I am honoured."

"I think the honour is mine, my lady. For an Ecumenic at the Aulunian court, a friendly smile is beyond price, and yours does me gladness. I am forward, I know, but it is the way of Gallic men." Self-deprecating humour lit his eyes and curved his mouth for a moment. Belinda had been right: with passion, his thin features could be handsome. "Would you walk with me, lady?"

"You are forward," Belinda agreed, amused, but when he offered his arm, she took it. "Outside, perhaps?" she suggested. "The courtroom . . . I am unaccustomed to so many people, pressing so close." Du Roz nodded, escorting her through the crowd to a side door.

"You've never been to court before, then?" he asked as they slipped out of the courtroom and down a hall. Arrow-slit windows allowed patches of soft grey winter light to blotch the floor and change the aquamarine shade of Belinda's overdress. She shook her head as they approached the end of the hall, du Roz pushing open the iron-bound wooden door for her. "Then you must see Alunaer from the palace walls," he announced. "There are a dozen times in a day when it's most perfect to be seen, dawn and noon and darkest night."

Belinda laughed, carefully gathering up her skirts to avoid slush and half-frozen mud. "But it's none of those times, Baron. It's mid-morning."

"Ah! But it has snowed lately, and the city is quiet under snowfall, and so that is perfect too. Have you a fear of heights, my lady?"

"No, my lord."

"Bold and beautiful," du Roz murmured. "This way, then: think you to risk the guard stairs?" He gestured extravagantly as he led her around a corner. Icy, steep stairs shot upward, a short wall of calf-height the only barrier between the stairs and a long fall. Belinda blanched, then nodded with determination. She took the first step, and felt du Roz's hands on her hips. "Fear not, my lady. I won't let you fall."

Belinda laughed again, breathless. "I trust you will not, my lord Baron." She climbed, placing her feet carefully. Du Roz took his hands from her hips in order to better balance himself. Nearly three-quarters of the way up, she paused, her hand pressed against her chest as she turned to lean against the high wall, looking out over the low. "Forgive me," she pleaded, taking in quick, shallow breaths. "I'm unaccustomed to climbing so many stairs, and the corsets are tight."

"Not at all. Even from here, the view is remarkable." He took a step past her, gesturing over the palace walls at the city beyond.

"It is." Belinda studied his shoulders, falsely broadened by his doublet, rather than the view, and her father's voice echoed in her flawless memory.

"And this is how it shall go, my Primrose. Heed me well. Du Roz visits Aulun for one purpose and one purpose only: he is sent by the Essandia court, by Rodrigo the prince, to bring down our beloved queen and instate an Ecumenical pretender on the Aulunian throne. He is too minor a noble to be suspected, too hungry for land and wealth. Should he be found out, Rodrigo can easily claim no knowledge; du Roz will be called an opportunist, working alone to impress a foreign prince."

Belinda touched a hand to du Roz's shoulder. He turned, avarice filling his eyes. She smiled, and he stepped closer.

"The man you believe I mean you to marry," Robert's voice murmured in her mind, *"is the man Aulun needs you to kill."*

Stillness filled her, a calm centre. Belinda smiled again, putting her fingertips gently against du Roz's chest. He made a pleased sound in his throat, edging closer on the icy steps.

Belinda straightened her arm, full force of her body weight behind the shove. Astonishment filled du Roz's eyes, then panic as he fell, silent, hands clutching uselessly at thin winter air. It took a surprisingly long time for him to crunch against the flagstones below. Belinda stepped forward cautiously, looking down. The body, small, puppetlike, convulsed twice, then was still.

She edged back against the wall, lifting her gaze to the snow-covered city. In the far distance, chimney smoke rose up, blue against grey clouds; the scent of wood smoke, rich and sharp, intruded on her senses, now that the task put to her was finished. Closer, black-branched trees with snow-dusted caps littered the parks that surrounded the palace. There were distant voices, lifted in argument and in laughter and carried on the wind. "You were right," Belinda murmured. "It's beautiful."

Only then did she begin to scream.

2

Ten years later

Belinda came awake with a start, the lurch more emotional than physical: stillness was inscribed so deeply in her soul now that she sometimes had to remind herself to react in ordinary company. At times she even thought she might have to tell herself to breathe, the silence in her so complete. But not now: her heartbeat was too fast, breath shallow from sleep. Dreaming of du Roz was never a good sign.

Nor was waking to the scratchy beard and bad breath of a Khazarian lover. Belinda exhaled, and carefully slid her shoulder out from under his head. He grunted, burrowing further into blankets in lieu of the pillow she'd made. She sat up, rubbing away stinging prickles left by his beard, and drew a discarded sleeping gown around her shoulders. Linen, silk-soft from age, hissed as she slid it from beneath the Khazarian's weight.

Belinda frowned at him, trying to remember his name. Vlad? Vasilly? Valentine? No, it had been shorter than Valentine. Sharper. She had spent weeks in his bed. She ought to know his name with some certainty. But then, there were reasons not to. It was Viktor, she thought. It hadn't been he, attentive but unimaginative in bed, who had inspired dreams of du Roz. No, there was more. Something coming awake in the belly of the little palace, its stirrings pressing into Belinda's mind and making her sleep restless. That was unusual; she often slept lightly, but the prickling awareness of things arriving harkened back to her childhood and the night her father had ridden so hard to his estates to make his daughter an assassin. Something had driven her out of bed that night; something now did the same. She could not recall that itch coming over her once in the intervening decade.

She slipped out the door without bothering to fasten her sleeping gown with more than a ribbon. The sky, pale with summer twilight, told her it was still early, perhaps three in the morning. Without winter's chill to ward off, no other servants were likely to be up, not within the house itself: no fires needed building, no breads to set baking, not for another hour or two. Belinda had the narrow servants' halls to herself.

They ran as shortcuts from one part of the little palace to another. The count, a stark man with grey at his temples and an eye for beauty that led to tales of sexual prowess, would not stand for delay. Not with his women, not with his wine, certainly not with the wealth of which he enjoyed showing unsubtle flashes. The ancient buildings that had stood his family for generations had been torn down, stone by stone, and rebuilt again to his pleasure. He was master and architect here, and now, with the back halls well-laid and well-lit, it took a maid, running at full bore, no more than two minutes to fetch any hot tea or cold drink from the kitchen back to her master in his study. Belinda had made the deliveries herself, all too aware that downcast eyes and a heaving breast were as much a part of what Gregori delighted in showing off to guests as the astonishingly rapid service. Her gowns were cut accordingly, square necklines a nearly imperceptible fraction lower than decorum permitted, breasts shelved high and mounded against the stiff bodice fabric. The line of propriety was so narrowly skirted that it was a rare man indeed who noticed Belinda's face. Gazes locked on the sharp line of fabric pressing into pale flesh instead, searching for a blush of pink. Other women used rouge to suggest that colour, but Belinda left nature alone, trusting men's imaginations over cosmetics.

The deliberate heavy bindings of daily wear made traversing the halls in little more than a shift against her skin all the more delicious. From kitchen to bedroom, library to dining hall, it was the same. Delicate bells with half a dozen tones strung the upper walls of the servants' halls: the deepest tone signaled a runner from the kitchen, and the highest, purest of them bespoke the bedrooms. Belinda had learned within a day which halls ran where, and to stand well back from the crossroads when a bell rang. Causing a wreck in the servants' halls earned even the most beloved servitors a beating. Rumour had it that more than one maid had left the count's service after such a beating, bellies rounded with disgrace. Many men blurred the line between violence and passion, and there was no one to press Gregori Kapnist to a gentler hand.

Belinda had made neither the error of clumsiness nor wanton sensuality; her position in Gregori's household was one of unobtrusiveness. When she was gone, no one should remember her face, only generous breasts and dark hair tucked away under a tidy white cap that emulated the rich snoods of the wealthy.

It was unfortunate for Viktor, snoring away in Belinda's bed, that her need for him had passed once she was ensconced in Gregori's household. The nights she'd spent with him since were necessary payment to keep a lustful man happy; most of all, to keep him from naming her a whore to his lord and master. No one believed the legendary chastity of the serving classes, but neither would anyone employ a maid denounced as a slut. A rough man like Viktor, in his lord's employ as an armsman, could and would destroy her, unless she turned him away by means of finding a lover of more power within the household hierarchy. To do so was beyond Belinda's needs, and meant a sad end to Viktor's days.

A breeze caught her gown, cool and unexpected. Belinda curled her fingers into the fabric at her throat, feeling her body react to the brief chill. She stepped back against the wall, lowering her head while shifting her gaze left and right. She'd come from the servants' quarters behind the kitchen, small and uncomfortable but private. The halls opened to the outside in two places: the east wall, the servants' entrance around the corner from the main southern entrance, and the north wall, where the stables lay. The breeze lifted her hem again, and she turned her head to the right.

To the north, the stables. Someone's assignation, likely, no more legal than her own. Belinda loosened her hand from the throat of her gown, pushing the fabric open to bare her collarbones. She folded one arm beneath her breasts, lifting them, and judged the effect from above before twisting her hair over her shoulder in dark, artless curls. She clutched the skirt of her gown in one hand, letting her stance and body language claim she was afraid of being caught.

But stillness washed over her as she lowered her head and gaze. Sometimes it seemed that the childhood memory came real again, and that men and women looked through her as if shadow had swallowed her whole, even when no shadows were to be seen. The sense of certainty that had accompanied that one frozen moment had never reasserted itself, and so each time now she was made to wait, and to see if she would be seen.

A man's footsteps, taking long, sure strides. Belinda watched the floor through her eyelashes, marking the swiftness of steps. Her breath barely stirred her bosom as she inhaled, and with the exhalation, the man strode by. Expensive boots, black and well-made, the stitching impossible to see at a glance; well-shaped legs. A scent of the outdoors, of horses, of perfume made with an exotic spice: a rich man's scent. Perhaps Gregori, returning from a visit with Akilina Pankejeff, whose grand duchy put her out of line for the throne, but far above what a count might call his own. There were a few who whispered that Gregori eyed the widowed imperatrix, and laughed in their sleeves at the idea. She was born too high, and he too low, though no one could fault him for his taste in women, and some admired the long reach of his ambition.

A hand closed in Belinda's hair, knotting in the curls she'd pulled over her shoulder. Her coquettish downward gaze had lost her the chance to watch, and there had been no change in his pace to warn her the man had turned back. She forbore to flinch or squeal as he pulled her head back, forcing her chin up to make her meet his eyes. Hazel eyes, dark with patchy light from well-spaced torches, and a well-shaped mouth thinned with anger. "Better, I suppose, to have it here than wake whatever cock you've got roosting in your nest."

Dmitri! Belinda knew this man, the expressive mouth and low voice a match to the one she'd heard as a little girl, in her father's own home. Surprise dilated her pupils, one of the few reactions she couldn't control. For a few seconds the halls seemed brighter, as if early-morning sunshine had somehow spilled through stone and around corners to light the place where they stood. Her pulse betrayed her by bumping higher in her throat, just one beat before she swallowed it down. "My lord?" A soft voice, properly cultivated as benefited a servant of a wealthy house, but with country vowels. Her Khazarian could be high- or low-born, less learned than absorbed in infancy, as had been her native Aulunian tongue. Gallic she spoke like an Aulunian, but that was artifice; she could swallow her accent and make herself sound a native if she had to.

But a country-born serving girl in a Khazarian palace would have no speech but her own, and Dmitri had spoken Aulunian. "My lord?" she asked again, eyes wide with uncertainty that was only partly feigned.

"Do not play me for a fool," he growled, fist tightening in her hair. "I've travelled long and late to meet you, and morning comes on harder than I'd hoped. Time is running out." Belinda's chin came up with the weight of his hand, exposing her throat. His gaze flickered to her pulse, and pleasure she couldn't allow on her face warmed her belly. She had him: the tiniest signs of vulnerability were the ones men could resist the least. The slightest signs of a man noticing weakness were the ones she could exploit the most.

"My lord," she whispered a third time. "I don't understand." He couldn't recognize her; he'd only seen her sleeping, and that more than ten years ago. He'd changed very little, only the style of his hair, cut shorter now than Belinda remembered. His beard was still thin and trimmed to the line of his jaw, his cheekbones and figure as sharp as they had been a decade earlier. She recognized in him now what she'd been too young to see before: he was, if not handsome, at least deeply compelling. His features might never grace the classic busts of ancient Cordulan emperors, but they would damn a woman's heart to break. He had, even in repose, what du Roz had lacked: passion.

And he was not now in repose. Irritation turned his eyes from hazel to murky black as he slid his hand behind her neck, pulling her head back another degree or two. His hands were unexpectedly soft, though the touch was not; the hands of a man who had never done heavy work or held a sword. Belinda's stomach tightened and she pressed her back against the wall, feeling her dagger dig against her skin.

"I think you do," Dmitri breathed, still in Aulunian. His accent, which had marked him as Khazarian in Belinda's childhood, was gone, words untainted by any other language. He pressed his mouth against the pulse in her throat, leaning his body into hers. His clothes were still cold from the outdoors. Belinda's flesh went to goose bumps against the chilly fabric. There was no extra padding to the man, not in body nor in garment; his thighs, slender and muscular, trapped one of Belinda's between them, his sex hard against her hip bone. Belinda ghosted her fingers at his hip, rather than reach for her dagger. A man's own weapons were the best ones to use against him.

"You are Belinda Primrose," Dmitri rumbled against her skin, so quietly that a passerby would hear nothing at all. "Adopted daughter of Robert, Lord Drake, favoured of Lorraine, queen of Aulun, and you are here to see to the death of Gregori, favoured of Irina, imperatrix of all Khazar. I am here to tell you that time is shorter than we believed, and the thing must be done now." The words vibrated through her skin, leaving warmth that spread as surely as chill from his clothes had. The spice that lingered on his skin was cloves, fresh and clean. Belinda willed herself to loosen her jaw, trying to fight off the heady pulses of desire that were too poorly denied, in light of the words he said. She didn't know him, other than a moment's encounter in her childhood; he could be a spy, a test, a trap. Belinda dared not risk that he might be otherwise.

"My lord—"

Dmitri snarled and struck her, a backhanded blow that caught her cheek and knocked her to the floor. Belinda crumpled, lifting the back of her hand to her cheek and injured eyes to the dark-dressed man above her. Her dressing gown had come open; through flashes of pain she hoped it had done so artfully, for her own vanity's sake. Men, in her experience, rarely cared for art, so long as a breast was bared or a thigh exposed.

Dmitri seemed no different. He took her in, the tears tracking down her cheeks and falling to follow the curve of a breast. Under the trickle of dampness her nipple hardened, and even through a blur of tears Belinda saw his gaze darken. He crouched, mouth pressed thin, to lift her breast and close his fingers over the nipple. She caught her breath, lips parting, and he knotted his other hand in her hair again.

"If there were time," he said through compressed lips, voice thick with desire and anger, "if it were not so urgent that I be far gone at dawn's coming." He pinched her nipple again, making her stomach jump with distress and want, then yanked her dressing gown closed and stood up. His eyes were black and furious, his cheeks flushed. "Within the week, Belinda. We have no time. Ill winds ride in Gallin."

He turned on his heel and stalked back down the corridors, leaving Belinda on the floor, cold and afraid.

It was because he hadn't taken her that she was convinced it wasn't a trap. That, and her childhood recollection of him; that, and the itch of warning that had sent her from her bed faded as she watched him ride away. She had climbed to a palace turret to watch him leave, a place where serving girls were certainly not supposed to be, but it wasn't fear of discovery that made a thick pulse of nausea pound in her stomach. It was malevolence, some small degree of it directed at Dmitri as the dawn took him away, but most directed at the count whose life she held in her hands. They conspired between them to take away the elegance of her assignment, Dmitri by insisting on speed and Gregori by his too slowly declining health.

For weeks she had slipped tasteless, colourless arsenic into Gregori's drinks and onto his foods. It was a slow death, meandering from illness to madness to the grave, but discretion had been more important than speed. Now, if the thing had to be done with all haste, other poisons would do, but they left their mark in discoloured skin, in distorted features, in distended tongues, no more subtle than the cut of a knife. That was arsenic's beauty as an assassin's tool: it left no traceable sign. With large enough doses she could have him dead in a week, but the necessity of forcing her hand where time had only lately been a friend rankled in her.

Belinda curled her hands in front of her stomach as if she could take the sickness she felt there and turn it into a weapon itself, forcing it upon the count. As if it were a canker that could be put on another.

A tremble of sweat dampened her upper lip and her temples despite the cool summer morning as the bellyful of illness broke and passed from her, leaving her momentarily light-headed and disoriented. Then sense returned, sharp and clear: she ought to return to her room, ought to convince Viktor the bruise on her cheek was his fault, and ought to do it all before guards came to find her on the palace turrets where she should not be. It would be job enough to blame Viktor without having to worry about another man or two to fuck or leave for dead.

She pressed her fingertips against her cheek gingerly, wondering if the bruise might be used to her favour. Belinda drew her gown around herself again and hurried back to her tiny room. Viktor was a lout, but not cruel. She could see in his eyes that he didn't remember the night, and took no pains to ease his fear. He rushed on the errand to fetch cosmetics that would disguise the mark on her cheek.

Disguise, but not entirely hide. Belinda stood in shadow, her head deliberately lowered for the morning inspection. The palace's castellan looked twice, but not closely, and gave her the typical morning approval for dress and demeanor before the day began. Once the castellan was gone she tucked her breasts higher, fetched a tea tray, and went to wait on her master.

His morning rooms were already too hot, low fires built at either end, drapes drawn closed against morning light. Belinda inhaled the warm air deeply, setting her tray against her hip as she pulled the door closed. There was a faint scent of sickness in the air, unexpected. Gregori should show signs of arsenic poisoning soon, but for the smell to linger already in his private rooms gave her odd heart: perhaps the smooth workings of her plan would be less disrupted than she'd thought.

The drapes needed opening; the room needed light and air to clear away that telltale scent. Better for her, if worse for Gregori, if no one noticed the count's illness in such early days, and besides, the scullery maids ought to have their ears bent for leaving their lord and master's rooms in the dark. Tray balanced on her hip, Belinda stalked to the windows, yanking a handful of heavy curtain back.

"Leave them."

Twice in a single morning she'd been taken off-guard. Belinda, facing the curtains, allowed herself to press her eyes closed, nostrils flaring. The cut of discovery ran deeper within herself, a tightening in her stomach and groin. Not panic, but something akin to desire.

"My lord," she said in a low voice, curtsying even as she turned toward the voice. "I'm sorry, my lord. I didn't see you." She kept her eyes lowered, more to hide her irritation with herself than out of deference to the count.

"You're injured," he said.

Belinda lifted a hand to her cheek, then twitched it away again as if aware she'd betrayed herself with the gesture. "It's nothing, my lord." Now her eyes were downcast to hide the light of success: she'd read him correctly. He noticed what his castellan had not.

"Come here."

Now she dared glance up through her eyelashes, if only to gauge the distance.

Gregori languished on a divan, startlingly pale against the heavy greens and golds. He was dressed loosely in sleeping gowns under a brocaded robe; his hair, usually swept back and tidy, was in disarray. Belinda was surprised to see how much curl, and how much grey, it had. His eyes were unnaturally bright, reflecting more light than the room had to offer.

Belinda came forward, setting his breakfast tray on a small table, and knotted her hands together below her waist. The stance bespoke fear and respect, and protecting herself; it also drew his gaze to her hips, where it lingered a few moments. "They call you Rosa, do they not?" he asked without lifting his eyes. She tightened her fingers in front of her groin, knowing he saw her knuckles whiten.

"Yes, my lord." The name was a safe one, part of her own and repeated in one version or another in nearly every Echonian language, and oft-used in Khazar as well. "My lord, are you well?" She whispered the words, hearing a quaver in her own voice, and nearly believed her own performance. A serving girl had no right to ask after her master's health.

"Well enough." Gregori put his hand around her wrist, pulling her hands away from her belly. His hand was feverishly warm, thumb and forefinger more than encircling her wrist. Belinda stumbled a half step forward. Gregori bore down on her wrist, and she dropped to the stone floor, hard enough to bruise her knees even through skirts and carpets. Her gaze darted up to meet his, her eyes wide. He kept his grip on her wrist as he lifted his other hand to touch the bruise on her cheek. Belinda hissed, jerking her head away a fraction of an inch, then held as still as she could, eyes intent on his expression.

He wet his lips, pressing his thumb against the masked bruise. Pain stung at the back of Belinda's throat and in her eyes, dry and without tears. "What happened?"

"N-nothing, my lord. Only my own clumsiness. I opened a door too quickly—" Belinda had heard a dozen women use the same excuse. Gregori believed it no more than she had.

"A door with knuckles, and a round stone ring. Have you a lover, Rosa?"

"No, my lord!" Horror shot Belinda's voice up, and she clapped her free hand over her mouth. Gregori's fingers tightened around her other wrist.

"Have you ever?"

Belinda dropped her gaze again, shivering. "Yes, my lord." Let him think she was too frightened to lie to him. The truth now was better than the outrage of a man later denied virgin blood. To her surprise, Gregori chuckled.

"You're either very foolish or very wise to admit that, Rosa.

Which is it?" He took his hand from her cheek and settled it at her bodice, plucking at the ties with the casual confidence of a man who knew time was in his favour. "Do these stays and ties hide other bruises, I wonder?"

Belinda shook her head mutely, amending the answer privately: *not yet.*

"You've lied to me once and told the truth once, Rosa. Which is it now?" He smiled at her for the first time, and as she took a breath to answer her bodice loosened. He slid his fingers, hotter and softer than Dmitri's, under her shift, catching the weight of her breast in his smooth hand. Too smooth: there wasn't enough water in his body, the heat speaking more of fever than desire. Belinda thought of the desire she'd had to force sickness on him, and wet her own lips, semiconsciously copying his behavior of moments earlier.

"The truth, my lord."

His smile broadened. "But you don't deny that you lied?"

She shook her head silently a second time.

"I cannot keep on a serving girl who lies, Rosa." The chastisement was light and mocking. "Do you think it can be trained out of you?"

Belinda swallowed again, letting her eyes drift shut. Gregori's skin was too hot, his eyes too bright, his colour bad. He had been well yesterday, and his symptoms were not those of the arsenic. Perhaps Dmitri need not have worried: this once it seemed nature and the queen's bastard had the same agenda.

But fevers could be healed from, if a man had strength, and the hold Gregori still had on her wrist told Belinda that he still had strength to spare. She remembered the strong dose of poison in his cooling tea, and certainty warmed her: the drug wouldn't hurt as she worked to achieve her ends, but there were other ways available, too. Cutting a man's hair wasn't the only way to drain his strength.

"Rosa?" His voice was more pointed, angrier now. Belinda lifted her chin to meet his eyes, letting a tremble come back into her voice.

"Perhaps w-with a strong hand, my lord." Let him take her hesitation for fear. Let him revel in his stronghold, while she eked the soil from beneath fortress walls.

Gregori's smile sharpened, and Belinda steeled herself against pain.

Viktor's mouth thinned with anger when she undressed that night. "No," she said, before he had time to fling the accusation. "It wasn't you." She kept her eyes lowered, though she watched him through her eyelashes. "I drew the count's attention this morning."

Jealousy struggled with loyalty, thinning Viktor's mouth to white beneath his dark beard. "I wouldn't betray you," she continued, voice low and beguiling. "You must know that." She didn't call him by name; she never called them by name. It made it easier for most things, although in moments like this it would be useful to play that card. Men—and women, too—liked little more than the sound of their own names being spoken. If only she were sure it *was* Viktor, and not Vlad, she might calculate the risk and take it. Instead she let her shift fall a little further around her breasts, clutching it loosely. "I had no choice."

"If he gets you with child, I'll marry you." The man's words were blunt and hard in the quiet room. Belinda forgot coquettishness in astonishment and let the shift drop, only catching it at the last moment. She drew it up too late; the bruises against her throat Viktor had already seen, but the others, on her arms and breasts, she'd thought to hide until twilight dimmed to darkness. Viktor curled his lip and came forward, using both rough hands to pull the shift down. Belinda folded her arms over her breasts as he scowled and knelt, putting his palm over marks left by Gregori's hands, without touching them. Her ribs, her hip, her thigh. The last he put his hand on, making her pull away, making her open her legs. The marks there, against the backs of her thighs and curving inward, were welts, not bruises. Viktor's hands, usually warm, felt cool against the raised marks. "Do you like this?" There was so much anger in his voice that the words scraped from his throat. Belinda answered truthfully, surprising herself.

"Not particularly." It was true, although not the whole truth. Lust rode a dangerous border between pleasure and pain, and she was well-versed in giving herself over to desire. When the line blurred, she rarely minded in the moment, riding it as a kind of power of her own. Even now she could reach back to the morning and feel Gregori's strength waning; feel it as though she drew it away like a succubus, increasing her own vigor. That was heady enough to savor, though days of soreness and bruises after made her sullen, and she never eagerly anticipated the lick of a cane or a hard hand.

"Do you like him?"

This time she smiled, more a sound, breath snorted out, than a curve of her lips. "Not particularly." She unfolded one arm from over her breasts and touched Viktor's hair. It was cleaner; he'd washed today. The realization clicked in her mind and she lifted her chin, staring sightlessly at the far wall. "You knew."

"Everyone always knows." Viktor's voice remained gruff. "So? Will you have me?"

Gregori would never get her with child. It took a simpleton of a servant girl to not know the sharp-flavoured flowers that grew, the seeds of which could be brewed into a strong tea and prevent a child from quickening in the womb. But men didn't like to think of such things, taking the very idea of an unrooted child as an affront to their masculinity. Belinda, touched with a rare compassion, closed her fingers in Viktor's hair as gently as she could. "You deserve better than I can give you." She meant the words, if not in the way the guardsman heard them. He hawked a rough sound, denial.

"You think I don't believe you when you say you have no choice? He's the count. You're nothing."

Anger flared up in Belinda's chest, taking her breath with it. She was far from nothing; she was a secret weapon, a secret child, a secret truth, and for a shocking moment the impulse to lay that bare hammered within her. She subsumed it, astonished at the emotion's violence; not in all the years since she had realised her hidden heritage had the desire to share it struck out. To do so was disaster for all; to discover that the notion to confess, or declare, lay in her thoughts astounded and frightened her.

"We serve, all of us," Viktor went on, oblivious. "No one, not serving maid or guardsman, says no to the master's whim."

Belinda's eyebrows arched slowly. "A guardsman?" Now that was a secret she hadn't so much as heard a whisper of, which meant either Gregori was incredibly discreet, or she was misinterpreting. Viktor's face curdled red under her hand, and she masked a laugh by forcing a lie of wonder into her voice. "I didn't know men could . . . could—but not the count, surely."

"I only know rumours." Viktor moved his hand up sharply, bisecting her sex with thumb and forefinger, ending her speculation. She closed her eyes briefly; the flesh was tender, and his touch hadn't been gentle. "I've never understood the need to hurt a woman," he said in a low growl. He pulled her closer, sliding his other hand over her bottom, bumping his fingers over welts laid there by Gregori's cane.

"Do you wish to explore it, my lord?" Belinda whispered. The hard hands of three men in a day was more than she remembered counting before, and Viktor usually laughed when she gave him the appellation normally reserved for the master of the house.

Not so this time. He pushed his thumb into the cleft between her thighs, pressing his finger against the already-abused centre of pleasure there, and ignored her question to say "You haven't answered me."

Belinda's stomach tensed, the small of her back tightening at his rough touch. She moved her hand through the guard's clean hair, savoring the feeling. He had known. Had taken care to wash and clean himself, knowing that his lover would come back bruised from their lord's ministrations. Had come to offer her a path out of disgrace and had got down on his knees like a love match, even if the wherefores were not love. It was a generous gesture, showing more kindness than she was accustomed to. It was his misfortune to have landed in her bed; he deserved a better ending than he was likely to find there. And now he rhythmically stroked the welts on her backside as he waited for an answer.

"Yes."

Viktor groaned and twisted his hand to drive his fingers inside her. He dragged her forward as she gasped, burying his nose in the thatch of her dark curls, tongue seeking the spot his thumb had abandoned. Belinda clutched at his hair and for a wall, shuddering as her ill-fated suitor brought her to come.

"He is ill." The castellan waggled his jowls, turning ponderously from the fires to face the assembled maids and manservants. It was barely dawn; for the count's illness to be worthy news already meant he was more gravely unwell than Belinda had counted on. There had been loud voices in the halls at three of the morning, and now she knew what they all did: a doctor had been called. Nothing less would precede so early an announcement. Belinda twisted her hands in her skirts, mimicking the girl next to her, and kept her eyes lowered. Her dress today was exceedingly modest, covering her from throat to toe and wrist to shoulder, the only way to hide marks on her throat. The bruise on her cheek had been covered expertly by cosmetics; today she didn't need to catch the count's attention. The castellan droned on, more taken with the sound of his own voice than the imparting of information: the count was sick, and it was serious, else the doctor would not have come, but his words implied renewing energy and restored health. Maid and manservant alike knew them for lies, but no one would dispute the truth with the castellan.

"Rosa."

Belinda allowed herself a startle, knotting her fingers more tightly in her skirt. "Yes, sir?" She barely lifted her eyes; the castellan liked his women dim-witted and submissive.

"The count asks for you to attend him today."

A whisper rustled through the other servants, knowing looks and glances of bitter jealousy. Everyone always knows, Viktor had said. Belinda knew it was true. She dropped a curtsey, fingers still clenched in her skirt. "My honour, sir."

"That will be all." The castellan flipped his fingers dismissively; the standing crowd stepped back, breaking apart. A girl hissed "Harlot" at Belinda's back, and a man's low chuckle followed it.

"And wouldn't you be, too, if the master bade you spread your legs," he muttered. The girl let out a gasp of outrage, then a squeak as he slapped her on the arse, hard enough for the sound to be recognizable through layers of skirts and petticoats. "Hold your tongue," he said. Belinda waited two breaths, then looked over her shoulder to meet the speaker's eyes. A coachman, awake enough to have been the one who fetched the doctor, unimportant enough in the household that Belinda didn't know his name. He gave her a wink and she inclined her head, the only thanks he'd get. She gathered her skirts, curtsying again to the castellan, and went to fetch Gregori's breakfast and tea.

Even knowing the doctor had been there, the count's colour was worse than she'd expected, and made worse still by comparison to the rich brocade duvet he lay beneath. "My lord," Belinda murmured as she set his tea tray by the bed. She'd wiped the cosmetics from her face, leaving the bruise an ugly greening mark on her cheek, and even in sickness she saw his eyes go to it, before amusement curved his mouth and he lifted a hand—thin-boned and pale, far more so than a day earlier—to curl his fingers into the high collar of her gown that hid the ring of bruises he had left.

"I'm disappointed, Rosa. Do you always hide the marks of love?" His grip had less strength than it had the day before, but he was still strong, stronger than she was.

"I had not thought to see you today, my lord, else I'd have taken more care in my dressing."

"Did you not?" His voice sharpened. "Do they tell you I'm ill, Rosa? That I must be coddled and treated like a child?"

"That you're ill, yes, my lord. That the doctor has been and gone, and that you'll be well enough soon." Belinda straightened; Gregori's hand in her partlet pulled the fabric tight, and buttons slipped free. It was made to do so, all the easier for assignations. His mouth thinned with pleasure and he yanked hard on the fabric. Buttons flew loose, the partlet tearing away. Belinda lifted her chin half in response to the pull and half to display her necklace of bruises. "It seems to me you're neither ill nor weak at all, my lord." The hollowness beneath his eyes and in his cheeks gave lie to her words, but nothing in her voice or gaze did. Later, when she lay with her teeth set together against the pain of too much use, she thought that nothing in his passion gave lie to her claim, either.

But the next day she was flush and healthy, and Gregori all the worse, and the doctor's face had grown deadly grim. Whispers ran wild among the staff, fears for the count's life and tales of what illness bore him down. Belinda shivered when a canker of the stomach was hinted at.

And the word spat after her then was not whore but witch. That gave her pause, her heart seizing with the fancy that the accusation held merit, and then simply seized, a place too cold for the stillness to fill opening inside her. Witchery was a forbidden craft; an impossible one, by any rational thought. But rational thought had never ruled, and very little stood between a woman and a stake to burn her at when the word flew. Belinda's heart lurched from one beat to another, staggered with the weight of real fear. Bitter thoughts on a midsummer morning did *not* bring on sudden illness, no matter how useful that illness might be to her. Dismayed nausea at a task interrupted did not leap from her frustration to poison a man's body.

It was not herself she had to convince.

Hands relaxed, disdain and insult in her eyes, Belinda turned back to face Ilyana, petite and blond and jealous, and looked down at her from the advantage of height she held. She said nothing, only looked; after a steady moment or two Ilyana blanched, then gathered her skirts and ran.

"You ought not have done that."

Belinda smoothed her skirts without lifting her eyes to meet the coachman's. "Perhaps not. A woman named whore will be run out of house and home, but a woman named witch will be burned." She looked up then, without humour, without betraying the pounding of her heart or the cold spurts that made her hands thick as they stroked her skirts again. "One I can live through. The other no one can."

"You've made an enemy."

Belinda shook her head. "No, sir. An enemy can do you harm. Ilyana can't do anything to me." She curved her mouth into a smile, still without humour. "Certainly not so long as I have the count's eye."

"And if he's as ill as they say?"

Interest lit Belinda's eyes. She swayed her hips forward, her smile turning fuller. "You drove the doctor. Do you have more than servant's gossip?"

The coachman shrugged, easy loose movement. Viktor, Belinda thought, would never move with that much grace. Viktor, though, would do her bidding, and the young catamount here might have ideas of his own. "Yesterday the doctor came away shaking his head and frowning, as bad a sign as I've ever seen. Today . . ."

Belinda edged forward again, inviting intimacy, her gaze wide on the coachman's. "Today?"

"Today he's silent."

Belinda caught her breath, wanting it to warm the coldness inside her and instead feeling the accusation of witchcraft dancing in the chill. Arsenic and a bad summer cold and a woman willing to spend all of Gregori's spare strength—that's what brought the count low, not spells chanted over an animal's spilled blood. It was not witchcraft, only coincidence and cruel, deliberate machination. She forced sluggish fear away, wrapping herself in the memory of sunlight cloaking Robert's shoulders. Slow warmth replaced the cold, calming her breathing and her heart, and, protected by stillness, she nodded to show the coachman she understood.

His mouth twitched, not with amusement. Recognition, rather, and the acknowledgment that she understood what he learned from silence. "You've known a lot of doctors, then."

"A few," Belinda said. "Enough." She glanced down the hall, then dipped a slight curtsey. "If you'll excuse me now, the count wants his tea."

"And his girl," the coachman said without malice. "If he's not stronger by morning, watch yourself, Rosa. Ilyana's got a mean tongue in her."

"Thank you." Belinda let his warning slip away as soon as her back was turned, and Gregori was dead with the sunrise.

She heard it with the others, being nowhere near important enough to sit out his death watch with him, for all that she'd been closer to him in the last days of his life than anyone else in the household. No, his son from a first marriage had come, riding in late the night before, and the regal, sharp-featured woman who was his noble lover had arrived in the small hours of the morning. Belinda had stood awake on the palace turrets, watching the hurried arrivals, and knew that morning would bear the news of the count's death.

Now, with it spoken, she heard the shrieks and wailings of Ilyana and other women, and stared thoughtfully at her own feet. She'd been in Gregori's employ only a few months; to leave immediately would call more attention to herself, even make her suspect. To stay with Ilyana and her spiteful tongue might cost her far more. The young count wouldn't want to risk her carrying his father's child, and the high-born lover would likely as soon see a bruised servant girl dead as not.

Over Belinda's thoughts and over the cries of the women, the castellan boomed that no one was to worry, that the young count would not put them out of job and home, and that if he did it would surely be with handsome recommendations. The others' alarm lifted the hairs on Belinda's arms, making her run a hand down one as she pursed her mouth. There would be chaos for a day or two while the estate was reordered. Most pressing was the matter of Ilyana: if she left off her cries of witchcraft, Belinda would stay. She lifted her eyes to consider the blond girl, who seemed to sense the look, and turned on her.

"It's your fault! Whore! Witch! You charmed him and did him to death! Been here no time at all, and now the lord is dead! It's your fault!" Shrieking, Ilyana pitched herself at Belinda, who fell back, catching the other woman's wrists more clumsily than was her wont, but with more ease than Rosa the serving girl might have done. Anger fueled by fear rose up in her, and she let them both show through: the coachman had been right after all, and no one should have been as calm in the face of an accusation of witchcraft as Belinda had been.

"Did him to death, did I?" She shoved Ilyana backward, throwing the smaller girl to the floor. A part of her sang with the truth of it: yes, she had done the count to death, but it had not been witchery, simply a stupid man more interested in showing his prowess than conserving his strength. That, and the arsenic, and perhaps a touch of lucky fate when she'd looked for nothing of the sort at all.

And beneath that, far beneath it where she barely allowed the thought to form, she wondered in terror and hope if Ilyana was not somehow right, and she had pulled a killing power from within herself. She had hidden in shadow once, as a child, and had been forbidden that talent by her father's interference. If it was witchcraft, if she was born to a dark art, he might have done well by her to hide it. If this was its maturity, the ability to murder a man by her will alone . . . what a gift that would be, and what horror.

Belinda thrust those thoughts away, refusing to linger on the possibility or the fear or the hope, and instead plucked her partlet from around her throat to show Ilyana yellowing bruises. "Would a woman who could do a man to death let him do this to her? Is this what you're so eager for?" Sharp inhalations seemed to thin the air, greedy eyes trying to stare and look away all at once.

"You bespelled him," Ilyana snarled. "Maybe bruises are the price you pay for your magic, bitch."

"Ladies." The castellan, face bleak with anger and grief, stepped between them. "We are all too emotional now. Forget this, and let us behave with the decorum that best suits us."

Yes, Belinda thought, the serving classes, so much more concerned with propriety than their wealthy masters. But she didn't miss the castellan's eyes lingering on her, or the suspicion and doubt that had been planted behind them. "Sir," she murmured, and backed away, eyes lowered. There would be no time for a discreet exit, then. Ilyana would expose her to angry nobles looking for someone to blame. Belinda had no intention of dangling her slender neck in a hangman's noose. She stepped into the first servant's crossed hall off the kitchen, pausing there to consider the ends that needed tightening.

"I leave within the hour," the coachman said from across the hall. Belinda raised her head, eyebrows lifted. "To bear tidings of the count's death to the capital city." He hurried down the hall, booted heels snapping against the stone floors. Belinda watched him go, then gathered her skirts. Viktor could not be found in her room.

3

SANDALIA, QUEEN AND REGENT
27 June 1587 ✝ Isidro, capital of Essandia

"I've waited twenty years, Rodrigo." Sandalia whirls herself across her brother's private rooms, fully aware she s giving in to the histrionics of a much younger woman. "Javier's long since old enough—"

"Javier," Rodrigo interrupts, "is his mother's most loyal subject, and doesn't itch for a throne. You haven't been waiting, Sandalia." He stands, cutting a deliberate swath across Sandalia's stormy path to pour cups of wine and hand one to her. She glowers, knowing he's trying to settle her agitation, but takes the cup regardless, sipping quickly.

The years have been kind to the prince of Essandia. In his sixth decade he's still slender, with streaks of silver highlighting his temples and beard. Noble women still dance their daughters past him, and negotiations have never ceased between the royal families of Echon. Sandalia's own curvaceous figure will be unlikely to fare as well over the next decades, but for now she knows she, too, makes a striking figure, especially at her brother's side.

A side that is not supporting her the way she wishes it to. "I *have* been waiting—"

"Waiting suggests doing nothing. Complacency. Idle hands.

You've gathered your strength, made the Gallic people love you—and that, princess of Essandia, is no small trick—kept Lanyarch's heart beating from afar, and have raised a son to follow you. You have kept an army strong enough to stave off Reussland's encroachments onto Gallic territory, and you have done so without crippling your people with taxes, or building their resentment so high that they refuse to fight in your name. Any . . . *any* of those things," Rodrigo emphasizes, lifting his voice over Sandalia's protests, "is not waiting. All of them together are preparing. You would have been a fool to move after Javier's birth, Sandalia. So soon after Louis's death. No one would have supported you, and Aulun would have crushed you and taken Gallin and Lanyarch in Lorraine's name."

"Aulun would have crushed me, and you, backed by Cordula, would have decimated the Aulunian army and destroyed their fleet," Sandalia retorts tartly, but sighs and looks away. "It's easier to see it as preparing from the outside, Rodrigo. I was a girl then, and suddenly heir to two thrones."

"Three," Rodrigo says mildly. "I still have no heir."

"You should marry Irina. She's been a widow ten years now, and no one misses Feodor. Let Ivanova take the Khazarian throne and have the imperatrix breed you a son or two of your own."

"Irina." Rodrigo lifts an eyebrow and sips at his wine, casual curiosity in his actions. "That's not one of the more popular suggestions. Khazar's church isn't Cordula's."

"Think of it, Rodrigo. The Echonian states would be caught between Khazar's massive power to the north and east, and Essandia's long arm south into the Primorismare. Couple that with me on the Gallic throne, and you would hold over half of Echon's coastline. Aulun would come to heel or be left in the cold, unable to trade."

"We would surround Reussland," Rodrigo says with thoughtful dismay. "The kaiser might take exception to that."

"We'll marry Javier to his daughter," Sandalia says. "He should be married soon anyway."

"This urgency is new, Sandalia." Rodrigo puts his wine cup away and does the same with hers, so he can fold her hands in his. "What prompts it?"

"There's nothing more to prepare," Sandalia says. "Either I move or I accept waiting for Lorraine's death before Lanyarch is released from Reformation hold. I move now, or I've spent a lifetime preparing for nothing. I'm not willing to wait, Rodrigo. As heir to Lanyarch's throne through Charles, I have a claim to Aulun's, and Javier will look well upon that seat. If I do nothing, I am only a woman. Not a queen, not a visionary, not an expansionist as all of us but you want to be—"

Rodrigo laughs. "You and Lorraine and Irina are women, Dalia. You rule well, all of you, but none of you have been to war. It's not that I don't want to regain Aulun for the Church. It's that I know war's price personally, and prefer my expansions to come through the signing of a treaty. You're determined to make this move?"

"Soon." Sandalia nods. "There'll be a moment when the stars align, when the time to move is clear. Maybe Irina—"

"Irina," Rodrigo says, "has proposed a treaty with me."

Sandalia picks up her wine again, using the motion to cover surprise. "Over a wedding bed?"

"Over a fleet. It seems the imperatrix hungers for economic expansion, if not new lands."

"Khazar's five times the size of Echon as a whole. Irina doesn't need any more land. What will she give in return, Rodrigo? The thing you need most—"

"It is not a marriage proposal," Rodrigo says firmly. "She offers troops, not an heir."

"Troops. For the war you don't want to fight?"

"It's not always necessary to meet battle on the fields, Dalia. They can be fought in mind and heart and on paper, and if I have Khazar's military to call on, the Red Bitch can't possibly hope to rally an army of equal size. All the better if she can be pressured into capitulating without a drop of blood spilt. Aulun will come back to Cordula." Rodrigo's voice deepens, a passion for his religion dominating all else. "We lost too many faithful in the aftermath of the Heretical Trials, and Aulun's rebellion only sparks more radical thought against the Church. Aulun must be brought to heel within our lifetimes, or Cordula seems weak. I will not have the world worshipping a false god, Sandalia. I will not have it."

"And so you'll threaten and bluster with Irina's army and hope for Lorraine's acquiesence?"

Rodrigo focuses on her again, putting God away for the world he must live in. His expression goes dry, and drier still are his words. "God save Echon from women who rule. The kaiser and the caesar in Parna must shudder every time they think of their neighbors."

"But not the Essandian prince?" Sandalia arches her eyebrows, teasing, and is rewarded with Rodrigo's grin.

"The Essandian prince believes God's divine touch graces us with the leaders we deserve, my sister. We've known a stretch of peace through these years. Perhaps God feels we've needed the gentle touch of female regents to guide us through it."

"Or perhaps we have peace because women don't look to war first." Ambition rides Sandalia's words, and she repeats, "Not first," beneath her breath. "But no true leader shirks from it when it's necessary. Lorraine's too old to pitch a battle herself. She won't see me coming, and if Irina is offering you troops—"

"She offers *me* troops, Dalia, not Gallin."

"Gallin and Essandia are allies, my lord."

"You would have me take Khazarian troops to conquer Aulun in your name?" Danger warns in the edges of Rodrigo's question. Sandalia ducks her head, making herself petite and pretty and harmless, then looks up again with a flirt of eyelashes.

"In Cordula's name, brother. In Cordula's name."

ROBERT, LORD DRAKE
27 June 1587 † *Alunaer, capital of Aulun*

"We are unobserved?" The question is a matter of ritual, thirty years' habit forcing it to Robert's lips even when he knows as well as his queen that their meeting room is cloistered against all listeners. Knows better than she, indeed, though he can never confess to the unearthly skill that allows him to be absolutely certain of their privacy.

"Have done, Robert," Lorraine says with ill-concealed impatience. "We have yet to hear whispers of anything discussed in this room hissing around the court. We are unobserved, and the lusty pair playing at our voices in the bedchamber will be obliged to violate our virgin reputation if we do not hurry. What have you for me?"

A smile shifts the shape of Robert's beard, prickling his skin. Lorraine's shields are unbreachable, her restraint and control beyond any he's ever met, but she can let her guard slip in words. When she does so with him, allowing herself the familiar *me* or *I*, it means more to him than the tasting of her thoughts ever might. "Gregori is dead. Irina is free from his pursuit and is indebted to us. Our negotiations may proceed."

"The Khazarian army," Lorraine breathes. "Think of it, Robert. Aulun's fleet and the masses of men who can be called to arms under Irina's banner. We might hold all of Echon in the palm of our hand, a summer hence."

"We might." Temperance fills Robert's voice. "But Essandia and Gallin will rise under Cordula's call, and Reussland will not take easily to Khazar rolling over it. We must maintain caution, Your Majesty."

"Caution!" Lorraine spits the word, coming to her feet in a rustle of heavy skirts. No longer the Titian Bitch in truth, her hair flames false red above a white-painted face that makes mockery of the striking youth she once was. "We have been cautious our entire life, Robert. We tire of caution. We would have confidence in our legacy, the measure given a man, not the weak-legged tripping steps of a woman."

"You have consolidated and held power for a lifetime, Lorraine." Robert softens his voice, daring the use of the queen's name. "You have played men against one another and kept yourself free, a regent in your own right when too many thought the throne ought not be yours. You have made yourself an icon whose name will never be forgotten. Kings would weep for lesser legacies."

"And Sandalia de Philip de Costa has done the same in the name of two thrones, and stands on my northern border, mocking me and waiting for me to fall. She has years, Robert." Bitterness taints the admission. "She is fifteen years the younger. I must command at least a fraction of Irina's army to hold my own country should my health fail. We have waited long enough." Her shoulders draw back, wattle tightening with the resolve that the formal *we* announces. "We will ally ourselves with our sister queen on the Khazarian throne. We will offer Aulunian ships and privateers to run their ice-blocked harbors and coasts so they might more easily enjoy the trade treaties we have built. In exchange we will accept some small part of her army under our command, so that we might all understand our delicate relationship to one another, and we will *not* threaten her throne in any way, for we understand what it is to be a woman alone at the head of a country." Lorraine takes a breath, satisfaction glinting in her grey eyes. "And in time we will enjoy discussions of where our alliance might further bring us, and what it might mean to the Ecumenic Church and Cordula."

BELINDA PRIMROSE
17 July 1587 † *Aria Magli, Parna*

It was Aria Magli; it was always Aria Magli. The city's peculiar streets, littered with gondolas and filled with vice, were the one place Belinda thought of with anticipation. She sat in a gondola now, leaning forward from under its canopy, allowing herself an unfeigned, unrestrained smile as the boy at the back of the boat poled it along the busy canals.

Rich and poor brushed elbows here; it was thus in any large city, but the possibility of a wealthy lady being dunked in the canal made watching the passersby much more entertaining than in the streets of Alunaer. A man with a rooster balanced on his head leaned out over the canal, one hand firmly wrapped around a water-way pole. Around his feet were caged birds, squawking with indignation. His voice rose over the din, over the sound of water lapping and the voices that bounced back and forth between the canal-separated buildings. The Parnan language rang liquidly in Belinda's ears, every word a promise, even if the speaker was only hawking chickens. He waved as he caught Belinda's smile, and she lifted a hand, snapping her fingers to gain the gondola boy's attention.

"This one will rob you blind, madam," the boy warned. "I know a better man, much better, and handsome, too. Almost as handsome as me."

"But are his chickens as healthy?" Belinda asked with a laugh. "I'm not buying a man, I'm buying dinner."

He clucked as sorrowfully as the chickens did and pushed the gondola toward the lichen-covered canal wall. "What kind of a woman doesn't want a handsome man to sell her things?" he asked mournfully.

"The kind who wants a handsome man to buy her things," Belinda suggested.

"If I buy you a chicken, you will see my man!" the boy enthused, and leapt forward to snatch up one of the cages from the hawker's feet. They fell to bargaining, speaking too low and too quickly for Belinda to catch the words. She settled back beneath her canopy again, entirely certain that the price of the chicken

would be added to the fare for her afternoon ride. Another gondola slid by, an expensively dressed woman reading from a book of
poetry to a man who doted on her. Belinda watched them go until
the curve of the canal took them from her sight, then smiled and
searched for another such pair.

Courtesans. Their days of great power in the Maglian courts
were over, brought low by the plague and the Heretical Trials half
a century earlier, but their stories were still told throughout Echon.
Had she been born to the warmer Parnan climes instead of foggy
Aulun, Belinda thought she might have been one of them. Not
necessarily beautiful, but well-educated in studies forbidden to
most women, and then taught to be hedonistic lovers as well. Their
lives weren't so different from Belinda's own, although a courtesan
worked for money, and Belinda for—

A cage with a shrieking chicken was dropped at Belinda's feet.
She looked up to see the gondola boy, who stood with his chest
thrust out and arms akimbo. "You see!" he crowed. "I have gotten
you a chicken, and now you will see my man."

"What do I need to see him for," Belinda asked, "if I've already
got a chicken?"

The boy's face fell, comical and quick as melting wax, but he recovered with lifted eyebrows and widened eyes. "He's wealthy and
handsome, lady. Maybe he's a good husband for you, huh?"

"Or maybe he's a thief who wants my necklace. Tell him it's
paste and have off with him, boy. I want my afternoon ride."
Belinda searched for biscuit crumbs from the lunch she'd carried
with her, and dropped them into the chicken's cage. The bird
stopped protesting and fluffed its tail feathers into the air, pecking
at the crumbs. The gondola boy pushed the boat back into the
canal, still entreating her.

"But he has asked for you, lady. He says he will give me two
guineas for bringing you to him."

"Two, hm? I must be very important, then." Belinda smiled

again, watching a girl above the canals lean out of her room and wave. Someone smacked her skirts, making her jump, and she fled back inside, but not before Belinda returned the wave and a young man caroled out a ribald poem.

"Yes, lady," the boy said, undeterred. "He said to look for you, to not take any other riders but you."

"And how did he tell you to know me?" Belinda asked, willing to continue the banter. It was the courtesans, her sisters in all but name, that made her feel as if she belonged here. She knew rare moments of peace and satisfaction in her life, but only in Aria Magli did she know happiness. Until her father or one of his men met her, she would spend her evenings slipping uninvited into parties, hiding behind masks to speak of politics and poetry to women whose names she would never know. It was the closest thing to freedom the queen's bastard had ever known.

"He said you would have fair skin," the boy all but sang, "and hair like the rich brown earth turned up to the morning sun. He said your eyes were the green of new leaves, and your smile softer than a thousand roses." Belinda twisted to look over her shoulder at him, astonished. The boy looked immensely pleased with himself, and she laughed out loud. "He also said you would be wearing a dress of blue and gold, and gave me the address you lived at. I waited half the morning, lady, and missed many commissions," he added more prosaically. "Now we have to go to him, or my father will beat me for losing so much money on a day like today."

"Would he really?" Belinda asked, the question mere noise to hide the dismay that dragged her heart down. There were patterns to follow in Aria Magli: dresses of particular colours, each selected for the day of the week; one address of a half dozen to stay at, rotated through. Either her father or one of his men was here to tell her more of Dmitri's cryptic message, and to give her a new assignment. There would be no long nights trading whoring secrets and stories with the courtesans, not this time. She lifted her hand, gesturing that the boy should take her where he'd been told, and looked, without expression, at the contented chicken. The boy answered her in the affirmative, babbling on with tales of his father's heavy hand and the eight, or fourteen, or twelve, brothers and sisters who all scrambled and worked to keep him in his drink and happy. Belinda laughed in the right places, gasped dramatically when it was called for, and heard nothing he said.

He had been waiting, then, her father or his man. For days, perhaps, even weeks; the journey from north of Khazar all the way to Aria Magli was easiest in high summer, but still not quick. She'd parted ways with the coachman—a more inventive lover than poor Viktor—in Khazar's capital city and travelled alone, only arriving in Aria Magli late the night before. They had been waiting for her, watching. The morning's taste of freedom had been a false one, and the open, sun-lit canals seemed a mockery now, instead of a pleasure.

The chicken finished its snack and bwocked with irritation. Belinda turned a faint smile on it. "You may have found a stay of execution, my little friend. I may not be here for supper." And if she were not, the bird would go to the boy and his eight or fourteen or twelve siblings, perhaps a finer meal than they'd had in weeks. Then again, a chicken hadn't the sense to comprehend false hope, and Belinda did. It left a taste of bleakness in her throat, bitter as almonds.

The boy poled the gondola beneath a low bridge. A coin glittered down off the bridge, landing at Belinda's feet with a flat tap. She leaned past the chicken cage to collect it, gold a heavy weight in her hand, warmth undiminished by its brief sojourn through the air. "Here," she said. "At the next steps."

"No," the boy said with determination. "The man told me—"

"He told you wrong," Belinda interrupted. "Here, boy, at the next steps, and this is yours." She lifted the coin between two fingers and all but felt the avaricious leap of the child's heart. For a

few seconds the image caught her, the stamped golden coin brilliant in the afternoon sunshine, giving a warm cast to her fingers.
Beyond her hand, in poor focus, was the water, blue with reflected
skies in direct light, brown with debris in shadow. Farther still were
figures on the streets, mostly in the strong shades favoured by the
wealthy. Probably not her father, then; he preferred the less ostentatious parts of Aria Magli for meetings such as this. Belinda had
long since learned it was often as easy to hide in plain sight, as
plumed as a peacock, but Robert would have no changing of his
ways.

"If you like to dawdle," she continued, "stay a while. It may be
that I'll return."

"My father," the boy hazarded. Belinda smiled a little.

"A bargain," she suggested. "Wait an hour, and if I haven't returned, you have the guineas, this coin, and this chicken here to
take home to your father."

"And if you have?" he demanded.

"Then you've all of those things and my fare for the rest of the
day," Belinda replied. Another chicken could always be purchased,
or dinner taken at one of the inns in the traveller's part of town.

But she'd reminded the boy with her words, and he hopped forward, a palm extended. "Your fare for the morning," he said.
"Four guineas."

Belinda lifted her eyebrows. "Two."

The child looked affronted. "Three and a half."

Belinda laughed. "Three, and it's done."

The boy spat in his palm, offering it to her before he thought.
Then dismay filled his eyes and he wiped his palm hastily against his
grubby shirt, offering his hand a second time. Belinda dropped the
guineas and the larger gold coin into his hand, watching as he se-
creted each coin into a different, heretofore unnoticed, pocket or
pouch in his clothing. "An hour," he said with the air of an ag-
grieved parent. "Not a minute more, fine lady."

"Not a minute more." Belinda gathered her skirts and climbed from the boat, her picnic basket swinging from one elbow. A young man with dark gypsy eyes and a ready white smile offered her a hand up, and she took it against her better sense, murmuring, "*Grazie.*"

His smile flashed deeper, showing dimples. She pressed a small coin into his hand and moved away, climbing up the steps and turning to walk back to the bridge the gondola had passed under. When she looked back, the gypsy man was staring at the coin in his hand with an expression of indignation.

A woman waited on the bridge, leaning over stone that made up railing and wall both, watching her reflection in the water below. Belinda took up a place on the far side of the bridge, several feet down from the other woman, and studied her as she waited for her contact. She was lovely in the expensive way of a courtesan, not the more demure beauty of a well-behaved wife: she wore chartreuse, the strength of the colour far beyond what Belinda would ever be able to wear. Her corsets made her torso long and slender, narrowing her hips and pushing her breasts high. The skirts were full but light: Belinda imagined the woman could ride a horse astride in those skirts. Her hair was dark, highlighted with gold in the afternoon sun, and her forehead high. Lorraine would approve, adoring the popular theory that a high forehead was a sign of intelligence. The women of Lorraine's court plucked their hairlines to emulate the queen. Belinda stilled her hand before it wandered to explore her own hairline; she already knew it followed Robert's more closely than Lorraine's, and that was just as well. Lorraine's widow's peak was distinctive, and a girl marked with it would draw comment and speculation that the queen could not afford.

Belinda deliberately inhaled, changing the tilt of her head to help chase away thoughts of Aulun and the queen. The woman across the bridge laughed unexpectedly, flinging a hand out. A gold coin sparkled through the air and hit a passing gondola's deck with a thunk barely audible above the sound of water lapping against the canal walls. Belinda went still within herself, keeping her expression mildly animated as her gaze went to the gondola passing beneath her. A delighted pole-boy scampered forward and scooped up the coin that had landed on his boat, shouting, "Thank you, signora!" up at the bridge.

"You're welcome!" the woman shouted back. She turned toward Belinda, looking through her and beyond her, a smile curving her full mouth. She waved; Belinda looked over her shoulder to see the gypsy man bowing deeply and extravagantly. The woman laughed and turned away again without meeting Belinda's eyes; without giving her any sign that she was to be approached.

Belinda looked back at the water, watching the shadow of another bridge swallow the second gondola the woman had gifted with a coin. She tapped one finger against the stone wall, and decided: she would wait, and see how fate ruled a third time.

When it ruled in favour of another coin thrown to a bright-eyed young gondola lad, Belinda tilted her face up to the sun and swore under her breath.

"Gone and left you then, has he?" The woman across the bridge had a warm alto, a burr to her voice that gave it an edge of sultriness. A voice practised for the bedroom, Belinda thought, and glanced at the woman. There was still a chance; her father had never before sent a woman to meet her.

"Abandoned and left cold," she replied. "Ungrateful bastard."

The woman laughed again, a rich comforting sound, and crossed the bridge to lean next to Belinda, her hands turned wrist-out against the stone wall. "Was he rich?"

"No," Belinda said. "Nor handsome, either."

The woman arched finely shaped eyebrows. "What's the point, then?"

"I suppose it's all in what we do for God and country." Belinda spoke the coded words with a shrug. The woman's eyebrows shot up.

"Sod God and bugger country. I want a palmful of coin and a feather bed."

Belinda let herself laugh aloud, relaxing against the rail. The dark-haired woman at her side was certainly not her contact. Despite what had seemed to be the signal coin, her answer left everything to be desired as a pass code, though not as a brazen woman. "With four posts and a canopy?" she asked. The woman shook her head vehemently.

"Canopies gather dust, and the only thing more foolish than a naked man is a naked man sneezing his skull off."

"Oh," Belinda said, drawn into surprise, "no. A naked man in naught but stockings is worse yet."

The woman's laughter rang out once more, and she put a hand out. "Ana. You're not one of the usual bunch."

"Rosa," Belinda said. Ana's grasp was as solid as a man's, slender bones in her hand full of strength and conviction. "And no, I'm not."

"Would you like to be?"

Belinda looked down at the patient boy in the gondola, waiting for her, and thought of the contact somewhere farther down the canal who expected her. "Yes," she said. If only for a little while.

"It is not among my assets," Belinda insisted over a cup—another cup, but she had lost count of how many *anothers* she'd had—of small beer. Ana waggled her head and her finger in tandem, dismissing Belinda's protest as the women gathered around their elbows giggled and prodded at one another. Sunset had long since come and gone. Fish pasties baked in a good light dough had been ordered, demolished, ordered anew, and demolished again. The group of boisterous women had altered somewhat over the hours, but its core, made up of Belinda and a now entirely drunken Ana, remained the same.

"Your assets are quite clear. That—" Ana was interrupted by the vocal rise and fall around her, as happily drunken women cried "Oooh!" and pushed Belinda to her feet, examining her assets. Belinda waved her beer over their heads, shaking her hips in a fruitless attempt to loosen their hands. "Lovely," an outrageously coifed redhead proclaimed, and another girl sniffed. "Her tits are too small."

"We haven't all got docks big enough to tie a gondola to, Bernice." Ana mocked tossing a rope toward the girl, who sniffed again and subsided as Ana turned back to Belinda with a sniff of her own. "She's only jealous of your throat. Long and lovely, that. Aristocratic, or meant for hanging."

"Thank you," Belinda said drily. "Dangerous thoughts, Lady Ana." More dangerous than the courtesan could know, and to be headed off as readily as possible. Belinda edged back toward her seat, trying to reclaim it.

"Not a bit of that." The woman seated behind her lifted her feet to plant them against Belinda's bottom and keep her away from the chair. "You owe us a song."

"My voice," Belinda protested again, "is not chief among my assets." The woman behind her straightened her legs, sending Belinda stumbling up onto her toes. Ana stood up and grabbed her wrist, climbing onto the table and tugging Belinda with her.

"That's not the point." She clutched Belinda's waist as they both swayed dangerously on the tabletop. Belinda leaned on Ana and squinted at her own feet, alarmingly distant.

"Was the table this crooked before?" she asked in a low voice. Ana snorted laughter.

"You haven't spilled a beer tonight, have you? There's a terrible puddle at the end of the table. A drunk man built these." She nodded, exaggerated, and slung an arm out, lifting her voice into a bellow. "Hey! You there! Me and Rosie, we're going to sing you a song!"

Three-quarters of the bar's patrons turned expectantly. Belinda elbowed Ana's ribs. "Hold your tongue! I told you, I can't sing!"

"So what'll it be then? Do you know 'Era Nato Poveretto'?"

"God," Belinda said, "barely. Born poor?" she brazened, then caught her breath, searching for another song. " 'C'è La Luna.' Will it do?"

"Well enough," Ana said with a firm nod.

Belinda drew in a deep breath, gave Ana one dismayed look, and began to sing.

"My God," Ana gasped at the break between verses, "you'd best be able to fuck like a dream, with a voice like that."

"I *told* you," Belinda snapped. Ana snagged her arm through Belinda's as they began the second verse, starting a jig that made Belinda's voice even hoarser with breathlessness. In counterpoint, Ana's voice rose and strengthened, until she was carrying the whole melody and Belinda only croaked out a word or two when she caught her breath. The crowd's cries blurred from jeers into shouts of approval.

A hand clasped around her ankle, making her stumble. She looked down to find a cheerily drunken man beaming toothily up at her. "Give us another one, bonnie Rosie," he begged. "Your voice makes my wife's sound like a golden harp, and God knows I need something to take away the edge!"

Belinda shook him off with a kick that missed clipping his temple by a scant inch or two. Then she found laughter bubbling up inside her chest, pressing against her breastbone, and after a moment she let it free. Her singing voice might shame a crowing cock, but her laugh was bright and warm.

"Oh, so *that's* how you do it," Ana said with a knowledgeable and approving nod. Belinda leered at her, flung her own head back, and began to sing the raunchiest song she knew.

Howls of approving laughter roared up to the rafters, while stomping feet shook the floor as the pub patrons kept time. She couldn't, perhaps, sing, but she could keep a beat, and now she was caught up by it, consequences be damned. As if sensing her abandonment, even the men who had shouted her down earlier courted her for more now. Torches twitched with exuberance, hopping in their nests and sending puffs of black smoke up to the ceiling. Ana grabbed her arm again and Belinda swung her around the table, slipping in spilled beer. The aroma splashed upward, hops mixing with wood smoke in a rich thick scent that made one part of her mind sleepy even as she reveled in the raw country life of it. Her circumstances allowed her few opportunities for unconstrained play, and her temperament fewer yet. It was a chance, rare in a lifetime of duty, to forget who and what she was, and why. Most of all, why. Belinda drank it in, letting the raucous music she made settle all the way down to her bones, where it might leave an impression. A memory for another time, when she would not be able to allow herself the freedom she had tonight.

Stolen freedom. The thought flickered through her mind and she banished it again. The coin from the bridge was a common signal from her father's men. That it had this time been happenstance leading to rough decadence was . . . *not her fault* would be too strong. Belinda had chosen her path for tonight, chosen to deliberately misinterpret and forget. Her voice broke on a high note and she laughed with everyone else, dropping into a deeper register to try the remainder of the verse.

Her corsets pressed into her ribs too tightly in the thick air; her throat felt constricted, though her gown was fashioned with neither collar nor hat-ribbon wrapped around her neck. Her hair had been up earlier in the day. Now it tumbled around her shoulders and down her back, sticking with sweat. If she took too shallow a breath she could smell herself, and so she breathed more deeply, drowning out her own sharpness with the woody scent of spilled beer. The dress would be forever in the cleaning, peacock blue fabric stained not just with sweat but with beer and the invading scent of the wood smoke. Belinda wondered if she could procure a sausage, and spill its grease on herself, just to irretrievably mar the gown.

Calling out, midsong, for a sausage, was an error in judgment. More than one man leapt to his feet, scrambling to undo his trousers, while others cupped their codpieces and swore it was all real. Ana laughed so hard she wept, and Belinda's dance ended as she leaned on the courtesan, gasping back laughter herself.

In the stillness brought upon by laughter, emotion swept through Belinda like fire. Not her own: that she recognized, even as rare as tonight's outburst was. No. It came from somewhere else— *everywhere* else, as burning and uncomfortable as the sickness she'd felt while standing in the dawn watching Dmitri ride away. It ate at her, feeling larger than she was, reaching inside her so it could claw its way out.

From Ana, her nose all but buried in Belinda's bosom as she tried to keep her feet while she laughed. Beneath the laughter there were tears, forced back by the night's gaiety. They were buried deep within her, tearing her soul apart. It was only through outrageousness that the dark-haired courtesan was able to keep them at bay.

From the man who'd grabbed her ankle, a fierce and abiding lust, not for the women dancing above him, but for the harpy-voiced wife he'd left at home. He would go back to her soon, trusting she'd be as happy to make a nest for his prick as he was to find one.

From the courtesans surrounding the table upon which Belinda and Ana danced came a pragmatic and determined approach to beauty, youth, and brains. As a unit, they stood together rather than apart simply because there were so few of them, and they needed what sisterhood they could get. Jealousies, petty and profound, were put aside for the few hours of shared companionship that had no guinea price on it.

And from the pub at large: desire and laughter, pleasure and pain. It rolled over Belinda in waves, tickling her in secret places, and discomfort broke as if rising emotion found welcome in the most private parts of her being. She gasped with it, knotting one hand in Ana's hair. Ana, still mirthful, lifted her head: she knew that tightness in Belinda's grasp as well as Belinda herself did, a precursor to violence and passion. They met gazes, both aware of their bodies crushed together, both aware of the hard straight lines of corsets that pressed against curves better explored in a more secluded room. Ana's lips parted and she wet them. Belinda felt her own mouth curve in an avaricious grin. Like a shock wave, those closest to them felt it, the sudden pound of desire that had, for one rare and sweet moment, nothing to do with commerce.

Then rage crashed through Belinda's belly, smashing need before its strength. She fell back; she saw Ana's eyes shutter, disappointment hidden away inside an instant. She wanted to speak, to explain, but the fury that beat its way through her only brought a film of blood to her lip as she bit into it. She fell back another step, staggering under the onslaught of unfamiliar anger, and caught the edge of the table with her heel. Her arms pinwheeled as she toppled, knowing she couldn't catch herself, hoping her new acquaintances might. Knowing, too, that they would not: she had slighted one of theirs, pink-cheeked Ana who had already gone back to dancing as if nothing had passed between her and Belinda.

Strong hands, big hands, clasped her around the waist, and the tang of fury ballooned in her so strongly that blackness swept up through her vision, and silence fell.

She did not want to waken.

She did not want to waken for a host of reasons, the first and least comfortable being that someone was carrying her, rudely, over his shoulder. Her nose smacked against the small of his back and she forced herself to let her arms dangle, instead of searching for the small dagger nested beneath her corset. Even if she could snatch it before she was noticed—unlikely—there was the second reason not to. The second reason she didn't want to awaken: she knew who carried her, and his anger would be great.

The third reason she would have preferred the oblivion of unconsciousness was that dangling like this, the uncounted number of beers she'd partaken of were eager to spill on the cobblestones. Belinda coughed and choked, then twisted as she heaved, trying to get away, less for worry of the man's clothes than to alleviate her own discomfort. He swore and dumped her on her hands and knees, holding on by her waist, while she cramped and vomited more liquid than she thought she'd drunk. Bright orange bits of carrot and chunks of half-digested meat mixed in with the runny bile. Belinda groaned, pushing up to her knees and wiping a hand across her mouth. Her captor swore again and grabbed her wrist, hauling her to her feet. She'd barely caught her balance before he flung a short door open and shoved her through it, in front of him. She tripped, stumbling to catch herself, and he caught her upper arm, hauling her around and throwing her against the wall. Belinda hit hard enough to lose her breath, and stood with her head turned, eyes downcast as she panted for air.

"Are you mad? Are you eager for the ruin of us all? I've been waiting since noon, girl!"

"Father," Belinda said in a low voice. She didn't want to look at him yet, to see the dark eyebrows beetled down in anger. She didn't want the moment of surprise she always felt when she saw how well the years had treated him: she could imagine, without looking, the well-trimmed dark hair with no more grey at the temples than he had borne when she was a child. The dark eyes that would now be clouded with fury, with a crow's nest of wrinkles around them that seemed to have more to do with eternity than age. If he held as well for another few years as he had the last ten, Belinda would appear to be his sister, not his daughter at all. She had faith that he would, for all that he was already old, nearly forty-five. His still-youthful appearance helped keep him dear to Lorraine, who wore more cosmetics now than she had in earlier years, re-creating the blush of youth. If her darling Robert aged so little, certainly she, too, must be clinging to a more tender age than a loyal populace could believe.

"Have you no answer? Look at me, girl!"

Belinda lifted her chin and her gaze, meeting Robert's eyes. "How did you find me?" she wondered, feeling as though the question came from a distant place inside her. Robert snorted and caught her arm again, pushing her up the stone steps that began barely a yard inside the door.

"The gondola boy, not that I needed him."

Damn! The force of the curse startled Belinda, making her clench her hands in her skirts. She ought to have paid the child off, sent him on his way instead of telling him to linger an hour and wait on her return. "How long did he wait before going to you?"

"Until the dinner bells rang," Robert spat. Belinda allowed herself a faintly curved smile, well-hidden from the man who followed her up the stairs. At least the boy had allowed her a few hours of freedom, instead of leaving the moment her back was turned. By dinner she and Ana were well away from the canal where Belinda had left the boy, stretching Robert's search out that much longer. She should have expected that the child would find the man who'd paid him, but hope and naïveté had won out. It had been a badly played hand.

"Someone threw a coin." Belinda offered the words as explanation, not excuse. There was no point in making excuses, not with Robert. Another man might be seduced out of his anger, but her father held as stubbornly to outrage as another man might to money. "I thought it was my sign, and only too late realised I was mistaken." Robert's hand moved past her head, pushing open a door at the head of the stairs. Fire's heat swept over Belinda. She lifted a hand against it, protecting her face as she stepped into the room.

It was well-appointed, if not extravagant. A fire burned higher than necessary for a summer night, throwing warm and wavering shadows about the room. It brought out the gold in a brocaded armchair a few feet from it; the rug that lay between chair and fire had burns from embers popping free and sizzling there. A footstool to match the chair sat opposite it. Belinda glanced around for another chair and found one lacking: it would be she who sat on the footstool, and Robert in the fine upholstered chair. Her mouth twisted a little, memories of childhood spoiling coming back to her, and she sighed as she gathered her skirts and went to the footstool.

She passed the bed, the only other piece of furniture worth noting in the room. It was a renter's room, without a kitchen or visiting area. Windows looked over a canal, but nearly every window in Aria Magli did; a room without a canal view could be far more dear than those with. The surfeit of noise from traffic that never ceased, day or night, was sometimes worth the cost. Belinda smoothed her skirts over her thighs as she sat, watching Robert move through the fire-cast shadows.

There was something in warm orange light that brought depth out in his handsome, craggy features. All the things she had remembered before looking at him were still true: he was aged enough to be sober and trustworthy, young enough to be playful and charming, but in firelight he looked dangerous as well. And he was—more dangerous than most anticipated. Lorraine's court granted him a measure of power, because he was beloved to the queen, but few of them regarded him as personally ambitious or worthy of note. Only his oft-discussed romantic liaison with Lorraine made him interesting.

Belinda knew better. Her father was Lorraine's secret spymaster, and had been for as long as she herself had lived, maybe longer. Cortes, a showier man, thin and clipped and rude, was Robert's disguise: he held the title Controller of Intelligence, and had a network that extended from nobles to playwrights and into the common populace. Behind Cortes's shadow, Robert worked, answering threats to Her Majesty in a brutal, efficient manner that could never be traced back to the queen or even her notorious spymaster. And of those secret spies, Belinda was the best-hidden of all.

"You know Sandalia," Robert said abruptly, coming out of shadow to take his seat by the fire. Belinda lifted her eyebrows a telling fraction, mildly offended by the question even though she understood it as rhetoric.

"Rodrigo's sister, who sits as regent in Gallin," she answered, keeping her tone patient. This, too, harkened to childhood ritual, Robert testing and quizzing her on whatever sprang to his mind. Things she ought to have studied, and usually had. Belinda had not been caught out by his unexpected questions since her fifteenth birthday, and had no intention of letting Robert take the upper hand in their little game now. She went on, voice lilting as if she lectured a child.

"Wed and widowed twice before she was eighteen, Sandalia and her son, Javier, stand heir to three thrones: Lanyarch, left to her by Charles, who, by the by, would have been Lorraine's heir should he have lived and should she never marry. Then there's Gallin's throne by way of her second husband, and finally Essandia's, should her brother, Rodrigo, produce no heir." Javier would have to be a strong leader indeed, when Rodrigo passed on, to hold the thrones of Essandia and Gallin both, much less add Lanyarch to the mix. If he managed, it would be through the strength of those religious ties, and a fair amount of luck besides. Luck arranged, perhaps, by Sandalia de Costa. "I do not," Belinda added, "know her personally."

Robert gave her a black look. Belinda lifted an eyebrow again. Her father subsided, pushing away her snip, and any acknowledgment that his question had been foolish, with a wave of his hand. "When were you last in court, Belinda? In Lorraine's court."

"Eight years and some. After du Roz, but not long after." Belinda watched her father warily, uncertain of where his question led. "Not since I was a child. You know this, Robert." Calling him "Father," as she had at the foot of the stairs, was a bladed luxury Belinda indulged herself in once each time she saw him. Someday she thought it would sting when she used that weapon, but in the ten years since she'd learned the truths he and Lorraine Walter hid, he had not yet flinched. She wondered, sometimes, if he did not realise what she knew; if to him the change from "Papa" to "Father" and "Robert" was nothing more than a sign that Belinda had become an adult and put away childish things. They had none of them confessed the circumstances of Belinda's birth and heritage, and certainly Lorraine never would. It seemed impossible that Robert could not know that Belinda had, since the day she became the queen's assassin, also known that she was her mother's weapon.

But then, memory did not stretch so far back, and a babe still wet with birthing blood should not recall a narrow, regal face and titian curls spilling over pale skin. That was a recollection Belinda kept close to her heart, and had never spoken of to her father. It seemed impossible that he could not know, but perhaps it was even more improbable that she could.

"I do. And I wonder if there are any who might know you."

"In the Aulunian court? A few, perhaps. More who would claim to," Belinda began, but Robert lifted his hand again, stopping her words.

"In Gallin. In the regent's court at Lutetia." Robert brushed his hand over his eyes. "It is a risk." The words were low, spoken more to himself than to Belinda. "The straits are not so wide, but the godly gulf is deep. And ten years might be ten decades in this place."

"My lord?"

Robert's gaze snapped up again and he shook his head. "Forgive an old man's ramblings."

Belinda snorted, loud and undignified. Robert looked chagrined, then laughed, bringing his hands together in a solid clap. "Which is it you'll claim? Not old, or not rambling?"

"Not either, my lord," Belinda said, smiling. "Your every word falls like a precious gem on my listening ears. I have not been placed somewhere so high as a regent's court, Robert, and you have not come to see me yourself in a long time. D—" She broke off, remembering abruptly that her childhood memories were supposed to be asleep. Dmitri had not given her his name, in the Khazarian north. She ought not know him or his name. "—the man who came to me in Khazar—"

"It was nicely done with the count," Robert interrupted. "What did you slip him to bring on that conveniently bad summer cold? The symptoms were unexpected."

Belinda held her mouth in a long moue, hiding a fluttering heartbeat behind a wry examination of her father before she lowered her gaze with a smile. "That would be telling, sir, and a lady never tells."

But only because there was no answer that would satisfy. The one she wanted to offer was arsenic, but uncertainty lay beneath it. She hadn't let herself linger on Gregori's death; it had been achieved, and that was all that mattered. For the second time that evening she remembered the alien emotion pounding through her. In Khazar she had trusted it must be her own; at the Magalian pub she had been certain that the emotion she'd known belonged to those around her. It tasted of witchery.

No. Belinda clamped down on a shudder, unwilling to release her control even—especially—in her father's presence. She would not show fear, would not give in to the power of childhood stories. Illness was brought on by arsenic, not wishes, no matter the desire she'd held in her heart to bring Gregori low, for Lorraine and for the bruises Belinda herself carried from his hand. Pretty, bitter Ilyana was superstitious and jealous, her accusations of witchcraft the creation of a small, frightened mind. It could not be otherwise.

Prickles of cold washed over Belinda's skin in spite of the fire's heat, and she set the discomfiting thoughts aside as her father laughed again. "A lady never does," he mocked her. "A gentleman never tells."

"You know far fewer ladies than I do, then, sir," Belinda said drily. "Not that I would wish to malign the reputations of any of the fine women I know." She thought, briefly, of Ana, swinging her around on the table, and let herself smile. The stolen afternoon and evening had been worth Robert's anger, which seemed to have fled quickly enough once she was back in . . . custody? she wondered. It was not a term she was accustomed to using for herself. "The man who came to me in Khazar said time was of importance. What's stirring in Gallin?"

Robert's expression blackened for a few seconds. "If time is so much of an essence, and you are aware of that, what excuse do you have for dallying away your day today?"

Belinda exhaled a quiet long breath. "Even the queen takes holidays, my lord. If one day is so desperate a difference, you ought have sent me to Gallin straight away rather than coming here as we always do."

Robert steepled his fingers and pressed his lips against them, frowning at her. "Yes," he said abruptly, eventually. "Yes, you have the right of it there. Damn you, anyway. Who taught you cleverness?"

"My nurse, my lord." Belinda lowered her eyes demurely, remembering the staid old woman, then peeked up with an arched eyebrow, not bothering to hide her amusement. Robert guffawed and came to his feet, catching Belinda's hands in his own. He pulled her to standing and into a rough hug.

"My lass. There's my girl. Outwitting the old man. Soon enough there'll be no place for me."

"Robert," Belinda began, but he shook his head and put her back from himself, holding her shoulders.

"Not yet. This old dragon has a few flames left in him yet. There is rumour of insurrection from Gallin, Belinda."

"Who? Against Sandalia? Or the boy? Javier?"

"He's your age, lass, not such a boy at all. Twenty-two years old and holding back from claiming the throne out of respect for his mother, that's what they say."

"Or out of a fear he'll never see another day that belongs to his own self and isn't owed to another."

Robert's eyes darkened again, this time with thought. "That may be some of it, too. No, no. Sandalia visits with her brother Rodrigo in Essandia, and my people warn that their cloistered discussions say she chafes at her boundaries and eyes Lanyarch and Aulun. You named the threads that link her to Aulun's throne yourself. Sandalia may think a pretender's crown would look well upon her head. You will not let that happen."

Belinda closed her eyes, absorbing Robert's orders along with the decade-old ritual that set them into place. *This is how it shall go, Primrose. Heed me well.*

When he was done she opened her eyes again, all but swaying with the music of his words. "It's a chess game you're playing, my lord, one where the black queen is not yet even on the board. Why send me to Lutetia and not Isidro in Essandia?" She passed off the question with a wave of her hand even as she asked it. Passed off, too, the chiding, flat-mouthed glance her father gave her; she went to Lutetia because Sandalia was *not* there, and that gave Belinda space to insinuate herself in society before the queen's return. "Does it matter to you how I become close enough to the throne to watch it and judge its actions?"

"Has it ever?" Robert asked lightly enough. It had not; not from the night he'd murmured Belinda's duty to her, and set her on du Roz. All she had known was the man's death must be accomplished, and even at not quite twelve, that it should look like an accident seemed obvious. Robert had been astounded at the swiftness of her actions, and at the method of du Roz's death. Belinda recalled with exquisite clarity the brief admiring expression on her father's face as she'd swooned and trembled in a guard's arms during the aftermath of sudden, dreadful death. No, if even then she had accepted her tasks and determined her own path to achieving them, Robert would not likely now commanded her walk a road of his choosing.

"Find a way to shove Gallin from the parapets; that's all we need," he said, as though following her thoughts of du Roz. "Sandalia has never had Lorraine's caution, and an ill-advised word spoken to an ear *we* can trust is what we need. Find that weakness, Primrose. Find that ambition, and exploit it. We cannot allow Aulun to fall into Ecumenic hands again."

Belinda widened her eyes in a mockery of innocence, a hand placed against her breastbone. "Why, my lord, do you say that you trust me so very much, then?"

Sudden unexpected fondness deepened Robert's eyes, and Belinda glanced away. "You are a good girl, loyal and true," her father said, as if from a distance, "and I would trust no other beyond you."

Belinda stood, gathering her soiled skirts, and dipped a curtsey of unnecessary depth. "Then I'm away to Gallin in the morning, my lord, to prove your faith in me."

ANA DI MEO, COURTESAN
17 July 1587 † *Aria Magli, Parna*

A door opens, almost soundless, breaching the space between rooms more thoroughly than a handful of spy holes can do. A man enters, long strides eating the space in small rooms. His voice, his question, is abrupt with unusual uncertainty: "And?"

Ana taps a fingertip against the arm of her chair, a soft thump of flesh rather than the rat-tat of longer nails. She leans on the other elbow, one knuckle pressed over her lips as she watches Drake pace in front of the fire. In another man such action might speak of nervous energy. In Robert, it has more of the predator to it, heavy solid movements that threaten to back quarry into position for the kill. He is the only man who has ever refused to pay her in coin.

He is the only man she can imagine permitting that refusal.

"She is lonely, my lord."

Robert turns in astonishment. "That hardly matters."

Ana tilts her head, eyebrows drawn down. "On the contrary. Almost nothing else does matter. Women will do things to ease loneliness as men will do them to ease the pangs of love."

"Not Rosa." Robert makes a sharp gesture, dismissive. "No more than I." Silence falls before he makes another gesture, still sharp, now demanding. "What might she do?"

"Besides ignore your summonings for hours on end?" Ana's eyebrows arch with challenge. "Robert, emotion is not a predictable thing that follows step to reasonable step."

He arches an eyebrow back, and Ana laughs. "All right, maybe for you, my lord, but those of us who are merely human are made of weaker stuff." She gets to her feet and comes forward to slip her arms around his waist, smiling up at him. "My lord Drake. Do you know that 'drake' means 'dragon,' Robert?"

He frowns at her with good humour, the lines of his short-cropped beard making the expression all the more dramatic. "Aulunian isn't your native tongue, Ana. How do you know that?"

"Neither is Reinnish, Robert, and that's where the word comes from. I do have some education."

"Yes." He cups her cheek wonderingly, shaking his head. "The loveliest women, trained for bedding pleasure and stimulating conversation. I will never understand Aria Magli."

"Aulunian reserve," Ana says, "will never understand the rest of Echon at all. Do you know there are people who believe you Aulunian are all knitted out of the fog that haunts your island? All so cool and pale and emotionless."

"And what do you believe?"

Ana smiles. "That you're unlike most Aulunian men I've met."

"Then I believe I'm flattered." Robert shakes his head again. "But you're not here to flatter me. Tell me how Rosa will jump."

Ana sighs and steps back, brushing her knuckles across her own mouth. It had been easy, in the moment, to believe that the young woman might have forgotten her duties to spend the night in the arms of another who shared similar duties. But then she'd drawn back, repulsed and panicked, and had fallen into a swoon. Ana keeps her eyes lowered until she's certain her expression won't betray the hurt she felt at Rosa's rejection, until the pulse in her throat has slowed a little. It's only a few seconds before she lifts her gaze to meet Robert's eyes. "She is bound to you, Robert. She won't betray you."

"And I can trust that?"

Ana snorts, all semblance of delicacy left behind as she turns away. "You can trust there's not a much better judge of character than a whore. What are you afraid of with her?"

Robert holds his tongue so long she finally looks over her shoulder. "It is my experience," he says with the delicacy she's abandoned, "that females are far more pragmatic than males. I did not mean to question you quite so . . . rudely." The deference in his voice is astonishing, his gaze lowered and shoulders rolled as he tries to make himself smaller. They've been lovers on and off for sixteen years; it isn't the first time Robert has questioned her judgment and abased himself at her snappish replies. It never ceases to amaze her. "It's unlike her to abandon her duty as she did today. I must be certain of her loyalty." His voice remains soft, apologetic.

"No wonder your queen is so fond of you." Ana comes back to him, touching his chin to make him lift his head. "I'd like to meet the mother who trained such deference to women into you."

Robert smiles, thin. "No," he says, "you wouldn't. Now *there* was a dragon." More humour lights his eyes and he shakes his head. "I need you to do something for me, Ana."

"Will I get a lot of money for it?" Impishness prompts the question and she's rewarded by Robert throwing his head back and laughing aloud.

"Expenses. I won't pay more than that, you know that."

"I do." Ana holds her breath a moment before plunging into a question that's plagued her for years: "Why is that, my lord?"

Robert's heavy eyebrows lift. "Because in my world, a woman chooses her lovers. A man might woo, but it is an honour to be chosen. To offer coin would be . . . a killing offense."

"That," Ana says drolly, "is hardly the Aulun I've heard of. Perhaps you nobles are more genteel than the fog can bear news of. Maybe I should visit there, or even stay. That sounds much more pleasant than spreading my legs at the drop of a coin."

"Not all Aulunian men," Robert murmurs, "dance on the whim of their queen."

"True. All right." Ana claps her hands together, curious. "What do you need me to do, Robert?"

"Follow Rosa to Lutetia."

Ana laughs as loudly as Robert did a moment earlier, her humour fading as Robert's expression remains serious. "You can't possibly mean that."

"Why not?"

"What would I do there? Why would I follow her?"

"You're a resourceful woman, Ana. Come up with an excuse. An evening of dance and drink awoke an unbearable longing in your loins for the lass. A wealthy patron finally made good his debt and you can retire; whatever it takes."

"I thought you said you trusted her."

Robert nods. "I do. But this is . . . important. If she's lonely, as you say—she's used to playing the part of a poor woman, Ana. A worker, not a lady. I cannot risk the feel of silk against her thighs and wealthy men distracting her, and I must know from other sources if she is focused."

"I'm not going to Lutetia unless I can travel comfortably, Robert. Expenses will be dear, for this." Ana speaks the Gallic language, but she's never travelled beyond Aria Magli. This has been her home, her cage, and until a moment ago, she would have never imagined leaving. It surprises her how willing she is to consider it, but then, she has confidence in the financial incentives Robert will agree to. His crooked smile tells her she's right to be certain of him.

"I wouldn't imagine anything less. You won't leave for a week. I don't want any chance of you meeting on the road."

"And if we meet in Lutetia?"

Robert lifts her hand to kiss the inside of her wrist. His mouth is warm, making a shiver of desire ripple over her skin. He looks through his lashes, unfairly seductive, and offers a teasing grin. "Improvise."

"Ya think God gave ya teats 'cause he wanted ya ta think?" A barrel-chested Gallicman thrust his face into Belinda's and exhaled breath laden with the stench of beer. She allowed herself the luxury of gagging, turning her head away to cough out the odor she'd inhaled. For a moment she thought of Viktor and his bad breath, and sent an apology to him, wherever he might be.

It was the curse—well, one of many—of being a woman: there was nowhere for women to gather and talk in the way that men did, at least not women above a certain station. Belinda dared not play a part too close to the street, not when she ultimately needed to walk into the palace, but for her first days in Lutetia she saw no other choice.

Chances were good it didn't matter. She would shed her identity and create a new one within the Lutetian walls as many times as necessary. So long as she moved from one part of the city to another, she remained anonymous: as in all Echonian cities, the classes rarely mixed. This was her third tavern in as many nights, and there would be more before she was satisfied.

Her costume was as much disguise as she needed. The corsets were thick and weighted, giving her the bulk of a larger woman.

She went barefoot in the August heat, subtracting inches from the height a noblewoman would stand at, and wore her hair in a rat's nest that approximated the smooth coifs of the upper class. It would take a week to comb out. Between all that and her breasts being shelved as high as they could be without popping out of her dress, she had reasonable confidence she would go unrecognized between tavern and a rich man's church.

"All I'm sayin'," she gave back to the blowhard, in language as base as his own, "is that it seems like the only godly thing to do."

"You're mad." He sat back on his stool so hard it creaked and one leg bowed out dramatically. "Do you know what a crusade is, lovey?"

It would hardly do to show surprise that a base-born Lutetian had any especial grasp of crusading, though interest piqued in Belinda's breast, flickering her eyebrows upward. "Naw. What is it?"

"It's a lot of people thinkin' like you do getting together and riding off to some foreign land to correct their religious beliefs." The bulky man raked a hand through sandy hair, signaling for another tankard. Half a dozen people reached to pay for it. Satisfaction glinted in his eyes as he lifted it to them all in thanks.

"So I don't see what's so wrong with that," Belinda snapped. "Someone's gotta save the heathens, don't they now?"

"Mebbe, mebbe. But it's the noble houses leading 'em, lovey, and it's the likes of you and me who die for 'em."

Belinda put all her suspicion into a squint. "How d'you know so much?"

"My granfa three hundred years back went to the Holy Lands."

Belinda snorted. "And my grandmother was the Aulunian consort. You're full of shit."

"She coulda been, with the way that bastard went through women." Raucous laughter split the air. Belinda leaned forward to pound on the table.

"That's what I'm sayin'! All them wives and divorces and what have you, and leavin' the Church behind! It ain't right! Don't the regent have a *right* to Aulun, better'n that red-headed harlot they got on the throne? How long's the Reformation bitch sat on the throne, anyways?"

"What's the point in changin' out one woman for another?" the man demanded. "God didn' give any of them teats so they could think, neither."

"But the regent is a godly woman," Belinda protested. "The son's been raised in the true church. I've got no call against you, mister, women don't belong on thrones but for holdin' 'em for their sons. But that woman, Lorrene?"

"Lorraine," someone said. Belinda waved a hand at the man in thanks before hitting the table again.

"Lorraine. She's got no get and no chance of it now, as long in the tooth as she is. Does she think she'll live forever? We got a *duty*! Think of all them souls being damned to hell because the regent won't act!"

A rumble of discontent swept through the men and women gathered around her. Her debate partner snorted and drank from his tankard, watching her with hazel eyes less bleary from drink than she expected. Others refused to meet her gaze, letting theirs slide uncomfortably away from her even as they exchanged little nods to one another. "It ain't right," someone agreed.

"Mebbe not," someone else said, "but I'm not lookin' to die for it."

Belinda's drinking partner leaned forward, crooking a finger at her. She folded her arms under her breasts and leaned on the table, watching his gaze drop to her bosom before he lifted it to her face. "You're trouble, lass," he told her in a smelly growl. "There's them that agrees with you, but it ain't good for your health to be spouting off like you're doin', you understand me?"

"No one cares what I say," Belinda said, infusing it with all the bitterness she could. "A woman without two coins to rub together. No one cares."

The man smiled, lecherous and foul with beer. "Can't do a damned thing about the womanhood, but the coin, now. Might have a few to spare for a woman as eager in bed as she is about politics."

He was, Belinda thought later, considerably less coarse than she'd expected.

BELINDA PRIMROSE
23 August 1587 † *Lutetia, Gallin*

The priest's fingertips touched her tongue. For a gleeful instant Belinda let herself wonder what he would do if she caught his finger in her mouth and suckled it as she gazed up at him through long eyelashes. Then again, what she'd heard of Ecumenic priests suggested it would be a gesture wasted, as she had a woman's curves and not a boy's narrow hips. She swallowed the sweetened bread, sipped the wine—better wine than she expected—and kept her eyes lowered. A fit of giggles in the magnificently silent cathedral would not do at all.

The grey flagstones beneath her knees were worn in smooth hollows from centuries of parishioners taking the blood and body of the Lord as she had just done for the first time. Belinda had more faith in her queen than in the God she'd never seen, but worshipping in an Ecumenical church made the hairs on her arms rise in discomfort. She had never played a role so close to her own and at the same time so diametrically different.

A queen's life depended on hers; that was as it had always been. But now, for the first time, it was not Lorraine's length of days, but Sandalia de Costa's, that she held in her hands. Sandalia had a viable claim to Aulun's throne and a lifetime of preparation behind her: if the rumours Robert had heard were true, the time for waiting was over. Sandalia intended to make a play for Lorraine's country, to take her throne and restore Aulun to Ecumenic rule.

Belinda had spent a decade slipping through the lower ranks, taking lives and ruining reputations to protect the Aulunian queen. Robert's whisper came back to her: *This is how it must be.* She would insinuate herself in court, make herself as close to Sandalia as she could, and seek out any hint of perfidy that might condemn Sandalia as an active, physical threat to Lorraine's person. She sought written confirmation in the form of treaties or ambitious letters if it was to be found, or to become embroiled in a plot to set Sandalia on Aulun's throne herself, if pen could not be pursuaded to parchment. For a rarity, she was not commanded to do murder, though Robert had left that dangling, neither condoning nor condemning it as a possibility. A queen might die at Belinda's hands, that another might live.

The priest bade her rise, and she did, murmuring thanks and crossing herself as easily as if she'd done it every night of her life. She stepped back, then turned, retreating to her seat, closer to the back of the cathedral than the front. Merchants and bankers sat here, the wealthy working class caught between nobility and poor. Belinda allowed herself a seat toward the front of that class, in keeping with the small wealth her persona commanded. More than one mother examined her critically, judging her clothes and bearing. More than one son caught her eye, judging her breasts and hips. Belinda took note of them without watching, her eyes fixed piously toward the front of the cathedral and the magnificently dressed priest who lectured there. Around her, women whispered the words of worship they had learned by rote; Belinda instead listened to his speech, delivered with passion. His voice carried up the cathedral walls, rolling to the back without effort.

Ancient Parnan was not her strongest tongue, but she could do more than translate a sermon with it. The priest never faltered, his voice rising and falling until the lecture sounded almost like a song.

Belinda drifted on it, listening less to the speaker than to the cathedral itself. Morning light slashed down through stained-glass windows, sending a multitude of colours over the congregation. It looked, Belinda thought, as if God had stretched out His hand and graced the believers with the light of faith. She turned her head and discovered bright patches of yellow speckling her shoulders, and thought perhaps He graced the less faithful as well. She smiled, turning her face back to the sermonizing priest, but not before meeting the gaze of a young man a few pews away. He offered a brief, hopeful smile that lit brown eyes, making him even more youthful than an unruly cascade of brown curls suggested. Belinda quelled the impulse to curl her fingers, as if snagging the man with her gaze put him in the palm of her hand. Marius Poulin, whose sturdy loyalty lent him friends of higher rank than the son of a merchant family might aspire to. She had studied him and half a dozen others from her gutter-rat station, hiding at the back of the cathedral to hear worship and watch the young men who might fall to her traps. Marius, handsome and good-hearted, was her first choice. Belinda let her eyes flicker back to his after a moment, and his smile brightened.

It was simple to let him catch her after the service. She dawdled, adjusting her shoe, and when she straightened he was there, offering a hand in support. "Marius Poulin. Forgive me my forwardness, but I haven't seen you here before."

Belinda smiled. "Do you know all the congregation by sight, Marius Poulin?" If they were well-dressed, certainly, though he'd passed her by a dozen times in the past two weeks without ever seeing her as she crouched with the poor on the steps or inside, near the cathedral's doors.

"Close enough. For a large cathedral, it's a very small church. May I be so bold as to escort you a little way, lady? And perhaps to beg your name? And to ask from whence you came?"

"Too many questions." Belinda laughed and slipped her arm

through Marius's. "You may escort me a little ways, but the rest I fear I must be judicious with. Lutetia," she confided, "is such a very large city, and a woman cannot be sure of whom she may trust." Her Gallic was more than flat; she endowed it with the burr of Lanyarch, the contentious, Ecumenic holdings in Aulun's north.

"From Northern Aulun, then," Marius said. Belinda's expression went cool and she pulled away very slightly.

"Lanyarch."

Marius tightened his hand over Belinda's at his elbow. "Lanyarch," he echoed. "I apologize, lady. It's difficult to know—"

"Were I a sympathizer to the Reformation, would I attend worship here?" Ice slid through Belinda's voice, her spine stiff with restrained indignation. "I have not chosen Gallin as a retreat entirely for the food, sir. If you will excuse me." She shook off his hand and swept forward, her skirts gathered away from the cobblestone roads. A few quick steps put passersby between herself and him, and she heard him call out a quick, frustrated apology before cursing. Smiling, she let the crowd take her away, confident of a hook well set. The midweek worship would be early enough to see him again. If she were a good judge, he would be there, fretting at his lost chance and hoping for a new one.

He was not. Nor was he at the following Sunday sermon. Belinda searched the cathedral pews, quick glances to the left and right. If Marius was there, being caught looking for him would undo her cool dismissal. But the staid and proper merchants hid him nowhere in their ranks. Other young men caught her eye, and she let her gaze soften; if she had to begin again, it would be easier if the first impression she left was not an unapproachable one.

She didn't like doubting herself; it wasn't like her to be such a poor judge of character. She heard nothing of the sermon, but rather watched the priest with blind eyes, considering her own tactics and wondering where she had gone wrong. Perhaps she'd been too cold, too challenging. Perhaps he had less of the hunter in him than she'd anticipated. Or perhaps it was merely something as simple as his mother having higher sights set for the boy, though she would still expect him to attend church.

Belinda exited the cathedral with the crowd, casting a judging eye at the morning sun. It was not yet noon and carried little of the day's heat with it. She stepped out of the line of traffic to shake open a parasol, grateful for the reduction in glare the moment she set it over her shoulder. Certainly Marius's mother would not forbid him worship entirely. She would try a final time, at the afternoon gathering, and accept disappointment and defeat if he were not there. She would find another mark, but it galled her. What gossip had told her of Marius Poulin had made him seem the perfect catch, and she was unaccustomed to having to try more than once to set her line.

Arrogance, she admitted to herself, the thought bringing a small smile to her face. Arrogance served her well; it gave her the confidence to gain the attraction of nearly any man, from soldier to noble. Confidence made up for lack of beauty; few people understood that as thoroughly as she did. And beauty was its own handicap. It was safer to slip through courts and intrigues as a pretty woman rather than as a beautiful one. Beauty, like that with which her mother was bestowed, would be remembered where mere prettiness would not. Of course—Belinda found herself smiling again, and men smiled back at her—of course, Lorraine had power as well, which made even the most unattractive of women beautiful. But it, too, carried its price. Power meant a lifetime of political bargains. Lorraine's choice was the power of solitude, her beauty aging and fading as she played one suitor against another, knowing none of them held love in his heart for her. Even desire was questionable, except desire for the throne she sat on. Not for the first time, Belinda wondered if Lorraine entirely trusted the feelings Robert Drake harbored for her. More, Belinda wondered if she should. He had never pursued her hand in marriage, choosing never to threaten her autonomy or power. If anything kept them together, it was that, Belinda thought. Robert was willing to accept a more subtle power, to let a woman sit above him. He was an unusual man, and for that Belinda felt a small, startling surge of pride.

Her mood restored, she shook herself and began down the cathedral steps, still smiling. Confidence had failed her, this time. It was no doubt good for her to lose one once in a while. It reminded her that she was only human.

"Mademoiselle?" The pleasant male tenor came from behind her. Belinda straightened, her smile turning pure with recognition before she schooled her features into calm curiosity and turned. Only human, perhaps, but not so poor a judge of character after all.

"Marius Poulin." She offered her hand, a delicate arch to her fingers, trusting he would curve his hand beneath hers. He did, bowing very slightly over her hand. As he came to full height again he lifted his eyebrows in question, the faintest pressure on her fingers. She inclined her head as slightly as he'd bowed, and he stepped forward, turning to tuck her hand into the crook of his arm. "I thought," Belinda said, "that perhaps you had abandoned me."

"Not at all. I've spent the past ten days cloistered in my garret, beating my brow and rending my breast, searching for a way to undo what damage my careless words had done to our burgeoning relationship." His eyes lit with hope and humour, making Belinda smile. Perhaps Lutetia was good for her; smiling seemed to come almost as easily here as it did in Aria Magli. The silence and stillness within her retreated a little. Not far enough to leave her in danger of exposing herself, but enough that it took less conscious effort to act as the women around her did.

"Relationship," she echoed, letting amusement warm her voice. She could see appreciation in his eyes, in the way his pupils dilated, black swallowing brown. A touch of red came to his cheeks and she almost laughed; he was an innocent. The laughter faded in an instant. Innocence made him easily used, and easily damaged. Marius Poulin would not forget the woman he escorted on his arm, not until the day he died. If his Heaven were a kind place, he would leave her memory behind when he entered through its gates. Belinda knew too well that first love found with her was a dredge that never lost its bitter flavour.

"Do we have a relationship, Marius Poulin?" Belinda asked, trusting her own instincts, long and well trained, to have not let the silence between them grow too deep or distressing. "And dare I ask—" She hesitated, wondering how far decency would let her play before she actually shocked the boy. Far enough, she decided: her part was that of a widow, after all, not a virgin with no teeth. "—what sort of relationship you have with women whose names you do not know?"

Color scarred his cheekbones again, but he smiled, making Belinda's smile return. Innocent enough to be embarrassed, but not undone by her flirting. He would do very nicely, if his friendships reached as high as rumour said they did. "Not the sort I would discuss with a lady," he confessed. "Perhaps you might tell me your name, that I might pursue a relationship of a more delicate nature with you."

Curiosity stung Belinda, making her tilt her chin up to consider the line of his jaw. He was only a little taller than she was; tall enough, but not imposing. He would follow men larger both in stature and in spirit, never doubting his own place as second or third in command. He would be well loved among the lower ranks for generosity of heart and for his faith in following those with authority over him. She had known men like him, essentially gentle of nature and true of soul, always followers, lacking the certain spark that made them bold and fearless in the eyes of others. Men like Marius were too predictable to be dangerous, but without them it seemed to Belinda that the world might cease to function. She had judged him correctly in his inability to resist the temptation she provided; she knew him well enough, already, to guide him where she needed him to be. There was strength in his jaw, pink still lightly touching his cheekbones. Belinda smiled once more, pleased with the young man at her side. He would do admirably.

"Tell me," she asked, a note of teasing command in her voice, "do you truly not know my name?"

He glanced at her, eyes widening with startlement before his smile broadened. "A gentleman wouldn't confess to knowing it if he did, Lady Beatrice."

Belinda had not heard the name spoken aloud before, not by someone of comparative rank to her assumed persona. In Marius's light tenor it settled around her like a cloak. Hairs rose on her arms very briefly, as if cool silk slid over soft skin. She felt the chill settle into her bones, airy and temporary, reshaping her from the inside out again. Belinda Primrose was left behind in the naming, a new woman born in her place. She breathed in, and found laughter would come more easily to Beatrice than to Belinda; she must take care to ward against it becoming dangerously easy. Beatrice must marry well, to guard her small fortune and have children that would support her in her later years; she had terribly little to do with the woman she had been made from.

Wearing the garb of Beatrice's life like a new skin that caressed her body, Belinda smiled up at Marius, letting delight, so easily mistaken for adoration, widen her eyes. "And if you know it, as you do, what, then, are you, if not a gentleman?" She felt the laughter bubbling up inside her and for a disconcerting few seconds found herself unable to release it, her own nature quelling it with more ferocity than the newly worn Beatrice had strength to support it. Marius, beaming at her, didn't see the internal struggle that Belinda fought with herself, denying a decade of stillness to let a noblewoman's laughter rise to the surface and froth over.

"Desperately curious," he answered. "Beatrice Irvine, a widow—" His smile faltered, eyes lowered for a few seconds. "I am sorry to hear of your loss, lady."

"He was old when we were wed." The note she strove for was a narrow one, simple fact mingled with small regret and a degree of both strength and relief. Marius lifted his eyes to meet hers, and in them she saw that all the things she had meant her voice to say in place of her words had been heard as clearly as she hoped. Her husband had been old, but she was young and vital; an old man could not have hoped to satisfy her, and she was a woman who wanted satisfaction. Colour warmed Marius's cheeks again. Belinda allowed herself another smile, mild and edging on regret that neither she nor her persona truly felt for the death of an imaginary husband. Society dictated that she must put on a show. Marius knew as well as she that she put on as little as possible, laying truth between them in the silence after her words.

"Widowed without children," Marius went on, his voice lower and huskier. "A crueler fate than a gentle woman deserves."

Whatever, then, Belinda wondered, did *she* deserve? But she lowered her own gaze briefly, acknowledgment before she looked up again. "But God has granted me health, and I am still young enough," she murmured. "Perhaps there is meant to be more to my life than a widow's lonely years."

Triumph and hope blended together in Marius's voice to lighten it again. "Perhaps, Lady Irvine, you would be so good as to join me for supper tomorrow evening? I would be delighted to introduce you to a few of my friends, so you might not be so alone in a strange new city. Lutetia must be very different from Lanyarch." Through hope came strain, his words so careful as to be forced. Such shyness was beyond her expectations of him, and Belinda dimpled, tightening her fingers around his arm.

"I would be delighted. One of the only kindnesses of widowhood, sir, is that as a widow a woman is thought respectable, and permitted to attend to her own duties and pleasures without a chaperone. I would enjoy dining with you very much."

"At seven, then?" Marius asked, voice still tight with strain, newly tempered with pleasure. "I should be glad to send my carriage for you, if you would tell me your address."

Teasing sprang into Belinda's words. "Are you telling me that you don't already know it?"

To her utter delight, deeper red than before rushed to Marius's cheekbones. He cleared his throat and pushed his lips out, staring firmly at a child across the street. The girl caught his gaze and darted toward him, holding her box of summer flowers out. "Buy a peony for the lady, sir!" she caroled. "A lady likes nothin' better than a pansy! Won't you buy a flower for a penny, sir?"

Marius released Belinda's hand to dig in a belt pouch for a coin, handing it to the waif as he plucked a bouquet of bright pink and yellow flowers from her box. Belinda stood back, her own concentration caught up in a struggle between letting a pure, full smile come through and the reticence she had long since built into herself wanting to forbid it. Instead of the forceful smile, she felt tremendous amusement twitching her lips as Marius turned to her, offering the bouquet. "Forgive me," he said, grinning openly. The flower girl's interruption had given him time to regain equilibrium, and he was able to laugh at himself now. "I do know your address, and if you will be so good as to take these beautiful—"

"Weeds," Belinda interrupted, unwilling to push down her own laughter any longer. Marius looked at his handful of flowers in dismay. "Weeds," Belinda repeated. "Dandelions, these," she fingered the yellow flowers, "and red clover."

"I had thought to do you better than a handful of common weeds," Marius said dolefully. Belinda laughed aloud, half startled at the sound of it, and stepped forward to take the flowers from his hand.

"The right sort of woman might take them as a compliment,

M'sieur Poulin. They have their own beauty, if perhaps a little coarse, and they are pernicious. A weed need not be nurtured and coaxed along. Instead it springs up when and where it will, to show its colors brilliantly and without fear. Even the most stubborn gardener of all," and she lifted her eyes, looking up at him through her lashes, "must root and dig and force himself upon them, to have a chance at the upper hand."

Marius blanched, then reddened again. He cleared his throat, glancing at Belinda's handful of flowers, then made himself meet her eyes. "I shall endeavor to be the sort of gardener who encourages weeds, then," he said, voice gone rough and soft again. "A woman who appreciates the beauty in such things must be worth cultivating for."

Belinda pressed her fingertips against her throat, smiling. "You honour me." She stepped forward again, close enough to sway her hips and brush them against Marius's. "I am sure," she murmured, "that being cultivated will be an experience all of its own." She swallowed back laughter—this Beatrice she wore laughed far too easily and Belinda was not at all certain she approved of her chosen persona's gaiety—as Marius swallowed and tried not to let his gaze rest too obviously on her bosom.

"Tomorrow night," Belinda said brightly, "at seven. I look forward to it, M'sieur Poulin. Good afternoon." This time, as she left him dumbfounded in the street, she threw a smile back over her shoulder, and lifted the flowers to find a scent in them as she walked home.

"Good Lord, Marius has brought a woman among us." Rich sounds for all the nasal inflection of the Gallic language—nobility, then. Another voice, less cultured but still well-schooled, something familiar in its depth, answered:

"Not gaudy enough to be a whore—"

"—unless she's a damned expensive one." A third voice, laughing. A woman's voice, with rougher tones and perhaps an edge of jealousy.

"Marius can't afford that. How'd he get her through the front door?" The second voice again, cheerful in its near-recognizable growl, before the first interrupted with, "Hush. They're here."

Belinda doubted her escort had heard the exchange; through the constant low noise of the Lutetian club, she was surprised she had. But then, it was necessary for her to pick out even the faintest comments concerning her. There were times her life depended on it.

This was not such a time—not yet—but even so, the place in which Belinda found herself was not one she was accustomed to. A gentleman's club, where women were not meant to be allowed at all, though prostitutes were of sufficient use that a blind eye was usually turned to them. A decent woman, certainly, would never find herself here, escorted by a courting gentleman or not. She had hesitated outside the door, drawing on Marius's arm to ask, "Are you certain, m'sieur? You will do damage to my reputation."

Marius had looked down at her, and she saw his intent clear in his eyes. Her reputation was safe: he intended to marry her. Even, perhaps, to make her an equal partner in his marriage, in his business. Bringing her into his club was a risk, but one he was prepared to take in order to lay himself before her as a man who trusted a woman's strength and intellect. Belinda admired him as much as she thought him foolish. "Very well," she murmured. "I look forward to this adventure."

Marius's smile had been tempered by a wink. He and Belinda had held their heads high, Belinda's gaze haughty and direct as the doorman began a strangled protest. He had faltered before her confidence and lowered his own eyes, allowing them passage into the club.

And now they came the last steps through smoky air, to the table Marius's friends had claimed. The club itself was extravagant, booths built against the walls and cushioned with red-dyed leather.

Each booth stretched to the club ceiling, heavy velvet hangings muffling the overall noise and making the booths into private spaces. Lattice-worked windows behind mesh lace broke the monotony of velvet, but thick silk cords hung low into the booths, ready to close soft walls over the windows.

Manservants, well-dressed and discreet, carried bottles of expensive wine and crystal glasses to the patrons. Those who wished less privacy sat in closely placed chairs, some surrounding the fire, others scattered in small groups throughout the main floor of the club. Everyone had paused in conversation to watch Marius escort Belinda by; it was part of how she had heard his friends' commentary. Once she was past, talk struck up again, most often about her, the former topics forgotten. A smile played at Belinda's mouth. She had hoped for recognition in the Lutetian social circles. This was not exactly how she had intended to achieve it, but it would almost certainly prove effective.

The three gathered in the booth watched her with open curiosity and, in the case of the single woman, clear hostility. Belinda's eyebrows rose in surprise.

The woman was extraordinary. Even dressed—extraordinarily—in what appeared to be *men's* clothes, and not even fashionable men's clothes, but rather peasant breeches and a wide-necked blouse that had once been white but was now yellowed with age and use, she was absurdly, almost obscenely, feminine. Her black hair was cropped ridiculously short, exposing her ears and nape, a tiny fringe over her forehead. She had small, well-shaped ears, pierced with gold loops, the only adornment she wore. Her eyes were wide and dark; the startling shortness of her hair made them seem larger and made the bones of her face even more delicate. Her mouth was drawn in a challenging scowl.

It took a conscious effort of will to glance away from the woman, to not allow astonishment and envy to darken her own gaze. Belinda saw surprise, then offense, from the corner of her eye, as the woman realised she'd been dismissed, or written off as merely ordinary. It was a dangerous sally to make: the woman would be accustomed to men and women alike being unable to look anywhere but at her. She would be used to tired and trite acclamations of her beauty, expecting them even as she judged poorly those who offered them. To brush her off would make her either an enemy or an ally for life; as of yet, neither she nor Belinda knew which path she would take.

The man across the table from her was a stocky youth, broadshouldered and broad-waisted both, yet without carrying too much weight. His hair was sandy, full of thick curls, and his eyes hazel, forthright, and shockingly familiar: it was the same man whom she'd shared a tavern bed with, weeks earlier, all his baseness gone and replaced by well-cut clothes and a clean smile. Belinda seized control of the pang that shot through her heart, refusing to allow herself so much as a clutch at Marius's arm. She herself looked as different as he, even more so, her dress no longer adding two stone to her weight. There was no flicker of recognition in his eyes, though his gaze was frankly appraising as it swept over her. He was more handsome than might have been expected from her first encounter with him, though he had nothing at all of the woman's beauty, and seemed all the plainer for being seen after her. He looked to be an honest sort, a man who would say whatever came to mind without a moment's thought for consequences.

And she knew already how untrue that must be. Unexpectedly, she found herself liking him for it, though she was not given to impromptu judgments for friendships. He clearly had cunning in him, and the impulse to like that could be dangerous to her. For a moment she cast thoughts to that night, wondering if he'd made her laugh; if anything, it was her laugh that might give her away. But he hadn't, and until she could learn more about him, her only need was to remain certain he didn't recognize her, and that could be best accomplished by playing her role as Beatrice Irvine fully.

"And has Marius found love at last?" The second man at the table sat forward, taking himself out of concealing shadows and into the light. "Who is she, Marius? Is this the woman who's had you addled the last two weeks?" He laced his fingers together on the table, long fine fingers with bone structure nearly as elegant as a woman's, and lifted his eyebrows.

He was red-headed without being sallow, a golden cast to his skin and to his hair brought out by the capped torches that lit the club. In that light, his eyes reflected gold, as if they had no color of their own. He was tall, even sitting, and full of grace. Belinda caught herself staring, and was grateful when Marius, proudly, said, "It is. May I present the Lady Irvine. Beatrice, these are my friends. Eliza Beaulieu, Lord Asselin, and—"

The second man's fingers loosened from each other, a slight movement, and straightened, staying Marius. He saw the gesture; Belinda was certain she was not intended to as he finished, "And Eliza's brother, James."

"M'mselle," Belinda murmured, dropping a curtsey. "M'sieur. My lord. It is a pleasure to meet you all."

"Yes." The coarseness was gone from Eliza's voice, replaced by cool disdain and vowels as expensive as the ones James produced. "I'm sure it is."

"Don't be nasty, Liz," Asselin said. "They've gotten used to you. They can get used to another woman, and so can you."

"At least I dress the part," Liz snapped. A curious silence fell as the other four party members looked at her, examining her clothing and her hair.

"What part," James finally asked, as mildly as he possibly could, "would that be, exactly? Sister." Eliza's scowl deepened and James flashed a grin, gesturing for Belinda and Marius to sit. "Come on, then. No need to stand on ceremony just because you've got a woman now." He scooted over until he bumped into Eliza, sending her out of her sprawl and into a more dignified position. "Asselin, move," he commanded, and the stocky man did, taking James's former place at the back of the booth. Marius offered Belinda a hand as she sat, deliberately allowing her to move in to the place across from James so she wouldn't have to face Eliza directly. Belinda saw what he was doing and smiled. Eliza saw it, too, and her glower darkened further.

"All right, now, tell us how you've bewitched him in just two meetings," Asselin demanded. "We can all see some of it—" His gaze dropped to her bosom, an entirely matter-of-fact and friendly leer. "But his wretched mother's been trying the last three years to get him married off and not a woman's caught his eye."

Belinda felt Beatrice draw around her again, stiffening her spine a little and making her chin lift. Felt her own reservations crop up as Gregori's death came back to her, as the night of dancing in Aria Magli turned cool in her blood. Those were not real things, she told herself, coincidence and drink, nothing more. But they framed her response in ice, making the provincial of her: "In Lanyarch, my lord Asselin, bewitchment isn't a word used lightly."

Oh, yes: the noblewoman whose skin she wore would make a fine player in Lutetian politics, one part warm and approachable and one part Lanyarchan provenance. Half the court would think she could be used and the other half would want to use her. Asselin rolled his eyes at that country rudeness, but James again made a small gesture, lifting his fingers from the table fractionally. It stayed Asselin as effectively as it had Marius, and the stocky lord let out an explosive, apologetic breath.

"Forgive me, Lady Irvine. I spoke lightly. I confess to knowing very little of your homeland. Perhaps a discourse on the topic would lend itself to my greater understanding of Marius's sudden"—he glanced at Marius, whose expression was guarded and warning, then at James, who held one eyebrow in a faint arch—

"infatuation," Asselin finished with all due diplomacy. "Perhaps I'll even find myself moved to visit there myself, and find as fine a wife as Marius seems to have done."

"Surely you speak too hastily, my lord," Belinda said with a faint smile. "I'm a widow as of yet, and not a wife again."

"He does speak hastily," Marius growled. "Leave off, Sacha. Jealousy ill becomes you."

"Oh, come, Marius, you wouldn't have brought her here if y—"

"Sacha." James interrupted, the name as mild as his question to Liz had been. Asselin held another irritated breath and let it go with an outward splay of his thick fingers. There was more argument in him than Belinda had expected, more wit and therefore more reason to be cautious.

"If I did not think the lady might enjoy the finest company Lutetia has to offer . . ." Marius said blandly. "Although if this is the best I can do, perhaps I should consider moving. They're not usually this dreadful, lady, I promise you that."

"No." Belinda smiled, watching Eliza's eyes darken with resentment. "But I've unbalanced your equilibrium, haven't I? I'm sure you've all known each other—since childhood?"

Three of the four looked accusingly at the fourth; Marius lifted his hands in a supplication of innocence. "I've told her nothing, lords and ladies. Can I help it if she's of a quicker wit than the rest of us combined?"

"Speak for yourself." Eliza looked Belinda over as if she were a side of meat gone bad. Belinda's eyebrows rose very slightly, wondering at the distaste behind the other woman's attitude.

"Is it only that I've disrupted the power balance?" she asked Eliza, forthright curiosity overcoming subtlety. "It must be appealing, having three handsome men ready to jump to your service. But is another woman really so challenging?" She smiled, knowing she was very likely setting the scales against herself, but Eliza's enmity was worth the blank anger that slid through the stunning woman's eyes. "Do you doubt your position here that much, mademoiselle?" She was aware of the fascinated, noisy silence of the three men, and knew Eliza must be equally aware. There was one more step she could take, a final taunt she could press, but she waited instead, watching nuances of expression flick across Eliza's face.

Eliza finally gave the only answer she could, moments before silence stretched out unbearably. "Of course not." She inhaled, about to make further excuse, then turned her head away and snapped her fingers, gesturing for wine. The soft sound broke tension in the booth and laughter replaced challenge. Sacha pressed her about Lanyarch, and Belinda answered, more than half a mind given to her part. The four she sat with had been friends long enough that they were given to answering questions put to another; long enough that they finished sentences together, often using precisely the same words. Eliza's vowels never slipped from the upper-class accent; it was the only detail that left Belinda uncertain. The woman's dress was outrageous, her hair unbelievable— many women wore their hair that short, but only so extravagantly coifed wigs could be more comfortably worn over it. Belinda had never seen a woman dare public scrutiny with her hair shorn. That she did laid to rest a lingering question Belinda had; only a woman who had a protector of great power would buck convention and wear her hair in such an astonishing style. Even so, there would be a story behind it.

Belinda nearly laughed at her own interest. It could wait, though. It *would* wait, while she bared herself to the four friends, pouring out a life's history for Beatrice Irvine. It was she who must be accepted; even for a union she never meant to consummate with Marius, the muster she had to pass was not the approval of his mother or father, but of these three, a family he had made for himself. This trio represented the reason she had selected Marius as her target, though to have been introduced to them so quickly was beyond her expectation. Once she'd passed the barrier they created she could feed her own curiosity, perhaps most particularly regarding Asselin and the life he led, as duplicitous as her own.

"No," she said for the second time, to Sacha, letting exasperation and amusement fill her voice. "We do *not* still paint ourselves orange and blue and go into battle naked. Lanyarchan nights are too cold for such things."

"I'm crushed," Sacha replied. "I've always hoped we might pick a war with Aulun so we could see the northern savages in their full and painted glory."

Belinda leaned in, dropping her voice to confidentiality. Sacha, an easy mark, shifted to hear her better. To her delight, the other three, Eliza with a degree of reluctance that was overcome by interest, leaned in as well, leaving them all clearly within hearing distance as Belinda infused her voice with both gentleness and mockery. "I assure you, the women of Lanyarch have long since been too sensible to join such war parties. I can only gather, then, that you have an abiding desire to see the full glory of a naked man. I cannot promise the wonder that's a Lanyarch man, but if you are truly desperate for the sight of armies of naked men, I suggest you visit the baths, my lord Asselin."

Asselin spluttered. James threw his head back and laughed, pure as bells. Belinda sat back, smugness playing around her mouth. Beside her, Marius puffed with pride and delight, his own cackles of amusement a deeper counterpoint to James's laughter. Even Eliza's mouth curved with disapproving humour as she poured Asselin another glass of wine.

"You lost that one, Sacha." The final score was voiced by James, who shook his head, grinning, and gestured at Eliza. "All around, sister dearest, and let's have a drink to Marius's good taste in women."

The request slowed Eliza, her gaze darting to Belinda before she shrugged, an expression built more with the faint twist of her mouth and a flare of her nostrils than with a lift of her shoulders.

Belinda saw it; the men did not. In response, in gratitude and in acknowledgment, Belinda lowered her head and eyes very briefly. Another degree of tension faded away, given voice by the full measure of wine Eliza poured into Belinda's glass. Belinda curled her fingers around the stem, thanks offered in the lifting of the glass and the glance through her eyelashes. Submission, not challenge: Belinda had no desire to oust Eliza from her family of friends. To do so would offer far too much disruption, and Belinda's purpose was to infiltrate, not destroy.

"To young love and new friends," James suggested. The toast was echoed around the table, music of crystal tapping against itself cutting through the warm thick air for a few seconds and lingering as the five drank.

"We make a habit," James said when the toast was drunk, "of meeting here on Monday nights. I think I speak for all of us when I say you would be welcome to come again, Lady Irvine. And not only because we fear we might never see our Marius again if we failed to extend the invitation." He grinned and lifted his glass to Marius, who returned both expression and gesture before they drank.

Satisfaction broke through Belinda's breathing, making her feel as though she had been taking shallow, careful breaths all evening. It loosened a band of risk from around her heart and she inhaled deeply. "So I've passed," she said, a little surprised to hear herself voice the words aloud. James and Sacha exchanged startled looks and laughter, while Marius stiffened with indignation and Eliza slumped with wry acceptance. Belinda found a smile in herself and bumped her elbow into Marius's. "Don't be ridiculous," she murmured to him. "It was a test. You know it as well as I do." To the others, she said, "A test that I'm both relieved and pleased to have passed. You're a somewhat overwhelming lot."

"You do a remarkable job of not seeming overwhelmed," Asselin said drily. "So remarkable, in fact, that neither your wit nor your beauty appear to be in the slightest bit damaged by your quaking fear of us."

"Beauty, my lord? Without meaning to seem trite, beauty is only diminished or granted in the eye of the beholder." Belinda hesitated, glancing at Eliza. "At least in my case." She let a trace of honest envy creep into the words, and Eliza's eyes narrowed, although not in anger. "I think if you find me beautiful you have become too jaded by the presence of genuine beauty in your life. I know where I can and cannot hold a candle, my lord." Belinda looked back at Asselin, then let herself smile, bright and quick. "I will grant you, though, that my wit is nearly unmatchable. Even when the company has me quivering in my boots."

"Enough," James said with an amused snort. "As I've said, Lady Irvine, we'll have you, if you'll have us. What say you?"

Belinda let stillness fill her, its soothing darkness calming her from the centre of her being to her extremities. It felt cool enough that she wondered if the wine in her glass might chill slightly from her own extending reserve. She knew her answer; there was only one she could reasonably give, but she needed the few moments away from Beatrice, to examine her own position and what she was about to broach.

The red-haired man sitting across from her was the linchpin of the foursome; it was he whom they acknowledged in subtle ways as their leader. He made the toasts, made the invitations; he made the other three answer to his will by nothing more than a tiny gesture of his hand. His long fingers were steepled in front of him now, eyebrows lifted as he waited for Belinda's answer. He was the reason Belinda had been permitted into the club on Marius's arm.

Belinda let stillness go in a quiet, deep exhalation, and laid her cards on the table. "My lord Javier," she said into waiting silence, "I would be honoured."

5

Dismay made sharp by anger penetrated Belinda down to her bones, rolling in waves off the men and woman she sat with. Accusation hung in the air; Javier turned his gaze, mild and direct, to Marius.

"No," Belinda said before Marius could protest. "He's not at fault, my lord. Even with our queen in exile we know what the heir to our throne looks like." Her voice remained quiet, but sharpened with intensity. "We know what the true heir to the Aulunian throne looks like." She felt the passion behind her own words, pure conviction as spoken by a noblewoman whose religion had been suppressed by a calculating and heartless foreign queen. Javier lifted his head sharply, flexing his fingers outward in the same small gesture that had stilled his compatriots. Belinda, abashed, ducked her head and turned her face to the side in apology. Her heart pounded too hard, blood coppery and thick in her throat. She tried to swallow the taste back, but it stayed lodged there, and she realised with slow surprise that she was genuinely afraid.

"You are too bold, my lady Beatrice." The reprimand in Javier's voice was as profound as any Belinda had heard from her father or even her queen. It was nothing in the words, themselves innocuous enough, nor the tone, as mild as milk. Rather it was the combination, and her own personal awareness of who it was she faced. That, Belinda thought, was the measure of true power and strength. She hunched her shoulders, her belly tightening, and tried not to squirm under Javier's steady gaze. Finally she whispered, "I apologize, my lord," and Javier lifted his chin with satisfaction.

"We were pleased with our charade, my lady. Why did you not let it continue?"

Belinda dared a glance up, unable to judge from his voice whether the "we" he employed was royal or encompassed the other three at the table. Eliza's dark gaze, unreadable, caught her with a stab of guilt. Asselin, to Javier's other side, watched with a faint smile. Marius would not meet her eyes. Belinda took in a shaking breath and forced herself to straighten her spine. She saw a glimpse of something in Javier's eyes. Approval? Amusement? The other three were more easily read than the prince.

"I did not like to begin a relationship under false pretenses, my lord." Internal amusement at her own audacity boiled over for a moment, breaking through habitual stillness. Belinda dropped her eyes, to don the apparel of Beatrice again before she looked up. "Had I not recognized you, the power would have been yours to betray, but I . . . I prefer an honest hand, my lord. It is, I am told, a Lanyarchan weakness." She quavered a smile, and, not receiving one in return, let it fall away in discomfort.

"You might have lied," Javier said. "Might have kept up the pretense, confessing great surprise and shock at the truth when it was granted you."

Beatrice, not Belinda, stared across the table at the prince in forthright astonishment. She heard Asselin's chuckle, and saw Eliza roll her eyes in disgust. "It's not in her, Jav," Marius said from beside her, as quiet as could be. "I told you. She hasn't got dissembling in her."

Oh, Marius. The thought struck through Belinda with a bright ache, making her breath catch with its clarity. *You sweet, innocent fool. There is no such thing as a woman without deceit, no more than there is a man.*

"I did not mean to give offense, my lord," she heard herself whispering. "I am not good at play-acting. Please. Forgive me if I've gone too far." Belinda lifted her gaze again, letting it soften in hope and fear. Her father could withstand the pleading expression, but most men, even many women, mellowed under it.

Javier was no exception. He snorted, a sound of exasperation that meant the moment of tension was over, and waved an elegant, long-fingered hand, as if clearing the air of deception. Eliza rolled her eyes again and Belinda's shoulders relaxed fractionally. "Too clever by half, Marius," Javier said. "This one's too clever by half."

"Yes, my prince," Marius said with such complete obsequience that it was clear he masked overwhelming smugness. Laughter broke, clearing away the remaining strain that lingered around the table. Javier sighed, leaning forward.

"It is occasionally tedious—"

"Occasionally?" Asselin asked with a snort very much like Javier's of a moment earlier. Javier shot him a look of exasperation and Asselin widened his eyes in pretended innocence, then made himself ostentatiously busy pouring wine. "Frequently tedious," Javier said, acknowledging Asselin drily even as he looked at Belinda, "to be royalty, my lady Beatrice."

One corner of Belinda's mouth quirked. "I wouldn't know, my lord." She tried, very briefly, to reach for the idea of a world where she would know, but she had put away those dreams and imaginations so long ago that it was as if they lay behind a thick glass wall. They were visible, but obscured and twisted by the warp of glass, no more reachable than the moon.

Her male companions laughed. Eliza sat back, sprawling in the booth seat, her shoulder brushing Javier's as she reached for and held her wineglass.

"Think of all the aspects you don't care for of nobility," Javier suggested, "and multiply them tenfold."

Belinda's eyebrows lifted a little. "Wealth, a good home, food on my table, warm nights? My lord, even the most dull evening spent embroidering is a vast improvement over sleeping with the pigs. I wed nobility, minor as it may have been, and have found very little cause for complaint in it."

Her eyes were on Javier, but it was Eliza she watched. Eliza whose shoulder pressed into Javier's a little harder, and whose mouth became a thin line. Her gaze dropped, a smirk flaring her nostrils before she looked up again, full of easy confidence and dis-like for Belinda. Belinda allowed herself a tiny burst of satisfaction, deep inside. Unlike her friends, the stunning woman had not been to the manner born; gutter vowels and rough words were natural to her, not the cultivated tones she'd no doubt learned from Javier himself.

And the prince seemed to hold no awareness of Eliza's wordless mockery. Belinda wondered if he had ever seen the other woman's real home, whether he could truly appreciate the difference be-tween his station and Eliza's. Whether he grasped on any useful level that sleeping with the pigs was not a colourful expression, but that people did it, for their own warmth and to keep safe the lives of animals upon which their own lives depended. Belinda did; Belinda had lived that life more than once, out of necessity. But that was Belinda, and not the role she played; Beatrice had been born landed, and not come from a place that low. Belinda could see no way to use the common experience as a bridge be-tween herself and Eliza, not without damning her own persona as a liar.

Javier, as Belinda watched, leaned back into Eliza with the affec-tion one might show a large dog: rough and tumble, awareness of her presence without acknowledgment of her astounding beauty. Belinda thought she was right: years of exposure had dulled the men to their companion's comeliness. She doubted very much that Eliza was equally unaware of the prince's charms.

He wasn't as pretty as Marius. The ginger hair and accompanying complexion lacked Marius's warmth and ruddy health. His eyes were yellow in the firelight, absorbing its color rather than holding forth with any of their own. He was more delicate, more elegant, than the young merchant sitting at her side, and next to Asselin's sturdy form he looked elfin. Eliza, at his other side, made an excellent dark mirror to his grace; if she were nobility, Belinda imagined they would already be wed. She thought Eliza might imagine the same thing, and was sure the idea had barely crossed Javier's mind.

He was studying her now, pale eyebrows drawn down in thought. "Are you chastising me, Lady Irvine?"

"If you feel sufficient guilt in your station that my comment strikes you as chastisement, my lord, then yes, I probably am." Belinda arched her eyebrows slightly, knowing she lay down a challenge. Javier's eyes narrowed. Beside her, Marius inhaled a deep breath of caution, but the words were already spoken, and she met Javier's eyes with her own forthright gaze, waiting.

The air between them . . . flexed. Belinda saw the subtle hand motion, the stretching of Javier's fingers that had stilled not only his lifetime companions, but even herself, not so long before. But this time it accompanied something more, a test of Belinda's will versus Javier's own. It was as if he put his shoulder into a stubborn, stuck door, expecting it to give way with a single shove. Belinda had felt men wield power before, knew the confidence that came with a lifetime of making decisions and being respected.

This was more. This was imposition, Javier's will intending domination not through fear or respect, but simply because he could. And even that didn't go far enough; Belinda had known men like that, too, who forced themselves and their desires on others because they had the strength that others did not. Javier seemed to have none of the impulse toward cruelty that such men—like Gregori—had, nor any apparent lack of confidence that often fed the need to domineer. This was less hurtful than those things; this was merely an extension of the man, an extension that edged on familiarity. He expected to triumph; he would, without question, triumph. His centre of confidence held, waiting for her to break.

Instead, she understood.

It felt like the stillness. Externally imposed, active rather than protective, but it carried that calm centre of invulnerability. Nothing could touch that force of will, and because nothing could touch it, no one could resist it. The thrill of recognition shot through Belinda's body in sensual excitement, bringing on a shiver. Never in her life had she felt anything like her stillness within another; never, in fact, had she even imagined she *might* encounter such a subtle and personalized power. Her pulse jumped in her throat, excitement desiring to overwhelm her facade of calm. She pushed it down, tingling with curiosity and enthusiasm, and for a moment another emotion swam over her, as it had done in the Maglian pub. Expectation radiated from Eliza and the other two men, and from Eliza, too, a sense of smug satisfaction. They knew, all of them, that Belinda would succumb to the prince's will and offer up an apology. It was as sure as the sun rising in the east.

Belinda lifted her chin, her fingers wandering to stroke the hollow of her throat, vulnerable and inviting. Javier shifted his weight forward, barely enough to perceive, and Belinda held her breath, judging the spark in the air between them.

It didn't flex again, Javier's will already loosened, but the core— so *different*, what she felt from him, compared to the stillness she had learned to hide herself in. He had chosen to channel his energies another way, into activity. That dynamic core within him pressed its advantage, seeing Belinda showing weakness in the most flattering form a woman could offer it, sexual availability. She could feel, almost as if she were in his skin, the heat of want that spread from his groin and fed his hidden strength. Belinda encouraged it a few seconds, retreating into herself. Javier leaned forward another fraction of an inch.

Belinda wrapped golden stillness around herself so nothing could touch her, and met the prince's gaze without fear.

Javier flinched.

He flinched, then straightened, mouth slightly open with surprise. He wet his lips, tongue caught between his teeth for an instant, before a slow, appreciative smile lifted the corners of his mouth. "Then I had best reconsider my complaints, had I not? Perhaps I speak of things that I do not well understand."

Eliza's scowl darkened again; beside her, Belinda felt Marius slump in unsurprised dismay. There was danger in introducing any woman to a friend, but especially when the friend was a prince. Marius had not expected to lose her so quickly, but he felt the change in energy between them, knew something invisible had passed between them, and laid open a new path for them to follow. Then he squared his shoulders, jaw set with determination. Belinda almost smiled at his resolution: he could not have said it more clearly if he'd spoken the words out loud. Javier could not be expected to wed a minor noble from a country so ill thought of it was often called Northern Aulun rather than by its own name. Marius would not give up his own hopes yet. He would fight for the lady's hand, and only accept defeat graciously when he had no other choice. Belinda admired him for it even as the prince's curious energy drew her toward him. Only Asselin watched without changing demeanor, the lying, raw honesty that defined him in Belinda's mind seeming to shield him from the shock of a woman crossing swords with his prince.

"It's a rare man who admits he may not fully understand a thing." Belinda chose her words carefully. "My father would have said, a wise man." She imagined Robert preaching the line, and let her own laughter echo through the stillness she still held wrapped around her. It warmed her without coming close to the surface, without darkening her eyes or curving her mouth. Javier inclined his head very slightly.

"I thank you, Lady Beatrice. I doubt I have the years for wisdom, but God granting, perhaps someday I'll grow into it. And if lovely women are to dispense it, so much the better for all of us." He flashed a grin, disarming and bright, at his companions, and they slowly loosened their hold on confusion and suspicion. All but Eliza, whose sulk deepened. She had no more idea than the men did what had passed between Belinda and the prince, but her position was already jeopardized. She would trust nothing of Belinda without a direct order, and even then would keep one eye on her purse. For a fleeting moment Belinda considered taking her aside to promise her own innocence in matters of pursuing the prince, but to make a liar of herself with actions would do no one any good.

Javier was speaking; Belinda turned her attention back to him, replaying the words she'd heard without listening in her mind. *There is to be an opera this Friday evening,* he'd said. "I dare say between the four of us we might scrape up enough to add a ticket to our party," he suggested. "If the Lady Irvine might care to join us?"

The Lady Irvine turned her gaze on her erstwhile companion of the evening. Marius's cheeks were flushed with more crimson than the heat of the club warranted, but he bowed his head gracefully. "Would you accompany me, lady?" The penultimate word was stressed very faintly, as if the tiny declaration of possession would go unnoticed by the others if he was careful to bring only a little attention to it.

"The opera," Belinda echoed, both amused and embarrassed to hear a thread of genuine apprehension in her voice. "I don't know operas, my lord." She did, though only in the abstract; fables in music, she'd read, with extraordinary songs and costuming. The art form had been birthed in Parna, and only lately; to find it burgeoning in Lutetia surprised her, for all that Gallin's capital city thought well of itself as a centre for art. "What does one wear?"

Pure malice, disguised as delight, from Eliza: "Don't worry, darling." Her smile was so sharp it made Belinda want to laugh. "I'll help you."

Not even the men missed that. They exchanged guarded looks, and Javier cleared his throat. "Perhaps between my sister and I, we might provide some assistance." His teasing reminder of their purported relationship only fanned Eliza's anger. She sat back, eyes snapping and bright, and made a short chopping gesture with her right hand. For the first time Belinda noticed jewelry there: a ring carved of stone, something pale enough to nearly blend against her translucent skin. Alabaster or maybe marble, Belinda thought clinically, and wondered who had given her the bauble.

"As you will," Eliza said. As if her desire could override the prince's, Belinda thought, but it wasn't her purpose to destroy the group. Not yet at least. She didn't know enough about them. They might prove more useful unified than they would separated.

"I would never presume to doubt the prince's taste or knowledge of women's clothing," she began. Javier let out a snort of laughter and lifted his wineglass.

"By which you mean, you are about to doubt it in an extravagantly polite fashion. And here I thought the Lanyarchans called a spade a spade, Lady Irvine." He drank deeply of his glass, never taking his eyes off her as she let a smile of acknowledgment ghost across her face.

"A spade is one thing, my lord. Insulting royalty is rather another."

"And yet," Javier said. Belinda smiled, and turned her eyes to Eliza.

"I would rather trust a woman's judgment," she murmured, putting herself into Eliza's hands entirely. She might pay for it by appearing at the opera in a whore's costume, but the risk was worthwhile. Eliza's gaze shuttered, small triumph obscured by uncertainty. "Lady Eliza, would you help me in finding a gown for the opera? I would be in your debt."

She felt Marius relax marginally. By putting the onus on Eliza, Belinda circumvented both owing the prince anything, and left the field fractionally more open to the young nobleman. It was not a direct refusal, which would have risked too much—might even have risked a breach in Javier's friendship with Marius—but it lay out rules of engagement. Belinda was not yet spoken for, and a prince's power and wealth were not quite enough to turn her head.

Eliza, having made the offer, could find no way out of it. "Perhaps tomorrow," she said eventually. "So that there might be time for adjustments to be made. I'm sure we can find something appropriate at one of the dressmaker's businesses near the palace."

"At what hour?" Belinda asked. Eliza glanced at her friends.

"That depends on how late we stay here, and how far into our cups we go."

"We haven't gone nearly far enough." Asselin poured another round.

The cathedral bells rang incessantly as the quintet staggered from the club, leaning heavily on one another to keep their feet. It had begun to rain; Belinda slipped in a puddle and nearly brought the whole train down with her. Marius hooted and howled, yanking her back to her feet. She stood with her face mashed against his chest for a few seconds, listening to the alcohol-induced rapid thump of his heartbeat. He snickered and put an arm around her shoulders, trying to reel her around into a more typically upright position. She swung too far; Javier caught her and set her on her feet. Beyond his shoulder Belinda could see Eliza, drunk enough to verge on belligerence, and leaned around the prince to blink wide-eyed at the other woman.

"Not before ten," she pleaded. "I pray you, we mustn't go out before ten. The very thought of sunlight makes my insides crawl." She shoved away from Javier, trusting the drink to be apology enough, and lurched the few steps toward Eliza, so they propped each other up. The bells continued to ring, banging out numbers that went far beyond any hour of the clock. Belinda rolled until her shoulders were pressed against Eliza's, and flung her head back to stare accusingly in the direction of the cathedral. "What the bloody hell time is it?" She let herself forget Gallic, her question slurred thick with a Lanyarchan burr and too much wine. "Why won't the fucking bells stop?"

It was Javier who answered, in Aulunian, as she expected. "It's the half hour. They go on for five minutes. You've heard them during the day, haven't you?"

"But they weren't so ear-bleeding *loud*," Belinda protested, then said, "Shite," with overwhelming enthusiasm. "I've forgotten my tongue."

"Let me find it for you, lady." Marius wrapped his arm around Belinda's waist and pulled her into him. Eliza staggered and swore. Belinda heard her mutter a thanks to Javier an instant later as he rescued her from her own tangled feet, but her own attention was taken by Marius's kiss: sensual and soft, his mouth hungry and tasting of wine but curtailed with just enough reserve as to make it a promise rather than a demand for more. It went on until the bells stopped; until Belinda heard Asselin's staccato applause and sharp whistling.

"Bring her home already, Marius, and stop teasing the rest of us. Jav, your carriage, please be to God we're not walking home."

"I ought to make you," Javier threatened idly. "It'd be best for all our heads. Marius, you've your own carriage tonight?"

Marius looked up from Belinda's upturned face, his eyes heavy in the rain-streaked torchlight outside the club. "Carriage," he repeated as if it were a foreign word, then chuckled and tossed his hair back. "Yes, yes of course, we'll be fine. Come. Come, Beatrice, let me take you home."

Belinda hung back a moment, even as Marius captured her hand and tried to draw her away. "Ten, Lady Eliza? No earlier? We could breakfast together—?"

Eliza flipped her fingers out, the same gesture Javier used to still his friends, but in her it was acknowledgment and dismissal both. "I'll wake Marius at dawn for your address," she threatened. Marius groaned dramatically. "Tomorrow," Eliza said. "At ten." She nodded, and Belinda let herself be drawn away into the rain-speckled street.

"You didn't tell me," she said to Marius, minutes later. They huddled together more than necessary, the coach protecting them from the rain well enough, but drink and laughter and the lingering effects of the kiss held them close. Marius sighed with a dozen kinds of exasperation, and settled on "Would you have believed me?" as the one to voice. Belinda cackled and leaned against him more heavily.

"No. Forgive me, but no. You're not royalty." She blinked, overexaggerated in the darkness. "Are you?"

Marius flung himself back into the cushions, making the whole coach lurch with the force of it. "Not at all. Sacha and I were friends first, and his family is better-placed than mine."

"Ah," Belinda said lightly, teasing, "then it's he I ought to set my cap for."

Marius gave her such a distraught look that she laughed, taking pity, and nestled against his side. "Lord Asselin is too short for me," she assured him. "A lady likes a little length in her men."

She said it without wickedness, trusting Marius to take it places he oughtn't, and from the brief shocked silence she knew she'd succeeded. She grinned broadly against his chest, letting fabric and the night conceal not only the expression, but the amused memory that what the stocky lord lacked in length was made up in breadth. That Marius Poulin had friends in high places she'd known when she'd sought him out as the first step in pursuing Javier, prince of Gallin. Asselin had been named one of those friends, but not even rumour had breathed hints of his cheapside whoring and rabble-rousing. She wondered if Marius—if Javier—knew of his revolutionary thoughts, or if he worked for the prince, searching out dangers to Sandalia, Javier's mother and the pretender to the Aulunian throne.

Questions to be answered later. Belinda schooled her smile to innocence as she look up again, wide-eyed. "My lord?"

"Nothing." Marius cleared his throat. "Nothing, Lady Irvine. Forgive me, my mind . . . wandered. Javier . . . is a tall man. What did you think of him?" Cautious words, testing waters he had trusted only hours earlier.

Belinda shrugged thoughtfully. "He seems a very nice prince. I don't meet a wide range."

"He admired you." Marius kept his voice carefully neutral. Belinda sat up, eyebrows crinkling.

"To what end, my lord? He has charm; he is attractive. He is also royalty, and my nobility comes through marriage, and is minor at best. Am I to aspire to being his royal hand-me-down?"

Marius met her gaze sharply. "There are women who would give their lives for so much as that."

Belinda lifted her chin, full of pride and indignation. "I trust I think better of myself. I might have thought you did, Master Poulin."

"Yes." Marius's voice roughened and he leaned forward to take her hands. "Forgive me, Beatrice. Jealousy makes a man say foolish things." He drew her forward and kissed her again, this time kissing her forehead, an apology. "Forgive me," he murmured a second time. Belinda exhaled and allowed him to settle her at his side again.

"Forgiven," she murmured. "I shall endeavor to prove immune to his charms, my lord. I think a woman might, should she put her mind to it."

The rest of the journey they made in silence.

A curtain drew back; piercing, vicious light stabbed through Belinda's eyelids and into the back of her skull, illuminating every dark thought and memory she held. She flung her arm over her eyes and flipped onto her belly, burying her face in pillows with a groan that vibrated in her bones.

"My lady." A servant spoke, timid and apologetic. "You asked to be wakened before ten. It's a quarter to the hour now."

"I lied. Hang me instead." Belinda dragged a pillow over the back of her head and groaned again. She hadn't had so much to drink as that—less than her antics the night before had suggested—but the part was made to be played, and she couldn't remember the last time she'd had the opportunity or desire to revel in noisy misery.

"My lady," the maid said, with the proper note of stubbornness, "your guest will arrive soon. You must be up." Even through the shielding of pillows, Belinda could tell that the girl was pulling back more curtains in the room, letting in mellow morning light that, despite Belinda's dramatics, was unlikely to sear the very flesh from her bones. Belinda flung the pillow away and rolled onto her back again, her arm draped over her eyes.

"You're a cruel taskmaster, Nina. A calculating and heartless bitch."

"Yes, my lady," the maid said with such mildness that Belinda laughed. She pitched the duvet back with as much drama as she'd flung both herself and the pillows around, and it slithered off the far side of the bed, farther out of reach than she'd intended. Dismayed, she found herself obliged to sit up, no longer able to burrow beneath the covers again.

"All right. I'm up. Pray God there's tea." She moved her arm enough to fix a one-eyed gimlet stare on Nina, who ignored her entirely as she finished opening curtains.

The room was well-appointed; every time Belinda looked around she felt a little surge of pleasure. Not extravagant, and not fashionable, at least not according to Lutetian standards, it was small enough to be cozy and warm. For this room, her private bedroom, she had forgone the cool yellow and blue silks that brought the rest of her little house up to local expectations. Here she had decorated in the colors of Lanyarch, rich greens and reds, the wall-hangings of sturdy wool that didn't flutter with the open windows. The maids clearly thought her eccentric, but she paid them on time and made relatively few demands, and so they found no cause for complaint.

Nina came back to the side of the bed, a silver tray in her hands. "There is tea," she said. Belinda reached greedily for a cup. Nina took one precise step backward and clucked her tongue. She was pretty, as nearly all serving maids were, and had been caught servicing her former employer's son in ways that ruined her reputation. Belinda felt a fierce sting of sympathy for the girl, too familiar with the pattern that women with no means of their own were so often caught in. One could not refuse the lord and master, nor his son, but neither could one afford to accept their advances. The price of seduction always lay on the woman, never the master.

And so when a neighboring wife had made passing mention of the little slut who'd whored herself to her son—a fine, upstanding young man, who could never be tempted by such raw and primal behavior if it were not for little bitches like Nina twitching her skirts at him—Belinda had requested to hire the girl to begin at her household the very next morning. The neighbor's eyes, already beady to begin with, had all but popped out of her head, while Belinda shrugged with imposed calm. *There are no men in my household,* she'd said. *There is nothing to tempt a girl to wayward behavior, and her reputation need not be destroyed.* And she'd smiled apologetically and offered, *Perhaps we Lanyarchans are a peculiar lot,* and the woman had no choice but to hastily agree to the hiring, or to insult her new neighbor. It had been an excellent choice: Nina was grateful for a new place in a reputable household, and believed her employer to have an inexplicably soft side.

Which was what now allowed her to dare step out of Belinda's reach and say, firmly, "You must be out of bed before you may have your tea, my lady. You always spill on the sheets and the stains never come out."

"Nina." Belinda utterly failed to reach a threatening tone. The serving maid widened her eyes, innocent as the newborn day.

"And besides, my lady, it gets you out of bed. You must be in at least a dressing gown before your guest arrives."

Belinda groaned again and struggled for the edge of the bed. Eliza would not only arrive on time, but she would already be dressed. The maid was right. Turning out in a dressing gown would be bad enough. Eliza would mock her with those lovely dark eyes, and Belinda would deserve it. "All right, all right."

She climbed out of bed and dropped her sleeping gown to the floor, absently touching the thread that held her dagger against the small of her back. Nina had gaped once at the tiny weapon and forevermore seemed not to see it, even when Belinda strode across her bedroom naked as a babe, as she did now. An elderly gentleman lived across the street. Belinda never looked, but always hoped he might have the presence of mind to be watching from his own bedroom windows when she got up in the morning. She thought of herself as less prone to exhibitionism as she was an appreciator of voyeurism. Nina made distressed clucking sounds as she did every morning when Belinda insisted on putting on such a display, and managed to shake a chemise down over her lady's shoulders while Belinda stood in front of the wardrobe trying to select a gown.

"How dreadful is my hair?"

A calculating silence left Belinda smiling as she reached for a gown. Dark amber, it brought out the warmth of her hair. She hesitated over it, then selected a less flattering dress. Eliza might find herself tempted to plume a sparrow well, but presented with a peacock she was likely to snap in the other direction.

"It has seen better mornings, my lady," Nina said judiciously, and then in dismay, "And that color will not help at all, my lady. The amber is better."

"I know. Don't argue, girl." Belinda brushed away her complaints with a snap of her fingers and spread her arms so Nina could wrap the corset around her. The overdress was of pale green; half a shade truer and it would be springlike, lovely, complimenting Belinda's complexion and making her hair dark and soft. Instead it bordered on the color of limes, too startling to flatter a woman of Belinda's skin tones. She thought, briefly, of Ana in Aria Magli, and wondered at the stab of regret. "I'll be trying on dresses. A hat won't do to hide my hair today."

Patience filled Nina's voice. "Don't worry, my lady. I'll have you presentable in time to make a fashionable entrance."

The girl was as good as her word. Belinda came down the stairs within minutes of Eliza's arrival, as properly bedecked as she could be. Her hairstyle wasn't extravagant, but neither was it unfashionable, swept up in a twist that emphasized her forehead and the length of her neck. Belinda felt quite smug until she saw her guest.

Eliza's close-shorn locks were hidden beneath a wig of such fine blackness that Belinda was certain it was her own hair. She wore it down, against fashion, but it made not the slightest difference; the dark shining waves coiled around her bare shoulders in a seductive

manner that made even Belinda want to brush it away from pale
skin and drop a kiss against the delicate bone there. She wore blue
so dark it bordered on purple, the cut of the gown more than simply fashionable, but predating fashion: Belinda knew within weeks
the women of Lutetia would be wearing such gowns, and that Eliza
set fashion with Javier's help and approval. She must: the gown's
hue itself was a challenge and an admission both, stating her closeness with the prince and daring Belinda to make anything of it. For
all of the woman's callous and deliberate disregard of her own
beauty the night before, today the rules were different, and it was
clear Eliza intended that Belinda should know that.

"My lady Beaulieu." Belinda curtsied more deeply than necessary, her own acknowledgment that she was far outstripped in
looks and attire alike. "You look well recovered from the night's
revelries."

Eliza's eyes glittered with suppressed irritation. "I'm not made
of such delicate stuff as most women, Lady Irvine. I'm surprised to
find you up and about."

"Blame my excellent servants, rather than my sturdy constitu-
tion," Belinda suggested, then tilted her head. "You haven't eaten,
have you? I would like to breakfast with you, if not . . . ?" She gestured toward the morning room, trusting that Eliza would remember the invitation made the night before.

Eliza nodded graciously and preceded Belinda into the arbore-
tum. It was small, hardly enough to be granted such a lofty name,
but its size made it warm, and morning light encouraged greenery
that would make the air fresh and scented even in the coldest
months of the year. Eliza glanced around perfunctorily, then
turned to Belinda. "I ate some hours ago, but tea would be lovely."

Bitch, Belinda thought, almost cheerfully. Let Eliza be superior
in her morning habits. It might get Belinda that much better of a
gown. "Then tea it shall be. And fruit, if you care for any. The
strawberries are very good." Real pleasure crept into her voice;

Belinda had missed the fresh fruit of more temperate climes during the months she'd been in the Khazarian north plotting Gregori's downfall. She was spoiled, she reminded herself as she sat. Eliza sat across from her, accepting the fruit—not just berries, but apples and pears as well—with more enthusiasm than Belinda expected.

Belinda studied the cut of Eliza's gown as they ate, letting the envy that was appropriate to her role bubble over a little. "I wager I'll find nothing of that ilk in the dressmakers' shops. You'll set fashion on Friday, at the opera." The envy was real, as was the admiration. "I have never dared to break the mold myself." It was true; her position was to be unremarkable, to hide in plain sight. Risking a gown with the daring cut plunging between her breasts, the slightly shortened waist that turned a figure from a V into an hourglass, would draw attention. Aulun, and therefore Belinda, could never risk such a show.

And so the truth of it lay in her eyes as Eliza frowned at her, then shrugged. "It's easy enough to do when someone like Jav supports you."

"I lack such support," Belinda said so wryly that Eliza almost smiled.

"Not for long." The smile fell away into rivalry and dislike again. "Jav doesn't make a habit of inviting everyone who comes along to the opera with us."

"Should I make a refusal, then?" Belinda asked, sensing a chance. "I think you won't believe me, but I really have no wish to intrude." She kept her voice quiet, seeking guidance with such earnestness even she believed it. "You four are clearly a close-knit group. I wouldn't presume to interfere."

"You presume by thinking you could," Eliza said, sharply. "Jav made the offer, I won't gainsay him. You're welcome enough."

As welcome as a bout with the plague, perhaps. Belinda caught her breath, held it long enough to still the smile she felt, then nodded. "Your candor is . . . appreciated."

Eliza's eyebrows snapped up and she stared at Belinda for a few long moments. Belinda, wrapped in the safety of stillness, waited, and Eliza relaxed. "Thank you for the fruit, Lady Irvine. Perhaps we should take our leave—the dressmakers get busy after noon. When most of the women of town are finally prepared to leave their homes." She didn't try to disguise her disdain, and Belinda found herself smiling.

"We should all take lessons from you, M'mselle Beaulieu," she said with absolute sincerity. "The world would be a more interesting place."

Eliza gave her another sharp look, and Belinda smiled again as they gathered themselves to leave.

The carriage was Javier's own, marked subtly with his signet. Belinda, allowing the coachman to help her down from the steps, knew she had been outdone: no one delivered to a dressmaker's shop in the prince's carriage would be allowed to pay for her own gowns. A tailor would bankrupt himself giving away wares, if it meant even the briefest notice in the royal household. He might gnash his teeth and pull his hair later, but in the moment, he would find himself without a choice.

And such was the expression on each owner's face as they explored the row of dressmakers and tailor shops. Gratitude, delight, dismay, relief. There were gowns by the dozen to admire; Belinda asked for more than one to be set aside so she might consider it, but it was Eliza's approval she waited on, and the street-born woman's eyes remained shuttered, and no purchases were made. Not until the row was exhausted and the carriage regained did Belinda turn to Eliza with a curious tilt to her eyebrows. "I saw them, Lady Beaulieu. I saw their eyes on your gown, on the cut and workmanship. None of them have anything like it; they would have brought it out. Now they'll copy it, but my lady, who designed the original?"

Hidden pleasure lit the brown of Eliza's eyes, although she turned her head away to mask it. "No one who can make another soon enough for the opera."

"I would not presume," Belinda said, surprised by her own vehemence. "Fashion is yours to set, my lady. You are the prince's friend; it is to you all eyes will look for guidance as to the season's garments. I would not presume." The passion left her and she exhaled more quietly. "But it seems nothing in these shops met with your approval. Shall I purchase a gown without your guidance?"

"Javier would know." Wry irritation tinged Eliza's voice. Belinda's eyebrows rose.

"How?" Could it be that Javier shared the *knowing* that sometimes overwhelmed Belinda? The *knowing* of thoughts and desires that had so overwhelmed her in the Maglian pub? Hairs lifted on Belinda's arms, remembering the unasked for intimacy in the overheated room. She shivered. Her thoughts had been unquiet all night, not letting her sleep until too close to dawn, but she had only considered the portent of Javier's indominable will and how closely it seemed to match the silence she wore within herself like a shield. She hadn't thought to wonder if that sense of self he'd tried to impose on her might run more deeply, might give him an uncanny awareness of the emotions that swam around him. Fascination and unwarranted hope shot through her, and she turned her attention to Eliza's response with more interest than anticipated.

And Eliza shrugged, easy dismissive motion. "He knows my tastes. We've been friends for a long time."

Belinda let go a breath of laughter, and with it a sting of disappointment. Javier was a prince, and his strength of will likely born from that, not any childish recognition of her own defenses mirrored in another's eyes. "How long, my lady? If asking is not presumptuous."

Eliza's eyes glittered darkly as she glanced at Belinda. The carriage was moving through streets Belinda didn't know; she hadn't heard Eliza give the destination. The houses beyond were still wealthy, though, the streets mostly clear of beggars. No one here would accost the prince's carriage, whatever their destination might be. Belinda let her gaze flicker back to Eliza's, aware that the other woman studied her mistrustfully.

"Since I was ten," Eliza said, "and he was eight. The entire city seems to know the story, so I suppose there's no harm in telling you. I wanted a pear. I'd never had one, and they talked about them being grown in the royal gardens. My mother forbade me from fetching any, as the price for trespassing is imprisonment or death."

"Certainly not for a child," Belinda said, startled. Eliza made a small gesture with her hand, very much like the one Javier used. Belinda wondered if it had been Eliza's first, or if she'd copied it unconsciously from years of exposure to the prince. She guessed the latter; there was grace to the motion that seemed inherent to royalty, although the prejudice of that made Belinda smile faintly.

"I could say that was what I thought." Eliza shrugged again, watching the streets outside. "But truthfully, I never imagined I'd be caught. And I wasn't, not by guard or gardener."

"Javier." Belinda smiled. Eliza gave her a sharp look and she realised with a start that she'd used the prince's name with no honourific in an appallingly familiar fashion. Heat rushed to her cheeks, enough admission of guilt that Eliza went on without taking further note of the transgression.

"Javier. I was scrambling back over the wall when he asked, very politely, if I needed assistance." Eliza's mouth curved in a smile, gaze distant out the window. The smile, unexpectedly, reduced her beauty. It took her from untouchable to merely extraordinarily pretty, warming her eyes to a considerable degree. It made her approachable, Belinda thought curiously. She had seen many women in whom laughter brought out beauty, but never one in whom it brought out something more ordinary and human. "I fell off the wall," Eliza went on, "and landed on Jav. I had bruises for a week, but he had a broken arm."

"Oh!" Surprise pulled laughter from Belinda. "Oh no!"

"I've had pears any time I wanted, since that day. Jav made them let me stay all through his convalescence, and we've been friends ever since." Eliza glanced at Belinda as the carriage drew to a stop. "You're home, my lady."

Belinda blinked and tilted to look out the window at the building beside her. "But a dress—?"

"One will be delivered to you on Friday."

Belinda straightened, excitement speeding her heartbeat. She felt heat come to her cheeks again, and thought that Beatrice Irvine was a somewhat silly woman, to be so unexpectedly thrilled at the prospect of an unseen gown as a gift.

The coach door opened, the coachman offering his hand to help Belinda step down. Summarily dismissed and caught between offense and amusement, Belinda accepted it, inclining her head to Eliza as she stepped from the carriage. Vanity caught her and she turned back. "But if it needs alteration—?"

"It won't," Eliza said. "Good afternoon, Lady Irvine."

It didn't.

Eliza's vanity had won through as well, pluming a sparrow too enticing a challenge to pass up, or her relationship with Javier too genuine to embarrass him with a poorly dressed companion at the opera. Three days was too little time to dye fabric, to make the cuts and sew the gown together, but color and size alike seemed to whisper that the dress had truly been made for her. The fabric was green silk, shot with counterwoven threads of brown, until the shade echoed and strengthened Belinda's eyes. The cut was less daring than the gown Eliza had worn—no doubt than the gown

Eliza *would* wear—but it flattered and was fashionable, the lines clean and long. There were fewer layers to it than she was accustomed to, the petticoats abandoned for a more natural shape, making the weight of the gown so slight as to be all but unnoticeable. It reminded Belinda a little of the gown Ana had worn—she could ride a horse astride in this dress without its weight pressing her thighs. She never would; it would damage the silk beyond belief. But the sense of freedom in the dressing was there, and made her smile breathlessly at her own reflection.

Nina, caught between scandalized at the cut of the gown's neck—far from off the shoulders, but a more open square, with angled sides that left a little more collarbone bare than current fashion dictated—and envious of the chance to wear it, reflected in the mirror as well, finishing the last touches to Belinda's hair. It was worn up, exposing the delicate length of her neck, scraps of leaves and pale green flowers woven against the brunette waves.

Belinda heard carriages outside, and the thunk of the knocker that thudded through the entire house. "Will I do?" she asked Nina, amused. The girl rolled her eyes.

"I suppose, madam. I won't be completely embarrassed to let you out of the house." They smiled at each other in the mirror as the bedroom door popped open, another breathless servant—Marie; Belinda wanted to remember their names, just as she deliberately failed to remember men like Viktor—Marie forgetting to knock in her excitement.

"My lady, he's here."

Belinda stood, smiling. "He's just a man, my dear. They're not worth quite all that much fuss." Her eyebrows lifted slightly, though the smile remained in place. "They're certainly not worth forgetting manners over."

Pink-cheeked guilt overcame the girl and she ducked her head, hands clasped together at her hips. "I'm sorry, my lady, please forgive me, it's only that—"

"You're forgiven," Belinda said, still amused. Ten years of playing the lesser parts, filling household roles such as the one that was this girl's livelihood, had done nothing to prepare Belinda for the constant source of delight that playing an upstairs role brought. She had let the stillness fade away far too often the last several days, allowing herself to be caught up in good cheer and the pleasantries of wealth. She could play lady disdain, but for Marius there seemed no point; he was caught already, and charmed by the openhearted and good Beatrice. Until she had to meet with his friends again— a time when reserve would more suit her anyway—Belinda could allow herself the revelry of simple joy. Capturing a light cloak from her bed where it lay, she followed Marie downstairs, fully aware the girl trailed after to watch Marius's reaction to the gown.

But it was Javier who stood alone in the lobby, his hands folded neatly behind his back as he studied a painting—a particularly awful portrait of Beatrice's late father—that hung in a place of pride near the door. The prince wore grey, both incredibly subdued and unexpectedly flattering to his complexion and hair. As he turned from the portrait, a smile of appreciation already settling on his face, the maid gave Belinda a desperate glance over her shoulder, as if to say, *You see, my lady? He* was *worth forgetting to knock!*

And Belinda, astonished, gave the girl absolution in the form of a faint nod. "Your Highness." She had no need to hide her surprise, nor did she think Javier would find insult in her gaze searching the corners of the room and landing in confusion on the door before finally returning to him. Beneath the heavy brocaded vest he wore white, startling against skin to which torchlight and fading sunlight gave a golden cast.

"Please," he said, "Javier. If my friends court you, then we must be friends, too."

"Javier," Belinda said faintly, then smiled. "Not James?"

"Good Lord, no," Javier said with a smile of his own. He was more attractive in evening light than he had been in the club.

"James is a construct, meant to hide behind, and evidently a poor one. No, my lady, please, call me Javier."

"Then you must call me Beatrice." Belinda spoke reflexively, stepping forward to take the arm that Javier offered with another smile. "But my lord . . . I had thought Marius would be here tonight . . . ?"

His eyebrows drew down over eyes that ate up the color of the lights with the same faint gold sheen that his clothes and skin did. "Marius's mother has taken ill. He will not be joining us tonight after all."

Surprise splashed through Belinda with such alacrity that for the first time in days she deliberately curtained it with the stillness, letting her heartbeat slow in the few moments before she spoke again. "He hadn't sent a message. I hope she'll be all right? It was kind of you to come for me instead, then." Suspicion flowered at the back of her neck, a hot feeling of certainty that had no root. "Lord Asselin and Lady Eliza wait for us in the carriage?"

Javier's frown deepened a little. "They've both sent their regrets, each of them vying for who is more disappointed to not see you in your new gown, which is," he took a perfunctory breath, "lovely. I'm afraid it's my company and mine alone tonight, Lady Beatrice. Forgive us all for the change in plans." The words and the tone were perfectly matched: polite regret, a vague aura of discomfort, mild humour at the situation. It was a flawless performance.

Hot flares wrapped around Belinda's throat and crept over her scalp, making her shiver even in the warmth of the room. The stillness within her gave her room for certainty, even without being able to make sense of it: beneath the prince's words lay no surprise, no dismay, and an unmistakable air of triumph. The emotions were strong enough to be her own, as if they came from within her own skin, rather than from the prince whose arm she was on. She gazed up at him, balanced between fascination and fear. He quirked his eyebrows, waiting for her answer, and she found it in herself to smile back at him, easily.

"I think I can forgive you, my lord. I look forward to the evening's performance. We must remember it well, so we can share it with the others, and especially relate it to poor Madame Poulin. Thank you for thinking of me even as your friends were unable to attend. I'm honoured."

Thoughts awhirl, she didn't hear his reply as he escorted her to his carriage.

6

The opera held nothing of interest, compared to the man at her elbow. Belinda watched without seeing, aware of its majesty and the skill of the players, and recorded the pageantry into memory for discussion later while remaining herself unmoved. Javier put on a show as excellent as the one below them: leaning forward, eyes intent on the stage, a smile playing over his mouth from time to time, as benefited the production.

It was all a lie. Now attuned to it and focused, not overwhelmed by an onslaught of emotion as she had been at the Maglian pub, she could feel the prince's true intentions, hidden beneath the veneer of grace and nobility. Not that he lacked those things in any fashion, but now they were distraction, a surface performance for the benefit of others. Below, triumph had faded into burgeoning interest, smugness into curiosity. At the edges of emotion Belinda thought she could almost pull individual thoughts free, but they slipped between her fingers and disappeared. She glanced at her hands and allowed herself a faint smile through the stillness. Metaphorical fingers, at least; she doubted she could slide her very hand into Javier's head and capture those thoughts in their entirety.

His curiosity was tempered by something more: apprehension. Fear was too strong a word, his own confidence too great to truly fear the woman at his side. But she was a new thing in his experience—from the conflict of interest and caution within him, Belinda could read that.

It hardly surprised her. The stillness she knew as a part of herself was alien to anyone else she had ever met. Especially—*especially!*—the moments in her childhood when the shadows had held her safe within their arms. Her father had meant her to forget, but the memory came on strong now, sitting in the darkened hall. It was unlike any theatre she had ever known, roofed over to keep in heat and to bring the full force of the singers' voices reverberating around the walls. Even the floor had seats, rather than the crowded, standing-room only areas she knew from Aulun's open-air play-houses. This was not a place the poor came into for an afternoon's entertainment, paying their ha'penny to a drunk who kept the gate. The darkness of it protected her, letting her drift in memory even as she tried to puzzle out a way to broach an unspoken broth-erhood with Javier. The will of *not being there* which she'd drawn so tightly around herself all those years ago, she could remember that. The triumph of knowing she was hidden from all eyes, and the shock of Robert discovering her. She could remember all of those things. How, then, could the moment of hiding be so fully erased from her memory?

Had she faded? Belinda rolled her shoulders forward, making her chest concave as she closed her eyes. Was it memory or imagi-nation that encouraged her down that path, telling her that *fading* was right, something important about *fading* . . .

"It ends badly," Javier murmured by her ear. Belinda caught her breath and lifted her chin, called back to the theatre and the music with a pulse of irritation.

"My lord?"

"The story ends badly, in death and despair for all the principal actors. Perhaps we should retire early, so you might be spared the anguish?"

Belinda arched an eyebrow as she tilted her head toward his. "I am all but certain," she breathed, "that the actors will rise up anew from their death throes and live to perform another night. I think I am bold enough to sit through another half hour of make-believe. They will notice if you leave, my lord. Your exit could end this show tonight, even as it opens."

Javier quirked a smile, his head angled with interest. "You're a gentle soul, aren't you? You think of things that I never would. Nobility suits you, lady. The world might be a better place if all gentry were as well-heeled as you."

Belinda returned her gaze to the stage, unwilling to meet the amused admiration in the prince's eyes. "I am perhaps closer to the land than you, is all, my lord. My station is not so high. Perhaps it is easier to see those who make their livelihoods on a prince's whim from where I stand."

"Then perhaps a prince requires your wisdom." Javier's tone changed, more weight given to the words than the conversation had warranted. Impatience grew in him, pushing aside apprehension and replacing it with avarice. Belinda glanced at him again, unable to read what goal greed sought. There was always one safe gamble, though, particularly with a handsome man of power. She lowered her eyes.

"I would be proud to serve you, my lord. My wisdom is at your disposal, as are all my faculties."

He glanced at her, sharp, then allowed himself a chuckle that altered the emotions she read in him more than it broke through into sound. It was marked by desire, thick and interested, and a trace of complacency. Belinda was not the first, nor would she be the last, woman to make such a blatant, if coded, offer to the prince. The uplift of his amusement was heady, sweeping up Belinda's spine and curving around her body as needle-sharp tingles of want in her breasts and groin. For a few seconds she rode the delicious pain of it, letting it rob her of breath, knowing Javier would note that breathlessness on a subtle level. She shivered. He put his hand over hers, and for a shocking moment, his thoughts were hers to savor.

. . . *ckable if nothing else—but there's more. Witchbreed.* The word hung in his thoughts, pulsing deep red with anguish: it was a word he would never speak aloud, one he feared, one that never strayed far from his mind. It accused and it denied all in one, forcing internal confrontations that led to an outpouring of power. The alternative was to subsume it, to swallow it up and deny its existence, but what then if the vessel, his weak body, should crack? What if the unspoken ability he held, one that no one, not even Mother, seemed to share, could burst forth if bottled too long? No, better to focus it, wield it like a sword, make use of it to influence and encourage the men around him. It could be done subtly, *must* be done subtly, else certainly Hell itself would rise up and take him back to its depths as one of its spawn . . .

Belinda jerked her hand back, every modicum of stillness, every ounce of control she'd ever known lost to her. A blush flooded her cheeks as her heartbeat crashed so loudly, so hard, that she thought it would tear her apart, and she couldn't say if it was terror or joy that drove it so fiercely. Fire danced through her, burning her face and demanding her breath to fuel it, and the heat it made spilled through her until nameless emotion was subsumed beneath raging desire.

Javier turned to her with surprise so enormous it forgot offense. There was nothing of his thoughts in his gaze, no hint at all of the flood of words that had swept her, and yet she was certain, achingly certain, that she had not imagined what they'd shared. What she'd stolen. *Witchbreed.*

The word tasted of fire, gold and bright at the back of her throat. It was new to her, not a term she would allow herself even in the most fanciful of moments, and it fluttered in her mouth, wanting to break free and be spoken. She wondered, if she kissed him, whether Javier would taste of the same enflamed power that his word burned with. The thought caught her breath, boiling away everything else, until she remembered herself and jerked again, harder than before. Choice, that time, she told herself fiercely. Choice, and not control deserting her.

"Forgive me, my lord." She let the breathlessness of discovery turn her expression wide and open, and then embarrassed at its freedom, eyes dropped as she adjusted the stays of her corset. "I hardly meant to be so rude. But it's nothing," she said quickly, softly, to the concern that overrode his surprise. "Nothing, save my corset seems to have taken a dislike to the soprano." The woman below lifted her voice to an astonishing note as Belinda wrinkled her face, twisting once more to adjust the lines of the maligned garment. Javier grinned and returned his attention to the stage.

Witchbreed. The idea hung in her thoughts now, not with the apprehension she'd felt in Javier's, but with heart-pounding curiosity. It defined him as surely as the words that had haunted her since birth seemed to define her: *it must not be found out.* So, too, felt Javier about this *witchbreed*; it was what he had named himself. Belinda had turned her need inward, making it internal and silent. Javier had extended outward with his; perhaps it was the difference between a man and a woman.

He knew, then. Without reflecting on it, he recognized, as she did, that they had something akin to each other. *Witchbreed.* Belinda watched the remainder of the opera in thoughtful silence, no more seeing it than she might see the wind. As the curtain fell and applause echoed through the theatre, she leaned toward the prince, her decision made.

"I'm curious, my lord."

"Mm?" Javier glanced at her, smiling, then back at the stage with arched eyebrows, clearly expecting her question to regard the performance.

"You would not have sent them away deliberately. It would have caused too much hurt among old friends. So I wonder, did each thing that arose to keep them away surprise you, or did you fashion their excuses with your own need and desire, and lay them like yokes on their shoulders?"

"*What?*" Javier's smile fell away and darkness clouded his eyes, a mixture of anger and fear. Belinda wet her lips, chin tilted up to give the prince a slight show of throat, one tiny acknowledgment of the power structure here.

"There is too much coincidence here tonight, and you know it as well as I. And, again, I wonder. Does the world order itself to your desire with or without your conscious will, Prince Javier? I have felt it in you, my lord."

"Felt what?" His voice snapped with fury, though Belinda noted he was careful to keep it quiet. She leaned in, close enough to brush his ear with her lips, and breathed the words.

"The *witchbreed* magic."

"You felt it, my lord." Belinda might have shouted the words out loud, for all the chances of being heard among applause and people leaving the theatre. She didn't; she kept them pitched for the prince's ears alone, a murmur edged with intensity. "You felt it in me, just as I felt it in you. Don't belittle us both and deny it."

There was nothing of horror or fear, no anger or deliberation in Javier's eyes. He bowed a brief gesture of approval to the opera cast, a smile playing his mouth. But standing beside him, Belinda could feel the bursts and sparkles of temper and fear, like fireworks of silver hue, snapping off him. Bending toward her, trying to shape her to his will, to shape her toward silence or caution or obedience.

Anyone so close as she would feel the energy of the man; anyone else would admire his vitality and never question that it sharpened the desire to serve him. In her, it birthed fascination at the utter opposites that choice allowed. Javier's strength poured into her, failing in his intent to dominate. Belinda folded it into herself, letting it increase the core of stillness within her. Frustration splintered the edges of Javier's power, turning it dark and blue, as if ice caught it and encroached inward. He was unaccustomed to defiance. More than unaccustomed: entirely unfamiliar with. That Belinda stood beside him without quailing or making apology was enough to put his doubts, if not his fears, to rest.

"Perhaps you would enjoy a tour of my gardens," he offered pleasantly, no hint of strife in his voice. Could she not feel uncertainty and a need to understand rolling off his skin like air over heated stones, Belinda might have believed his offer to be nothing more than seductive politeness. "The hour is late, I know, but the night should still be warm, and I can offer a cloak if yours is insufficient."

As bound by curiosity and desire to know as was the prince, for all that hers was tightly contained, Belinda bobbed a curtsey of agreement. "I would be delighted, my lord. Eliza tells me that you grow pears."

"Yes, and they're just at the end of the season." Javier escorted her from the theatre, meaningless pleasantries exchanged for the carriage ride to the palace grounds. He himself offered her a hand in leaving the carriage, and without asking slipped her fingers into the crook of his arm. No woman would pull away from a prince; the gesture was instinctive, but also intended to confer honour. "Are you warm enough?" he asked solicitously. Belinda dropped her gaze and reveled in allowing herself a tiny smile in place of laughter.

"Yes, my lord. Thank you." Bland and polite, they left the carriage behind as Javier guided her through a series of gates and into a midnight garden. They walked in silence, the charged topic between them set aside as Belinda loosened her fingers from Javier's arm and took a few steps ahead of him into the warm, scented grounds.

Fruit-bearing trees clustered together thickly enough around pathways to cut evening moonlight into dapples and strips of white-blue light, shifting with the slight breeze. The air that stirred between them was warm and light with sweetness, the rich scents of ripening fruit. The paths were well-tended but not pristine; smaller bushes overflowed and tangled their thin branches into the walkways, easily torn if a wanderer did not watch his feet.

Belinda turned back to Javier, catching the prince standing still in a shaft of pale light. The moon was a harsh mistress to him; her blue tones made lilac shadows in his hair and hollowed his cheekbones. She took blood from his lips and made his skin seem fragile over the bones, too pale for life.

But she brought out the lightness of his eyes and named their true color grey. In her light he looked like a creature from another world, perhaps one of the underhill dwelling *shee* the Hibernian island west of Aulun had legends of. Belinda gazed at him, entranced, then shivered, trying to cast off his spell as she lifted her chin. "My lord?"

Javier shook himself, as she had just done. "Forgive me. I was only admiring how well the moonlight suits you." He made a moue and brushed the words away disparagingly. "For though it sounds like it," he said, and Belinda started to smile, "that is not a line I try on most women. Forgive me; it sounded absurd."

"It sounded charming," Belinda corrected with amusement, then extended her hands a little as she turned to encompass the gardens with her embrace. "This is all yours."

"Yes."

"And we're alone here. Without guards or spies."

"Yes." Javier's voice lowered as he came closer. "No, my lady Irvine. There is nowhere in a palace without guards or spies. Your country estates may be more forgiving, but here there is nothing that cannot be bought and paid for, and so there is nothing that goes unwatched." His hands came around in front of her throat, unfastening the clasp of her cloak with an easy twitch of his fingers.

The cloak fell away and Javier put his hands on her hips, stepping closer. The freedom Belinda had felt in donning the gown that Eliza had sent was compounded by shock: through thin silk, without the weight of petticoats between the fabric and her skin, she could feel the heat of Javier's hands with far more intensity than she was accustomed to. His lips brushed her shoulder and she shivered, letting go a soft laugh that had more in common with desire than amusement. Javier pulled her hips back against his, mouth brushing her shoulder a second time.

"There is one sort of assignation that is hardly unexpected." His breath spilled over her skin, warm compared to the surrounding air. Belinda's stomach tightened, knots of responding need making bright aching points in her breasts.

"My lord," she whispered, then wondered what she thought she might say next. A token protest? A refusal? Javier chuckled as his hand lifted from her hip and found, unerringly, the pins that held her hair up. He tugged them loose, dropping them to the ground as her hair loosened and fell around her shoulders. He inhaled the scent, then brushed it out of the way and slid his arm around her waist, mouth against her shoulder again.

"My lord?" Mocking words, although gentle. "Do Lanyarchan men not bring their women to lovely places for seduction, Beatrice? Surely you didn't think we would have an innocent walk in the gardens, a quiet talk about the *witchbreed*—!" The final word was no louder than the others, but with it he pulled loose the laces that held her gown in place. It fell away more easily than Belinda expected it to, Javier pushing the sleeves from her shoulders and letting the fabric rumple to the ground around her ankles. Belinda could feel her tiny dagger pressing itself into the small of her back, bound in place by the corset that was all she wore now. Javier ran his fingertips along the lower edge of the corset, over her hips. She could feel his smile against her shoulder and the hardness of his desire pressed against her bottom.

"I believe I approve of this new fashion, Beatrice. One single piece of outerwear is far easier to overcome than the dozens of petticoats and layers women usually wear. Did you do this for me?" He traced the corset to its lowest point, ghosting his fingers over curls. Belinda shivered, tilting her head back against the prince's shoulder and making him breathe laughter. He pressed his palm over the thatch of curls, holding her hips against his as his other hand wandered free, following the stiff lines of the corset up to where skin was bared again. He brushed his fingers over rounded flesh, then delved into the scant space afforded by the bindings and forced her breast free of the corset, scraping her nipple against the hard edges of the stay. Belinda whimpered and Javier growled, a hungry sound of triumph as he pinched the nipple and slid his fingers between her thighs.

The liquid sound of pleasure that escaped her was loud enough to call any nearby guards with an impulse for watching. Javier pressed his thigh between hers, pushing them apart. Belinda's ankle twisted, the shoes she wore for extra height not intended to be moved sideways while weight bore down on them. She collapsed; Javier caught her with his hand hard on her breast and his fingers curving inside her. For a blissful moment there was relief, pressure against the sweet spot on the bone within, but his fingers left her again when she was steady on her feet. Belinda made a mewl of protest, opening her thighs further and winding an arm back around Javier's neck, uncertain of her own ability to keep her feet. He smiled again, against her throat.

"Now." He drew his fingers, wet with her need, up through curls, sifting the coarse hair. Belinda gasped with dismay, pushing her hips forward and squirming her thighs further apart as he chuckled. He thumped a fingernail forward, sending a paralyzing combination of pain and need surging through her body, and she let out a strangled cry.

"Please, my lord. Please!"

"Do they grow all Lanyarchan women so lusty?" Javier murmured, pleased. His fingertip flicked over the centre of her pleasure again, this time light and quick and repetitive. Belinda whimpered, trying to hold still so the touch could build to release. Javier let warm breath spill over her neck again, a quiet sigh, and murmured, "Now. Tell me what you know of the witchbreed."

Laughter ripped from Belinda's throat, helpless and gasping. "*Now?*" Remembering her own name was in question; she wanted to give in to sensation, not force thought into coherent words.

"Now," Javier said for the third time. "Now is the only time listeners don't hang on every word. Who wants to listen to the soppy, false endearments spoken during lovemaking?" His own voice carried soft amusement and detachment; it was not the first time he'd used love as a guise for secret conversation. His touch glided over her again and Belinda groaned, half laughter, and tightened her fingers in his hair.

It wasn't that it was impossible. In fact, it was easier than most men's egos would like to know, detaching the physical from the mental. Calling stillness all around her helped, the use of long years forbidding the body's reaction to pain and pleasure both. It allowed her to order her thoughts, ignoring her body's shivers. Javier felt the withdrawal and bit her shoulder, contrary to his own orders, redoubling his efforts to call them to the surface again. Belinda allowed herself a tiny whimper through the distant ache of need, unwilling to divorce herself entirely from the sure touch of his hands and the pleasure they brought. If there were spies on the garden walls it did no good to stand like a stick in the prince's arms, ignoring the work he did to please her.

"I know very little, my lord." The words came as a sigh. "I've never met anyone else like me." She shuddered again, tightening her fingers in Javier's hair. "Like us." Her voice was low and liquid, a plea in itself as she pressed her hips into his touch.

Even as she spoke, though, realization sparked through her,

bringing its own kind of pleasure. Her father had to share the power Javier called witchbreed, or he never would have seen her through the shadows. And if Robert carried that kernel of power inside him, so, too, did Dmitri, whose presence she was now certain had roused her from sleep in the Khazarian north a few months ago. Dmitri, who had been with her father the night he took away Belinda's memory of how to hide in the shadows. There *were* others, then, but Javier's fingers had found a quick rhythmic circle that threatened to shatter her concentration. Beyond his touch was the weight of his will, impressed upon her stillness, external force to her internal. One or the other she could withstand; the two together gave her over to abandonment unlike any she'd known. For long moments she shuddered and cried out in Javier's arms, until her thighs were wet with desire and the only thing that kept her on her feet was his grip on her.

"I call it the stillness," she finally gasped. Javier chuckled, his hands abandoning her. Belinda locked her knees to keep her feet, swallowing hard. "It was a game. So no one could hurt me." There was very little sound as the prince disrobed. Belinda turned her head toward him, wetting her lips, but he stayed too close to see: a pale shoulder in moonlight, the play of muscle, nothing more. "I used it to hide in shadows once," she blurted, abruptly desperate to confess what she knew so she might no longer need to divorce body from soul and could focus wholly on Javier's touch. "But I—" Her breath caught, his hands on her hips again. She heard the smile in his voice, mouth brushing her shoulder.

"But you what?" His hands weighed heavy on her hips, bringing her down to the grassy earth. Her gown, wrinkled beyond repair, let blades of sharp grass prickle her knees as she whimpered again and pressed them further apart. The corset was too long to let her arch her hips back in offering. Instead she fell forward, but Javier's hand in her hair stopped her with a forceful jerk. The impulse to submit weakened her and her head rolled back in his grasp, the weight of her body following. "But you what, Beatrice?" Javier asked again. He kept his fist knotted in her hair, pulling the skin of her throat taut. She swallowed against it, yielding to his strength.

"But I've forgotten how, my lord." Need parched her throat and she swallowed, raw. "The stillness is all I can do." Even as she spoke, memory washed over her, the cacophony of emotion in the Maglian pub and the very words she'd plucked from Javier's mind earlier that evening. "Oh . . . *oh!*" Thought left her in a rush as Javier claimed her, a hard thrust demanding submission without causing pain. He settled back on his heels, spreading her over his thighs. Her skin rolled at the shoulder blade, pinched between the hard line of the corset and Javier's chest. She fumbled her hand back, scrabbling for the corset cords, but Javier caught her hand and twisted it further up, until her spine arched despite the stiff boning in the undergarment. Her breath came more shallowly as he curled her fingers into the laces, a wordless command to remain as he arranged her. An ache throbbed through her shoulder joint, made worse as he teased her nipple with a touch so light she thought she might only be imagining it. She arched again, trying to press her breast into his fingers, making the ache in her shoulder worse. She bent her other arm back, half to try to alleviate the ache and more to hear Javier's low chuckle and the breath of praise that spilled over her skin. He freed her other breast from the corset bindings, the nipple tightening with desperation at the touch of cool air.

There was a deliciousness to being helpless to the prince's gentle strength. Belinda's hair tickled her own spine, her head bent back so dark waves were caught between her body and Javier's. He put his fist into her hair again, pulling her head further back until she arched more sharply into the corset bones than her lungs could bear. Her own fingers tangled in her hair, pulling hard enough for pain that blossomed into the sweet ache of desire, keeping her in the pose he had placed her in. She had had men treat her thus before, but without tenderness; for them pain and discomfort were meant for domination. Under Javier's touch she felt sculpted, shaped and made beautiful for the pleasure of extremity, her breasts pushed forward and her hips back in an exaggeration of woman-hood. She trusted his desire implicitly, knowing without reserva-tion that he might bend and mold her, but he would never deign to break her. That was for lesser men.

"Tell me more."

That he spoke sent a paroxysm of shock through her, tightening her nipples and her belly again. He pulsed his hips upward, taking what little breath she had away and leaving her unable to catch more, the corset stays pressed too tightly against her. Black fire-works sparked and trailed across her vision, brightening as she closed her eyes and struggled to take a breath. "Can you not tell me more?" he murmured, teasing. Even teasing, his intent to pursue conversation triggered both laughter and offense in Belinda. She strained to lift her head, determined to drag in enough air to make words.

Javier's fingers slid between her thighs and clasped the swollen nub of flesh there. Her words were taken by a shallow cry, too lit-tle air behind it to give it full voice. She shuddered around him, too breathless to struggle violently as orgasm smashed through her. In moments she was boneless in his arms, held there by the stern corset lines rather than any willpower of her own. Her head was fallen so far back the corset pressed painful lines into the flesh of her shoulder blades, her breasts offered up to the moonlight. Javier kissed her throat with a murmur of appreciation, ghosting his hand over her nipples again. When she shivered he laughed and captured her clit between his fingers again, drawing out a whimper of pain brought by too much pleasure.

"Then let me tell you what I know," he breathed. He lifted his hips into hers, purposeful strength burying himself more deeply in her. Half swooning with breathlessness, Belinda gasped and fell fur-

158 • C. E. MURPHY

ther into his grasp, spreading her thighs another scant inch to afford him greater access. His mark of approval came with another torturous touch around her aching clit, and as she shuddered he whispered secrets of sorcery against her skin.

Dew soaked the green silk of the dress, morning too young to warm the air yet. Belinda shivered under her summer cloak, curling her legs up to move her feet under the comparative warmth beneath the cloak. She found Javier's shin with her feet and tucked her toes between his legs, making him inhale a sleepy laugh. "Why do women always have cold feet?"

"In this case, because I've been sleeping on wet, cold ground for hours." Belinda rolled onto her back, still keeping her body pressed as closely to Javier's as possible. "Why are men always warm?"

He slid his arm over her ribs and the still-stiff lines of her corset. "Because the human race would surely die out if we couldn't keep our mothers and wives from turning to ice every night. Unbend your knees, woman. Now my feet are uncovered." He crunched up, resetting the cloak over them, and threw the hood over their heads. The cool air warmed almost instantly and Belinda realised her nose was numb. She clasped it between her fingers and Javier chuckled, moving her hand to cover her nose with his hand instead. She could smell her own scent on him, musky and faint hours later. As if sensing her reaction to that, Javier shifted the cloak and lowered his head to cover her nipple with his mouth. The heat was exquisite and shocking after hours of chill. Belinda arched into it and he let go another low laugh, lifting his head again. "Do it."

"My lord—"

"Beatrice." Command filled his voice, expectation bordering on irritation. "Power is begotten by desire, and I know you desire." He put his hand over her lower stomach, just where the corset ended. The warmth of his hand was distracting, waking heat in other places—but that was the point. Belinda inhaled deeply, watching Javier's gaze snap back to her breasts. It was something, at least, and thus sated she wrapped the stillness around her, letting it protect her more thoroughly than any cloak could do.

They had done this twice during the small hours of the morning, once with Belinda following Javier's guidance and once on her own. There was a wall of resistance in her, one that weakened as she shoved against it, calling her *need* through it and to its other side. That wall, she didn't understand how, tasted of her father, as if his broad shoulders and scent of chypre had somehow taken up residence inside her own mind. Beyond it was the power that had let her hide in shadows when she was a child. Robert's very will lay between her conscious desire and that power, making a barrier to her accessing it.

But there was a weakness in the barricade: she could almost see the words around the place where it ran thinner. *It cannot be found out. Not yet. It's still too early. The time has not yet come for you to know such things.*

Not *yet.* That admonishment had been made well over ten years earlier. Now, finally, whether her father meant for it to be or not, it was time. Belinda was no longer a child. She served her queen and her country, but her will was her own, and the long years of wondering were coming to an end.

She had broken through twice, and now felt it giving way before her desire again. It didn't shatter, but rippled and spread outward, as if she'd thrown a stone into a pool and her point of access was the tiny centre of the vortex it created. She pushed through that centre, widening it, then withdrew. A trickle of power spilled forth, golden and warm as sunlight. It was the stillness, made visible within her own mind. In itself, it was nothing, not even potential; it merely lay beyond the barrier in her mind and waited.

Waited for desire. It warmed her as much, more, than Javier's touch, filled her with a completion that no mere man could achieve. She cupped her hands together beneath the cloak, as if she might catch water in them, and took a breath deep enough to strain her ribs against the corset. "*Light*," she whispered, not in Gallic but in her maiden tongue of Aulunian.

A glow stained her fingers, soft and warm. It lit the underside shadows of the cloak, a tiny, gentle ball of sunlight cradled in her hands. Pride and delight bloomed in her, well-hidden from the surface but enough to warm her within. A smaller part of her mind crowed with alarm, Ilyana's accusations of witchery proved true, and death by burning should Belinda ever be caught. She should be more frightened; she *knew* she should be more frightened. But with the soft glow of power in her hands, most of that fear was drowned beneath confidence. She only had to go carefully, and she would never be found out.

Javier clucked approval and she moved her hands slowly, carrying her little palmful of light closer to his face. His eyes picked up the golden hue, reflecting the silky sheen of the cloak they lay huddled beneath. "Better," he breathed, as if the stirring air might put Belinda's light out like it was a candle. "It came faster this time. Did you feel it? Witchlight, Beatrice. Your light."

"Our light," she whispered back, though it wasn't true. Javier curled his fingers around the back of her hand, pale silver light springing from his palm as easily as he might point a finger. It warred with her golden sunlight, and dominated, for all that it was the color of moonlight. He had years of practise and skill over hers, and, Belinda thought, access to power that was not hidden behind a wall built by a well-meaning father. She caught her lower lip in her teeth, eyes closed as she wrestled the bleak wall within her mind, prodding and poking at the pinhole she'd made in it. It tore, and her eyes flew open as power stung her palms and brightened the sunlight held in her hands. Javier put his palm against hers and brought more of his own power to bear, smothering golden sparks with the cool light of the moon. Belinda gasped as her witchlight winked out and Javier pinned her wrist against the ground.

"Our gift," he corrected. "All that's best of dark and light. But not too bright, lady. Such secrets must be studied in the quiet of night, when there are fewer eyes to watch."

"My lord?" A sudden blush came over her, an honest reaction; the art of blushing on demand was one she had tried to learn without success. She watched Javier's eyes follow the rush of pink down her throat to where it stained the upper swells of her breasts, and wished not for the first time that she could achieve the effect at will. She could prevent it; that much the stillness gave her, but never call it. He lowered his mouth to the tinted flesh, then followed the curve upward until he caught her nipple in his mouth, all tongue and teeth. She arched and he rolled his weight over her, cock pressed against her belly.

"Now you blush?" Amusement enriched his voice. "A wanton woman under the moon's light and come morning you blush and look away? Yes: at night, Beatrice, in the long small hours. Is it your reputation you fear for? You wouldn't be the first woman to be named the prince's whore. It may even boost your marriage prospects, if we part on amicable terms."

"Marius . . . ?" The question was poorly judged. Javier's eyes darkened as he put his fingers against the hollow of her throat.

"Is it he you prefer, my lady Beatrice? Is the prince merely a feather in your girlish cap?"

"No," Belinda breathed. She reached for the drip of power inside her, infusing her answer with its light, all the truth she could muster into the soft word. Belinda had seen jealousy in a hundred men, but wouldn't have imagined that this man, a prince, would allow himself such a petty emotion. Her life might depend on defusing it. She parted her lips and swallowed tentatively against the pressure on her throat. She had not confessed to the prince her burgeoning ability to sense emotion and even thought; the moment to do so had come and gone, and she was no longer tangled in passion that washed even the clarity of stillness away. If Javier didn't know of the faculty, he might fall prey to it. Belinda poured all the power she could reach into her whispered words, filling them with subtle adoration and trust. "Marius is a boy in his heart, my lord, no matter what his years. I prefer men."

Javier's fingers tightened, then loosened enough to let her swallow. The darkness in his eyes diminished, leaving them colorless in the filtered light through the cloak. Belinda tilted her head back, letting the weight of his hand press into her throat again. Submission, now that danger was past, only reinforced his position relative to hers. It could do her no harm.

"Marius should aim so high as a royal cast-off," Javier said after a moment. "And I think I will not tire of you for some time, my little witch. You have much to learn."

"You honour me," Belinda whispered. Flat amusement shot through Javier's gaze.

"Yes. I do. Enjoy it while it lasts, Beatrice. Nothing ever does."

7

ROBERT, LORD DRAKE
11 September 1587 † *Khazan, capital of Khazar,*
north and east of Echon

Irina, imperatrix of all Khazar, is a beautiful woman.

Not like Lorraine, whose striking features made her beautiful in her youth. Time has stripped that beauty, her long face falling with age. She might have found a way to move through her later years gracefully, but instead she fights every year as if it is her bitterest enemy, and that, too, has left marks.

Not like Sandalia, either, who has never been beautiful, only devastatingly pretty. She still holds the edge of youth that maintains loveliness, but in a few short years her figure will fail to a fondness for sweets, and her curves will turn to plump softness. It will look well on her, but it is not beauty.

No, Irina Durova will be beautiful when they lay her down in her grave. Time will not be able to take the elegant square bones of her face away, and her skin is of the quality to hold wrinkles tight around the corner of large dark eyes. She is in her forties now, and her hair is silvering. She lets it do so naturally, taking gravitas from aging; she does not believe youth is the only potent drug there is. Then again, she has true beauty to see her through the years.

It is more difficult to be angry at a beautiful woman than a plain one, but Robert is trying.

"I do not understand, Your Majesty." It was a falsehood; he understood perfectly, as did Irina. "What does Essandia offer that Aulun can't? Our fleet is better-trained, and a treaty with my queen is unique in its advantages. There can be no backdoor pressure to marry." He stresses the last sentence, making it a clear reminder to those who know—in the audience chamber, that means himself and Irina—how much trouble Irina has faced on the marriage front lately, and how Aulunian resources slipped into Khazar to divest her of that problem.

"Aulun stands alone against Cordula," Irina says, full of genuine-sounding sympathy. Her voice is as rich as her face and body: deep, for a woman, and warm. The imperatrix's laughter is said to melt snow from the eaves, a gift of some renown in icy Khazar. Robert has never heard her laugh, nor seen snow melt through force of personality, but he likes the story. "We do not share Cordula's faith, but we are cognizant of the dangers of rejecting it blatantly. My father recalled the Heretics' Trials, Lord Drake. We are reluctant to draw attention to our own borders by making hasty treaties with Cordula's enemy."

Robert bows, a light and almost teasing action, to hide the grinding of his teeth. "Aulun is certain Khazar never makes hasty decisions, Your Majesty. Aulun would also like to remind you that while much of southern Echon is held in Ecumenic sway, the northerly states, like Aulun, have found their own spiritual paths to follow. An alliance with Aulun is not an alliance against Cordula."

"We are certain that is a point worth remembering," Irina says, and now there's a tint of humour in her large eyes. "We are, after all, only a woman, and must heed the advice of the men around us."

Robert nearly chokes: he knows this trick. It's one of Lorraine's favourites, and it makes him mad with exasperation.

And then suddenly, abruptly, he sees what he should have seen before: that Irina's gown is the one Lorraine sent her twelve years earlier, in congratulations on Ivanova's birth. It has been modified, made more fashionable, of course, but the jewel-encrusted fabric is the same, the cut still subtly Aulunian rather than the broader lines of Khazarian fashion.

He is too masterful a player to let his eyes widen, though irritation spills through him. He, of all people, should know that words spoken in political debate mean little, and Irina has given him answers in her dress and in her phrasing that few others would know to read. That he nearly missed them himself is an embarrassment, and he bows again now, in part to cover that embarrassment and in part because Irina has effectively dismissed him. "Aulun trusts your counselors will guide you well, Your Majesty. I hope we'll speak again before I leave Khazan."

Irina flickers her fingers, neither agreement nor disagreement, and Robert catches a smirk on a courtier's face as he turns away. He allows thunderous frustration to darken his own features, playing to that smirk; playing to Aulun being stymied by Khazar, and he narrowly avoids stomping as he leaves the audience hall.

His mockery of temper is thrown off by the time he leaves the palace, though there's a hint of true anger simmering inside him. Irina took him by surprise, and he hates being off-balance.

"Dmitri!" Robert finds the hawk-nosed man in the stables, the scent of straw and manure rising up. The horses snort as he stalks by to catch Dmitri's arm. Robert is a big man, his hands powerful, and Dmitri flinches. "Irina is making treaties with the Essandian prince, Dmitri. Don't tell me you didn't know." He digs his fingers into the tender flesh of Dmitri's inner arm, as if leaving a mark will earn him the answer he wants.

Dmitri's mouth thins and he drops his gaze to the offending grip, then stares at Robert until Robert releases him. There is a note of grace, of chagrin, in the way Robert averts his eyes and offers apology. Dmitri, satisfied, takes a deliberate moment to straighten his sleeve, fussing like a man more fastidious than he normally is. Robert, still irritated, remains silent, waiting.

"A queen doesn't always heed her advisers," Dmitri finally says, as close to an admission of failure as Robert's ever heard from him. "Her strength will be divided," he adds in a grumble. "Her army will be split between Khazar, Essandia, and Aulun."

"Or she'll have Essandian and Aulunian ships alike and her own troops here to put on them and send where she wants. Dammit, Dmitri, you should have told me. You should have stopped it. She hints at favouring Aulun, but I want her to have no choice. Warp the missives from Essandia. Make it seem as though Rodrigo seeks her hand along with her troops."

"A dangerous game," Dmitri murmurs. "What if she accepts?"

"She wouldn't have come to Aulun about Gregori if she were of a mind to marry. These three queens hold a unique place in Echon's history. So many women have never held such power simultaneously, Dmitri. None of them are willing to cede it. She'll reject a marriage offer, or dance around it like Rodrigo and Lorraine have done for twenty years." He exhales, explosive sound, and the line of horses down the stables responds in kind, shaking themselves, stomping feet, huffing and puffing. "Do you know where Seolfor is?"

"I don't" is Dmitri's eventual answer. "Are you losing control, Robert?" There's interest in his eyes, flashing, bordering on avarice. Robert nearly allows himself to seize Dmitri's arm again, more intentionally threatening.

The truth is there are moments when Robert loses sight of his goal. Moments when the politics of Echon and Khazar overwhelm the end game. Moments when it's difficult to remember his queen's face, her image replaced by an aging redhead whose power is blunt and worldly and the centre of his everyday existence. He has spent thirty years guiding Aulun and her regent, coaxing reluctant love and desire out of a woman determined to stand alone. He has never threatened her, never shown interest in stealing her power for his own, and this is why she trusts him. It's as well she has no need to understand that her power is transitory and unappealing to him. She is a vessel, and she has long since done her part in ensuring the downfall of her world.

There may yet be one thing left for her to do, though, and until that thing is done, he will love, honour, and manipulate her, and regret none of it. When it's done, he knows he might find that frail human emotion has gotten the better of him, and that he might love the Titian Queen until the end of her days.

Robert has no objections to that. She's a formidable opponent, all the more so for being a female regent to a society that believes women to be weak and inferior. How they can stand before Lorraine, before Sandalia, before Irina, and retain that conviction is beyond him, though he's heard it said many times that all of those women are unnaturally masculine. The idea that they are wholly feminine and wholly capable doesn't appear to have occurred to anyone, or if it has, they've found it such an appalling and frightening thought as to put it away again and never let it see the light of day. There are moments when Robert has wanted to smack courtiers alongside the skull, not to defend Lorraine, but out of simple exasperation at their determined thick-headedness.

He wonders, briefly, if Dmitri might suffer the same loss of focus if the invasion were his to conduct.

"No," he says, and makes it light, refusing to allow himself the luxury of physically threatening the slighter man. It's a closer match than it might look, anyway: Robert has bulk, but Dmitri's slenderness holds wiry strength. They were always well-matched, even before. It's why they were selected.

Seolfor, though . . . Seolfor is their third, waiting, and Robert has no doubts of his loyalty. No one would: breaking faith with the queen is a concept that has only slowly become even conceivable, and that only through long years of watching human betrayals. The idea turns Robert's stomach, makes him physically sick, and Seolfor is no less staunchly the queen's own than he. But Seolfor is a renegade, if any of them are; Robert believes, though he'd never ask, that this is why the queen sent him on this one-way journey. Because of that, Robert has preferred to keep him off the playing field until his participation is critical. "But with kings and queens playing at pieces as if their lives were their own to direct, it may be time to activate him. Seolfor can be a charming bastard when he wants to be, and there'll be no taint of foreign courts to him."

Curiosity darts across Dmitri's angular face. "Is that why you've kept him out for so long? Where will you send him?"

"Essandia," Robert says drily, "to plant a woman on Rodrigo's cock long enough to make the child she bears seem reasonably his. I'll never understand the hold Cordula has on these men. The women are more pragmatic. I only wish Sandalia'd given in to you soon enough to make her son seem Charles's, instead of catching by that foppish Louis."

"So does she." Dmitri lowers his eyes, oddly womanish in his apology, then looks up again, all sharp hazel eyes and hawklike features. "But Gallin is under control, isn't it? I thought your girl was there."

"She is, and Sandalia will be there soon. My Primrose will have slipped in quietly, made herself a part of the court, and be waiting to gain the queen's confidence." Of all the tasks he's set Belinda to, this one is both simplest and most difficult. Murder is easy to achieve; sedition much harder, particularly spoken from royal lips. But they need so little, and Belinda is so very good at her winsome ways. It's why Robert sent her, and not someone of lesser import: even *he* finds himself inclined to trust his daughter; and that's why he sent Ana de Meo to watch over her, in turn. Trust is a weakness that hides flaws; better to set a second pair of eyes over that which he dares trust. "One wrong word from Sandalia spoken in Primrose's ear, and we'll have our war."

"And then it will be properly begun."

Robert nods and claps his hand on Dmitri's shoulder. They stand like that a moment, Dmitri covering Robert's hand with his own. Then they break ways, no more words needed between them, and go about their separate duties.

There is a rapping, not at his door, but from within a wall. He knows, though he should not, that the passage there leads to three different bedrooms. None of them is Irina's, which is a shame: even Robert isn't above the secret thrill of a queen coming to him in the night.

He's at the hidden door before the tapping comes a second time, his head tilted against it, listening, scenting, seeking. The first two garner nothing; the door is too thick for subtleties to slip through. The third encounters a woman's mind, not agitated, but calm and focused. Again, not Irina: she, like Lorraine, is all but impossible to read, her throne granting and demanding an indomitable will. The woman who has come to him is not thinking of who she is but of what she wants: a high-born lover to replace the one she had.

Robert will take no pains to remind her of his own lowly beginnings.

He finds the mechanism that opens the door, slides it open, and looks down at Akilina Pankejeff, a grand duchess within Irina's court. She, like Lorraine, is not beautiful, but in her age she will be terrifying. Black hair sweeps back from a violent widow's peak, one that rumour says grows sharper with every lover who dies. Akilina Pankejeff has outlived two husbands and three well-placed lovers, the last of whom was Count Gregori Kapnist, and she is only thirty-two. The superstitious and fearful—nearly everyone in this stars-forsaken place—call her Yaga Baba behind her back, and make the sign of God to ward off witches. She has a golden cast to her skin, and eyes as black as her hair; there is nothing soft about her, not even when she comes to him dressed in loose sleeping gowns. They only play up her narrow shoulders, her small breasts, and the length of her limbs.

The door hisses shut behind her and Robert kneels without speaking, putting his hands on her hips. Her eyes can't darken any further, but surprise colours them and she touches his hair as he gathers her nightgown, one palmful at a time, toward her waist. He is attentive and delighted to please; Akilina is lusty and ready to be pleased. Minutes later she stands slumped against the wall, fingers still knotted in Robert's brown hair, gasps chuckling from her. "Not what I came for," she breathes, "but well worth coming for. No wonder the Titian Bitch keeps you at her side." She pushes Robert's hands away, not unkindly, and lets her sleeping gown fall again. Robert wipes his beard without a hint of discretion and climbs to his feet still licking his lips.

"Then why are you here?" He's surprised for the second time in a day; that doesn't often happen. Akilina smiles, unexpectedly predatory, and walks her fingers up his chest. He, too, is dressed for sleeping, and her touch is warm through the soft linen of his shirt. He does not catch her hand and pull her back to the bed to roost above him; that decision is hers.

"I require an escort, my lord Drake." She offers another smile, as pointed as the first, and leads with her hips as she steps into him. "I'll pay you in whatever coin you prefer."

He kisses her fingertips, politeness, not ardor. "An escort, my lady?"

Playfulness falls out of her gaze, leaving it flat. "Our winters are long and cold, and my lover's five months in his grave. I'd intended to retreat to my estate for the winter, but if I can go farther afield that's much to be preferred. A woman might travel safely in your party, Lord Drake."

"I travel light, my lady." Robert isn't trying to dissuade her. More likely to convince a snake not to bite, he thinks, though he's far too diplomatic to let the thought anywhere near his expression. "Myself and a handful of men, and with winter coming on we'll set a hard pace. Can you keep up?"

The challenge glints in her eyes. "I won't travel as light or as fast as you'd prefer, my lord. Wherever I winter, I can have new gowns made, but a woman of my stature can't arrive in a new city with nothing but what's on her back. Give me an extra day for every three you travel in speed, though, and I'll keep your pace."

"Where will you go?"

Akilina smiles. "I've always wanted to see Aria Magli."

BELINDA PRIMROSE
15 October 1587 † *Lutetia, Gallin*

My Dearest Jayne;

The letters were etched into parchment, retraced so many times they might have been inked onto the table beneath it. In the deepest of the grooves, ink sat in shallow puddles, the parchment's ability to absorb it lost. Belinda picked up her quill for the dozenth time, scraping it over the shapes of the letters. She had thought too much; she must simply write, and when the words had spilled out of her she could choose and decide what she ought and ought not say in a letter to the Aulunian spymaster.

My Dearest Jayne;

Lutetia agrees with me more than I might have dreamed, and I have been remiss in writing to tell you of it. The weather is temperate—a blessing after stormy Lanyarchan nights!—and the people are kind. I have made friends both high and low, from a woman whose beauty is so extraordinary I would scarcely believe it

real had I not met her myself, to a man of the greatest power. I
would tell you his name, though I think you will not believe me: he
is Javier, prince of Gallin and heir to that throne and another:
Essandia, should Rodrigo fail to marry as seems so likely now that
he is in his fifties. And la: listen to me, calculating out the heirship
as if I might someday bear children into it. A good Lanyarchan
woman would not cast her gaze so high—and yet there are moments, dear sister, when I wish it were otherwise. He is handsome,
and commands power. Any woman might dream of such a husband, even a woman widowed with no sons to prove her fertility.

He is very kind, the prince, and has taken me into his group of
friends—

All but on cue, Nina knocked on the door and opened it, ducking her head in a brief curtsey. "Marius is here, my lady." She smiled,
full of bright hope and cheer; in the weeks that had passed since the
opera, Marius had given no sign of being daunted by Belinda's
friendship with the prince, and called as often as his duties would
allow. The merchant's son was a good match, bordering on excellent, and Nina was determined that her mistress should not miss it.
Belinda felt a brief unaccustomed pang of guilt through her belly,
wondering how long the young man would continue courting her.

"Thank you, Nina. Tell him I'll be down momentarily." Belinda
set the quill aside with more care than was necessary and scooped
a palmful of sand over the paper, shaking it to take away excess ink.
Tilting the paper sent fine grains sliding back into their cup,
though several stuck in the deep-scratched lines of the salutation,
glittering as the light caught them. Her father would be amused by
the emotion wrought in those deep lines. Belinda scowled at them,
determining to rewrite the letter even if the words came out flawlessly. She stood up, exasperated, to discover Nina still hesitating in
the door. "Well? What is it?"

"Do you not like him, my lady?" the servant asked timidly. "He
is a fine match, and, forgive me, my lady, but—"

"But royalty is beyond my grasp, no?"

Nina blushed and dropped her gaze. Belinda put her hands on the desk and leaned heavily on it for a few moments, letting the weight of her head stretch an ache into her spine. "I like him well enough. Are you too polite to tell me that my chance is slipping away?" She looked up. Nina's eyes remained fixed on the floor, but she nodded, a minute gesture that spoke more by daring to be made than the sentiment expressed. "And how do you know that, Nina?"

Guilt rolled off the girl in waves, thick enough to flavour the air. Belinda took a deep breath of it, closing her eyes and savoring it. It was her secret, her one secret from the prince in the matters of witchcraft. For six weeks, through summer's end and into autumn, they had stolen as many hours as they dared, pressing the borders of the longer nights to study together. Study, and more. Even with the mixed blessing of too-clear memory, Belinda could only hazily remember a time when she felt as if she'd had enough sleep.

But the walls that Robert had placed in her mind had softened. Where there had been a hard-won pinhole of access to her witchbreed power, there was now a pool, serene and calm at the heart of her. There was more yet to be gained, but she no longer struggled every night simply to cup her hands together and call witchlight to them. Even now she felt the impulse to curl her fingers and light the tiny glow, curtained by her palm. It was a small thing, but each new lesson gave her ideas as to how she might increase her gift and her strength.

Behind it all, though, was the talent she had been stayed by need from sharing with Javier, and which she kept close to her heart now for the joy of secrets. The little things she had learned paled by the depths to which she could now read emotion. Fear and lust, delight and anger were all writ in the air around the men and women she encountered. Contentedness and ambition, hope and despair, so heavy around them that Belinda wondered how she had never seen it before. The difficulty was no longer in delving for those secret emotions, but rather in fending them away. It took no more than a thought to know if a man desired her, and what kind of needs he had in bed. No more than a wish to know, to discover if the neighbor's wife feared her husband discovering he was being cuckolded. It lent Belinda glorious confidence, and she resented her father's decision to lock that gift away behind a barrier in her mind. Only a little: she could not afford resentment or anger to any great degree—the stillness wrapped around her and tightened on her bones when she pursued rebellious thoughts. They ill-suited her; at the core of her, beneath newfound power and even beneath her precious, long-nurtured stillness, Belinda knew herself to believe, without reservation, in her duty to a mother who could never acknowledge her. She let herself wonder, very briefly, what she might feel now from Lorraine, with this burgeoning power at her disposal.

It would not, she was certain, be the guilt and discomfort that made Nina squirm in the doorway. "He complimented you," Belinda guessed with a faint smile. "Did he impose himself upon you, Nina?"

Surprise replaced guilt, washing off the girl as her eyes jerked from the floor to meet Belinda's. "No, my lady. Only—" She swallowed and flinched through the chest, making her breasts twitch with the motion.

"Only told you that you have lovely breasts, and lovely eyes." Horrified embarrassment swept over her, Nina's ears burning red. Belinda smiled and touched the girl's bodice as she passed by. "He was right."

Nina's confusion and startled desire followed her down the stairs.

"There is snow in the air." Marius walked with his hand at the small of Belinda's back, a touch that was barely there. It made her aware, as she rarely was, of the tiny dagger she wore there, nestled beneath layers of clothing. Not for the first time she let herself smile at the ridiculous placement of the thing; trapped against her skin it did no good whatsoever for defense, and more than once she'd had to palm it away into the fallen folds of her gown when a man undressed her. It didn't matter. The knife was sentimental, a reminder of who she was and a reminder of the stillness, not a weapon. She turned the smile up at Marius, curiosity in her eyes.

"Does it snow this far south, my lord?"

"Beatrice," Marius said with mild exasperation. "How many times must I ask you to call me Marius?"

"At least once more." Belinda smiled again, letting her gaze drift from the boy at her side. It was harder among intimates of a higher class, she was discovering, to follow her own rule of never calling a man by his name. Formality drenched every move to such a degree that the calling of names became far more important than it was as a serving girl. She found herself unable to forget Marius or Javier's names, unable to not learn them, as she'd been able to not learn . . . *Viktor,* she reminded herself. Poor Viktor.

Asselin was easier; she saw him less, and his gaze on her was frank and lustful and open, like most men's. Over the weeks he'd given no sign of recognizing her as the strumpet from the tavern. Without that concern threatening their play, it was clear he understood the game between men and women in a fashion that Marius did not, and Javier disdained. Asselin called her Lady Irvine, openly mocking the formality, and she called him Lord Asselin with all the sly wit and sexual rejoinder that he sought.

Eliza was different. Belinda's own law didn't stand in the face of women. Women only rarely had power and most of that came through the men they wed or whored themselves to; it was rare indeed that Belinda was sent after a woman. There was no need to misremember Eliza's name, or call her by a formal one.

Then again, friendship had not blossomed between them,

though they were not quite enemies. Eliza had too much respect for her friend—and Belinda wondered for the dozent time, lover? The answer was there for the taking if Belinda chose to read either of them deeply enough, but the curiosity was more thrilling than the answering. Eliza would not declare open warfare on a woman Javier chose to invite into his circle of friends, or his bed, until he tired of her. Belinda admired Eliza's loyalty, recognizing it for the bitter draughts of unrequited love. *That* was a cup of poison Belinda had no desire to ever drink of, and it left her with a trace of sympathy for Eliza's position. She refused to be drawn into cat fights with the other woman, frustrating Eliza and amusing Asselin.

"You are not with me."

"What?" Belinda cursed herself, turning her gaze back to Marius, who watched her eyes older than his years, not so much sad as weary. "Forgive me, my lord. I was lost in thought."

"Thoughts of Javier." It was half a question. Marius lifted his hand to brush his fingers across Belinda's cheek. Her eyebrows drew down, then lifted.

"Eliza, my lord."

Surprise and a trace of hope graced Marius's expression. "Eliza?"

"She doesn't like me."

Marius smiled and looked away. "Eliza doesn't like anyone who lands in Jav's bed."

"I do not believe you're supposed to know that, my lord."

Marius looked back, eyebrows elevated. "That Eliza doesn't like anyone who's in Javier's bed, or that you're there, my lady Beatrice?"

"The latter." A faint smile curved Belinda's mouth. "The former seems eminently obvious."

"The difficulty," Marius said, turning his gaze away again, "with being friends with Jav is that women do not dare tell him no, even when they might otherwise wish to." He glanced at her again, folding his arms across his chest. "Spare me the insistence that you are bound to me heart and soul and that you only spread your legs for him because you have no other choice. Jav's hard to resist."

"Then why did you introduce me to him?" Belinda put her hand on Marius's forearm. "Women are not so different from men, my lord. We, too, are drawn to power. Why introduce me to him?"

"Because he is my friend." Marius withdrew a step, making Belinda's fingers slide away from his arm.

Another voice came out of the distance, not so far away that their conversation might have gone unheard: "And because we're all damned in our lovers by knowing him. No way to go forward or back without his permission, so we must introduce our paramours whether we will or won't." Asselin stalked up to them, shoulders hunched against cold more threatened than felt in the air. "Marius, may I borrow your fine lady for a little while? My sister's giving another damned recital and my mother expects me to bring a comely woman of marriageable age."

"You couldn't find one of your own?" Marius sighed with resignation. "Beatrice, his sister has a voice like a harpy. Your ears may never forgive me if I let you go."

"But she's got the body of an angel, Marius. Turn up alone yourself and my mother might see past the merchant street to consider you a prospect. No offense to our lady Irvine, but a Comtesse is a rank worth aspiring to."

"I'll come," Marius said sourly, "if only to be certain Beatrice isn't being mistreated by the lout I call friend. Shall we all go together?"

Asselin's gaze, appraising, raked over Marius, then Belinda. "Irvine will do," he said after a moment, "but Mother would never let you past the front door in those clothes, Marius. Meet us there. I'll save you enough wine to stop the sound of my sister's voice from scratching out your ears. Beatrice, if you'd do me a few moments' honour?" He extended his arm, heightening Belinda's awareness that Marius had stepped away from her, abandoning her to stand on her own. A flash of unkind playfulness prompted her to take Asselin's elbow, her gaze direct on Marius.

"If no one else will offer me an arm and warmth against the cold, I suppose I'm forced to your side, my lord Asselin." She transferred a look of mocking adoration to the stocky man, watching a flush creep up Marius's cheek before he sketched a short bow.

"My lady. Forgive me. It seems I am inappropriately attired to be seen in the company of nobility. I'll join you again shortly." He turned on his heel, clipping across brown grass at a brisk pace. Belinda pursed her lips, looking to Asselin.

"Was that really necessary, my lord?"

"Oh, yes, it was. Tell me, Irvine. How long has the Reformation bitch sat on the Aulunian throne?"

Stillness wrapped around her so swiftly that a chill shot over Belinda's body. It prickled her breasts and her spine, nestling icily in her groin, and lingered there, a cold throb of desire. She had no fear of betraying herself; she felt her head tilt, a curious smile playing at her mouth, the coldness entirely within. No hairs raised on her arms or neck and her heartbeat remained steady as her own words from a night months earlier were thrown back in her face. "Longer than my lifetime, certainly, my lord." A moment's hesitation before she said, "Nearly thirty years. I think there will be a Jubilee held in Alunaer soon."

"Well done," Asselin breathed. "Ah, well done, my lady Beatrice, but don't bother. Marius pointed you out to me days before he introduced you. I know you, Irvine, or whatever your name is. I've held your tits in my hands and buried my cock in your cunt, and I've known it since the moment he showed me his new true love. You've something I want, and that's all we've got to discuss."

Beatrice's veneer let a blush slide through, scalding Belinda's throat and jaw before she regained control of herself. Of the too-quick heartbeat whose pace never should have changed, even with

Asselin's accusations thrown in her face. Beatrice was a dangerous part to play, wearing Belinda down, too thin and close to the surface for the stillness to entirely protect her. She could feel witch-power rising in her, soft golden light that might distract Asselin's thoughts, might make him forget who and what he knew her as, if she could focus it enough. She had no doubt he'd recognized her, no underlying certainty that she could make him believe he was mistaken with less than the growing power she had at hand. And that, though a temptation, was too great a risk: she and Javier had been cautious in their studies, hiding them beneath the facade of an affair. The idea of flame and a stake to be bound to still edged her thoughts, and Javier's own fears ran to a far deeper sort of Hell, a true belief in his condemnation in the eyes of God. No; she was not yet prepared to try changing a man's thoughts through her own will.

Instead, she tightened her fingers on Asselin's arm, letting a wash of fear at having been recognized come into her eyes and sharpen her voice. "Perhaps this isn't the place to discuss it."

Asselin pulled her, without remorse, toward a copse of trees that made shadows and darkness in the daylit park. "Of course it isn't. But Marius will expect us at my mother's in less than an hour, and anywhere private enough to suit you will require more time than I'm willing to sacrifice. This will do, Irvine." Shadows enveloped them as he spoke, leafless branches making vicious lines against Belinda's skin. She reached for them with the witchpower, half wondering if she could disappear before Sacha's very eyes. They lengthened, seeming to penetrate her body, darkness as invasive and sensual as a lover.

The cold trunk of a tree pressed against her spine as Asselin pulled her around to face him, deliberately trapping her between the woods and his body. For the second time in a matter of minutes she became aware of her dagger, useless and reassuring at the small of her back. Asselin traced his thumb over the hollow of her throat, making her lift her head and swallow involuntarily.

"My lord Asselin." Her voice was dryer than she meant it to be, but the stocky lord read it as fear and a dark interest came into his eyes. She swallowed again, letting her pulse ride high and watching his gaze dart to it. "Will you denounce me, then?"

"I've got more use for you than that. I knew you weren't base-born the moment I heard you talk. No uneducated woman cares that much about the politics of another country, not even a good God-fearing one. I don't know who you are. I don't *care* who you are."

"Then what—?" Genuine curiosity filled the question, draining tension away. The shadows deepened, writhing around her protectively, as if they could help eyes pass her by. Power caressed the darkness, encouraging it, draining out of her and leaving her feeling pale and wanton beneath the weight of Asselin's body.

"What I want is your passion."

Belinda laughed, startled bark of sound. "So you think to take me in a park, in broad daylight? I thought you had more reserve than that, my lord Asselin."

"Not for me." A leer, sudden and good-natured, curved the blunt man's mouth and he looked down her body, one hand still at her throat. "Well, but that's an aside we'll take care of in a moment. It's Javier I want you for, Irvine. He's not the sort to get distracted every time a woman flaps her skirts at him, and a good thing for all of us, too, else he'd be so busy fucking Eliza that no one would see him for months on end."

"Eliza," Belinda said, breathlessly, "wears trousers. Perhaps that's her mistake."

"Have you ever looked at a woman's arse cupped in pants, Irvine? It does things to a man even skirts can't." He dismissed the statement with another lustful sneer, pressing his thumb into the hollow of her throat. "You've kept Jav's attention for weeks. Trying to earn his trust. Trying to make your voice heard. Tell me it isn't so. Tell me Marius wasn't a means to an end."

Belinda tilted her head back against the bark, swallowing again beneath the pressure Asselin kept on her throat. Desire piqued again, and with it, curiosity. "You've made up your mind to that already. What do you want, Asselin?"

"It's time to move. Push him. Jav's complacent. He believes that when the old whore finally dies, Aulun will come back to the fold without protest. That in the people's hearts they are Ecumenics still and that blood will cease to be shed. He's naive, and he needs a shove."

"One you won't give for fear of it being your neck on the block," Belinda breathed. Asselin twisted a smile.

"That's the beauty of it, isn't it? What are your choices, Irvine? Refuse me and I'll turn you in for a whore and rabble-rouser anyway. Agree, and you might get what you want."

Belinda half-lidded her eyes, watching Asselin's eager features a few inches from her own. "And what is it you think I want? You don't think I'm so foolish as to reach for a throne." She made it a statement, too offended by the idea to phrase it as a question. Asselin crowded closer, the scent of his desire caught between bodies.

"I think you want so badly for the Red Bitch to be off the Aulunian throne you'll let a dog fuck you in the arse to get it." He caught her wrist, sudden impulse to twist her away from him clear. Belinda went solid, refusing to move under the direction and bringing surprise to his eyes.

"You are not a dog, my lord, and you will want me to be able to walk like a woman at your sister's recital. Does Marius know?"

A flash of acceptance lit Asselin's eyes, then faded. "That you're a high-minded whore? No, and I'm willing to keep it that way if you play the way I want you to." Belinda deliberately widened her stance as he spoke, unspoken acquiescence and understanding of his demand. A hungry smirk curled the broad-shouldered lord's mouth and he leaned closer. "That this push to make Javier move must be done? Yes. The only one of us who doesn't think Jav should push his mother or himself is Jav. Marius is a good boy, and I want you to understand that the sweet arguments he'll make will persuade you."

"Or else?" The question came lightly, Belinda wetting her lips. Asselin took a breath against her skin as if he could taste her with its depth.

"Or else."

He was, Belinda thought later, considerably more coarse than she had expected.

"Her voice," Belinda murmured in low accusation, "was not so bad as all that." Indeed, Asselin's sister had sung sweetly enough at her afternoon recital to gain the approval of more than one young man's mother. Like Asselin, she was sandy-haired, though tending more toward blond than her brother, and what were unruly curls on him were long loose ringlets on her. Belinda, left wanting from Sacha's decidedly selfish desires, had studied the girl's heart-shaped face and the soft, round curves of her body and wondered without remorse what the girl would look like pink-faced and flushed with need, or if she had ever known passion's hand. The impulse to find out hadn't faded, and Belinda had excused herself to walk in the gardens with Marius as quickly as she could. "She'd make a good match," she added idly. "Better than me, in truth."

Marius, dressed in a more gentrified manner than he had been earlier, touched her arm in alarm that was only partially mocked. "Do you grow tired of me already, Beatrice?"

She allowed herself one of Beatrice's easy smiles, tucking her arm around his. "On the contrary, I expect you to tire of me." She hesitated, then added, "Or for the situation to become unbearable."

Marius tightened a fist, muscle playing beneath Belinda's hand. She rubbed her thumb against the hard knot, listening with half an ear as he muttered, "That can't happen. I have no choice. Nor do you."

"Have we not?" Belinda slowed, turning Marius to face her. "It may be that I no longer do. A woman does not idly dismiss a prince and expect to walk away unscathed, but you, my lord . . ."

"You have something Jav needs," Marius whispered, voice hoarse. Belinda bit her lower lip, filling her gaze with uncertainty and sorrow.

"Me? I'm only a woman, my lord, how could—"

"You're a woman of faith." Marius gentled his voice as Belinda looked up at him in wide-eyed bewilderment. "I see you at church. You have no pretenses there. You understand politics. And you are the daughter of an oppressed land. You did not," he murmured, echoing words she'd spoken weeks earlier, much as Asselin had, "come to Gallin only for the food. How strong is your faith, Beatrice?"

Belinda lowered her gaze, letting calm settle around her again. "As strong as it must be, my lord," she whispered after long moments. An eyelash-shuttered glance upward took in the pain in Marius's expression and she went on, refusing the haste that might have eased his agony. "A generation has already grown up as Reformists. The queen is said to be in good health, despite her years. There may be another generation born and raised under her before her days are ended."

God willing, Belinda thought, a fierce and unusual prayer thrown silently into her enemy's teeth. She let none of it near her face or voice, watching Marius with the desperation of a woman knowing her path and fearing it. A woman wise enough to seek guidance from a strong man, pretending that any power she might have came from him alone. It was one of the few tactics she'd learned from the queen her mother, whose proclamations of weakness and womanly foolishness blunted her advisors' realization of Lorraine's sure military and political hand. "It is a fear we struggle with every day in Lanyarch. We are not quite forbidden our masses, but there are honours and praises for those who give up the true religion for the Reformation. Soldiers watch those of us who bow our heads to the Ecumenic church, and children drift away from God to explore the false hopes of the Reformation. In another generation, our religion might be lost."

"Rally him to his mother's cause," Marius said in a low voice. Belinda lifted her chin, eyebrows wrinkling.

"My lord?"

Marius glanced at her very briefly, then away again. "Even in Gallin, Beatrice, these are dangerous things to speak of." His voice remained low, making her step closer to him to hear him well.

"You speak of revolution, my lord."

"No." The word was sharp as his gaze, though both softened after a moment. "Something more dangerous than that."

"More dangerous than open war?" Belinda laughed, fluttering sound in the back of her throat. "What—" She let understanding darken her eyes, then shook her head. "My lord . . ."

"You said yourself, Beatrice. The Aulunian queen is in good health and could well survive another generation. Ecumenics may not survive that."

"You have so little faith in Cordula, my lord . . . ?"

Marius made another short gesture of irritation. "Island Ecumenics," he modified. "Our faith is stronger on the continent."

Belinda drew herself up, colour staining her cheeks as Beatrice's indignity filled her. "Do you doubt my faith, my lord?"

"Beatrice!" Impatience shot through Marius's voice. "I didn't mean you."

"Only my people. Only all of us who try to keep faith under a godless queen. We are not perfect, my lord. Fear and money bought even Judas. Do you condemn the weak among us for choosing the state religion over a loss of liberty and wealth?"

Belinda's hands shook with poorly suppressed anger. Marius's mouth turned downward in apology, and he reached for her hands.

"Forgive me. Perhaps I speak with too much sentiment and too little understanding. We are not persecuted here for worshipping God in the true church. Perhaps it is too easy to judge and too hard to understand."

Belinda turned her face away from him, her jaw set. It was long moments before the role she played softened enough for her shoulders to drop and the line of her chin to loosen. "You speak of things I dare not even say aloud, my lord. You speak of . . . death."

"Yes." Marius's hands tightened around hers. "Make him see, Beatrice. Make him see that Aulun will be lost without this."

Belinda looked back at him, stiff with caution. "You believe I have such . . . sway?"

He smiled a little, the expression leaving his dark eyes reluctant and sad. "Standing here now, seeing you argue, seeing your belief, yes, lady, I do. If you were a man yourself you might make a great general, to call the men to battle. But you are only a woman, and so the most you might do is inspire the men who can make such things happen."

"The most." Belinda breathed out laughter. "Is that not rather a lot, my lord? Some say men would never war, but for women." She fell silent, studying Marius's face and feeling the rapid skip of her own heart. A handful of words could lay the path to Sandalia's destruction, if only Marius would speak them. It was not written condemnation, but it might be the hint of chicanery against Lorraine that Belinda searched for. "You believe the regent supports this, my lord?"

His tone went guarded. "I cannot say what Her Majesty may or may not believe."

"But you called it her cause." Belinda lowered her voice further, stepping closer to him. She reached for the pool of golden power within her, shaping it with her desire. She wet her lips, looking up at the man through her eyelashes, and curled her fingers around his. "I would not betray you," she whispered. "I understand that she could not voice such beliefs in any way, for fear of being accused of plotting regicide. A royal assassination is a desperate measure, my lord. It breaks the laws of God and man alike. Worst"—Belinda crooked a tiny smile, letting wryness colour the desire she pressed on Marius—"worst, at least for a king, is knowing that to assassinate another royal opens the possibility that he, too, might die in such a way. I understand," she whispered again. "These are not things which we dare speak of aloud. But tell me, Marius, tell me in truth. Do you believe that this is what the queen and regent wants?" She brought his hands, over hers, up to the cool skin of her chest, pressing his warm knuckles below her collarbones. They looked like lovers, her mouth turned up to his, so close that a kiss might be exchanged instead of words. Marius's claims would carry no weight in a court, but Belinda had no need to justify herself to a judge. She only needed a place to begin, a thread of confirmation from the lips of a man close to the regent's son.

And he was desperate to please her. She could feel that in the lines of his body pressed against hers, could almost taste it in his breath. So close to him, and open to the witchpower Javier had awakened in her, it was easy to mistake Marius's desire for her own. Easy to accept thwarted pleasure from earlier as desperation now. She moved a half step closer, crowding her hips against his. Need flared in him, and the grip with which they held each other's hands abruptly opened a channel between them. Uninhibited glee shot through her, joy like little she'd ever known: this stealing of thoughts, the gift of witchpower, was what she was born to, even more than being her mother's tool. It burned through her so brightly she had to fight off laughter, had to swallow a yearning to take Marius's desire and make it her own, and then to ride it until they were both left exhausted.

But stillness won out, habit stronger than the urge to play, and she made herself listen to the young man's rapid-fire thoughts, savoring them as if each was a precious morsel.

She is faithful, he was thinking, *faithful to God if not to a single man (but if not to a single man then not to any man and I might have her, too). She trusts me, God above, help me, see how she looks at me, with trust (and desire, she wants me, it is only Javier standing in the way)*—a thought, Belinda realised curiously, that held no jealousy in it, merely hope. *I will never win her if I lie now (what would she do if I kissed her? would she scream? would she slap me? would she fold with desire and damn the consequences?) and I ask her to do something terribly dangerous*—

"I believe," he whispered, the true words drowning out the chaos of his thoughts, "that her majesty would look . . . favourably on a course that would free Aulun from its Reformatic prison." Thick emotion, caution and nervousness, swirled around him, sinking into Belinda's skin. "I believe that with the support of her son, she might"—he swallowed, slow and tense—"she might take action that might otherwise seem . . . unthinkable." So careful; he chose his words so carefully. Belinda bit her lower lip, then pulled herself even closer to him, releasing his hands so she might put her fingers into his hair.

"I will try," she promised, a breath below his ear. The embrace felt like a lover's, their bodies dangerous against each other. "For Aulun. For Lanyarch." She pulled back, meeting his gaze with wide eyes. "For you, my lord."

Marius groaned and sank his hands into her hair, pulling her mouth up to his for a kiss that drowned her with its need. The heat of his desire rolled through her, building until she was forced to break the kiss, hands against his chest again.

"We must not," she whispered. "We cannot. Not yet. Not if I am to do this thing with the prince. Forgive me." She looked up at him again, pulse leaping in her throat. "Forgive me, my lord. A day will come when I am yours."

"It cannot come soon enough." He shoved her away, not far away, keeping his hands on her waist but putting space between their bodies. "You must succeed, Beatrice. I cannot bear any of this if you do not succeed."

"I will." Belinda gave a jerky nod, stepping back. "I swear, my lord. I will." Then she smiled, fragile thing, and said, lightly, "When do you think it might snow, sir?"

Marius forced a laugh and offered her his arm. "Soon. Soon, my lady. Winter comes on stronger than we know."

Snow fell two nights later. Belinda stood in the shadows of Javier's balcony window, face turned up to the silent white stars falling through the night. The flakes tickled her cheeks where they blew past curtains to land on her, almost imperceptible weight gracing her eyelashes. They lingered a moment, then turned to drops of water, beading until their accumulated size spilled them down her face. Snow tears, Belinda thought. Precious as a virgin's. The air, heavy with the silence of snow, seemed warm and comforting. Belinda stepped out into it, and was caught by an arm around her waist. Javier drew her close again, lowering his head over her shoulder. "Discretion, Beatrice."

"Do you think we're fooling anyone?" Certainly not Marius, the one whom Javier might most intend to hide from. Belinda shook her head fractionally, in dismissal, and waited for the prince's answer.

"Yes," Javier said. "Not that you're here, not that you're my lover. But in our true purpose in meeting? They cannot suspect it."

"It cannot be found out." Belinda shivered, curling her arms over Javier's. Rather than relax into her closeness he stiffened, lifting his mouth away from her shoulder. Discomfort flared in him, the clarity of words and thought broken before she could read them, his skin taken from hers too quickly. Only uncomfortable familiarity lingered, making Belinda twist in his grasp to peer up at him. "My lord?"

"It cannot be found out." He echoed the words in a hoarse, low voice, strain suddenly telling tales. "You know what they would do to us, Beatrice."

"I do." Another tremble ran over her skin, too appropriate to forbid. "I don't like to think on it."

"Nor I, and yet it has haunted me since childhood. You have no idea," he said, abrupt and startlingly harsh. "Beatrice, to find even one other person like me . . . you have no idea. I only wish I knew if we were damned together, or granted salvation." He put his arms around her again, a wordless ache of loneliness answered rising in him and sweeping over her as their skin touched. "It must not be found out," he repeated. "Only the ignorant and superstitious would begin to believe what you and I know as truth, and they would free us from our curse with fire."

Belinda turned to smile up at him, deliberately pushing away nightmare thoughts. "Are you accusing me of being ignorant and superstitious, my lord? I believed you instantly." Her eyebrows rose, mocking horror. "Are you claiming it is *not* true love that brings us together in so many darkling hours? My lord, my heart breaks. How could you?"

"I make no such claims," Javier said promptly. "I would never dream of dashing a lady's hopes."

"Unless your mother or uncle instructed you to," Belinda said wryly, turning again so she could watch the snow fall. The balcony floor was too warm to sustain it, flakes melting where they landed. Turmoil coursing through Javier's emotions, a chagrined distress at odds with his calm exterior.

"I have no choice, Beatrice," he said eventually. "What would you have me do? I am who I was born to be."

"As are we all, my lord. I meant no harm. I know the obligations a man of your station has."

"Do you?" Javier said. "I wonder how the duties of a minor Lanyarchan noble compare to that of royalty."

Silent as the snow, Belinda let stillness settle into her bones. The act of Beatrice was too open; she let the stillness go too often in favour of thoughtless, appropriate reaction to the gentility whose class she'd joined. The part was easy to play, far more enjoyable than the serving girl role she was accustomed to taking on. Without the need to hide in plain sight or explain herself to her betters, she could taste a little of what she might have become, in a different world. Wealth and comfort were dangerous; they let her feel free. She hadn't known the cost of freedom was so high.

Fleetingly, she wondered what Javier would say, if she whispered the truth to him. That her blood was as royal as his, if on the wrong side of the bed. That her duties were as significant as his, all the more so because she might someday make a misstep, and when she was found out her royal mother would not reach out a hand to save her. Belinda couldn't easily name the emotion that lanced through her belly, could barely form words for the blur of wistfulness and might-have-been that she let herself imagine for a moment. There was no room in her life for daydreams or regret, so little room that she hardly recognized them.

"I think our duties lie heavy on us all at times, my lord. Forgive me. I didn't mean to cause you distress." Armoured by stillness, she smiled at the prince. His gaze softened and she lowered her eyes. Oh, yes. Freedom was dangerous. Belinda thought of the letter to her father, still half-finished, and let herself shiver as if with cold. "Forget freedom," she murmured, knowing she spoke aloud. "With duty, we know our places, my lord. Perhaps there is nothing more we can ask."

"Sound advice," Javier said. "Do you follow it yourself?"

"I try."

She heard the smile in his voice. "And with these new gifts, where do your duties now lie, Beatrice? Does it change with what you're able to do?"

Belinda spread her hands, looking at them. "A woman has only the power granted to her by men, my lord. At least . . . usually. No man has granted me this. Trained me in it," she conceded before he could take offense, "but not granted it to me. Perhaps it changes me. Perhaps it changes what I ought to do." She lifted her chin, looking out at the snow. "Although I command very little power, in truth. You . . . have more, my lord." Almost a lie. Javier had no walls in his mind, cutting him off from the source of his witch-power. For the moment, at least, he commanded greater power than Belinda could call up. And it flattered his ego, which was more useful than truth anyway.

Thusly flattered, the prince chuckled. "What, then, would you do if you wielded the gifts that I do?"

"Dangerous things, my lord," Belinda whispered. Javier's body against hers turned curious, hips tilting as he canted his head closer so she might answer even more softly.

"What things? Tell me." Command combined with desire in his voice; the thought of a powerful woman excited him. Belinda felt hairs lift on her arms anyway, reluctant to voice words treasonous to Aulun, even when those ideas were at the heart of the role she played. She wet her lips twice and swallowed before making herself speak.

"I would remove the Aulunian threat from Lanyarch, my lord. I would seek allies with Cordula's support and break the yoke of Reformationism that weighs down on island shoulders." Panic squirreled in her belly, spreading sharp claws of nausea up to wrap around her heart and tighten her throat. It trickled downward as well, pounding between her thighs and making her knees tremble. Belinda fought against banishing terror, knowing the calm of still-ness would push it all away and leave her untouchable.

But the words she spoke were terribly dangerous, and Beatrice Irvine was no more than a minor noble who answered to Aulunian law. Beatrice could be put to death for the things she'd said, and it would be Belinda's head that rolled. Javier himself might betray her, offer her to Lorraine as a gift to soothe troubled waters between Gallin and Aulun, betwixt Ecumenics and Reformationists, more importantly. A public execution, carried out by the queen's men—Belinda Primrose would be no more. She doubted, in the core of her, that Lorraine would waste so valuable an asset; far more practical to behead some poor woman with similar features. Belinda herself would be safe to pursue the queen's wishes under cover of another identity, but she would no more be her beloved uncle's niece, no more be able to claim that thin line of heritage. Panic brought chills and sweat both at once, the air too thin to breathe. Why did he not *speak*? Belinda shuddered, afraid to move, afraid to speak, afraid to do anything but wait.

Javier's silence brought her frayed nerves to the shattering point before he inhaled and straightened. "And then?" Light tone, almost playful, but Belinda felt the undercurrent of intensity in it. Acute desire pushed through him, pricking at Belinda's skin, but she couldn't determine *what* the man desired. She closed her eyes, wetting her lips again.

"I named you true heir to the Aulunian throne the night I met you, my prince." Her voice quavered, so weak and small she barely recognized it. She swallowed again, trying to strengthen herself without lifting her voice so loudly that a spy might overhear. "The Aulunian queen is the child of an illegitimate marriage, and there are no other Walters to follow her father Henry. Moreover, your mother's first husband was heir to the Aulunian throne, and you, though no child of his, are a child of hers. He made her queen, and in doing so made you heir."

"Oh, but it's more complex than that, isn't it?" Javier's voice was as low as her own. "Henry Walter's first wife was my grandaunt, and if she was the only legitimate wife, then perhaps I can lay claim to the Aulunian throne through those means, too. But Gallin is mine already, and Uncle Rodrigo looks unlikely to wed, so Essandia is likely mine as well. Would you have me conquer all of Echon, Beatrice? Would you make yourself a king-maker?"

"I cannot make what God hath already wrought, your highness." The fervor in her voice was such that Belinda believed herself for a moment.

"You would get on well with my mother." Javier released her and Belinda's heart lurched as he stepped back into the warmth of his chambers. He had not before made mention of Sandalia in her presence, certainly not in such intimate terms as *my mother.* It offered the first glimmer that her approach to the Gallic court had been a good one; that the prince should say such a thing so easily and carelessly hinted that there was a chance Belinda would be introduced to Sandalia so such comparisons might be made. No triumph rose within her; it was far too early for that, but a hint that she'd taken the right slow road pushed down some of the nerves that had come over her as she'd whispered her daring thoughts. Patience, patience; to trap a queen was a long and dangerous path, but finally she felt herself on it, one stride closer to success.

Buoyed a little, Belinda turned to watch Javier as she waited on his indication that she should join him. He dropped into a chair by the fire, sprawling his legs out. Slender calves, well-muscled under his tights, backlit by the fire. Belinda let herself admire the lines of him, the graceful turn of his fingers as he pressed them against his forehead.

"My lord?" she ventured when silence drew out too long. Javier lifted his head and crooked his fingers, the dismissive acknowledgment he might call a dog with. It was the way of men, especially men of power. Belinda crossed to him, kneeling at his feet in a rustle of skirts. "Forgive me, my lord." Eyes lowered, she felt his touch on her cheek, drawing her gaze up, before she saw it.

"There's nothing to forgive. I did ask. Watch your tongue, though, Beatrice. You do speak of dangerous things."

"Yes, my lord." Belinda lowered her eyes again even as she lifted her chin, giving her throat to the prince. Javier chuckled and leaned forward, wrapping his hand behind her head. She came to her knees, breath gone short, and smiled up at him.

"Another man might be less lenient."

"Then I am fortunate to be wi—"

"Jav!" The door banged open, a feat in itself: the weight of oak and the woven rug it dragged across precluded such enthusiasm under nearly any circumstances. Asselin lurched in, his weight making the door bounce against the stone wall a second time, barely muffled by hanging tapestries. "Oh, bugger and bollocks, Jav, get rid of the tart, there's things to discuss." Asselin waved a flagon of wine around with more drama than care; red droplets flew and splattered across the walls and rugs. He focused on Belinda, blinking heavily, then sketched a bow so deep it bordered on ludicrous. "Forgive me, Irvine. I didn't see you there. Shite, Jav, why can't *I* find a noble girl who'll go down on her knees for me?"

Blood drained from Belinda's face, then rushed back in a pound of scarlet. She scrambled to her feet, knotting her hands in her skirt and staring fixedly at the floor. Stillness kept her a safe distance from laughter while she played out the part of Beatrice's mortification, trembling with humiliation and embarrassment. Javier climbed to his feet with languid poise, brushing his fingers across Belinda's crimson cheek in apology. "Sacha, you're a pig and a fool," he said mildly. "What the hell are you doing here?"

Asselin still watched Belinda. "Praying to God you're as free with your women as with your wine, old man. Look at her, Jav, blushing like a maiden. You're a widow, Irvine, and even if you weren't Jav here would've had your head a hundred times by now. Come on, Javier, can't we share a bit of a shag?"

Belinda jerked her eyes up, horrified on Beatrice's part and startled beyond belief on her own. Asselin waggled his eyebrows at her with such exaggeration she wanted to laugh. He sauntered over to her, leading with his hips and both hands held high, wine droplets spilling carelessly down his wrist. "Never dreamed of that, did you, Beatrice? A woman's got more than one hole, might as well put them all to good use." He took a few dancing steps around her, and came up against Javier. "Shite," he said into the prince's closed expression. He let his arms fall and shrugged liquidly. "You can't blame a man for trying, now, can you, Jav?"

Javier remained expressionless, staring his compatriot down. Asselin exhaled noisily and fell one step back. "My apologies, Lady Irvine. Drink has got me, and I take more pleasure in her than good sense might allow."

"It . . . it is—" Belinda cast a frantic look at Javier, expecting, and finding, his slight nod. "It is all right," she whispered. Heat still stained her cheeks, a flush that would be attributed to shame, not amusement or arousal. She locked her eyes on the floor, aware that she still held her hands clutched in her skirts, fig-leafing in a useless show of modesty. Everything in how she stood bespoke her embarrassment, but keeping her gaze down let her indulge in curious imagination without betraying herself.

"What's so damned important, Sacha?" Javier settled back into his chair, gesturing for Asselin to take the matching one opposite him. Asselin flung himself into it hard enough to knock it back a few inches, and leaned forward to bring the front legs down again. "What about her?"

Javier's gaze flickered to Belinda. "Beatrice, there are wineglasses in the front chamber. Enough for all, please."

"My lord." Belinda bobbed a curtsey and took care not to stomp as she left the room. A woman was a serving maid no matter what her station, shy of being a queen. Carrying the rank of lady only made for better dresses to sweat in.

Asselin's drunk had passed by the time she returned. He sat forward in his chair, flagon dangling from his fingertips and voice low as he spoke earnestly to Javier. The prince remained leaning back, ankle cocked over his knee and one arm dangling over the side of the chair as he listened. They were, Belinda thought, very much man and servant, for all the friendship held between them. Asselin straightened as she came back in. Belinda bobbed another curtsey, murmuring, "My lords," and took the flagon from Asselin's fingertips to pour wine. There was no moment of shared thought, as she hoped there might be; the fingertip touch was too brief, or her skill too little. His emotions were clouded with lust, as frank and open as it had been the night she'd met him in a low-class pub; as they had been when he'd taken her in the park days earlier. He was a blunt man, dangerous like a hammer, and Belinda found herself liking him for it once more, despite the threat he posed to her. Threat, though, could be dealt with without mercy if necessary, and for everything Sacha Asselin thought he knew about Beatrice Irvine, he knew nothing at all of Belinda Primrose. So long as their ends lay down similar paths, she was content to leave him alive, but should the knowledge he carried become a burden to her, her only regret in his death would be the hurt it would cause Javier.

Faint surprise coiled through her at the thought; Javier's emotions were irrelevant to her goals. Sacha's death might pull him away from the desire to teach her more of the witchpower magic, though, and that was enough to feel a twinge of dismay over. Belinda dropped her gaze briefly, then offered Asselin a filled wine cup. His eyebrows shot up as he took it. "Daring, to give me the first cup and not Jav."

Nerves bunched in Belinda's stomach. As a serving girl, she never would have made the error of serving the lower-ranked man first. She poured a second glass, offering it to Javier. There was no tremble in the liquid that betrayed the quiver she felt inside. Javier lifted an eyebrow, as aware of the slight as Asselin had been, but he took the glass. Belinda poured herself a glass as well, setting the flagon aside and smiling with cool reserve at Asselin. "You brought the wine."

"And I," Javier said, "did not rescue you quickly enough, hm?" His other eyebrow elevated to match the first, challenging. Belinda, trusting social propriety over Beatrice's embarrassment, tilted her head.

"My lord? I am sure there was nothing I needed rescuing from. Lord Asselin is a gentleman, and you a prince. How could a woman fear in such company?"

"Oh, she's good," Asselin said past her, to Javier. The prince arched an eyebrow again, warning, and Asselin subsided. Belinda inclined her head and drew a footstool a little closer to the fire, smoothing her skirt as she sat down.

"Now that the matter of Beatrice is aside," Javier said, "to what do I owe this unexpected visit, Asselin? You may have guessed: I had plans." Neither man looked at Belinda. She felt the weight of their avoidance far more heavily than she might have felt a knowing smile or wink, and wished she dared roll her eyes. Instead she lowered her gaze and sipped her wine, demure, as Asselin launched into talk of inconsequentialities. Belinda felt Javier's impatience as if it were her own, the witchpower stirring in him as he sought a way to bring Asselin to the point. It was her presence that stayed the young lord's tongue; they all three knew it, and that Javier had waved her to stay was . . . interesting. Belinda pressed wine against her lips, feeling them wet, imagining colour staining them.

Golden witchlight spread through the back of her mind, tempered into darkness by the stillness. Belinda was grateful for that; without the stillness she thought the bright power might burst out of every crevasse of her body, blinding her and everything around her. She gathered the light around her as if it were the stillness, tucking it around the corners of her mind. It tingled and itched; she could not remember the same sensations a dozen years ago when she tried to hide in the shadows. But she had been less aware then, she reminded herself. More powerful, perhaps, but less aware. The prickle over her skin was bearable, even ignorable, but fascinating. She stopped herself from spreading her fingers to investigate, knowing she could try again another time when she would not call attention to herself with the action.

She took a slow breath, calmness washing through her as it suppressed the skin tickle that power had awakened. Excitement tasted of copper at the back of her throat and made her fingertips ache; the calm was so profound it had the weight of chains. She knew the sensation, like the frightening quiet at the heart of a storm. It held her prisoner and safe both at once, denying her the ability to break free even as it offered the consummate certainty that nothing could reach her. Belinda's lungs burned, heart pounding sickly in the cavity of her chest. She dragged in a shaking breath that only served to prove how little air there seemed to be around her. With the breath, tranquility stretched taut and snapped. In silence, it surrounded her, tucking her safely into the shadows. The wine in her glass darkened, no longer reflecting the warmth of firelight. Asselin's voice cut through, sudden and loud, amplified as if he stood in an echo chamber. Belinda lifted her head, confident in the shadows that held her, and watched the two men openly.

"It's Liz, Jav. You don't know—"

"Liz?" Javier glanced at where Belinda sat, clearly without seeing her there. "All this bother and dancing around the topic and it's Eliza? What could you not say about her in front of Beatrice, man?"

Asselin's silence fell almost as heavily as the solitude surrounding Belinda. "You are my prince," he said eventually. "My oldest friend and my brother, but my God, you're an idiot sometimes, Jav."

Javier turned a round-mouthed gape of astonishment on the stocky noble. "I beg your pardon?"

Asselin sighed. "Nothing. Suffice it to say that Liz would rather not be discussed in front of your lady Irvine."

"Liz," Javier pointed out, "would rather not be discussed behind her back at all."

Asselin waved a hand dismissively. "So would we all. But if she must be, let us not compound the injury by doing it in front of her ri—in front of Irvine."

"You don't like her." Javier sounded stiff, petulant. Belinda, safe in her shadows, allowed herself an open smile, and sipped her wine. Asselin let out a raspberry of exasperation.

"What's to like or not like? She's a pretty woman and she must be a good lay or you wouldn't keep bothering with her. It's not like you, though, Jav. We've been friends since boyhood, the four of us, and you're the one who's kept that sacrosanct. Now you invite this woman in without a hitch or hesitation?"

"Marius invited her." Belinda hadn't known the prince could be sulky. She smiled again, into her glass, and watched the men through her eyelashes. Years of long practise kept her from wriggling with amusement, or permitting herself the giggle that fought its way through her, but the grin she gave free rein to. Delight in success pounded through her like sexual arousal, thrills of excitement and interest making her overaware of her body. How easy it would be to carry out her missions, if she could sit unseen in a room with men who had moments ago been fully aware of her presence. If she could learn to walk within the shadows—she didn't dare try now—she might become the most successful and secret assassin Echon had ever known.

"Marius showed her to us," Asselin disagreed. "You invited her, Jav. You're the only one of us who can."

"Sacha, that's not true—"

"Yes, my prince." Asselin's voice softened, sympathy in it. "It is. It's why we're never more than four, Javi. We can only present outsiders. It's your will that takes them in or leaves them to the cold."

Javier slumped in his seat, expression unguarded and youthful. "You haven't called me that in a long time."

Asselin crooked a smile. "We haven't been boys in a long time, Javi. I don't like to use it around Marius and Liza." His grin went more sheepish. "We knew each other first. I think of it as my name for you, and if I used it, it would become theirs, too."

"Jealous lordling," Javier said, but he leaned forward to reach for Asselin's hand, grasping it a moment.

"Rarely." Asselin sat back with a sigh and kicked his heels out on the rug. "Which brings us, Jav, back to Eliza."

Javier lifted his eyebrows. "She's become a jealous lordling? Sacha—" The prince straightened, curious dismay wrinkling his forehead. "Is that why none of you have married? Because of me? Because you think you need my . . . approval?"

"Oh, God, Jav, don't tie the noose yet. There are moments when you're our only line to freedom. Marriage beds will come soon enough. They're political machinations, not full of love and romance. It won't make any difference if you like our wives. Hell, it won't make any difference if *we* like our wives. A woman's got no strength to come between the four of us anyway. *Which,*" Asselin said, "brings us back to Eliza, Jav. Again."

"All right, all right! God in Heaven, Sacha. What's the problem?"

"Her father's found her out, Jav."

Javier's eyes shuttered, light in them turning black. "Then I'll protect her."

"She won't let you, Jav. She never has."

"Don't be absurd. She has rooms here—"

"She'll refuse them as long as Irvine is here."

Javier came up short. "Is she as jealous as that? Beatrice is—"

"A distraction? A toy? Easier to believe when she's not on your arm every evening and in your bed every night. Are you going to introduce her to your mother?"

"God," Javier said with feeling, then exhaled. "I'll have to, if I continue with her. Mother's absence has been—"

"A gift?"

"Not unwelcome." Javier glanced at the stool where Belinda sat, as if imagining her there. She caught her lower lip in her teeth, watching with interest. After a moment he shook his head and turned his attention back to Sacha. "But once she's returned, I'll have to make the introduction. I can't put Beatrice aside right now."

Fascinated horror lit Asselin's eyes. "Good God, man, you haven't gotten her pregnant, have you?"

Javier blanched and shuddered. "No. My God, no. It's— There are other things. Other reasons." He shrugged, making an end of it. Sacha sighed explosively.

"You're bewitched, Javi. Look, Liz won't come to my home, either, but if she goes home her father will likely—"

Javier lifted a hand. "I think I have a solution. One she won't like, but it may appeal. Sacha, don't tell her you were here talking about her, all right?"

"Do I look like a complete fool?" Asselin demanded. Javier gave him a slow grin and Sacha laughed. "Some friend you are. All right. All right, Jav, but make quick work of it, because she's got nowhere to go." He looked around. "What the hell happened to Irvine? I thought she was bringing more drink."

Belinda cocked an eyebrow curiously, then gathered her skirts and stood to slip through shadow in search of wine.

8

Dawn came on before Javier brought the subject around to Eliza and offered up his plan. Belinda sprawled across his bed, hair twisted over her shoulder into a mocking semblance of propriety. Javier stood at his window, watching the mist-coated palace grounds as sunlight struggled to break through the grey. "So your women will all be under one roof?" Belinda murmured. "Convenient, my lord."

He scowled over his shoulder. "It's not like that between Eliza and myself, Beatrice. I thought you knew that."

"I do. I was only teasing, my lord." She stood and crossed to him, putting her fingertips on his shoulders. "Then why?"

"Eliza's father doesn't like her friendship with me."

Belinda's eyebrows shot up. "Doesn't like a friendship with the *prince*?"

"He thinks I . . ." Javier turned his head, uncomfortable. "Abuse the friendship."

"Abuse. A powerful man, a beautiful woman." Belinda's eyebrows remained elevated. "Few would call it abuse."

"They are very poor." Javier's jaw set. "Poor enough that a father might only see his daughter as a victim in such a relationship."

Belinda stepped back, letting surprise stiffen her movements. "Poor . . . ? She speaks so beautifully, my lord."

Disdain flashed through Javier's expression. "High-born tones can be learned. We've been friends a long time."

"Yes." Belinda stiffened further, flushing as she glanced down. "Of course, my lord." She knotted her fingers together in front of her belly, turning her palms up. "Another father might use such a relationship as leverage into a good marriage," she suggested. A glance at Javier through her eyelashes found him shaking his head.

"It might've if she wasn't as stubborn as the day is long. Her mother and three sisters died five years ago of a bad fever. Eliza was the only one who survived. She refuses to grow her hair back out and behave like a proper woman. Her father's hand . . . is growing heavy."

A shiver spilled down Belinda's spine, making the hairs on her arms stand up against the light fabric of the dressing gown she'd stolen from Javier. "Then why come to me, my lord? You must know . . ." She hesitated. "Eliza considers me a . . . rival." She chose her words with delicacy, watching the prince for his reactions. Javier let out a breath that bordered on laughter.

"I'm aware. But I can hardly place her with Sacha or Marius, can I? A woman at least has the gloss of appropriateness. Besides," he finally met her eyes again, "it would divert talk from our relationship."

"Or compound it, my lord."

Javier flashed a grin. "Which might do as well. Please, Bea. I don't ask favours that often."

Belinda lifted her eyebrows again as she offered Javier her hands. "Is she going to want to murder me in my sleep, my lord? Ought I sleep with one eye open every night from now on?"

"You sleep enough nights with me that I think you're safe." Javier lifted her hands to his mouth, kissing her knuckles. "Perhaps sleep with both eyes open those nights you don't."

"So you'd have me get no sleep at all," Belinda teased. "Very well, my lord. But I warn you: we may become fast friends and both toss our heads and laugh when you come calling. Women are strange creatures."

"Then I'll have gotten what I deserved for putting the two of you together. That dress, Beatrice. The one you wore to the opera."

She tilted her head, curious. "Aye?"

"It was Eliza's design. It's her true talent, making beautiful gowns. With your help, she might soon be able to begin a business of her own. It'd be good for both of you: she wouldn't be under your roof anymore, and she wouldn't be under her father's."

Belinda frowned, shaking her head. "If it's her design, my lord, why on earth hasn't she begun a business already? Certainly with your patronage—" Her chin came up. "Ah."

Javier quirked an eyebrow. "Ah?"

"She won't take your help, will she? Too much pride."

Javier inclined his head. "I remember, as a child, the beggars who flung themselves at mine and my mother's feet as we walked into church. I thought then that pride was a provenance of the wealthy. When I met Eliza I realised that the poor have an even more desperate pride than the rich. She's never let me help her, except when she was too ill to object."

"The fever?"

Javier nodded. Belinda's chin lifted again in new understanding. "Your doctors saved her but not the rest of her family."

Javier nodded a second time. Belinda stepped back, pressing her fingers over her lips. "Her mother. Her sisters." She didn't wait for the prince's nod, though it came again. "No wonder her father hates you, my lord. Four for one. I wouldn't trust your intentions, either."

"They wouldn't let me help," Javier murmured. "Her mother allowed me to take her, but not the rest of them."

"You are a prince, my lord. How could one poor woman stop you? And how could one wretched man beg your mercy for the rest of his family when you had shown preference to one?"

Javier met her eyes, helpless. "I didn't want to offend them. Does my rank give me the right to disrupt the lives of others as I see fit?"

Belinda laughed out loud, throaty and warm. "Isn't that what royalty does, my lord?"

Javier's spine stiffened, his face gone pale with anger. "Yes. And that is why I do not care to do it myself, Lady Irvine. I try to respect those around me."

"Unless they are too inconvenient." Belinda stepped forward again, curling her fingers in his shirt. "In which case, there is always the witchpower, no? An extension of yourself. You can hardly be blamed for making use of it." She stood on her toes, brushing her mouth against the pulse in his throat. "It is a peculiar and fine line to dance, my prince. But you are a rare man if you are willing to walk it at all. Most would never think twice of imposing their will as they saw fit, given the means and opportunity. I will try to help make Eliza a dressmaker with clientele all her own, as untouched by your helping hand as is possible, if you, my lord. . . ." She lifted her eyes, bright winsome smile teasing him, "will but come back to bed now. It's very early, and you've no duties until the tenth hour." Belinda put on a pout, then drew him toward the bed. "Is it not a fine bargain I make?"

Javier laughed and let himself be drawn.

"In a pig's eyes."

"Liza—"

"Like hell, Javier, no. I won't."

"I need you—"

Eliza snorted, derisive, and turned to stare challengingly at the prince. "I need you," he repeated with as much patience as he could muster, "to watch her."

Silence. Belinda held her breath, feeling herself barely more than a shadow under the starry skies. She was not supposed to be there, no more than Javier himself was: she could feel, subtly, his pleasure at having escaped the guards that evening. Not his thoughts; those were too well-shielded, only readable in a handful of moments when she touched his skin. The impressions were enough, though, carrying Belinda with them as if she belonged inside the prince's skin herself. She'd left his chambers well before duty called him to work, intending to return home and begin arranging for Eliza's arrival. Only a few steps outside his rooms, though, she found herself filled with burgeoning curiosity. It had been rare impulse that prompted her to follow him, less to observe his day than to see if she could manipulate the stillness and the silence into making people believe she wasn't there. If she could do that under the watchful eyes of a prince's guard, under the gaze of men who were supposed to see everything that happened around their ward, then she had discovered power indeed.

It was exhausting, draining beyond anything she knew. Even now, simply thinking of what she did sent trembles through her, as if conscious recognition threatened to shatter what control she had. It had been easier earlier in the day, and as the strain grew so did her intent to maintain it. Power of any kind was worth only as much as could be grasped and held. Limits were there to be pushed and explored, but more critically, acknowledged in a moment of necessity. She had slipped after the prince for nearly twelve hours now, following him into the privacy of his bedchambers and into the courtly halls of the palace. No one had noticed her.

No one would ever know. Belinda twisted her hands, a small gesture like she held a garrote and had a slender throat to wrap it around. It would take mere seconds in the pretender queen's presence to slaughter her, and with the stillness so profoundly wrapped about her, no one would ever see Belinda to blame her. The idea of that opportunity made her heart beat harder, sending heat through her core until it became sexual excitement. Robert had not told her to kill Javier's mother. Regicide was a dangerous game, and with one royal murdered, eyes might turn to another as the next possible victim. Her duty was merely to discover the breadth of plots against Lorraine, and end them.

Sandalia's death would be a resounding note to end them on.

And that was a childish impulse toward a glory Belinda would never be allowed to acknowledge. Should she succeed in assassinating the Essandian princess, Robert might know of it. Lorraine should, could, not, though in the secret places of her heart she might suspect.

Belinda's heart fluttered in her chest, spiking sickening joy into her throat. That would be enough. To have her mother know Belinda's loyalty would be enough. For a startling few seconds tears burned her eyes, heat scalding her cheeks as she thought of it. There was little enough that the queen's bastard could do to connect herself with her royal mother. A death offered from the daughter as a gift to the mother was the greatest intimacy Belinda could dare imagine, an insurrection stopped and a kingdom preserved. That was who, and what, the secret daughter was. Belinda curled her hands into fists against the heady fear she might fly away on the breathless hope of securing her mother's throne for years to come.

Shadows glimmered and twitched around her, sinking deeper into her skin as if they'd drink up the failing pool of witchpower from which Belinda drew. She allowed herself one last shaking sigh, a sound of desire that men would count themselves fortunate to earn from her, and straightened herself, letting go of powerful wishes in order to maintain her hidden presence a few minutes longer. She quested outward, careful exploration of nearby emotion, riding that as strongly as she dared. She wasn't yet ready to try influencing those emotions, but every experience of another's mental state would help her when that time came.

Javier was easier by far than Eliza, Belinda's hours with him helping her to read him even without the witchpower. She let her eyes lid, wetting her lips as tendrils of golden power threaded outward, settling around Javier and testing him, seeing what she could read without giving herself away.

The prince cast a wordless prayer in the guise of a glance at the heavens, leaning wearily against the bridge railing. His quiet pleasure at escaping the honour guard was still there, though muted beneath wry frustration at Eliza. She, like Sacha and Marius, could forget the guard, so long as they lingered at a semi-respectful distance. Javier himself never forgot. It made the few stolen hours when he shook them off all the more precious. Spending them arguing, even with a beautiful woman, was far from his preference.

Eliza held her mouth in a pinch, eyes guarded, though at least she listened. Belinda felt almost nothing from her: faint challenge, angry acknowledgment. After a few seconds she let her sense of the other woman go; Javier was the more important of the two to understand. Eliza's voice was low and cutting, distorted by distance as Belinda severed the faint link of power she'd held to the dark-haired woman. "Don't you trust her?"

Javier groaned and looked to the sky again. Thin clouds, pale against the blackness, blocked out patches of stars, and his breath steamed to wash away another handful of nighttime diamonds. Belinda's own gaze flickered upward, half expecting the stars to be blocked by the shadows that wrapped her. Instead, a handful of them glittered hard, picking out the form of a dragon in the sky.

It brought with it memory, a cold winter night when Belinda was a child, so clear that for a moment it overrode the discussion held by the two she watched. Robert had stood beside her, his warm arm around her shoulders to ward off the night's chill as he'd picked out figures in the stars. A lion here, a bear there, a hunter presiding. A dragon, his spray of fire a scattering of stars across the night sky. Belinda had turned a dubious look on her father, insisting, "The others are real. Are there dragons, then, Papa?"

Robert lowered his hand from the stars to study her with a grave expression. "There are, Primrose."

Belinda's eyes widened until cold crept into their corners, a chill of ice lacing through her vision. "What are they like?"

"Nothing like you would imagine, Bella. Nothing like you would imagine." He'd picked her up then in a rare and unexpected hug, and carried her back into the house to warm up over a cup of mulled wine and sweetmeats left out by the cook. Belinda smiled at the stars in thanks for the memory, then brought her mind back to the conversation she spied upon.

"I trust her," Javier had already murmured. "But my judgment may be clouded."

Eliza laughed, sharp in the chilly air. "What confession, my lord prince! How much did that cost?"

"More than I'd like." The impulse to snap was there, to draw himself up and wield insult like anger, cowing the woman into her place. It was an easy trick, a thoughtless flexing of the witchpower he carried inside himself. It was, to Eliza and the others, a mark of royalty, a sign of position he held over them. Javier could not remember the last time he had knowingly used the witchpower on his friends. When they were children, certainly, not more than twelve or thirteen. Before he understood that no one shared his gift; before he understood that using it could only deepen the space between his station and their own. Friendship was rare and precious to him, more fragile than his three companions understood. In his life, they were the only things he was truly certain of.

They, and now Beatrice. Relief and gratitude swept through him, an alleviation of loneliness that took Belinda off-guard. She bit into her lower lip, reaching for the bridge railing as she struggled to shake herself free of that passion. Struggled to ignore a similar welling within herself. Understanding Javier was one thing. Wearing his needs and fears on her own sleeve was a greater commitment than she was prepared to make.

"What is it about her, Jav?" Belinda heard the note of frustration in Eliza's voice and watched Javier drop his chin to his chest, exhaling heavily.

"I couldn't tell you." Merely an evasion. Belinda knew as well as he did, and knew as well that he couldn't—wouldn't—tell, not Liz nor their two brothers in arms. "But this is something I need."

Eliza snorted again. Javier half smiled, turning his gaze down the silent bridge. Belinda steeled herself, ready this time for the influx of sentiment from the prince. It was easier, prepared, to absorb what he felt without being subsumed by it. The bridge was one of his favourite places in the city, particularly at night, with the Sacrauna running through it undisturbed by daytime travellers. Torchlight reflected here and there against the black waters, and when the surface lay very still, the stars. As a child he had laid on the banks, reaching to touch those stars only to watch them ripple away when his fingers broke through the water tension. It left him melancholy, with a sense of loss he could neither explain nor share with others. Belinda curved a humourless smile at the water, familiar with the remoteness that Javier felt, and more comfortable with admitting it than she was with acknowledging the loneliness and recognition of a similar creature that she'd sensed from the prince moments earlier. Even so, she broke away from too deeply pursuing that connection, wary of anything that might alert Javier to her presence.

"What do you need me to watch for?" Eliza broke the silence, staring at the stones beneath her feet rather than meet Javier's eyes. "Her spending habits? If she keeps secret lovers? You could find those things out without me, Jav."

"I trust," Javier said tartly, "that there are no secret lovers." Eliza breathed out laughter.

"That's because you're a man."

"What does that mean?" He straightened, affronted. Eliza shook her head.

"Only that men see what they want to see, and women must see the truth. We have no other power."

Cold anger curdled at the back of Javier's throat, Belinda tasting it with sudden and aroused interest. "Eliza." His voice came low and dangerous, the witchpower responding even when Belinda could feel he would have it otherwise. A wind snapped up, icy and sharp, and Belinda retreated from her own investigation of his emotions, caution overcoming curiosity: with his power alert, the chances of discovery were far greater, and not worth the risk. Eliza frowned and drew her cloak around herself more tightly, lifting its hood. "Eliza," Javier repeated. "Are you saying that Beatrice has another lover?"

Her head pulled back as if she'd been hit, complete startlement in the movement. "Don't be ridiculous. I may not like her, but the woman's not a fool. I'm just saying if she did you'd be the last to know."

"No." The anger and power was still in his voice, deepening it. Belinda could see Eliza react to it, not in fear, she knew him too well for that, but respect, perhaps submission, though she barely lifted her chin at all. More telling than either of those, her stance changed, weight rolling forward through her hips, a subtle offering of desire. It was easier to see in Eliza, with her breeches and men's shirt, than in court-dressed ladies. Even burdened by her winter cloak, the lines of her hips were more blatant than any woman under a half dozen petticoats could hope for.

"No?" Eliza's voice had deepened, too, fueled by want, not anger. Belinda caught her breath, tip of her tongue between her teeth, and let her shaking power reach forth again, desire to read the truth of Javier's interest in Eliza far greater than her fear of being noticed.

Impulse rolled over her in heady waves, anger cutting away intellect. It would be easy—it would be *welcome*—to crowd Eliza against the bridge railing and take her. Her desire and his power had danced a knife's edge almost as long as either of them could remember. It was a dance that had to remain unconsummated; anything else would too drastically change the power structure among the four friends. Javier forced his hands to loosen and glanced away, Belinda finding herself doing the same, even to letting a breath out in a quiet sigh. Javier felt, and Belinda through him, Eliza's bright burst of hurt and anger, even without looking at her. He waited a few moments before looking back. Her expression was under control when he did, fresh and open but for a sliver of disappointment that would someday fester into hate. Belinda shivered with pleasure, not at that truth, but at Javier's recognition of it, and retreated again before her presence was detected.

"Liz. . . ."

"Don't." Eliza turned her head away sharply. "Don't, Jav."

Javier curled a fist again, then let it go. It was a visible moment before he trusted himself to say, lightly, "I wouldn't be the last to know, because you would tell me. But it's not her spending or her lovers I want you to watch. It's simply what she does through the day. I must know if she can be trusted."

"Do you intend to marry her?"

Javier's eyebrows went up. "*Beatrice?* She's practically a commoner—" And then his thought rolled across his face, so clear Belinda needed no power to read it: *ah, Javier, you are a fool.* Eliza turned a gaze of daggers on him. "Eliza—"

"You know I can't tell you no." She looked away again.

"Yes," Javier said, almost regretfully. He stepped closer, lifting his fingers to brush them over Eliza's cheek. She stiffened, refusing to look back at him. He produced a wry grin and added, "Because I could order you, anyway, and you're bound by oath of fealty to do as I say."

It worked admirably enough that even Belinda smiled. The tension broke, some of the sting leaving Eliza's eyes as her full mouth curved slightly. "I was ten, Jav."

"And I was eight. Do you think it meant less to either of us for all our tender years?"

"You were going to have me thrown in the dungeon." Eliza's smile grew, and Javier laughed.

"It seemed like a good threat at the time."

"I was terrified!"

Javier laughed again, shaking his head. "Now that, Liz, I do not believe. I don't think you've ever been terrified."

"I am." Amusement left her and she turned to lean on the railing, staring down into the black river. "But the fears that haunt me are very different from yours, Jav. Things you wouldn't understand. It's the worlds we come from."

"You've never let me understand." Javier leaned beside her, fingers dangling over the rail. Eliza shook her head.

"No. And I never will."

"Why?" Belinda tasted the impulse behind the question: he had wanted to ask it a hundred times, never daring. But there was something raw in the wind tonight, letting them touch on topics they had let lie fallow for fifteen years of friendship. Belinda found herself curling her fingers against the stone railing, wondering if that strangeness was her. She could sense tight control in not only the prince, but in his common-born friend as well. They never spoke of desire or the positions in the world that helped keep them apart. It was harder, too hard, for Eliza; that was what Javier told himself. "Haven't I been there for your life, Eliza?" He reached over to touch her hair, catching a short-shorn lock between his fingertips. "I remember when we cut your hair," he murmured.

"The first or the second time?" Eliza gave the river an unhappy smile. "Those were the best years, you know, Jav. Before God saw fit to grant me tits and hips that made sure I could never really pass as one of the boys again."

"You were a stick," Javier said. "Narrow everywhere."

"I was a child. We all were. But you're a man, Jav, you wouldn't understand the change in freedom." Eliza touched her own hair. "My hair was my vanity then, you know. And you three pinned me down." She laughed, clear sound that Belinda found herself savoring, just as Javier did, for its rarity. "You pinned me down and cut it all off."

"You were fashionable," Javier protested, grinning.

"For a ten-year-old boy!"

"I never asked," Javier murmured. "What did your family say?"

Eliza shook her head, the action draping stillness of soul over her. Her voice went quiet. "They were angry. But in deference to the station of my friends"—a minute shrug—"they let me keep it shorn so short for a whole two years. Until I got my blood."

"Is *that* what happened. I remember you being sulky for weeks and looking like a hedgehog while your hair grew out."

"No one would marry a woman with a boy's haircut, Jav. And an unmarried woman is only a burden on her family. My father had daughters enough without the added trial of trying to marry off one who wears a boy's haircut."

"I would have taken care of you, Liz. Of your whole family."

"Oh, aye. My whole family. And the cousins, Jav? And their babies? And the hangers-on and the families down the block who were related by blood three generations back? Until you had all the poor of Lutetia in your chambers, maybe. Maybe then you'd understand what you can't. It isn't your fault, Jav. You come from places that are too high."

"And you won't let me walk in the low ones, Liz."

"No," Eliza agreed. "Because you can't save us all. You can't even save one of us."

He reached out to touch her hair again. "I saved you."

"And my mother and three sisters died, Jav. Sacha and Marius should never have brought me to the palace."

"You had the fever, Eliza. What were they to do, let you die? They would have brought you all. They say your mother refused. That she only let them take you because you were so very ill. I remember the second time, too, Liz. You looked so damned fragile, so pale and sick. They were afraid your hair took too much of your strength, and you needed it all to live."

"And I looked like a shaved skull when I woke up. My mother thought I was Death come knocking on the door when I went home." Eliza fell silent. "And she was right, Jav. They all died."

"I would have tried to save them," Javier whispered. Eliza sighed and put her hand over his. Belinda flinched, feeling the warmth of the woman's hand on hers, and jerked her gaze to her own hand before looking back toward Javier and Eliza.

Eliza had long fingers, her hands nearly as big as the prince's, for all that he was a half-hand taller than she. He turned his palm up to lace his fingers with hers, holding on hard for the few moments that she let him.

"I know, Jav. But we all have our pride." She stared down at the river. When she spoke again her voice was carefully neutral. "It left me barren, you know that? The fever. I used to dream of marrying a prince." Her smile had no humour in it, only years of resigned sadness. "I knew it was only a dream. Royalty doesn't marry commoners, no matter how pretty they are. But still, I dreamed. Then the month after the fever my blood didn't come, nor has it in the five years since. Not just common, but common and barren. No dream can survive that."

"Eliza." Cold flooded Belinda's hands, Javier's horror her own.

He tightened his fingers around Eliza's, uselessly, and she flashed him another sad smile.

"Sacha knows, can you believe that? I got piss drunk a few years ago and he asked me point-blank, I don't know why. And I told him. Made him swear not to tell you. Then we fucked. It hasn't happened again, so he thinks I don't remember, but I do. Nineteen, I was nineteen and despite looking like *this*," she jerked her hand from Javier's so she could gesture at herself, "I was a virgin."

"Really?" Javier's voice broke with surprise and he glowered at the black river below. Eliza laughed without real humour.

"Really. I'd wanted—" She shrugged, stiff, and leaned on the railing, her elbows hyperextended with the pressure she put on them. "I'd make a fine rich man's mistress, Jav." She strove to keep her voice light, stretching her throat long to do it. "He'd never have to worry about by-blows."

"You're better than that, Liz."

She smiled and turned to him, putting both hands on his chest and patting her fingers against the soft fabric of his doublet. "Yes." She sighed and dropped her hands a few inches, putting her forehead against his chest for a moment. Then she stepped back, holding her right hand up. Gold coins glittered between her fingers, then jumped as she flipped her hand over and bounced the coins, three of them, across her knuckles. "I am."

Javier clapped his hand to his purse. "Eliza!"

She laughed, popping the coins over to land stacked in her palm. Javier picked them up, scattering them across his own palm; they were all faceup, all imprinted with the same year. "How do you *do* that?"

"Practise," Eliza said with a shrug. She bent her wrist in and fetched a fourth coin from inside of her sleeve, holding it up between two fingers. "Practise and a healthy disregard for other people's belongings."

Javier snatched the coin out of her fingers, grinning. "Are there more?"

Eliza spread her arms. "You'll have to look."

"Eliza. . . ."

She dropped her hands and shrugged. "It's your coin, Jav. I don't mind making it my own. Call it the cost of setting me on your lover."

"You'll do it, then."

She eyed him, turning back to the river. "Sacha told on me, didn't he. He told you my father found out what I'd been doing."

"Yes." Javier put his backside against the railing and studied his feet.

Eliza's mouth quirked and she shook her head. "Darling Sacha. I don't need your protection, Jav. I have enough money hidden away to make a fine life for myself."

"And yet you don't do it."

"Of course not. Your mother would never approve."

Javier frowned. "What?"

"Come on, Jav. Your streetside friend suddenly makes good? All of Lutetia would think I'd given into your wiles and you were putting me up in style. The prince's mistress."

"Is it such a terrible facade?"

"No." Eliza pressed her lips together, leaning more heavily over the river. "But I won't climb the ranks on rumour of royal bed, Jav. I'll find a way by myself or not at all."

"Let me help. Take the position in Beatrice's house. It's a place to begin, Liz."

"You're a hard man to say no to, Prince Javier."

"I know." He bumped his hip against hers, smiling. "And you won't, will you?"

Eliza's shoulders dropped. "I'm not a lady, Jav."

"You will be." Javier twisted to put his arm around Eliza's waist, kissing her temple. Belinda felt a sigh go through him, relief that the argument had ended without him making his plea an order. Below that lay gladness, not just that Eliza had agreed, but that he'd spoken earlier with Belinda, choosing his battles in the right order. Not, Belinda knew, that she could have refused the prince any more easily than Eliza could have. "I have to get back," he murmured against Eliza's hair. "Someone will miss me."

"*She'll* miss you."

"No. I only spend the night with one woman at a time. She's not in my chambers tonight. Tonight was yours."

"Charmer." Eliza turned her head to kiss his cheek. "Good night, my prince."

Javier left her on the bridge, less alone than either of them might think.

Eliza watched the river until the bells tolled the half hour after Javier's departure, nothing of her emotions readable to Belinda's weary investigations. Only when Eliza slipped away did she let the power go, staggering under the onslaught of stars after so many hours hidden in shadow. She reached for the railing, leaned heavily on it, forcing herself to shallow gasps when she wanted to drag in half-panicked lungsful of air. It would not do, *would not do*, to show weakness from use of power. Belinda curled her lip, barely an expression on the outside, but focusing all her remaining strength through it, forcing all her disdain at her own faltering vigor into it. A lifetime's training straightened her spine, steadied her breathing even when her legs trembled and her heartbeat scampered with speed and lack of air. This was what the stillness was for: to forbid anything external from seeing her frailty. The stillness had nothing to do with the power she'd used to excess; it was her own gift to herself, studied and learned. The witchpower might enhance it, but the stillness was not born of the witchpower, and Belinda would not allow herself to soften in its use now. She spread her fingers against the bridge railing, light gentle touch that forbade her leaning, and slipped a smile into place as she gazed out over the quiet water.

No wall stood in her mind any longer, the odd, inexplicable flavour of her father washed away, his barricade destroyed. The desire to act was no longer separate from the ability to do so, golden strength finally her own. What was left of it? The day's exercise had drained that pool so thoroughly she could only feel the emptiness where it belonged. She cupped her hands together as if she would call the witchlight to her, but in truth made no effort to—it would respond no more than a man exhausted by a hedonistic night. Like a man, though, it would replenish itself; Belinda had no reason to believe that, but found herself easily confident of it, the fear that it might not return as absurd as fearing the sun might not rise.

Taking her hands from the railing to cup them told her she had the strength to stand unsupported. Replacing them there made it clear how much preferable support was. An unexpected quiet laugh bubbled to the surface and Belinda leaned forward, catching a glimpse of her reflection in the dark water below. Returning home would be more of a challenge than slipping unnoticed into the palace had been that day.

Water rippled and distorted her features for an instant, adding a length to her face and peaking her hairline in a way that reminded her of Lorraine. Belinda straightened again, brushing her fingers against her forehead to wipe away the thought. Allowing herself to dwell on the Aulunian queen was always dangerous, but more so now. She could slip into the minds of others and sense their emotions, even share their thoughts if she touched them. Should Javier have a similar secret, then Belinda must be certain to keep her mind guarded always. Her duties to Aulun had to remain in the quietest part of her, lest she be exposed and die for her troubles.

There was a trick still left to be explored. Belinda put away thoughts of her work and turned to a thrill of exploration that brought another smile to her lips. Beatrice, she thought without heat, smiled too easily. Even now, when the Lanyarchan lass had been set aside for a while, her influence lay over Belinda like a cloak. Still, she chose not to wipe away the smile as she considered the last step she might take with her newfound skills.

She could read thoughts, gauge emotions. Influencing them would be a power worth reckoning with. An Essandian princess might be moved to suicide, if caught in the right mood, or her red-haired son made to fall in love with and rashly wed a barren commoner. Javier was a perilous target to test on, though; his own witchpower might easily make him immune to Belinda's influence. And if the power were a gift of royal blood, then Sandalia, too, might be difficult to sway.

But the weaker minds around them could be used. Asselin already moved toward sedition; with a little effort, he might betray himself and his compatriots. A plot against Lorraine, built by those close to Javier—perhaps, to succeed, Belinda didn't need so much as Sandalia's own hand in the pot. Sacha's ambition might well bring Belinda far closer to her goal, his plots the mechanism to undo them all. And sweet Marius would—

"Beatrice?"

Belinda startled more profoundly than she could remember doing since she was a child, a jolt flinching her entire torso as she twisted toward the sound of her name. Marius, in an extravagant hat and boots that showed off the shape of his calves, came up to her in astonishment. "Beatrice, whatever are you doing out here alone at this hour?"

"Has it grown so late?" Her question was distant even to her own ears, a flighty smile curving her mouth. "I suppose it has, hasn't it? I've watched my reflection in the dark water without thinking anything of it." Marius put his arm around her, warm and solid, just as the memory of her father had been. Belinda turned her head toward his throat, inhaling the scent of a tavern on his skin: wood smoke and ale.

"Are you all right, lady?"

"Better now," she murmured. Marius's pulse leapt and she put her lips against it, probing curiously with her tongue even as her own thoughts demanded to know what she was doing. Marius gasped, the soft sound of startled pleasure, and Belinda lifted her hand to knock his hat off and pull herself closer to him, closing her teeth over the rapid beat in his neck. The hat made a lonely splash against the water and Marius made a strangled noise, desire mixed with bewilderment.

"What, m'sieur, have you never had a woman act first?" Belinda kept one hand in his hair and slid the other down his body, rucking cloth out of the way to investigate what manner of man his codpiece concealed. He croaked and sagged, catching the bridge railing for support as Belinda let go a delighted chortle to tease his throat. "Less padding than a decent woman would imagine. What a lovely surprise, Marius Poulin."

"Beatrice . . . we . . . the prince . . . we cannot . . ."

"The prince is welcome to join us." There was sense in Marius's protests and none at all in Belinda's actions, but she withdrew her hand to unlace his ties and shoved his breeches down a necessary few inches. Need pounded through her, a desire for control and domination that was nearly alien to her. Her position was to be weak, attractive, usable; men of power, the sort she was trained to seduce and kill, did not in general appreciate a strong hand in bed. The sudden opportunity to take it was disconcertingly appealing, all the more so for the very problem that Marius had voiced. Belinda pulled him around until her back was against the bridge railing, put his hands on her waist in a demand he understood whether intellect ruled against them or not. He lifted her high enough to rest her bottom on the railing, Belinda twisting her skirts out of the way as she pulled him closer.

He muffled a cry against her shoulder as she sheathed him within herself, and she bit his throat again, hard enough to leave marks. "Have you ever shared a woman with your prince, Marius?" All her rules were shattering, stillness forgotten in the demanding rock of her hips. His name was on her lips, used more than once, filled with a hunger that confused her. "They say there's so little between a woman's walls that if you both take her at once you feel the other. Shall we invite Javier, Marius, my love?" She nearly laughed at her last word, its gratuitous nature garnering another cry from the youth buried within her. She slid forward on him, barely balanced on the railing for all that he groaned and pushed forward again. "Hold me tight and we'll pretend, Marius. Fuck me well and imagine the dangers of taking the prince's lover as your own."

For once, gloriously, her lover's enjoyment meant nothing to her. Her breasts ached, body throbbing with a need that she gave in to utterly, forcing her own hand between their bodies to seek out her own pleasure. Marius protested and she bit him again, drawing a sharp sound of confused pain and then the tilt of his chin, giving her his throat in acquiescence. She wrapped her legs around his hips, dragging him closer, trusting his strength to not let her fall, and his hands knotted at her waist in a promise that he wouldn't. "Harder, Marius." Belinda barely knew her own voice, low with demand and desire, but the youth in her arms whimpered as he drove into her, desperate to oblige. A sensation of rightness overwhelmed her, carried on climax beginning to crest; she had spent too long, far too long playing to the whims of others. Marius would be hers, marked as hers, and no one would dispute her claim.

She knotted her fingers in his hair, pulling his head back to force him to look into her eyes. His own were wide, glazed with desire, pupils dilated. His breath was harsh, the play of his mouth lost and sweet. Belinda brought his mouth to hers and when he begged a kiss bit his lower lip until she tasted blood. "You'll make me come," she whispered. "With your next thrust you'll make me come or I'll cut your throat and leave you here to bleed, I swear it on my soul."

Honest terror slid through him, delicious rewidening of his eyes as he believed a threat Belinda knew she could carry out. His body went still in hers, no bad thing with her own weight bearing her down on his cock, making a spot of desperately rising pleasure as she worked her fingers against herself. But she smiled against his mouth, shaking her head. "Oh no, love. Not now. You don't get to stop now."

She took her hand from his hair, his head falling forward over her breasts, though fear still held him still. She slipped her hand down his backside, fingers spread wide over his crack and then diving relentlessly inside him.

His voice broke, high sharp sound as he shoved forward, scraping her against the railing, scraping against the bone within her that brought violent spasms of heat spilling through her body. She bit his shoulder again, rolling against him with her own whimpers and cries knotted in her throat. Marius still dared not move, only clung to her and gasped in uncertain need as she took what she wanted from him. Only when she slipped her fingers from within him did he groan and risk rocking forward again, a plea that broke hard laughter from Belinda's throat. She pushed herself off him, balanced on the railing momentarily to shove him away and thump her feet to the ground.

Confusion filled his face, his hands spread in question, unsated cock jutting at a desperate angle through the folds of his tunic. Belinda straightened her arm, fully cognizant of another man she'd pushed away thus, a lifetime earlier, and watched Marius stumble back a step, but not to his death. "Come now, Marius." Her voice was harsh in her ears, mocking more viciously than he deserved. "Can you imagine the disaster of making me pregnant, with the prince as my lover? I can't risk your seed spilling inside me. Put it away and take it home to a serving girl." Her heart banged against her ribs, cruelty aching and distinct within her, as much in search of release as the fading throb between her thighs had been. She crimped a fist against the hurt in his dark eyes and brought her voice back under control, a greater struggle than she liked to admit.

"Go, Marius." Almost nothing more than a whisper. "Your sweet mouth, your eyes. I knew enough to resist, but it's hard when one man can't be denied where another is wanted." Sorrow etched the words and a flush came over Marius's cheeks, forgiveness too easily obtained. "Tomorrow," Belinda promised. "Tomorrow we'll talk, we'll try to see how this can be gotten through, when I know now I'm not strong enough to stand strong against you." Tears filled her eyes, tangling in her lashes and making hot lines down her cheeks as she turned her head, offering her throat just as he'd done for her moments earlier. "Forgive me, m'sieur."

"Beatrice." Marius's voice went rough and he stuffed himself back into his clothes before stepping forward to catch her in a hopeless, desperate hug. "There is nothing to forgive. You're right, of course you're right, about children, about . . . tomorrow." He broke his own near-apologies off and clenched her against his chest, a promise of safety. "I'll call on you tomorrow," he promised, then released her so quickly it seemed he feared what he might do. Within seconds he'd taken himself away, hurrying across the bridge without daring to look back. Belinda watched him go, licking the coppery taste of blood from her lower lip.

Feared what he might do, or, she thought, feared what she might do. Red fire tinged the edges of the reemerging golden pool of power within her mind, as if she had for the first time acknowledged her own strength. It made no sense; she had acted against her own character and reveled in it. She did not take, or risk, or demand, not in the fashion she had just done, and yet it felt more pure and delicious than any moment she could remember. She did not release the stillness she'd learned so carefully and rut without a thought for anything but herself. Less than a quarter hour earlier, she would have said she *could* not do so.

Fresh fire burned through her, spilling from the top of her skull down through her body, making points of desire in her nipples and groin. She wet her lips, eyes half closed as she considered the barrier that no longer lay in her mind. Perhaps it had held back this part of her, too. She had broken down that careful barricade, drained her witchpower to nothing, and in the aftermath given in to her own wanting in a way she had never imagined doing. If those things were connected, it was a lesson learned: using her power to its nadir was aggressively dangerous to her, destroying a lifetime's careful study.

Her perfect memory rose up with a gift: a serving girl's blush and shocked hunger following her down the stairs.

Belinda smoothed her skirts and set herself homeward, a predator's smile curving her mouth.

9

SANDALIA, QUEEN AND REGENT
19 October 1587 † Lutetia, Gallin

The queen arrives back in Lutetia with neither pomp nor circumstance. She has the flags covered on her ship and slips into port late at night, meeting a prearranged and nondescript carriage to take her from the docks to a country cottage on the palace grounds. She sleeps under guard, and awakens in the morning to the smell of breakfast in the outer room. Pulling on a dressing gown, leaving her hair tousled and down, she steps through the bedroom door to smile at Javier. "How do you always know?"

"What kind of son would I be if I didn't know when my mother came and left her home?" He stands, first to bow as benefits both their stations, then to step forward and kiss his mother's cheeks. "I thought your business with Rodrigo was only supposed to take a month."

"Petulant child." Sandalia walks barefoot to the table, greedy for a croissant and rich salty butter. "I hadn't seen my brother in two years. A visit was warranted."

"You've written to him." Javier retains the deliberately sulky tone, earning Sandalia's laughter.

"And I wrote to you. You, however . . ." She points her butter knife at him and laughs again to catch his expression of guilt. "Who is she?"

Javier's eyes widen. "She? She who?"

"Jav." Sandalia speaks the nickname fondly. "Even if you didn't write, my spies did. Don't pretend there isn't a woman."

"If you know there's a woman," he says easily, "then you know everything about her already, and there's nothing to tell." He glanced at her for permission, then sprawled in a chair, gangliness of youth briefly still apparent in his form. "Her name is Beatrice Irvine, and she's a minor Lanyarchan noble."

"Yes. I don't recall the Irvines, or her father. Roger, I think his name was?"

"Robert." Exasperation fills Javier's tone. "Mother, you lived in Lanyarch less than two years. For all the stories, I cannot believe you slept on *every* hearth in the godforsaken country. You can't be expected to know every parent and every child birthed there since you were fourteen. Even," he adds lightly, "if that was only a scant handful of years ago. How is Uncle Rodrigo?"

Sandalia laughs. "Handsome, but not as flattering as my son. Handsome," she repeats thoughtfully, "and, perhaps, growing ambitious at long last."

Quietude surrounds her son, an expectation that she's learned to recognize as a moment when those things that he desires will come to him. He has extraordinary will, and she wonders if he realises how easily he influences others.

"Aulun." He barely breathes the word, aware even in the privacy of her own small cottage how carefully watched he and his mother are. "Curiously," he says an instant later, tone normal again, "Beatrice may be of some use there. She's passionate, Mother." He leaves words unsaid, words that Sandalia has no need to hear spoken. Passion is an excellent vice, easily shaped to foolish behavior. Passion can be used to set flames from embers that have been too-long untended.

"Irvine," Sandalia repeats, and taps the flat of her knife against her mouth. The blade tastes of salt and butter and she licks her lips absently. "Have you looked into her family?"

"No, and I haven't checked her teeth, either. She's for rolling, Mother, not breeding." There's something tense in his words, something he wishes to hide. It's possible he's fallen in love with the girl, though it seems he still understands how she can be used.

"Javier." Sandalia puts steel into her voice, enough to make him flinch as if he were still a guilty child. "The Church says we must come pure to the marriage bed. Surely you haven't broken that covenant." She's teasing, but Javier's mouth flattens for a moment before breaking into an easy smile.

"Of course not, Mother. She's told me a little of her family," he adds more patiently. "Her father was landed but not noble, and that her title comes from marriage to some old man aged enough to be her grandfather. Aside from that, I haven't looked into her family, not beyond the painting of her father that hangs in her hall. I don't know if it was his face or the painter's skill that's lacking, but Beatrice must be her mother's daughter." Tension eased, he chuckles and reaches forward to dump jam onto a chunk of pastry.

"They always are, my sweet. They always are." Sandalia purses her lips, then holds out her hand for the jam jar. Javier puts it into her palm without her having to ask, and she smiles. "Let me set my spymasters to her. If she's all she seems, then I think you'd better introduce me."

"The courtiers will think you plan to marry me to her."

"A Lanyarchan provincial? Let them think it, if they're that foolish. My brother is making treatise with Khazar, Jav." Sandalia drops into her native tongue of Essandian, confident of her son's ability to follow. He speaks more languages than she does, his Khazarian fluent and his Parnan passable. She has only Gallic, Essandian, and Aulunian, though they've been enough to serve her. Nor does she think the change of language will truly hide her words from anyone determined to listen, but no one is supposed to know she's back, and the usual run of spies might only have one tongue. "With her help we might—"

"So we might," Javier murmurs. That something is in his gaze again, a far-awayness that she hasn't seen before. She knows ambition, but is hard-pressed to recognize it on her son's face; Rodrigo spoke truly when he said Javier was her first and most loyal subject. He's grown up in a shadow Sandalia has worked hard to cast long, and he has never shown resentment or hinted at plotting beyond Sandalia's own intentions. She is torn in understanding this; the idea that it's awe and respect that keeps him in line is appealing, but at desperate odds with the behavior of the men she knows. If he is finally facing his first taste of desire for a throne, Sandalia finds herself almost relieved, even as a part of her regrets the loosening of the hold she's had on him all his life.

"I have men," he says abruptly. "Friends loyal to me—"

"You have Sacha," Sandalia says, as gentle as he was abrupt. "And Marius. A lordling and a merchant boy, my prince. Will you send them into battle for you? Will you risk them that way? Is that what you want to propose to me now?"

Red flushes Javier's cheeks as it hasn't done since he was a boy. "They are, Sacha especially, ambitious, Mother. And I'm their prince. If—" He's stumbling now, eager embarrassment making for tongue-tangled frustration. "If events should move forward, and I know Sacha dreams they might, then he might earn himself a title or lands separate from his father's. How could I tell him no? And Marius—" Now colour truly curdles his face, ugly contrast with his ginger hair. "Beatrice was his," he says dully. "I owe him something."

"You're his prince," Sandalia says mildly. "You owe him nothing. Rodrigo reminds me that I have never seen war, Jav. Neither have you. Perhaps you should wait to see it before you consign your dearest friends to their glory. Besides, winter comes on and there will be no dramatics during the cold months. It'll be spring again before the ice breaks and the world moves forward again."

BELINDA PRIMROSE / BEATRICE IRVINE
19 October 1587 † *Lutetia, Gallin*

A gong and a whimper of dismay awakened Belinda, sunlight filtering through tangled lashes and turning her vision to red in the moment she became aware. The bell sounded a second time, and so did the whimper, the latter bringing a lazy smile to Belinda's lips. She slid a hand across the sheets, encountering a curve of flesh and following it upward to find the sloppy spill of a breast. The nipple reacted as she plucked it, hardening and earning another whimper, more bewildered and shy than the first. Belinda rolled closer, setting lips and teeth to the girl's breast, eyes still closed with lazy satisfaction, and slipped her hand down the girl's body, sifting her fingers through rough curls. Dismay squeaked in the girl's throat and Belinda lifted her mouth to speak even as her fingers delved inside the young woman, seeking a moisture that had not left her in the night.

"Is it different in daylight, Nina? You seemed eager under the stars. Is it frightening now? Is it wrong?" The need for domination had left her while she slept, content filling her mind as the pool of witchpower within her replenished itself. But an edge remained, though whether it was power demanding more or simply the irresistible toy in her bed, Belinda was both uncertain and uncaring. Her dark-haired parlour maid lay bound ankle and wrist, wide open for teasing and taking, far too sweet to ignore.

A cruelty that had left her had deliberately chosen to keep Nina spread through the night, a kerchief shoved into her mouth and tied so the girl's crying wouldn't disturb Belinda's sleep. Nina's hair was still damp with tears, pincurls slick and delicate as they stood away from her temples, and marks reddened the sides of her mouth where she was gagged. Viciousness was gone, but Nina's helplessness woke pulsing hunger in Belinda's veins, strong enough to kill any impulse to release the girl. "Shall I stop, lovely child?" Her thumb worked a quick hard circle between Nina's thighs, sending a shudder of confusion through her body. The protest she'd begun was swallowed, eyes wide and uncertain. Belinda chortled, rolling her weight on top of the young woman, who exhaled sharply through her gag.

The bell sounded a third time, sparking irritation. Belinda flounced off the bed, knowing full well she behaved like a spoilt child, and snatched up a dressing robe to run down the stairs in. Being left to answer the door herself was certainly her own fault, with Nina occupied as she was.

Marius, a high-collared cravat not quite hiding bruised tooth marks on his neck, stood outside the door with eyes dark and haunted. "Beatrice . . ."

Belinda caught him by the sleeve and pulled him inside, molding herself against him as the door closed behind him. "Did you sleep? Your eyes, my lord . . ."

"I could not." His voice was hoarse and Belinda smiled against his chest, then turned a sweet gaze on him as he clutched her upper arms. "I shouldn't be here, but I cannot think for desiring you, Beatrice. What have you done to me?"

"Young lust, m'sieur. Young love. This is its taste." Belinda loosened his grip on her by lifting her hands to touch his collar. "I was cruel. You must forgive me, please."

He hissed, jerking his head, though his pulse leapt as she touched the marks she'd left. "Did you find a girl to sate your need, my sweet?" Her own heartbeat rose too quickly, surprising her with the dark playfulness in the question. She'd thought her power replenished, with no need to take more, but the impulse to tease the young merchant rode her heavily, pressing her beyond good sense back into passion. Good sense: she clawed at the memory of

232 · C. E. MURPHY

it, aware of how quickly it had fled her the night before, and feeling it falter again as Marius shook his head with another quick hard motion. Laughter and desire, so tied together she could fight neither, spilled through her, and Belinda stepped back, taking his hands. "Then let me help you."

Hope flared in his eyes, so bright it made her laugh again, breathless. She shifted her shoulders, letting her dressing robe fall loose, so that only her arms, pressed to mound her breasts as she drew Marius with her, kept it in place. His gaze dropped to the soft flesh she displayed, arrested by it. "Lady Beatrice." His voice was thick, tongue clumsy with desire. "I would not have imagined you so . . ." He swallowed, unable to find the word.

Belinda wet her lips, walking carefully up the stairs, each step taken backward so Marius kept his eyes on her body. "So wanton, my lord?" Her own voice was hoarse, more artifice than desire, hiding laughter instead of showing need. "I said my husband was old, not well suited for pleasing a young woman. I did not say he was . . . unimaginative. He had a young wife, and certain . . . desires to play out." Laying the blame on a man who'd never existed, making him cruel and hard and creative, made it too easy to blur the line between herself and the role she played. Too easy, but necessary: Beatrice should never have Belinda's expertise, not without an excuse that a young man, half in love with the idea of rescuing a lonely widow, could accept. "Let me show you how I can ease your need."

She knocked her bedroom door open with her hip as she spoke, Marius fixated on her until Nina's shrill scream broke through the gag as a pathetic, high sound. She twisted on the bed, hands knotted, hips raised as she struggled against her bonds and only tightened them with her efforts. A blush scarred Marius's cheeks, his gaze torn between Belinda and the writhing, bound girl on the bed. "You have admired her, have you not?" Belinda whispered.

"She has known a man's touch before. Take your pleasure from her, and think of me."

Nina screamed again, bucking and flinging herself against the bed. Marius flinched, his colour still high, and spoke with no conviction: "She does not want me."

Belinda released his hands, letting her robe flutter around her as she went to the bed. "She will," she promised, confidence burning inside her. More than confidence: a drive to prove herself, to explore, to control; all things lying outside Belinda's sense of self, lying beyond her long-imposed stillness. There were reasons to draw back, reasons that seemed far away and faded behind a wall of golden fire. It was without hesitation that Belinda sat at Nina's side, stroking her hand down the younger woman's belly as she repeated, "She will."

Nina shrieked again, spitting a curse that spilled new tears from her eyes and turned to dry sobs inside a breath. Belinda leaned down, kissing tears away and touching Nina's breasts. She could taste her servant's thoughts if she wanted to, helpless repetitions of resignation struggling with the need to defend her own honour, discomfort at the erotic potential of her mistress's touch, a horrifying acquiescence that hungered for more. "Nina." Belinda whispered the name, taking her hands away and shifting to sit at the head of the bed, lifting Nina's head into her lap. "Are you afraid, Nina?"

The girl nodded, dying hope coming into her eyes, into her thoughts. Perhaps her mistress would let her go from the nightmare she'd been brought into in the dark hours, if she admitted to her fear. Belinda's soft smile made that hope blossom and Nina twisted, not in rebellion this time, but in supplication. *Love me, protect me, save me, I'll do anything* spun through the desperate action and Belinda's own body tightened with desire. "Do you want him to fuck you, Nina?"

Belinda felt hot tears spill along her own temples, felt the tension in Nina's neck as the girl shook her head frantically. Another smile curved Belinda's lips, offering another shard of cruel hope to her serving girl. Power sang through her, encouraging, dominating, and Belinda leaned closer to whisper against Nina's ear. "Do you feel any desire now, Nina?"

Nina shook her head again, coldness in her body and thoughts telling Belinda the answer was true. The witchpower needed no gathering: it was there, golden and heavy, exploring the nuances of Nina's emotions. It heated and shot a throb of need into Nina along thin tendrils of connection, so sharp and unexpected that even Belinda gasped with it, uncertain if it had been her own choice to fill Nina with aching want. Belinda knew that aspect of desire all too well, memories of a lifetime's training at learned arousal in a submissive position rising, then spilling into Nina. Caught by her own lust and the witchpower's strength, Belinda focused on the ache in her own body and the heat of need climbing in her.

Nina gasped, eyes unfocused. Her hips relaxed, then lifted in a different way. Her nipples hardened under the onslaught of desires chosen for her, and triumph blossomed in Belinda's breast. Hungry with the ability to do so, she sent shame through the witchpower, and watched tears fill Nina's eyes again, even as she whimpered behind her gag and pressed her knees apart. Emotion washed back to Belinda, need rising until it hurt coupled with Nina's humiliation at her body's sudden betrayal. Belinda let the shame go, replacing it with rage. Nina vaulted upward as best she could, straining and twisting, cords standing in her neck as she screamed deep, raw sounds of fury against her gag. Belinda fed that, her own breathing growing ragged, until Nina's eyes were shot with blood from the force of her protests and sweat soaked her body. Belinda sensed, more than saw, Marius hovering a few feet away, too taken with the sights to retreat and utterly uncertain of his place there. Nina's diametric changes in emotion excited him beyond his comprehension, as did the girl's dark head in Belinda's lap.

"Is that better?" Belinda whispered the question over Nina's hair as she released the rage. "Have you fought enough, love? Do you think we believe your anger?" Sensuality bred from exhaustion slipped in with the words, slow need throbbing again. Nina turned her head, whimpering as her body betrayed her again, and finally her gaze came to Marius. He took a rough step forward and she moaned behind her gag, lifting her hips. "Touch her," Belinda commanded, and he put his hand between the girl's legs as if Belinda manipulated his desires as well. Nina sobbed and Belinda flooded her with the impulse to submit and offer herself to the merchant youth. She accepted it, spreading her already-wide legs and pleading with her captured voice and eyes. A curve slipped over Belinda's mouth: she had no sense of Nina believing her emotions and needs were anything but her own, betraying as they might be. A servant girl was an easy target, bearing nothing like the will of a prince or queen, but it could be done. Her gift extended that far.

Belinda looked up, a smile still playing her lips. Marius was trembling, his hand sealing the heat between Nina's thighs. "Do you wish to be cruel to her, m'sieur? As I was to you?"

A flash of heat scored off him, then faded as he shook his head, uncertain of which woman to look at. Without touching him, Belinda couldn't know his thoughts, but the emotion that poured from him said despite the momentary impulse, his better nature was true. That he wanted the helpless servant was unquestionable, but he had no need to do her brutally. Belinda pulled her lower lip into her teeth, watching the youth with dark eyes, and sought out that instant of spitefulness that had sparked through him.

It was there, buried beneath an overwhelming eroticism at the strength Belinda had shown the night before. He was a man; he did not think of himself as submissive, and yet he'd given her his throat and, mortifyingly, his arse, and liked it all. Belinda grasped that moment of humiliation and played it forward, making it larger than it had been; making him think on and remember it, when he preferred to put it away.

There was a woman here who could not resist him, Belinda whispered into that sliver of embarrassment. A woman who could not use him the way he'd been used. A woman to regain his manhood through, a woman to dominate and show his strength to. She would not dare laugh at him as Beatrice had seemed to, or would she? Was that amusement in her wide eyes now, recognizing that he'd been taken by a woman? Was she gagged to stop her laughter, those sounds in her throat not need or fear or desire, but mocking?

Marius curled his lip, hand twisting at Nina's crotch to slam soaking fingers inside her. She cried out behind her gag and Marius's eyes darkened further, free hand fumbling at his leggings to loosen them. Belinda's heart raced, lip caught in her teeth as she leaned in, unable to stop herself from encouraging his building outrage with her own body language. Her breasts spilled forward, close to Nina's face, and she felt a spike surge through the man, as his imagination had the servant suckle the mistress.

Belinda nearly laughed with split concentration, feeding enough of her own raw want to Nina to keep the girl on the agonizing edge of fear and desire. At the same time she drew on Marius's barely acknowledged desire for domination, turning it and feeding it into anger that it had happened. He closed his hand over Nina's throat and replaced his fingers within her with his cock, a hard claiming that pulled a raw gasp of pleasure from Belinda. Nina cried out in bewildered pain and Marius tightened his hand at her throat, every struggle she made pushing him deeper into the violence Belinda had called up in him. She laughed, rocking her own hips forward with enthusiasm, floating on physical and emotional links to the two she had made unwilling lovers.

It was *easy*. Too easy, perhaps; sex and passion were easily built upon, the mortal weakness for pleasure. So easy she'd become lost in it, letting newfound power stretch and explore even beyond what she would have thought to be her own limits.

Beneath lust, beneath desire brought to the boiling point, the thought that the witchpower was controlling her made a cool angry place inside her. Whether it did, whether it could, she would not allow it to happen freely. Belinda licked a hungry tongue over her lips, rolling with the need that built between Nina and Marius until it lay so close to completion it seemed nothing could stop it.

She threw her head back and with all deliberate cruelty, as much to herself as to the bespelled pair beneath her, called the stillness. Proving to herself that she *could*. The witchpower was second to the stillness. It had to be, even if it could burn away that recollection with passion. It had controlled her. Now she must control it.

Stillness swept over her, a lifetime's practise stronger than any desire she had ever known. She distanced herself from the passion that wet her thighs, slowed her heartbeat and ignored the pain nipping at her breasts until it was gone.

Marius, unprepared for sudden flaccidity, croaked in disbelief, all his desire for violence, for sensuality, drowned as thoroughly in Belinda's calm as it had been built by her witchpower. Nina cried out again, dismay at the cessation of emotion; Belinda had not even left her her own dismay and fear at what she'd been brought in to. There was nothing left for either of them, no climax, no pleasure, so cold and wrapped in the survival trait Belinda had developed for herself were they.

Passion was easy. Cutting its throat was power, and that power lay in the stillness, not the witch-magic itself. Relief trembled deep inside her, that even lost in pounding want, she could bring herself back under rein. Belinda rose from the bed a paragon of tranquility, dressing gown gathered around her breasts and leaving her shoulders bared. Marius lifted his head, face twisted with befuddlement, and she touched his cheek, heartbeat slow through years of training. "Finish her while I dress, my love."

Not quite trusting her now-silent witchpower, Belinda released her hold on the lovers, leaving them nothing but their own emotions, Nina's fear and Marius's bewilderment. The young man scrambled away from the servant girl as Belinda left the bedroom, wrapped in carefully held stillness.

"I'm doing this for Jav." Eliza thrust her jaw out with the words, laying them flat between herself and Belinda. Belinda dropped her eyes, letting Beatrice's easy smile quirk her lips.

"So am I." She lifted her gaze, meeting Eliza's evenly. "With that in mind, we might make the best of it." Marius, flushed and flustered, had left before the noon bells had tolled. Belinda had climbed the stairs, skirts gathered and curiosity high in her mind, to investigate what he had left behind.

Nina, exhausted, confused, blushing to the tops of her breasts, had been left curled on her side, bindings released to let the girl huddle around herself, small and afraid. Surprise had wrinkled Belinda's forehead. She would have taken the order brutally, the finish she demanded was one the pretty serving girl would never wake from. But that was her training, her expectation, and her cold way of facing the world. Marius was, at his core, a kind man; if Belinda had doubted it before, she no longer did. Left with a living, breathing, blushing girl, she'd bathed Nina herself, finding herself unaccustomed to the gentleness she felt at doing so. She liked the girl, and if Nina were to live, then best to do right by her, as much as could be done.

Nina had been calm when the bath ended, able to meet her mistress's eyes. Whether a need to survive overcame humiliation or whether Belinda's careful attempts to alter the girl's memories were successful, Belinda was unsure. If her ministrations had worked, Nina's night had been spent in Beatrice's bed, indeed, against the cold and a fire that had burned out without new wood to feed it. Belinda told herself there was nothing of soft-heartedness in trying to rebuild the girl's thoughts, only a test to see whether she was able, but a thread of unusual guilt ran beneath the experiment. She had been roughly used often enough to wish the edge could be blunted, and she'd been trained for it. Nina had found herself caught in a web she had no chance of understanding, and it brooked unexpected sympathy within Belinda's heart.

She'd offered Nina a length of cloth to dry herself with, deliberately brushing her hand over the girl's naked breast. Nina had squeaked, a small sound of startlement that flooded Belinda with the same innocent confusion and desire that a similar touch had once brought, and Belinda had been satisfied with her investigation. Nina had been set to airing a room for Eliza, putting out bedding and wall hangings of equal quality to the ones in Belinda's rooms, and Belinda had gone to await her new housemate.

Eliza arrived with almost nothing. A stand for the wig made of her own lustrous black hair, a trunk barely touched with clothes. Her men's wear was blatantly folded on top of the few items within the trunk, and she shook them out now, as Belinda watched. "Nina will do that," Belinda offered softly. Eliza's lip curled.

"I don't need a servant, Beatrice. I've done for myself all my life."

"I know. But if we're to make the best of this, there's no harm in settling into the house like you belong, is there?" To her surprise, Belinda meant the question, oddly hopeful she could make a friend of the prince's beautiful friend. "Nina honestly won't know what to do with herself if she finds all your things already put away."

"Nina knows I'm a guttersnipe," Eliza snapped. "Just as everyone else does."

"Eliza." Belinda took a few steps forward, putting her hand on the taller woman's shoulder. Eliza flinched away, jaw set again. Belinda dropped her hand, but not her voice. "Have you noticed the prince has a friend from each obvious class, in you three? The nobility, the merchants, the poor. You were all too young, I think, for him to make that choice deliberately, but if you play it right now, it could make him even more beloved than he is. No one expects you to become something you aren't. You know where you're from, and God knows the nobility will never let you forget it. But if you're generous with your time and your money and bring the poor to Javier's attention, even the nobility won't be able to despise you outright. And the poor will love you for it."

Eliza spat, the sound so violent Belinda expected to see a glob of moisture land on the bedpost. "The poor will hate me as much as my father does for living."

"Javier loves you," Belinda said steadily. "The poor will see you as one of them who touches the stars. You can give them all a dream. Dreams are more precious than coin, sometimes."

"What would you know about it?" That was spat, too, but Eliza had stopped putting her own belongings away.

Belinda drew her lower lip into her mouth, searching for an answer honest enough to ring true without belying the persona she'd assumed. "I could see it from the prince's face," she said after long seconds. "That to him, sleeping with the pigs was a colourful expression. That it was outside the possibility of reality. I wasn't born to nobility, Eliza. My title came with my marriage bed."

Eliza's shoulders stilled as if she dared not breathe until Belinda's confession was through. For her part, Belinda took a deliberately deep breath, speaking to those squared shoulders. "We were landed, though not generously. No Ecumenic seems to be well-endowed now, not after a half century of Walter rule. My husband was old, his wealth a gift for loyal service to the Reformation queen. We had no dowry to offer him, not even my beauty."

Eliza's shoulders pulled back, a twitch as loud as words. Belinda cast a smile at the floor. "Don't bother," she murmured. "You're beautiful, Eliza. I'm pretty. I don't need protests to other ends. Besides, it wasn't beauty my husband desired. It was a girl well-born enough to not cause comment and ordinary enough to . . . not cause comment. He had certain pleasures," she said to the slight turn of Eliza's head. "Pleasures a beautiful bride might have dared object to, or that a father with his daughter's beauty to sell might have found ways to avoid. Pleasures a young man might risk saving a beautiful woman from. I . . . didn't offer those risks. I never slept with the pigs," she added more clearly, and out of all of it, that was the lie that stung to speak, "but I know more of that life, from my childhood, than I do of this one." She fluttered a hand at Eliza's room.

"Your husband," Eliza said in a high voice, "died of old age." There was a question around the edges of her statement, one that neither woman would allow to come to the fore. Belinda's heart went tight, internal expectation that she didn't allow near her features.

"I was fortunate." Her voice, too, was high and soft. "Perhaps there's someone you know whose age is creeping up on him."

Stillness, as profound as any Belinda knew, settled over Eliza again. When she spoke, it was not to the topic at hand, its weight too heavy in the afternoon-lit bedroom. "Do you really think they could be made to see me as something other than Javier's whore?"

"I think that if that's what you want, you'd better begin by growing your hair out."

Eliza turned, a startled hand going to her shorn locks, protest blackening already dark eyes. "It's that or wear your wig all the time, and hair's cooler than a wig. You're acting out of defiance." To her own surprise, sorrow curved Belinda's lips. "You're throwing it in their faces, that you're a woman protected by the prince and so you dare to do the unconventional. I know you don't like me, but I have no reason to lie to you when I say you aren't physically capable of being conventional. You'll be beautiful when you're sixty, when all the rest of us are merely old. Wear the wig," she said softly. "Grow your hair. Put aside the men's clothes and dress in your own gowns. Set convention. Be generous to where you came from, and yes, Eliza, they will see you as something other than Javier's whore. Not all of them. There will always be smallminded and bitter people. You'll have to be stronger than they are. But you *are* beautiful. You'll be able to make most of them love you." She sighed. "And you'll be able to make Jav regret all his life that he's not the one who can have you."

She kept her hands relaxed at her sides, against the impulse to curl them. The card she played was a dangerous one, using simple words and an unexpected truthfulness to ally herself with Eliza. The more—or less; she was as yet uncertain as to which it was— subtle manipulation of emotion lay within her capabilities, but Belinda found herself unwilling to indulge in that game. Alliances forged with words were better-known to her, more trustworthy, and would leave no mark of molding on Eliza's mind. Whether that was even a risk worth considering, Belinda didn't know, but better to avoid it if she could.

Besides, she admitted in a rare moment of honesty, she simply wanted the dark-haired beauty to like her. Friends were a luxury she was unaccustomed to indulging in, and a hazardous one at that, but Beatrice felt the lack more than Belinda ever allowed herself to.

"And will I have to share him with you?" Eliza's voice was still careful, her body still held in statuesque quietude. Belinda coughed out a derisive breath.

"A Lanyarchan provincial? His fascination for me is fleeting, Eliza. You'll have to share him with someone, but it won't be me. My sights aren't set that high."

"He's never shown even so much fascination for me." Strain cracked Eliza's voice now, making her sound more youthful than she was. Belinda finally dared move, taking herself to stand before Eliza and offer her a hand.

"There are four of you, and none of those men are your brothers. Giving yourself to any one of them changes the balance. Gives weight to that couple's desires over the other two. Javier is a prince. Royalty does not afford friends easily. It may be easier, and wiser, to refuse to see you, than to risk the only friendships that go back so far as to withstand the test of sovereignty. You were children," Belinda whispered. "Parents might care for the rank of person their children associate with, but children care nothing for it. You, I would think, most of all, more than Sacha or Marius, even, would stand that test. All you wanted was some pears." Her smile was fleeting and sad.

"How do you know us so well?" Eliza didn't take Belinda's hand, but her question lacked accusation, filled instead with resignation. Belinda lowered her eyes to the floor, self-same smile turning wry.

"Envy, perhaps," she replied, discomfited to find a degree of truth in that. Only a degree; the larger part was in needing to know, to see clearly, for her own survival. For the survival of her queen. "That, and I've been made a satellite around a body that works. Perhaps it's easier to see you from the outside, looking in."

Eliza sighed, turning her gaze away, and after long moments swore under her breath. "Have you ever had to grow your hair out from this length, Beatrice? It looks and feels horrible."

Belinda's mouth quirked, eyes bright. "We'll just have to find someone skilled enough with scissors to make it bearable. Or buy you a sheerly impossible number of wigs."

"With Javier's money." A note of bitterness sounded in that and Belinda, despite the earlier rebuff, deliberately reached for and caught Eliza's hand.

"Not if you don't want to. I have money of my own."

"I don't."

Belinda tilted her head, curious; Javier had accused Eliza of stealing more than a palmful of coin off him, and Eliza had claimed to him that she had cash. But that might have been a fob to make a prince cease worrying; there was no reason to suppose the cheap-side beauty still had the money. "Well, then. We'd better set about doing something about that, hadn't we?"

"You've taken her under your wing more fully than I'd expected, Bea." Javier lay sprawled on a divan in Belinda's sunroom, one long leg kicked over its edge, the other knocked up rakishly so his free hand could dangle over his knee. Belinda sat tucked into a chair beside him, allowing him her fingertips to pluck and drop idly as he watched her household run.

In ten days her home had been transformed. Eliza, given her head and a budget, had stalked through the Lutetian streets to make tightfisted deals with merchants bewildered by the stacks of coin she left even when they insisted a friend of the prince couldn't possibly be expected to pay for the wares she bought. She purchased cloth, bejewelments, threads, all manner of sewing material, and before the first day was out a quiet young woman appeared at Belinda's door, jaw set with determination. She would not, she explained hastily, be able to come back for the gown herself, but she would send her serving-maid. As it was, her mother believed her to be on the way to visit a friend, but rumour had sparked in the streets and she had seen for herself the gowns that Eliza wore. She wanted to be the first outside the prince's intimate circle to wear a fashion made *by* Eliza, and was willing to risk her mother's angry hand to have that first gown.

Eliza, irrationally offended at the link to Javier, had opened her mouth to refuse and Belinda had stepped on her toes with a solid heel, accepting the commission while Eliza's full mouth whitened with annoyance and pain.

"Don't be absurd," Belinda told her acerbically, once the girl was measured and gone again. "You've taken a loan out from me. I have no intention of letting you welsh on it through foolish pride. Now, unless you intend to sew every gown yourself, I'd suggest you turn some thought to hiring a seamstress or two, and if you've any sense you'll take one from your old address."

Eliza had spluttered, railed, and ultimately acquiesced. By morning she had three seamstresses, all from her old quarters, and Belinda had kept Nina running all morning to bathe the three more thoroughly than they'd ever known in their lives. Eliza's mouth had tightened, but she hadn't argued; there was no profit in staining expensive fabric with dirty hands, or holding it against bodies smelling of refuse and shit when there were baths to be had. One of the women nearly refused the hot water, until Eliza reminded her of the pay she'd be earning for a little cleanliness. Muttering about it being against God's will, the woman had climbed into the tub and emerged forty minutes later looking a decade younger than she had going in. She'd asked twice for a bath since then.

"It's not my wing," Belinda said mildly. "It's the chance unshadowed by your wings, my lord. I'm glad to help." She was privately delighted at how true that was; watching tautness fade from Eliza's stance as it became clear she could succeed on her own was worth the disruption to the household.

"Unshadowed," Javier murmured. Belinda shrugged.

"Close enough for her pride. They come to her now because of your friendship, but in six months' time they'll come for her creations, and in five years most of them won't remember she was your friend first."

"Will she make something for you?"

Belinda arched an eyebrow. "If I pay her, but if you'd like another gown to ruin on your garden floor, my lord, I'd as soon wear a muslin shift that can be replaced more easily."

"No." Humour curved Javier's mouth momentarily. "I want something to present you to my mother in."

"Your mother." Belinda's heart gave a sudden uncharacteristic thump, filling her throat. A note of panic cut through that fullness, Beatrice's shock at the idea of meeting the regent briefly overwhelming Belinda's own tense delight, though as seconds passed her own emotions conquered those of the role she played. She ached to meet Sandalia; after months in Gallin's capital city, waiting on the queen's return, she would finally have something to report to her "dearest Jayne." There had been no sudden move against Aulun in the months she'd spent in Lutetia; indeed, if a plot was moving at all, Belinda half felt it was she who lay at the heart of it. Perhaps Robert's intelligence was overblown.

Or perhaps the plotting of a queen's murder was a slow and careful thing. Belinda felt the prickle of hairs wanting to stand on her arms, and refused her body that tiny show of emotion. "I had not thought . . ." The protest was token, a whisper, something to ease the amusement on Javier's face.

"You can't go skulking about the back halls of the palace forever, and," he lowered his voice, "I have no intention of putting you aside just yet, for reasons you know well. Better you meet her," he said more briskly. "Become a part of the court. Perhaps you'll even find yourself a better match than Marius."

"Would you take me from him, then?" Belinda asked, allowing the question to distract her for a moment. "It's cruel enough what you've done. Would your friendship survive handing me to another noble?"

"Even if it were Sacha," Javier said with arrogant confidence. "Marius's heart would break, and in a week he'd find a new love. He's my man, Beatrice, and his soul is a true one."

"All the more reason to treat it well."

Javier sat up, copper hair falling into his eyes. "Beatrice, are you telling me you're in love with Marius? Do I keep you from your heart's match?" Teasing and jealousy both tinged the question, Javier's will flexing unconsciously toward her, as if to bend her to the answers he wanted to hear.

"No," Belinda said, neither influenced by his extended power nor lying. "But a loyal man should be treated well, not used callously for his good heart." As she'd used him, she reminded herself without rancor. His visits now were a paroxysm of discomfort, the merchant youth barely able to keep his eyes from Nina, nor willing to allow himself to look at her. Belinda's work on the serving girl's memory seemed to have held, and she showed no discomfort or interest in Marius's presence than was dictated by their classes. Belinda lifted a shoulder and offered Javier a smile, letting thoughts of Marius slip away. "No matter. I would be honoured to meet your mother, my lord prince. Is she . . . is she like you?" Belinda drew her fingers over his, the question light and cautious. He chuckled.

"Flat-chested and redheaded, you mean? No." A judicious pause. "She's a brunette."

Belinda laughed aloud, taken entirely by surprise. "I've seen paintings. She's not flat-chested, either. You know what I mean, Jav." Her voice lowered. "The witchpower." There was no more vital piece of information. She'd come to Gallin expecting the challenge of— Better not to think it, not when her own gifts could pluck thoughts from the air around someone she touched. She withdrew her hand from his, knowing Javier might keep a similar secret close to his own heart.

"Is your mother?"

Belinda thought of Lorraine, slender and elegant on her throne. She was fond of pearls, their creaminess playing up her pale skin. Belinda shook off the image as surely as she'd forbidden herself thoughts of her duties in Lutetia. "My mother died when I was born."

Javier shrugged, languid motion of dismissal. "Then there's no comparison to be made there. You and I are what we are, Beatrice. We won't worry about others, except in the impression you're to make on them. Have Eliza make you something innocent, Bea. Mother will know better, but she likes the illusion that the women I keep are nothing more than youthful playmates."

"As you wish, my lord."

10

There was nothing innocent to the gown's cut.

In a decade of learning to dress to hide herself, to please men, to make herself beautiful or plain, she had rarely worn something that made her feel as unrestrained as Eliza's design did. It was not that it was overly immodest, or lacking in underlayers; the gown Belinda and Javier had ruined had been more daring in that respect.

Part of it was the sleeves. Capped and ruffled, they followed the curve of her shoulder, just covering it, and left her arms bare. Belinda had objected: it was October, and the palace was often cold. Eliza sniffed without sympathy and handed her a cape.

Even that enhanced the gown. The cloak's ties, stretched across Belinda's collarbones, made the round scooped collar's dip seem all the more extravagant. Her breasts were shelved high, a new corset tucked beneath them, and a broad ribbon made a waist of the dress immediately beneath her bosom. It flowed loose from gathers below that, and above offered a shocking expanse of bared skin before a lace ruffle that scraped her nipples made a nod toward propriety.

Most extraordinarily, it was pink. Belinda had gaped at the fabric when it was brought in, unable to stop herself even as smugness played at Eliza's mouth. "I thought you were putting away mannish things," Belinda'd managed to protest, and earned Eliza's laughter for it.

"Who says only men can wear pink? Or would you pretend that you're too weak for the color, as they say women are?"

Beatrice might have stood her ground, but Belinda knew better than to fall for the taunt. She found herself eyeing the fabric more covetously despite herself, and had ignored Eliza's triumph. It was frothy muslin, so light it would take layer after layer to give it a decent weight. That, Eliza had agreed with, though the final dress still all but floated, and with the afternoon sun behind her Belinda knew full well her figure would be visible through the gown's layers. It was not at all innocent.

And yet, looking at herself in the mirror, her hair piled into ringlets that fell around her shoulders, even feeling lush and sensual, Belinda's reflection to her own eyes looked virginal and soft. Pure. The costume was so far from fashionable it would very possibly horrify Sandalia, but if its outrageousness passed muster, the effect was exactly as Javier had asked.

"What I want to know is what's beneath all that diaphanous material." Javier spoke from her bedroom door, his reflection appearing in her mirror only after his voice wrapped around her. Belinda tilted her head toward his image, smiling.

"I thought you were waiting for me at the palace."

"I thought I'd better investigate Eliza's creation, to make sure we weren't both to be humiliated." He came into the room, drawing the knot free from her cloak and catching it as it fell. "My mother may have a stroke, Beatrice."

"You said innocent," Belinda said lightly. "Would Eliza deliberately humiliate me in front of the queen?"

"No," Javier said so steadily Belinda believed him. "Mother likes Eliza, so far as she grasps her existence at all." He dropped a curious kiss on Belinda's bare shoulder. "Perhaps I should warn her you've been dressed by my friend. It might alleviate her shock somewhat."

"I have other, more ordinary gowns, Javier," Belinda murmured. "If you disapprove—"

"On the contrary. I approve enough that I'd prefer to keep you here and discover what's beneath that dress."

"I am, my lord." Belinda turned around with an impish smile and stood on her toes to brush her mouth against his ear. "Nothing you're unfamiliar with."

"You're a woman, Bea. It's a woman's gift to be eternally mysterious."

Belinda laughed aloud and kissed Javier a second time before threading her arm through his. "Your mother's taught you well. Shall we not keep her waiting, my lord prince? I do not," and for once Belinda spoke with all honesty, "want to make a bad impression."

"You won't," Javier promised, and with the murmured words, escorted her to the Gallic queen's court.

Sandalia, Essandian princess, queen of Lanyarch and regent of Gallin, was not a tall woman. Javier had done her a disservice with his teasing about her figure; even in the straitlaced corsets that were fashionable, her petite curves were hinted at. Nut-brown hair, richer than Belinda's, was neither dyed nor powdered to hide signs of aging; unlike Lorraine, Sandalia had years yet before age began to catch her. She'd borne Javier as little more than a child bride, her husband lost to battle within weeks of Javier's conception, and she had ruled Gallin in her son's name and with her brother Rodrigo's support for more than two decades.

Belinda was surprised to find her heart beating rapidly as she approached the throne. The assembly was far from the formal audience at which she'd met her own mother ten years earlier, but her own anticipation of the event was far more acute. Then, she had been preparing to kill a man for the first time, with no idea that meeting the Titian-haired queen would bring understanding to a vivid memory from the first moments of her life. Today she met another target, much higher in rank than the unfortunate Rodney du Roz had been.

Du Roz. Of the rose. A startling clarity and question fell over Belinda even as she heard Javier murmur her name, even as she curtsied deeply and kept her eyes lowered, waiting for Sandalia to assess her. In nearly all her guises she called herself Rose, or some variation thereof, stealing her father's pet name for her in deliberate deference to him, and making a purposeful connection to the girl she'd once been.

How much of it, she wondered for the first time, was an homage to the first man who's life she'd taken? Surprise burned her cheeks and she reached for stillness, then let it fade again: the flush might do her good under Sandalia's watchful eye. Let the Gallic queen think her a Lanyarchan provincial, shy and overwhelmed at meeting the woman who was arguably the rightful ruler of Belinda's homeland.

"Rise." Sandalia's voice was sweeter than Lorraine's, a soprano of operatic quality, if it could be trained to sing. Belinda straightened from her curtsey, daring to lift her eyes to the queen's for an instant, then dropping her gaze again as benefited her station. "We presume our son's little friend designed your gown, Lady Irvine."

Irritation flared in Javier's eyes, as open to Belinda as the impulse for a hard look that she doubted he would dare lay on his mother. A sting of sympathy went through her; Belinda, in Eliza's place, wouldn't care for the condescension in Sandalia's tone, either. That Javier felt outrage spoke better of him as a man than Belinda might have thought, and for an instant her heart softened toward him. There was nothing he could say, certainly not in public, that would not make him look the fool and insult his mother. One might be rude to street urchins, even, or especially, when they weren't present, but offending the queen was a mistake no one would dare.

"Yes, Your Majesty." Belinda's whisper barely reached the throne. Sandalia leaned forward, brushing her fingertips against her thumb, not quite a snap of sound.

"Come forward, Lady Irvine. Let us examine Eliza's artistry."

Javier's chagrin faded at the interest—no more than polite, but there—in Sandalia's tone, and at his mother's use of Eliza's name. Belinda took two careful steps up toward the throne, its daised height helping to make up for Sandalia's diminutive size. Jav's throne, angled to the right and a step below the queen's, still put his head nearly level with hers; she was, indeed, not a tall woman. "Turn," Sandalia ordered, and Belinda did, eyes cast out and up to examine the throne room briefly and thoroughly from the closest she might ever come to royalty's vantage.

Courtiers and hangers-on watched with envious eyes, belittling gazes, anger, and lust; they were a wash of colour, coveting Belinda's position above them and resenting her for it. It took no gift to understand that; she could see it from their expressions, painted with politeness that lay too thin over rage: there were daughters who belonged where she now stood, favoured of the prince. There were sisters who had been overlooked. Belinda would find no friends within the Lutetian court, though should she hold her place with Javier, she had no doubt that dagger-smiling women would flock to her side.

"Pink," Sandalia said when Belinda had completed her circuit. "An unusual shade for a woman, Lady Beatrice."

Sudden impishness caught Belinda with a smile. "It was that or a tartan, Your Majesty. Mademoiselle Beaulieu thought the dress better suited to pink." She let the Lanyarchan burr come through strong in her Gallic, everything about her delivery bright and delightful, though her heart hung between beats and she felt nothing but calculation as her gaze flickered to the queen again, seeking approval at her audacity.

Her heart crashed into motion again as Sandalia lifted an eyebrow so discreetly it didn't so much as mar the smooth skin of her forehead, then allowed herself a full-mouthed twist of a smile that reminded Belinda unexpectedly of Eliza. "We are inclined to agree." Sandalia's voice warmed a little more, her brown eyes curious on Belinda's face. "It is not an unattractive shade for a woman of your colouring. We're not certain we would see it as pink at all, if there were not so many layers to enhance it. Tell us, Lady Beatrice, do you think we would look well in Mademoiselle Beaulieu's fashions?"

Hope surged from Javier, so sharp and controlled it cut through Belinda's heart. She kept her eyes from him, knowing that the answer couldn't be tainted by seeking his approval; Sandalia would see that, and think less of her, and even more, less of Eliza, for it. But the queen had called Eliza by a title, far from the belittlement she'd first used, and that, combined with the question, emboldened Belinda to lift her gaze and study Sandalia's petite form with a cautiously critical eye.

"Your Majesty . . ." Belinda tilted her head, then took a deep breath, risking her place in Sandalia's court on a moment of truthfulness. "Your Majesty, if you will forgive a blunt Lanyarchan assessment, you have a form that women envy and men covet, and very likely the other way around as well." Dismay sparked from Javier's direction, but Belinda went on, eyes earnest on the queen. "This style of gown would enhance Your Majesty's finest assets and help to prove that youth's bloom is not yet gone from Your Majesty's face or figure. That said, Your Majesty is not especially tall, and truthfully, I would have to see one of mademoiselle's gowns on Your Majesty to say whether the straight lines of current fashion lend a gravitas and height that a woman of power might feel necessary, or whether the soft femininity of looser lines might enhance her strength in its own way. I would like very much to see it," she finished, deliberately wistful, then added a twist into her smile. "If for no other reason than I believe Your Majesty would look lovely in this fashion, and the idea of the Aulunian queen echoing it amuses me. It would suit Your Majesty; it would not suit her."

Nor would it. Belinda thought Lorraine too wise to fall for such an obvious prat, but she was vain and considered herself—rightfully, as a queen—as a maker of fashion. Moreover, there was something inherently youthful about the loose lines of Eliza's design, and Lorraine's vanity was tightly tied to an unaging, girlish self-image. To have such a fashion come out of Lutetia and to have it look poorly on her might injure an enormous pride that Belinda had no need to prick, but which suited Beatrice enormously.

Emotion raged behind Sandalia's mild expression. Belinda could all but taste it, sudden glee on the Essandian princess's part at the idea of flaunting the sixteen-year gap between her age and Lorraine's. Belinda had no need to touch the queen's hand and read her thoughts: amusement and avarice washed off her, almost as clear as words, and echoed the lines Belinda wanted her to follow. Setting a new fashion, one that played to her youth, would remind not just the Gallic and Essandian peoples but the Aulunians, that Lorraine was aging, and Sandalia still so young as to be able to bear another heir. That she was only just young enough hardly mattered; Lorraine, at fifty-five, still seemed to flirt with the idea, and if a people could accept that, they could far more readily believe that thirty-nine-year-old Sandalia might mother a second child.

Moreover, there was the question of Javier. Lorraine had no heir and Javier, as grand-nephew to Lorraine's father's, first—and by the Ecumenical church, only legitimate—wife, had in the eyes of many the only genuine claim to the Aulunian throne. Sandalia was comfortable in her position as regent, reluctant to give away her power to a son whom some murmured should have taken the throne at his sixteenth year. Reminding Aulun of Javier's presence, even in so simple a way as introducing new fashions that played to vitality and beauty, could benefit an intention to set the prince on Aulun's throne, leaving her own seat in Gallin unchallenged.

Belinda lowered her eyes, no longer certain if she followed Sandalia's emotion or her own—*plan*, she found herself thinking, and the stillness came over her whether she wanted it to or not.

We face insurrection against our own beloved queen. Robert's words hung heavily in Belinda's mind, his voice as clear as if she heard him speaking now. She had come to Lutetia to seek out a plot against a pretender reaching for Aulun's throne, and to whisper word of that plot in her father's ear when the time came. That the seeds of it lay dormant in the men and women she'd met, Belinda had no doubt. It was too soon, too soon by far, to know whether Sandalia herself strove for the ends threatened by Robert's warning, but something new shaped itself now. If those ends were not yet in place, then Belinda herself might put them there, might push and prod the pieces into place in order to devastate Gallin and Essandia alike, leaving Aulun and Lorraine and the Reformation unchallenged in western Echon.

Coldness spurted through Belinda's hands, alien ambition rising in her so rapidly that only the safety of self-imposed and uncrackable control kept her breath from quickening. All her life she had been sent to spy, to do murder, and to inspire treacherous lust. Never had she found herself so close to guiding strings with her own fingers. There did not have to be rebellion to root out, nor a queen piece to dislodge. She could *build* the rebellion, and damn a princess in the making of it.

Inexplicable joy tore her heart upward, giving it the wings of desire and excitement, so unfamiliar to her as to nearly undo her. For an instant even her control faltered, a smile of astonishment playing at her lips. Had Robert intended her to step into such a powerful position, or did his intelligence lead him to deeper plots than she had yet seen? The latter she would discover, and the former, if it was not so, would be a jewel in her crown of quiet triumphs.

Sandalia saw the smile that touched Belinda's lips and read it the only way she could, her voice light and amused. "It is a dangerous thing to heap laughter on one monarch's head when you stand in the presence of another, Lady Beatrice."

Belinda lifted her gaze to the Gallic queen and let her smile come more fully, no repentance in it. "Yes, Your Majesty."

To her delight, Sandalia laughed aloud and Javier, at his mother's right elbow, slumped a few inches in his seat, shooting Belinda a look that told her all too clearly what a fine line she'd chosen to walk. She didn't dare drop a wink of reassurance, both propriety and her own relief preventing it, but her smile crinkled her eyes, more emotion than she was accustomed to letting through. "We will see your Eliza in our private chambers next week, Javier," Sandalia said. "We prefer not to be offered pink. You may go."

Fierce delight and a thick wave of gratitude swept out from the ginger-haired prince, though he merely inclined his head and crooked a small smile of his own. "Yes, Mother. I'll tell her." He stood, executing an elegant bow to the tiny woman who'd birthed him, and Sandalia put a hand on his arm as he turned away.

"Do not become too attached, Javier." She spoke precisely loud enough for the command to reach Belinda's ears as well as her son's. "Your young lady is bold and clever, but Essandia and Gallin's crown prince will not marry a Lanyarchan upstart."

"I never dreamed he would." Javier pitched his voice as she had, courtiers straining to hear and to look as though they weren't trying to. "Nor did she."

"Women always say that." Sandalia released Javier's arm, then offered Belinda a token that would have the court dancing on her wishes: "We would enjoy your company at supper tomorrow evening, Lady Beatrice. Wear something impetuous, and be prepared to discuss Lanyarch and Cordula. I would fain to hear how our sister Ecumenics do under Alunaer's rule."

"Your Majesty." Belinda curtsied so deeply as to doubt her own ability to rise again, Javier saving her from an ignominious failure by offering a hand as she began to straighten. She ducked her head in thanks and slipped her fingers into the crook of his elbow, listening to a wave of murmurs crest before them and ripple after them as they left the hall.

Only outside it did she clutch Javier's arm in half-real alarm. "Wear something impetuous?" she whispered. "What would she have me do, wrap a sheet in ribbon and leave my breast bared, like the statues of ancient Parna?"

Javier laughed aloud, as easily as his mother had done moments earlier. "We'll ask Eliza to dress you, and your tongue will be impetuous enough. What were you thinking, Bea? Comparing Mother to Lorraine?"

"Comparing her favourably," Belinda retorted. "Sandalia is nearly as close to belonging on the Aulunian throne as my queen as you are to belonging on it as my king. She should sit in Lanyarch as queen and you are to be crown prince to—"

"To a land of rabble-rousers in skirts, by your reckoning," Javier said coolly, "as well as heir to Essandia and Gallin."

Ice flew over Belinda's skin, caution come too late. She drew her lower lip into her mouth, a show of contriteness that went deeper than she expected it to. "I'm sorry, my lord." The apology was whispered, all she dared. "I meant no disrespect for the position you now hold. It is only—"

"An endless desire to replace Lorraine with an Ecumenic ruler," Javier said, still cool. "Your lust, Beatrice, has better places to show itself. I will not hear words of sedition against Aulun spoken near my mother, not when the Titian Bitch seeks any excuse she can find to unseat her and have her put to death."

"Sandalia is a queen in her own right," Belinda said steadily. "It does not do to openly commit regicide, even if, especially if, you're another regent. Take her power, yes, I'm sure Lorraine would do that. But having her killed, Javier." Her voice softened. "I think even the Aulunian queen would balk at that."

More than Beatrice's naïveté allowed Belinda to speak the protest. Lorraine's reluctance to have another sovereign put to death was a topic at her court, discussed vigorously, well out of the queen's hearing. Men thought it a sign of a woman's weakness and her unsuitability to rule; women, if they thought anything, kept it to themselves, opinions private enough that not even Robert knew how the ladies of the court felt about the queen's reticence in securing her throne through bloodshed. Belinda believed them to think as she did, *because* she did, that regicide was a dangerous precedent, and should it be used it must be done untraceably. It was not weakness, but prudence, and moreover, a public and well-known horror of such means could only stand the queen well should her rivals fall unexpectedly.

A bloom of satisfaction took Belinda's breath, then eased it into a smile. She made it winsome, turned it on Javier in hopes of soothing his pique, and let herself ride pleasure that had nothing to do with gross physical delight and everything to do with a necessary job done well. *It cannot be found out.* It never would be. There were far worse things than a lifetime spent in the shadows: a lifetime of uselessness was a condemnation Belinda couldn't imagine. Lorraine could, and would, retain her moral stance, and might well never know the details of the dance that helped keep her enthroned. She did not, in Belinda's estimation, need to; impossible choices could be lifted from a queen's hands and given over to another to ease her way as easily as might happen for anyone else. More easily, perhaps: the royal name inspired a loyalty that an ordinary man might never command.

"I think you understand less than you imagine of the affairs of royalty," Javier snapped, unmoved by her hopeful smile. "Being on my arm does not make you privy to the thoughts or means of those above you." His witchpower was extended, an unconscious and indomitable expectation that she would acquiesce. Belinda permitted herself the luxury of imagining to grind her teeth, imagining tightening her fingers on his arm in irritation, all in a core of her so deep she barely felt relief from those internal allowances. Pride, strange thing that it was, would not allow her to actually roll beneath the prince's will, but unlike the moment of challenge at the drinking house, she at least did not stand against it, did not meet his urge to conquer with her own untouchable centre of stillness.

"I'll watch my tongue, my lord," she murmured instead. "Forgive me my impertinence."

Javier relaxed, confident of his supremacy. "It's easy to forget your provinciality," he offered magnanimously, then dropped his voice to add, "particularly knowing that which we share."

Belinda deliberately dimpled, stepping ahead to twitch her skirts at him, eyes bright with mischief. "A bed, my lord?"

Javier surged toward her with a laughing growl, and she skipped out of reach with an obligatory squeal. An instant later they were running down the halls of the palace, the one after the other, given over to playfulness that different circumstances forbade both from often indulging in.

"I am bored with these tricks, my lord. There must be more the power can do." Belinda lay on her belly on Javier's bed, shoes abandoned and her feet kicked up behind her, a palmful of witchlight glowing in her hand. It winked out as she spread her fingers, earning Javier's scowl.

"It took me months to call the light consistently, Beatrice. You can't abandon your practise after a few weeks because you find it dull, nor can we risk pursuing our gifts too far. You know what would happen if we were found out."

Beatrice flung away his protest with a wave of her hand, fully aware he was right and still too impatient to bow to his will. "How old were you when you began, my lord?" she said irritably. "I'm an adult, my power matured."

"I was ten," Javier admitted. "But that means nothing."

"It means everything," Belinda said. "You flex your power, Javier, weight others with your will. I wrap myself, hide myself, in mine. I'd been practising that for years by the time I was ten, long before power woke in me."

"Power you hid until I showed you it could be used," Javier said shortly. "Women fear strength, Beatrice. You should see that from your own behavior. Now make the witchlight again."

Unwilling to throw the truth in his teeth, Belinda schooled her features and called another palmful of light to her hands. She wouldn't allow irritation to fuel the soft golden orb; that would give Javier a score in a battle she could barely define. She wanted her strength to come from the control she'd learned through a lifetime's practise, not from raw, manipulatable emotion. She heard Javier say, "Good," and ignored him, subsuming annoyance beneath hard-won dominance. The witchlight wavered before stillness won out, serene confidence brightening her globe to brilliance.

"Javier." Belinda looked up, half-imagining warmth radiating from the light between her fingers. The prince turned to look at her, golden shadows warming his face and turning his eyes the shade of her magic. She sat up on her knees, cupping power, and flashed a smile. "Catch."

The impulse to throw it overhand, as hard as she could, shot through her. Instead she underhanded it, refusing the urge to use strength. It spun through the air in a delicate fiery arc.

The air between herself and Javier flexed, Javier's will thundering as though she'd offered an attack and he could end it by over-whelming her. Silver shot through the air, a shield of his own moonlit power. Belinda's ball splashed against it, golden fire rain-ing down in droplets, and she flinched back, feeling the impact as if she'd crashed against something solid herself. Javier's eyes rounded, youthful dismay that brought forth a laugh that Belinda usually kept well under control. An external focus of power certainly had its uses, but the prince would never match her ability to hide expressions. She stretched out her hand, calling the fallen sparks of witchlight back to her, and held them against her bosom when they'd returned, her eyes bright on Javier's. "Did you feel it?"

Javier's slow one-sided smile answered more thoroughly than words. "Try it again."

"And have my nose smacked up against a shield again? I think not." Belinda rubbed her nose in offense, then lobbed her power with her free hand, deliberately winging it wide.

Javier fell into a fighting stance, eyes snapping to the golden ball even as silver creased the air again. Belinda put intensity behind the desire to stop her power's movement, and it brushed against Javier's shimmering shield with a tingling caress instead of painful force. He split an astonished grin and she curled her toes under herself, lower lip caught in her teeth as they both stared at aspects of magic dancing with each other in the prince's bedchamber.

"We should stop." Javier's voice had no conviction. "Can you imagine what it looks like from outside? Fire darting across my room and light glowing bright and white like no torch anyone's ever seen?"

"The curtains are drawn. There's nothing to fear, Javier. Or will you be content with always hiding your skill, never pursuing its depths? I will not." Belinda tossed her hair as Javier's expression darkened.

"We dare not show it, Beatrice. Tell me you're not that great a fool."

"I'm not." Belinda brought a second ball of witchlight into

being, the first one flickering but holding its position as fresh light cupped itself in her palm. "But look what you've done here, with just a little push. Shields, Javier. What else is possible? Can you make it invisible, so it can be used in battle?" She sent her own magic rolling out of her palm, taking a slow and circuitous route toward Javier as he glanced first at her, then at his own shielding. Concentration made a line between his ginger eyebrows, and the silver sheen of power faded a little at the edges. He exploded a breath of air, nearly a laugh, and shook his head.

"I may have to claim it's Gabriel here to protect my royal arse. I don't know if I can take the moonlight away, Bea. It's always been there."

"Concentrate." The word came hard, Belinda's attention split three ways, but Javier gave no notice of her second attack until golden witchlight spun out behind him and wrapped itself around his eyes. He shouted, clawing at his face, and his shield failed. Belinda shot up onto her knees, hand extended to direct her first attack toward the prince, who roared in offense as witchlight invaded his chest.

Laughter burst forth from Belinda's throat and lost her concentration in doing so, both hands clapped over her mouth. For all her complaints, Javier was right: they couldn't afford to be found out. The witchlight blindfold she'd wrapped him with faded and he glowered at her, shooting a cautious look at the door. No one came to it, his guards on the other side evidently unconcerned with noise. Her laughter, Belinda thought, might have been the saving grace after Javier's shout.

For a moment they faced each other, both panting with effort before Javier curled his lip as if to damn the consequences and pooled silver light in his palms. With an instant's thought he split the ball of power into two and lobbed them, one after the other, toward Belinda. She shrieked, half startlement and half play, and flung herself across the bed, dodging physically even as she tried to focus on the idea of hardening the stillness, pushing it out of her as a force of its own.

Silver splattered against a brief golden shield, the reverberated impact less startling than her success. Javier shouted with pleasure and Belinda, half off the bed, lobbed another handful of power at him. He ducked, not bothering to shield, and power exploded behind him as it smashed into the wall, leaving a scar above unlit candles. They both gaped at the mark on the wall before Javier turned toward Belinda, censure warring with admiration.

Heavy pounding on the door startled them both badly enough to jump, and Javier's expression shot toward anger before he swept his hand over the mark on the wall and stalked toward the door, yanking it open. "All's well," he said sharply to a dismayed guard. Then, unexpectedly, a snigger ran over his face and he added, "A little disagreement over how the candles ought to be arranged. They said we gingers are tempermental, but God save me from the brunette in my bedroom. You've heard nothing at all, of course."

The guard looked in nervously, eyeing the scarred wall and Belinda in equal parts. She scrambled for the edge of the bed, twisting her hands behind herself guiltily, as though she might be holding one of the maligned candles. Something in the guard's expression changed, as though he was trying not to laugh at his betters, and then he stepped back with a rap of his fist against his chest. Javier closed the door and turned on Belinda, who ran to him, hands against his chest as she looked up with laughter and adoration in her gaze. "I am trouble," she whispered in delight. "And you, my lord, you are control and restraint and—"

He put his hands over hers, silencing her with the gesture. Belinda drew a sharp breath, words lost beneath Javier's grey gaze and the things his touch told her. Even in his irritation he sparked with life, a joy unrecognizable to him after a lifetime of solitude. She had brought that to him, saving him from lonely constraint;

saving him from the Hell that he was sure was his for all eternity. For a few aching seconds her heartbeat matched his, breath stolen beneath an exquisite agony that knew he could not keep her, and still found itself daring to hope he might find a way.

The strength of passion undid Belinda, leaving her gazing at Javier in astonishment. A lifetime of duty had never warned her of being needed, not for herself; only for what she could do. Hunger crawled up through Belinda's body, claws of determination curling in her groin and stinging her breasts, a taste of ambition burning away thought. She slipped her hands from beneath Javier's and knotted them at his hips, making a clean insatiate line of her body against his. "Look at who we are together, my lord, my love, my prince. Think of what we could do together. Think of the thrones we could hold."

But for all that he desired her, he went still, eyes darkening to silver. "We, Beatrice?"

Rage, pure and unexpected, took Belinda's voice and flooded her body until she felt as though heat poured off her. It captured her power, building it higher, alien and exciting. Javier had no right, no place, in questioning her use of *we*, not when her power was clearly as great as his. It burgeoned inside her, begging to be used. It would be easy, deliciously easy, to let that rage ignite the very air, to burn Javier where he stood for daring, *daring*, to question her—!

Belinda forced clenched teeth into a smile, internal struggle more violent than anything she could remember. Pushing away outrageous anger and slowing her heartbeat should be the work of a moment, the calm of stillness captured and wrapped about her. Instead witchpower flexed and fought her will, demanding Javier acknowledge her as equal, even superior: she could do what he did not, disappear from plain sight, manipulate others into acting as she desired. He could be used like any man, made to think well of himself and his cleverness while all the time doing her bidding.

That he stood against her was exciting, profoundly interesting, but his gambit would ultimately fail: he was only male, slave to her will.

Belinda shuddered from her core all the way to her skin, so profound Javier caught her out of concern, despite the challenge she'd laid at his feet. Eyes closed against another surge of unaccustomed ambition, she whispered, "We both know I could never stand at your side and share power, but I might offer it to you in support, from behind those thrones you conquered. I meant nothing more, my lord. Forgive me." She opened her eyes, procuring a weak smile that had more to do with deep-seated uncertainty about her own impulse to dominate than the sought apology Javier would see it for. "Once more I've failed to watch my tongue, and I'd only just promised I would do so."

Mollified, he drew her closer again, voice dropped as he murmured, "Then perhaps I should watch it for you, Beatrice."

Belinda trembled, subsuming the outraged witchpower as she tilted her head back and opened her mouth to the prince's.

11

JAVIER, PRINCE OF GALLIN
9 November 1587 † Lutetia

"She isn't your usual type, Javier." Sandalia is watching her son, making him uncomfortable, though he doesn't dare let that show. He left Beatrice sleeping off the aftermath of sex in his bedchambers hours ago, and he has been thinking, pacing, avoiding everyone ever since.

Even now he paces the confines of Sandalia's chambers, reaching for wine, nibbling on sweetmeats. He isn't hungry, but better to let his mother believe that's the problem than delve deeper. "She's pretty enough," Sandalia admits, "but you've always had an eye for the slender blondes." Amusement suffuses her words. He thinks of her as a happy woman, he realises. She is many things, of course—focused, intent, a queen—but in the end, to Javier, she is his mother, and she is happy. "Deliberately avoiding comparisons to your mother, I imagine. What draws you to her?"

Javier imagines, briefly, telling the truth. Daring to explain, as he has never dared, the witchpower that he thought was his burden alone. Daring to pool light in his palms and explain that his will is its source.

As always, since childhood, caution stays him. He believes, must believe, that his mother wouldn't condemn him as a monster, but while Sandalia is earthier than her brother Rodrigo, she's also a true Ecumenic queen, and he can't imagine making her believe that his abilities aren't the devil's tricks.

Especially when he doesn't believe it himself.

It's easier, now that he has Beatrice. Now that he knows he's not the only one gifted, or cursed, with the witchpower. He's continuously surprised that a woman should share his powers, but better a woman than a man. Beatrice's sex gives him an easy excuse to spend time with her. Should he have discovered another man with such skills, the hours they'd spend together training would have all of Echon snickering in their sleeves at Sandalia's only heir. It's not a path Javier has any interest in taking, all the more so given how desire helps to focus the witchpower for use.

"She's useful, Mother" is what he allows himself to say. It's all he can allow himself to say, even if he were to leave the question of witchpower itself behind. The pain that sears through him at the thought of losing Beatrice takes his breath, and to confess to more than her use would have Sandalia remove her from his life permanently. "The night Marius brought her to meet us—"

"You're the only son of a royal house I know who means more than one person when he says us," Sandalia interrupts. Javier smiles because she expects him to and waits a moment to see if she's going to follow that familiar path of scolding before he goes on.

"That night she named me the true heir to Aulun," he says when it's clear he's been given a reprieve from that particular lecture. "Even a brunette catches my attention that way."

"Did you stop to think that might be what she wanted?"

"Mother," he says impatiently, "I'm the prince of Gallin. I think the last time I met a woman who didn't want to catch my attention she was ten and trying to steal pears from our gardens. Of course I did. But even if she was, if she's bold enough to do it that way, then she may be reckless enough to help—" He breaks off, unwilling to speak specific terms, even in a room where no one is supposed to be spying. "Reckless enough to help," he repeats, and makes it a finished sentence.

Sandalia, less paranoid or more confident than he, laughs. "Help? What would you have her do, Javier? Wrangle an introduction to the Aulunian court and slip poison into Lorraine's tea?"

Javier exhales. "I had a different plan." This is a moment of danger, one he barely recognizes himself for risking. It borders on sentiment, a weakness Javier never thought himself to share, with the exceptions of his childhood friends. For those three he will do anything. To find himself about to propose what he intends to, in order to retain contact with the only other witchbreed being he's ever found—and in order to threaten the Aulunian throne, he reminds himself—speaks of something his mother might see as vulnerability.

It is never wise to show weakness to royalty.

Sandalia's eyebrows quirk, invitation to continue. Javier puts down his wineglass and picks it up again, cursing himself for the tell even as he does so. "This is not," he begins, "intended as a long-term arrangement." He has to say that first, or she'll never listen. He has to say it first, to establish to himself that it's true. Interest and amusement light Sandalia's eyes at that opening foray. She gestures to the wine, and he pours her a cup, brings it to her grateful for the physical distraction. "Lanyarch is without a king since Charles's death," he says as he does so. "Either out of respect for you or fear of Lorraine, no one has come forth to put on a pretender's crown since you fled the country."

"Let's pretend respect," Sandalia says drily. "I know this, Javier."

"Lanyarch is still Aulun's greatest threat as an Ecumenic neighbor to the north, contentious and chafing under Reformation rule. But the threads that tie us there are slender, Mother. You're a widow, not a daughter of any Lanyarchan nobility, and you have no children by Charles." He smiles suddenly, bright and disarming. "Unless you've hidden one all these years?"

"I'm beginning to consider claiming that," Sandalia says, though she's smiling. "If you don't reach your point."

Javier is avoiding doing just that, and knows it. He takes a sip of wine—a small sip, because he wants a large one—and says, "The Lady Irvine is Lanyarchan nobility, however minor."

Sandalia takes it where he wants her to, dark eyes widening momentarily. "You would propose marrying her to strengthen your claim to the Lanyarchan throne? Javier—"

"I would propose engaging myself to her to see if fear can shake Lorraine Walter out of her royal seat," Javier corrects. "If we can push her to invasion or war, Mother, then Lanyarch can call on Cordula for help. We all only seek an excuse." He falls silent a moment, caught by childhood schoolings, and beneath his breath murmurs, "How many centuries is it since Aulun held Gallin's throne in any meaningful way, or since Gallin has reigned with true power over Aulun? Two? More? And still we rattle back and forth at one another like angry children, each of us certain the other has stolen our toys. Hatred runs old and deep, the reasons long forgot."

His mother's gaze goes cool. "It's only a lifetime since Aulun splintered from the Church, and in that time her Reformation has spread to Echon's northern states. Our reasons are fresh, Javier, and born of a hope to see all the world safe in the arms of Christ, not led astray by weakness of flesh and mind. If you can't remember that now, how can I trust you with a war for a throne?"

Not so very long ago, Javier realises, that lecture would have sent his head ducking down and apologies to his lips. Now he lifts his eyes to Sandalia's with neither fear nor regret, and knows with certainty and a small shock of joy that Beatrice has helped him come this far. "The Church is an excuse, Mother, and if you can't admit it to yourself, at least I can. The wherefores of this plot run far deeper than Lorraine's father and his cuckholding ways. But let it be," he adds, smoothing away the disagreement with a gesture. "What matters is that if an engagement to Irvine can shake the

THE QUEEN'S BASTARD • 271

Red Queen's grasp on Aulun, her reign may fall beneath the combined might of Gallin's army and Essandia's navy."

Sandalia is silent for long moments before she nods and admits,
"Clever. It's a clever thought. But how much of it is born of sentiment, Javier?"

He will not allow himself a guilty wince. Instead he shrugs,
loose and casual, hoping the cost of that doesn't show. "Some. I
like her. But she's not meant to be a queen, Mother, and I know
that. I'll need to do better than her to hold even Gallin's throne,
much less Aulun's."

"There's Irina's daughter," Sandalia says thoughtfully. Javier's
eyebrows wrinkle until his head hurts.

"She's fourteen."

"As was I the first time I was wed," Sandalia reminds him acerbically. "Besides, if you're to do this she'll be more than old enough
by the time you're able to break with Irvine and still hold two
thrones." To his astonishment, he realises she's genuinely considering his proposal, and he wonders if it's not as rash as he first conceived. "For God's sake, Javier, whatever you do, don't get her
pregnant."

"Ivanova?" he asks lightly. "I'm overwhelmed by your belief in
my manhood, Mother, but I'm afraid it won't reach all the way to
Khazar by itself."

Sandalia gives him a sharp look that makes the jape worthwhile.
"Irvine no more wants a pregnancy than I do. Don't worry,
Mother." An impulse hits him, though: what would their child be
like? Heir to witchpower from both parents, trained in it since
birth? Echon might never have imagined such power in such a
ruler.

Sandalia interrupts his musings with a snort that belies her delicate prettiness. "The only reason a woman bedding a prince hopes
to not become pregnant is if she fears for her bastard's life when a
legitimate heir comes along. Ask her to marry you and she'll lose

that concern, Javier, so for God's sake, watch yourself. Make sure she watches herself."

He finds himself holding his breath, as if he's a child again. "Does that mean you approve?"

"It has merit," Sandalia allows. "It would have more if your Beatrice were of more significant rank, but the tie to Lanyarch . . ." Her expression turns sour, a sure indicator that she wishes she'd thought of the ploy herself. "It's well thought out. Making Lorraine nervous is an entertaining way to pass the winter, if nothing else."

"And come spring," Javier says lowly. Sandalia nods, slow and thoughtful.

"Come spring," she agrees. "Come spring."

BELINDA PRIMROSE / BEATRICE IRVINE
9 November 1587 † *Lutetia*

"Whisper seditious promises in my ear, Irvine." Asselin caught Belinda on her own street, dragging her toward evening-made shadows between houses. She protested, one sharp startled sound, and he curled a lip, crowding her into darkness roughly enough to make passersby studiously look away. Belinda put her hands against his chest, thrust him back, and for a moment imagined him falling many feet to a snow-covered courtyard below. There were damp patches of white stuck to the Lutetian streets even now, enough to make the momentary vision seem real, memory of a lifetime past overlaying the world in which she now lived. Irritation flashed through Asselin's hazel eyes as Belinda fixed him with a steady gaze.

"You will behave with decorum, Lord Asselin. Javier's favour still rests with me. He won't take lightly hearing you've manhandled me."

"Do you think that?" Sacha sneered. "You're a tool to be used, Irvine, nothing more, and I'll have my use of you as much as he will." He caught her upper arm, pulling her close with a hard grip. "You've gotten no movement from him. Nothing. No whisper of ambition. What good are you if spreading your legs doesn't make him jump to serve you?"

"Why the hurry, Asselin?" Belinda breathed the question, making it light and mocking. She sympathized with Sacha's impatience, eager for movement herself, but her life had taught her patience. The plot to create or kill a king was not a thing to happen swiftly in its beginning stages. Only when a certain critical momentum was reached did things begin to move at inevitable, unstoppable speed. They would all, in time, fall prey to the trap Belinda felt more and more certain was hers to build, a dangerous game to keep her own queen mother unchallenged on the Aulunian throne. "You're young. Javier is young. Surely you've no personal stake in making the prince a king so quickly, have you? Is it your own desire agitating for Ecumenic domination in Aulun again, or does someone feed your ambition and your pocket? Does someone hunger for results and heap recriminations upon your head and your bank because they are not swift enough in arriving?"

For all of Asselin's skill in dissembling, that talent could not deny the touch of his hand against her arm or Belinda's twist of witchpower, seeking his thoughts through that touch.

Guilt and anger surged through the link, powerful enough to obscure words. His actions hid emotion beautifully, used the anger to bury guilt as he closed a powerful hand around Belinda's throat. "Do not imagine I would hesitate to kill you for saying such things, Irvine. Javier is my prince and my loyalty is his. My impatience stems from a man in his prime dancing and dawdling on his mother's weak will, when he should move forward and claim what is his under Cordula's banner. Don't think his favouritism will protect you from me if you fail to move him, or if you question my loyalty again."

Belinda, incongruously, thought of the small dagger tucked at her spine, and opened her mouth to let go a shaking laugh that told Asselin she was cowed. Eyes averted, she swallowed nervously against the pressure on her throat and dared a tiny nod. The corsets beneath Eliza's fashions were looser, shaped more like a woman's natural form, only tightening to shelve the breasts against the low-cut necklines. There was no easy way, of course, to get to the dagger, not so long as she remained clothed, but stripped to her undergarments she could slip her fingers under the corset and free the blade. It had never been bloodied in battle, only in practise.

Someday, Belinda promised herself as she swallowed against the pressure on her throat, it would find Sacha Asselin's heart's blood.

"Forgive me, my lord. I spoke in jest, nothing more." As her laughter could be read as supplication, the quaver in her voice could be interpreted as fear, not the hard delight of an oath made. Triumph rose in him, obscuring anger and guilt, and words whispered through the grip he held on her arm: —*does not wish to wed a prince, but a king*—

He released her with a spat curse, Belinda's hand going to her throat as if she could massage breath back into her body, though eagerness for explanation behind the stolen thoughts overrode any discomfort she felt. Only one person she knew might dare to want a king instead of a prince, for all that the prince was far out of her grasp as it was.

"Perhaps you need Eliza on your side." Pragmatic Eliza's ambitions couldn't have risen so high, and yet it was far too easy to see how they might have. An ache of unfamiliar sympathy shot upward through Belinda's chest, spiking in her throat. She quelled it with stillness: it was not her place to care for the pieces that were moved on the board, only to make certain of their alignment. It was easier not to care from the guise of a servant girl, though, removed from the intimate interactions of lifelong friends. This would be the only time in Belinda's life that she played so public a role—indeed, to do so again would be to invite exposure—and she found that the larger part of her was glad. Caring made her vulnerable, and she was unaccustomed to and displeased with the sensation.

Sacha answered her unspoken question with a sharp look. "She's not to be any part of this. My name, Marius's money, those might save us. Eliza's got nothing. Not even the patronage of the queen could keep her safe if she were part of plans that went awry."

"How long have you protected her?" Belinda hesitated over the penultimate word, knowing Asselin would hear the pause and interpret it as hinting at another: *loved*. His lip curled, equal parts confession and dismissal.

"Long enough to know what I'm about. She shares your roof, Irvine. Make sure she doesn't share your secrets." He turned on his heel and stalked away, slush splashing around his feet. Belinda held her hand at her throat, her lips pursed as she watched him go. Whether he'd finished with her or whether Eliza was a delicate enough topic to drive him away, she wasn't certain. If it was the latter, that would be useful in the future, for all that the idea of using Javier's friends against one another sent a shiver of regret over Belinda's skin.

"Weakness," she murmured to herself. It was weakness to be concerned with any one of them. That thought fixed in mind, the stillness drawn around her like armour, she straightened her gown and her shoulders and stepped out of the shadows to climb her front steps. She would have to watch the mirror carefully for signs of bruising on her throat, and entreat Nina to find the best cosmetics to hide evidence of Sacha's visit.

JAVIER, PRINCE OF GALLIN
10 November 1587 † *Lutetia*

Of all people, it is Marius he feels he must ask permission of. He, a prince of the realm—a prince of several, to hear Beatrice tell it, and the truth is, she's right—finds himself at a merchant boy's door somewhere past midnight, further in his cups than any sensible man should be, most especially one of his status.

He cannot, for some reason, bring himself to knock. His carriage waits on the street, coachman patient or at least silent, and Javier de Castille, son of Louis IV and Sandalia de Costa, can't bring himself to knock on the front door of his friend's home. The coachman will wait all night. The coachman may have to. Javier sways, wine surging through his blood and making him dizzy. He reaches for the door to keep himself steady, and to his shock, it opens beneath his hand.

Marius, tousle-headed and bleary-eyed, stands before him with an expression that Javier can't decipher. He is not surprised, the dark-haired merchant's son, not at all surprised for a man who's appeared at his own front door for no obvious reason, somewhere after the small bells of the morning have begun to toll. He stands there, looking up at his prince—Marius is well-built, broad enough of shoulder and slim enough of hip, but has nothing of Javier's height, or Sacha's bulk, for that matter. He looks up at his prince, and his prince looks down at him, and finally Marius steps out of the door and says, "I expect you should come in, whatever it is." There's little doubt in his voice: he knows as clearly as Javier does that "whatever" is Beatrice. It's merely a matter of discovering what particular hell being the prince's friend will now cost.

Javier does, because his other choice is to spill—or spew, given how much he's drunk—his guts on the threshold. He asks, "What are you doing up?" as he steps in, and regards it as a stupid question. So, it seems, does Marius, who chuffs something like laughter and closes the door behind Javier. Darkness overwhelms them; Marius in his sleeping shirt and bare feet isn't so much as carrying a candle to light his way, and the flickering streetlights outside are too distant to penetrate the curtained windows of the entrance gallery.

"I heard the carriage, and then felt you pacing." Marius says this as if it's natural, and Javier wonders if it is. Suddenly the answer is important, and he grasps Marius's shoulder.

"Felt me?"

"You're a lead weight to be around when you've got something on your mind, Jav. You always have been. It brings the rest of us down, like you're a drowning man clinging to our ankles. You know that. No one comes out unscathed when you're in a mood."

"I didn't. I didn't know." Javier's not precisely sure that's true; he's been careful for so many years not to influence his friends consciously with the witchpower, it's never occurred to him that he might be doing so accidentally. "I'm sorry."

"You're soused," Marius says, not unkindly. "Come on to the kitchen. Some bread will sop up some of that drink." He guides Javier, who hasn't released his shoulder, down the dark hall and down a short set of wooden stairs into a kitchen lit by the banked embers of a fire. Only when Javier is seated in front of the hearth does it come to him to demand, childishly, "How do you know I'm drunk?"

"Two things." Marius tears off a chunk of bread from a new loaf; the cook will be outraged come morning. "First, you smell like a brewery." He hands Javier the bread and roots around for a knife, unwrapping cheese as he speaks. "And second, you never apologize for anything unless you're too drunk to remember your position." Now he brings his prince the cheese and pulls a stool closer to the fire, studying Javier in the red-tinted light. "Is she pregnant, then?"

"Fuck," Javier says, and for long moments can think of nothing else to say. "Fuck, Mar, you're not even supposed to know I'm swivving her."

"My lord prince," Marius says so diplomatically Javier knows the next words will be insulting. Nor does Marius disappoint. "Just how fucking stupid do you think I am?"

"I don't think you're stupid," Javier protests, and it's true. "It's only—"

"Only that when our royal friend sees fit to pursue one of our women that we're supposed to politely glance aside and notice nothing. Sometimes I envy Eliza, Jav. At least you don't look to her paramours."

Javier, distracted, demands, "Liz has lovers?" and then, offense managing to work its way through wine, adds, "You're cruel tonight, Marius. It's not like you."

"I think I may have earned it, Jav," Marius says, so softly that guilt burns hot through Javier's blood. It's an unfamiliar and unwelcome sensation, and it's the one that drove him first to an excess of drink, and ultimately to Marius's doorstep.

"I'm going to ask her to marry me." There has to be a better way to couch it, but the words blurt themselves out, not out of viciousness but desperation. And Marius pales in the ruddy light, shock widening his pupils until there's nothing but darkness in his eyes.

"Oh, my lord prince." The whisper has edges. "Do I not deserve better than that?"

Javier closes his eyes against the pain in Marius's question. "You deserve far better than I," he replies, and can't bring himself to look on his friend again. "So does she, and for being friend to a prince neither of you will get it. I won't marry her. I can't. But she's Lanyarchan, and even the threat of a fresh alliance between my mother and that country—" It's too much to tell the merchant's son, but Javier can find it in himself to say no less. Marius does deserve better, and the only offering he can make is the hard truth. And Marius is silent in the face of Javier's faltering, so quiet the prince is forced to open his eyes and gauge his friend's expression.

There is pain there. More than Javier ever wanted to cause the few people in his life whom he trusts implicitly. Pain and weariness and worst of all, acceptance. Wouldn't it be better for Marius to rail and shout, to hit him and stand his ground against Javier's desire?

No. The answer comes too fast. For all the friendship shared, Javier is still a prince and Marius still a merchant's son. He can't throw himself on Javier in outrage even when Javier most richly deserves it. Worse still, the witchpower would never allow it to happen, even if Javier should steel himself to cower and brace against the blows he so richly deserves. His power would work to protect him instinctively, either through the shielding that he and Beatrice have discovered or through the part of Javier that is, and will always be, royalty. No one may lay a hand on a prince, and even if Javier might school his conscious mind to other ends, the core of him would lash out and bend Marius to his will. Better that Marius hold in his betrayal and let it show in smaller ways than clear insubordination and threats.

"So you will act at last," Marius finally whispers. Javier isn't expecting that, and finds himself staring through the darkness at his friend. "Does she love you, Javier?"

"I don't know. I hope not."

"Do you love her?"

Only because he owes this man so much, in the form of Beatrice Irvine, will Javier answer that question. He closes his eyes, savoring the words as he speaks them: "I don't know. I hope not."

"I do," Marius says steadily. "Love both of you, and see no way for this to end happily. But then, that's not the point, is it?" He needs no more answer to that than he might need answer to the colour of the sky. He stands, gesturing toward the food Javier still holds. "Eat, my prince. You'll need to be sober if you're going to ask a woman to marry you."

Javier, unusually obedient, tears at the bread with his teeth, its aroma suddenly heady. For a few minutes he does nothing but gobble down the tender savory and the cheese. Marius hands him wine, so well-watered there's only a glimmer of flavour, and waits for him to drink that before he speaks again. "Will you tell her that she's only a mark to be used in a political game?"

The thought quite literally hasn't occurred to Javier. He scowls through the dimness, more at the fire than at his friend. "Should I?"

Marius breathes a sound like laughter. "How many women would say yes to a proposal like that, Jav? But Beatrice might," he adds more quietly. There is something indecipherable in his expression again. In another man Javier might call it subterfuge or canniness, but Marius has always worn his heart on his sleeve. The idea that he might now be trying to manipulate events is laughable. "Her passion for her country's freedom is great," Marius finishes, and Javier has to look away again.

"And being engaged to royalty, however briefly, might make her an even more appealing wife," he offers. Marius exhales again, another noise that resembles laughter.

"To those who care about such things, yes. I don't. I don't even think my mother does. Now, if you were to elevate her to some duchy or something, Mother might care . . ." He's joking, and his expression changes to startlement, then horror as he sees Javier considering the idea. "Jav, I don't need—"

"But it would make a magnificent bride-gift, wouldn't it," Javier murmurs. "So outrageous as to alarm Lorraine. Take a minor Lanyarchan noble, elevate her to a duchess, propose to marry her . . . short of slapping her face with a glove there could be no more obvious announcement of Gallin's intentions toward Aulun." He offers a smile that he knows is too weak. "And in the end my friend could become nobility, without me ever conferring the favour directly. It's a pretty setup, isn't it?"

"And where does it leave Eliza?" Marius wonders.

"Oh, hell," Javier says recklessly. "I'll marry her to Sacha and we'll all be happy."

Marius barks laughter this time, so derisive Javier straightens in offense. "Yes, my prince" is all the merchant lad will say, though, and Javier climbs to his feet unsteadily. Puts his hand on Marius's shoulder, gripping muscle as he leans heavily.

"Will you forgive me, Marius?" The question's asked thickly, more than just wine weighting it. Marius folds his hand over Javier's on his shoulder, then reaches out to grasp the back of the prince's neck, bringing his head in until they touch foreheads, an intimacy Javier would allow almost no one else. Marius holds them there a long time before his grip tightens and he sighs.

His answer, the only answer he can give, will haunt Javier for the rest of his days: "Yes, my prince."

BELINDA PRIMROSE / BEATRICE IRVINE
10 November 1587 † *Lutetia*

"The prince has sent his carriage for you, my lady." Nina bobbed a curtsey as she stepped into the sitting room with her announcement. Belinda glanced up with a faintly startled look toward the windows and the dimming afternoon sky. "The coachman says I'm to extend his invitation to dinner."

Amusement curled Belinda's mouth. "How forward of the coachman. I don't believe I've ever been invited to dinner by one before."

Exasperation flickered over Nina's face and Belinda's amusement turned to brief laughter. "I know. I have no propriety, have I? Have blankets brought out for the horses, invite the driver in to the foyer, and send Marie to my room. I'll have to dress for him."

"For the coachman, my lady?" Nina looked down her nose in half-teasing mockery, then bobbed another curtsey and scurried to do as she was told. Belinda climbed the stairs to her room, laying out the amber gown she'd dismissed for the outing with Eliza months earlier, only to earn Marie's cluck of disapproval as she swept into the room behind Belinda.

"'Tisn't the fashion, m'lady. Going to the palace you ought to wear the fashion you set."

"Eliza set it," Belinda said absently. "And I haven't any of her fashions warm enough for the weather tonight. The amber is flattering and warm. It will do."

Marie hummed, urgent little noise of dismay, but did as she was told, first settling her mistress into a chair so Belinda's hair could be made suitable, then arranging petticoats and skirts and corsets until the amber overgown could be settled into place. It took longer than Belinda preferred—it always did—but the result looking back at her in an unwarped mirror seemed worth the time. Even Marie clucked again, this time in satisfaction. "M'lady should have a winter gown in the new style made up in this colour. It does m'lady's eyes and hair good. Shall I have the dressmaker come round?"

"And insult Eliza? I'll discuss it with her," Belinda offered, and Marie, satisfied, ducked her head and backed out of the room. Belinda watched her go in the mirror, wondering, not for the first time, what kind of dragonish mistress had trained that particular obsequience into the girl. Only royalty expected such behavior, and even then it was usually only in the courtroom or private audiences. Servants were expected to be efficient, and backing through rooms wasted time.

Nina stood too near the coachman in the foyer, startling into a proper distance and blushing beyond her collarbones as Belinda entered the room. The coachman, only a few years her senior, held his expression steady, as though the flirtatiousness in it couldn't be seen if he didn't admit guilt in its being there. Belinda hid amusement as Nina helped her slip a cloak on, and watched the coach-man as he led the way down to the street. He was young for the job, which meant he had talent that might be parlayed, in a few years' time, to a position in the stables as a judge of horseflesh and a breeder. He could make Nina a good match, and she could be kept on as Beatrice's servant as long as Belinda desired her.

A dark smile played her mouth as she stepped up into the carriage with the coachman's hand in support. As long as Belinda desired her, or as long as Marius did. Nina'd lost none of her good nature or bidability in the weeks since she'd become their plaything, recollection swept away by the witchpower. She had not been taken advantage of since, out of fondness for the girl and out of no time or need to sate Marius, but Belinda was satisfied Nina's memory and body were hers to manipulate. With the girl safely wed to the coachman, any child would be assumed legitimate. Belinda would discuss it with Javier over dinner.

The prince met her in the courtyard, dressed in blues that shaded toward purple in the rising moonlight. He took her hand as the carriage door was opened, breathing a sigh that shone silver in the cold air. "You've chosen a more conservative dress. Thank God."

"My lord?" Belinda arched an eyebrow as she stepped down to the flagstones. "Have Eliza's dresses fallen out of fashion already?"

"No, no, God, no, not with Mother looking fresh as spring in them. No, a contingency from the Khazarian court is here. They arrived without warning this afternoon, and they look to a man as if they've walked out of another century. All dark and dour and fur-covered. Do you have any Khazarian, Beatrice?"

The impulse to reply, blithely, "Oh, I've had several" nearly strangled Belinda, the expression she imagined on Javier's face almost worth the cost of the answer. "None, my lord, except perhaps *yes* and *no*, which do me no good at a dinner. There is a dinner," she half-asked, and Javier let go an explosive breath.

"There is, and I'm sorry I didn't warn you. None of us had any warning, and all I could think was your presence would help to welcome her."

"Her?"

"There's a woman in charge of them all." Javier escorted Belinda into the palace's warmth as he spoke, keeping his voice low as he shared what he knew. "She speaks nearly flawless Gallic, and her hangers-on have words of it here and there. Eliza will be at the table as well. Her Khazarian's not as good as mine, but—"

"Eliza speaks Khazarian?" Belinda couldn't keep the astonishment from her voice, though even as she blurted the question she wished she hadn't. Javier's gaze darkened. "Of course she does," Belinda said. "You taught her. I'm sorry, my lord. It just never occurred to me. I meant no slight toward Eliza."

"I needed someone to practise with who would talk to me about something other than politics, so I made them all learn. Sacha and Marius are passable in Parnan, and Sacha's Reinnish is quite good, but Eliza's the best of them."

"She would be," Belinda murmured. Javier gave her a sharp look, eyebrows drawn down.

"What does that mean?"

"She had the most to gain from education, my lord." Belinda left unsaid that a street rat in love with a prince might hope innumerable languages could elevate her toward a throne; if Javier wasn't aware of that, there was no need to draw his attention to it. "Tell me about the Khazarian woman."

"She's a noblewoman of some sort. They call her *dvoryanin*, a lady's rank. Something like a countess. Outside the line for the throne, should something happen to Irina or Ivanova, but close to it in politics and friendship. She's the most dangerously beautiful woman I've ever seen," Javier said, so frankly it made Belinda smile. "All sharp angles and dark eyes. She looks like a witch."

Belinda's eyebrows shot up and her hand tightened on Javier's arm. He glanced at her and smiled, brief and faint. "I know," he murmured. "Of all the people to say that. But I don't know. I don't feel anything from her, but you were the one who named us alike."

"Is that why you really wanted me here?" Belinda asked, just as quietly. There was no censure in her question and after a moment to ascertain that, Javier dropped his head in a nod. "What's her name?"

"Akilina Pankejeff. She goes through love—are you all right?" Javier caught Belinda's weight as she stumbled, a moment of clumsiness, of losing control, unlike anything she'd felt in years. Her heartbeat soared and she fought down heat in her cheeks, knowing a blush could damn her. Golden witchpower seared through the back of her mind, seeking a channel for use. Belinda seized it, dominating it with her will and wrapping it around herself in stillness that shivered under the onslaught of shock.

"My ankle," she said, the lie coming easily to lips numb with cold. "Forgive me. I'm all right now. Alikina . . . ?"

"Akilina," Javier corrected, but his description of the woman was lost beneath Belinda's own knowledge.

She had only seen the woman once, briefly, in the early-morning hour before she escaped Count Gregori Kapnist's country estates with the help of a lusty young coachman. Akilina Pankejeff had been the latest in Gregori's stream of high-born lovers, just as he'd been the latest in hers. There was almost no chance Akilina would know her: she had not demanded to see the harlot serving girl whose sensuality had driven Gregori to his grave. Had Belinda stayed even an hour longer, with nasty-minded Ilyana waiting to make trouble, she might well have come face-to-face with the noblewoman, but as it was the raven-haired, hard beauty hadn't so much as glanced at the help.

And Belinda was now Beatrice Irvine, a provincial noblewoman from Lanyarch, hundreds of miles away from Khazar. Lutetia was as far as Beatrice had ever travelled, or ever would; to connect her with the Rosa at Gregori's estates was simply impossible. "I'll do my best," Belinda heard herself promising, and had to cast her mind back over Javier's lecture to learn what she'd agreed to. Ah: overtures of friendship with Akilina. The Khazarian ambassador, if that's what Akilina was, would have very little reason to be friends with Beatrice Irvine, but if Javier's favour lay on the Lanyarchan girl, then friends Akilina would make. "Why is she here, my lord? Does Gallin treat with Khazar?" That, above all, was a question that needed answering: Gallin's navy wasn't well-endowed, but the Essandian navy to the south was. A treaty made with Sandalia could very easily sway Rodrigo, and that triumvirate was a dangerous combination for Aulunian prospects.

"Don't worry about it," Javier murmured. "Those are politics outside your concern, for now. We'll discuss it later. For now, be charming, Beatrice. Be charming."

A few steps ahead of them, doormen opened the way to the dining hall. Belinda, on Javier's arm, swept into warmth and light and between a double-row of Khazarian honour guards, who, like everyone in the room, turned their gazes on the new arrivals. Training made her offer a brief, breathless smile at the guards; friends in low places were always good to have. None of them changed expression, save one, whose breath caught audibly beneath the sound of Belinda and Javier's footsteps. Belinda's curious gaze went to that one, and for the second time in as many minutes, a lifetime of control deserted her, sickness lurching in her belly. *Vassily, Vlad, Valentine,* sang through her mind.

Viktor.

12

She should have killed him.

The stress of running in tight corsets came back to her even now, breathlessness that had nothing to do with the rising illness in her belly. She had turned from the coachman, moving with decorum, and then gathered her skirts and run through the carefully laid-out halls of Gregori Kapnist's estates as fast as she could. She was young and healthy and running for her life in any sense that mattered, and it had seemed mere moments before she burst into her cell, breast heaving with the effort of haste.

Viktor had not been there. There had been no sign of him; there never was once he left, except perhaps a handful of thick black hairs sticking to the pillow. But it was early, earlier than a guardsman often needed to be up, and so to find her mattress cold and the blankets rucked and empty was a shock.

Belinda put it away almost instantly. All that mattered, all that truly mattered, was that he not be found in her chamber. It would be best if he were dead, his tongue silenced for good, but it was not necessary, and she had no time for unnecessary things. She loosened her corsets and stuffed partlets beneath them, needing enough to give her clothes the look of having changed without the risk of packing a bag that might draw attention. The coachman intended to leave within the hour. There might be time to find

Viktor, to slip a knife into his kidney or across his throat and leave him bleeding in a streambed.

But Gregori's death and Belinda's disappearance, coupled with Viktor's murder, might well shine too much light on the serving girl whom Ilyana had accused of witchery. Better to leave Viktor alive, out of the picture, than to play the dangerous game of silencing him.

A touch of sentiment made her shoulders tighten. It was not that he'd asked her to marry him, or made the offer as if it were a love match. That kind of weakness would be her undoing, and so it could bear no relevance on the decision to leave him alive. It was not that which stayed her hand, but raw practicality.

Belinda looked through the Khazarian guard now with the same brief and meaningless smile she'd offered all the guards, and told herself again that it had been the right choice, at the time, to let him live.

She did not, *could* not, *would* not, let the sickness in her stomach betray itself with her expression. She forbade a blush to rise, forbade any hint of recognition to light her eyes. Disbelief beetled Viktor's eyebrows, the outrageous impossibility of his onetime lover being in Lutetia and on a prince's arm doing more to maintain Belinda's cover than any action she might take could do. It was simply not possible, and in that lay her only chance at safety. It had been wise to let him live then.

It would be suicide to do so now.

They were past the guards, bowing, curtseying to the table; Belinda brought her curtsey low to Akilina, almost as deferential to her as to Sandalia. Both women noticed, Sandalia with a quirked mouth that hinted just barely more at humour than offense, and Akilina as if it were no more, and possibly less, than she was due. They were seated, Javier at Akilina's right and Belinda farther down the table, as benefited her lesser status. Pleasantries were exchanged, all in Gallic, Akilina complimenting Belinda on her accent, Belinda demurring and insisting it had improved greatly in the months she'd lived in Lutetia, but Akilina, to Belinda's ear, sounded as if she'd been born to the tongue. Polite, meaningless, charming; all the things that Beatrice Irvine should be in the face of so much nobility, so much greater than her own, and all the while with the weight of Viktor's gaze on her slender shoulders.

Akilina said something that brought Beatrice's laugh to the fore. Too easy, too easy; Beatrice laughed too easily, and in such free emotion there was, had always been, danger. Belinda's grace was not in her singing voice, but in her laugh, as she had once told a dark-haired courtesan in Parna. Viktor would know that laugh, impossible as it was, and yet to choke it back was unthinkably rude. Belinda quieted it as best she could, leaving merriment in her eyes and trusting without fail that her gaze and smile would bury true emotion so deep no one but she would ever find it. Akilina smiled at her, an open predatory expression that Belinda knew too well, and this time it was she, not her assumed persona, who wanted to laugh, almost in despair. There was safety in being a serving girl. No one saw her as a servant, no one cared or noticed, no one bothered. Belinda kept her smile in place and coiled stillness around herself, reaching back to the first days of training and remembering Robert Drake riding away, his cloak golden in the sunlight. That cloak was a thing of protection, keeping her safe, making her untouchable.

Witchlight gathered in her mind, comforting, as if its presence had always been meant to be there, and now that it was, as if it were unthinkable that it might ever have been missing. It reached through candlelight and fire for the shadows, pulling them closer, darkness soft and comforting. The amber of Belinda's gown seemed to fade and dim, and for a sweet moment Belinda felt panic bleed out of her. She had been raised to shadows, that was where servants belonged.

Serving girls did not make themselves part of burgeoning revolution.

The thought, sharp and clear, shattered the gathering witchlight and straightened Belinda's spine. She reached for her wineglass too hastily, nearly knocked it over, and spat a curse in Aulunian that silenced the table.

This time she let a blush come, able to stop it but unable to command it to rise, and murmured an apology in Gallic. "I've forgotten my tongue. I beg of you, forgive me, my lords and ladies. I'm told appalling language is a Lanyarchan trait."

"What did it mean?" Akilina asked after a moment, and laughter restored itself around the table as Belinda made a still-blushing confession to the mating habits of swine. She made a show of holding on to her wineglass too carefully from then on, earning amused looks and once, a mocking round of applause for managing to accept a newly poured cupful. None of the banter went beyond the surface, not only for Belinda, but at the table as a whole: it didn't take the witchpower to see judgment beneath smiling eyes, or the thoughtful perusal of the high-born blood seating placement. Javier, at Akilina's elbow, could easily be placed there as more than just a polite sop to a visiting guest; it could be read as potential, as a promise: the young prince might be wed to a powerful woman from the Khazarian empire, making an alliance there that would strengthen Gallin and alarm Aulun.

Unwilling to allow her body to betray herself again, Belinda didn't shift positions at the idea, but memory of a thought stolen from Sacha rose: *she intended to marry a king, not a prince.* Belinda had thought he meant Eliza, but the possibility that the stocky young lord's reach stretched beyond Gallin's borders arose as she studied Akilina. There had been guilt and anger both in Asselin's reaction to her pressure, and if his patron was making her way to Gallin, expecting results . . . the idea was intriguing.

From the distance down the table, even with her witchpower extended toward the black-haired Khazarian woman, Belinda caught no sense of plotting or turmoil. Nor should she, she thought; the fine meal and the company were intended for pleasure and the first forays into casual intimacy. That it also served to allow insight into some of Sandalia's court alliances was inevitable, and that Akilina should pay attention to those alliances was only to be expected.

And it set Belinda herself firmly in her place: four or five men and women separated her from the head of the table and the guest of honour. Eliza was even farther down the table, and caught Belinda's eye momentarily as Belinda looked over the gathering. They exchanged brief smiles, both aware of their positions literally and figuratively, and then Eliza turned her attention back to the heavily bearded Khazarian man beside her. He, like most of Akilina's people, was a minor dignitary, part of an entourage that was intended as a show of support rather than any expectation that they would do anything. Belinda caught a murmur of Aria Magli from Eliza's conversation, and turned to the man at her side, offering a smile of her own. "Do I understand that you travelled through Parna, then? You must have left Khazar early in the summer, to make so much travelling worthwhile."

He stared at her as if she'd said something unpleasant, and stuffed a joint of lamb into his mouth, blood drooling down his beard. Belinda, repulsed and startled, drew back, earning Akilina's laughter. "Forgive my men, Lady Irvine," she said, loudly enough to be heard. "Their manners are cruder than even the worst tales of a Lanyarchan's. I visited Aria Magli," she acknowledged, "but only with a handful of retainers. This honour guard caught me on my journey east. It appears I was embarrassing my imperatrix by travelling as lightly as I did. Have you ever been to Aria Magli, Lady Irvine?"

"Lutetia is the farthest I've ever been from home." Belinda let the Lanyarchan burr come through more strongly in her voice, then deliberately corrected it, trusting the show of provinciality to be considered charming. "I've heard that Aria Magli is the most beautiful city in Echon and the most vile. Is it possible that it could be both?"

"Oh, yes," Akilina said without hesitation. "I think the smell would be appalling in the heat of summer, and yet the music on the canals and the life of the city is irresistible. And, of course, there are the courtesans, who may be the breaking point for villainousness or perfection, depending on your opinion of them. What is yours, Lady Irvine?"

Belinda dropped her eyes to hide a laugh, her evident shyness garnering amusement from Akilina. "Is that a terrible question to ask a young Ecumenic woman?" she asked without remorse. "Can you even imagine such a life, Lady Irvine? Trained in pleasure, educated on all manner of topics—is it freedom, do you think, or is it Hell?"

"I believe we should not be so bold as to define Hell as an earthly conceit," Belinda murmured, and lifted her eyes. "Nor is freedom found in anything but walking God's path and casting off our sins to be welcomed in Heaven at the end of our days. I cannot say that I approve of a woman selling her body for money, but I wouldn't presume to say God had no reason for asking her to do so. My lady."

Akilina's dark eyebrows shot up and she leaned back to clap her hands together thrice, lazy staccato sounds. "The provincial has teeth," she said with an edge of admiration. "I think I see why Your Majesty holds such fondness for the country of her first crown, now. Forgive me, Lady Irvine." She leaned forward again to give Belinda a frank and appraising look. "I baited you, and you've set me in my place. Shall we be friends from here on out?"

Belinda smiled, an open and delighted expression, and thought that friendship was not made on words even as she murmured, "It would be an honour, my lady."

———

A near-commoner from Lanyarch did not refuse Khazarian nobility when the latter said, "Walk with me, Beatrice," regardless of
her feelings on the matter, or even the surreptitious glance given by
her high-born lover. Javier nodded, one barely visible dip of his
chin; Belinda thought she might not have seen it, had she not been
looking to the prince for a cue. Dinner was over, sweet wine drunk
by the bottleful after it, and the polite discussion that lingered was
Akilina's and Sandalia's to end. The duchess watched Sandalia for
weariness, and shortly after Belinda herself would have begged off,
did so with grace and self-effacing apology. Sandalia granted the
Khazarian contingent their leave, and only then did Akilina turn
her hawk's smile on Belinda and extend her invitation. The bells
had run the first small hour of the morning a long time since, and
Belinda, as much as anyone, longed for her bed. That Akilina knew
it she had no doubt, but while the Khazarian countess might not
dare put out a queen, she had no such qualms about inconvenienc-
ing Belinda.

"What do you think of us, Beatrice?" Akilina tucked her arm
through Belinda's and dawdled down the hall outside the dining
chambers, in no more rush to sleep than the moon was.

"I think all those beards must itch," Belinda said promptly, and
earned a laugh for her efforts.

"Lanyarchan men wear beards, don't they?"

"They do, so I have confidence that I'm right." Belinda offered
a smile and Akilina squeezed her arm with pleasure.

"What else do you think? I've never met a Lanyarchan, so I want
to hear everything. It's my small way of understanding the world,
in seeing how others see us." Akilina's explanation was guileless,
her expression open, and Belinda smiled again.

"Surely you're not old enough to be so wise, my lady."

"Surely you're not old enough to be so skilled at flattery."
Akilina laughed again, more easily than even Beatrice did, and
Belinda, walking so close to her, thought that there was no artifice

to her humour. Witchpower whispered of Akilina's curiosity about the Lanyarchan provincial who'd captured Javier's eye—for clearly she had, if he'd entered the dining hall with her—and a certain glee in keeping Beatrice from Javier's bed, even if only for a short while. There was more mischief than malice in the emotion, though beneath it all ran a river of intent. It flavoured Akilina's laugh, but lay deep enough that without touching her skin, Belinda couldn't read its meaning. "You watched us all very carefully during dinner," Akilina accused good-naturedly. "You must have come to some conclusions. Besides the beards."

"You laugh much more easily than rumour has it, my lady," Belinda said with absolute honesty. "The stories one hears of Khazar are all of dark and dour people, as if the long winter days have pressed the joy out of you. And you don't dress as I'd imagined. I think of somber colours when I think of Khazar, but—" She broke off briefly to gesture at Akilina's gown, so deep a red as to be heart's blood. "And the guards with their bristly hats and broad shoulders all done in such blues, with the yellow epaulettes. The eye wishes to drink your clothing down. It's wonderful," she added with a girlish enthusiasm more heartfelt than she expected, and almost laughed at herself. The serving maid role she'd played at Gregori's manor had never cared for the colours or costumes of the men and women she was surrounded with, and nor should she have; for Rosa those things were merely part of the patchwork of life. Beatrice's observations and excitement were charming, in a dangerous way.

"Perhaps I'll have a dress made for you. Your skin is very fair, and would look well in a strong tone." Akilina's offer masked a ploy so deliberate Belinda didn't need the witchpower to uncover it. A gift to the prince's paramour was a way to draw his attention without being unbearably obvious. Belinda glanced at the amber of her current gown and arched an eyebrow at Akilina, who threw her head back and laughed again.

"That was not an insult," she promised. "You know what looks good on you. Forgive me, my lady, if you think I'm that crude."

"I believe I hold the prize for crudity this evening, my lady," Belinda said diplomatically. "I would be delighted with a Khazarian-style gown, if your kindness extends so far. And perhaps I can introduce you to Eliza, who sets fashion here in Lutetia."

"The extraordinary woman at the far end of the table," Akilina said without hesitation. "She is a friend of his highness's, da?"

"Da," Belinda echoed, deliberately awkward. "That's one of the two Khazarian words I know. The other is *nit*." She made the word into a scrape in her throat, forcing it into unfamiliarity, and Akilina's laughter rose again.

"Nyet," she corrected. "Your Gallic is very good, so you do know how to make the nasal sounds. *Nyet*," she repeated, and Belinda imitated her again, retaining the *I* rather than the proper pronunciation. Viktor was somewhere behind them in the ranks of guards, and she had no intention of making her voice any more familiar to him than it must be.

"I'll practise," she promised. "Gallic didn't come easily to me. I fear I have little gift for language."

"What are your gifts, then?" Akilina asked lightly, but ice slid in beneath the question. Belinda flickered an empty smile down the hall, thinking of the answers she couldn't give. Loyalty. A talent for death. An ability to belong wherever she stopped moving, at least long enough to wreak mayhem and move on. And most freshly, of course, the witchpower, a gift she barely allowed herself to consider in Akilina's presence. She had no sense of indomitable will from the woman as she had from Javier, no recognition of power shared, but caution was a better path to follow when it came to a magic that could see her burned at the stake.

"Passion, I suppose," she murmured. "But even that burns out in time." She was not speaking of herself, and she knew it; so, too, did Akilina. The black-haired woman exhaled a short breath of sat-isfaction and squeezed Belinda's arm again.

"At least you have the intelligence to see that," she said magnan-imously. "Intelligence sees us further in life than either passion or beauty, Beatrice. Remember that, and you'll do well."

Belinda all but bobbed a curtsey even as she remained on Akilina's arm, then slowed at a cross-hall and looked around, sud-denly cheerful. "Now, tell me, Lady Akilina, shall I leave you to wander the palace halls all night, or do you know where you are?"

"Rosa."

There was no too-quick heartbeat of betrayal this time; Belinda had expected Viktor's voice to come after her once she'd escorted Akilina to her rooms. She was nearly back at Javier's chambers when the Khazarian guardsman spoke; he'd been waiting some dis-creet distance, not following her, not drawing attention to himself.

She ignored him, walking past the alcove he waited in, her gait unfaltering. He stepped out behind her, repeating the name with more urgency, though just as quietly: "*Rosa.*"

There was no one else in the hall, no one else he could possibly be speaking to. For that reason alone Belinda turned, eyebrows wrinkled curiously. "M'sieur?" Her performances always had to be perfect, but quiet urgency swilled in Belinda's stomach this time. It was impossible that she could be both Lady Beatrice Irvine and Rosa the serving maid. Viktor knew it, but suspicion rode so heav-ily on him that he couldn't let it go. Damnable sympathy for the man rose in Belinda's breast, complicating everything.

"Rosa, is it you?" He spoke Khazarian, of course; Belinda didn't think he had any more Gallic than her assumed persona had Khazarian. She offered an uncertain smile, and shook her head in apology.

"I'm sorry, m'sieur. I don't speak Khazarian." Unexpected

memory rose in perfect clarity: Dmitri's exasperation at Rosa's guise of incomprehension, and the bruise he'd left on her cheek for playing her part so well. Belinda would not allow herself to lift a hand to the memory of that bruise, but instead dipped a nervous curtsey and turned away again.

Recklessness drove Viktor forward to catch her arm. Belinda yelped, small soft sound of terror, trembling as she tried to pull away. Viktor would know nothing of the soft noblewoman's fear in her eyes, not from the Rosa he knew. He knew ardor and weariness, those being the primary emotions she had let show as the serving girl, and common strength. Rosa might have fought back; Beatrice cowered, tears already marking her cheeks. "No—no, you can't, you—please, don't hurt me, don't—"

Viktor, who had never understood the need to hurt a woman, let go with a look of horror and fell to his knees, offering apologies. Laying hands on a noblewoman, especially a prince's doxy, could far too easily lead to his own death.

Could, and should. It was by far the easiest way to protect herself: one single scream would have Javier's guards at her side in a few seconds; one babbled accusation would have Viktor in chains or dead. It would mar the relations between the newly arrived Khazarian contingent and Gallin, and that could only be to Aulun's favour. It was an opportunity to seize subtle control in Sandalia's court, gently crafted and offered up to her. Robert himself could not have planned it more perfectly.

Belinda did not want to scream.

A lifetime of training made her draw breath. Alunaer, clean and still under new snow, flashed through her vision. The flavoured memory of wood smoke in the distance, rich and sharp, tightened her throat against sound, and black-branched trees reached through ten years of survival to sink their shadows into her. She did not need to look down to see a body lying broken on the flagstones beneath her. To scream was to write an ending, as one had been written, bloodily, to end her childhood. To scream was to end studying with Javier and to move forward with revolution.

To scream was to let Javier go.

Witchpower thundered through her blood. Belinda reached out on its command, putting her fingers into Viktor's hair. It was clean, though not so clean as it had been the last time she'd seen him, when he'd knelt before her in just such a way and offered marriage and sex. Recognition jolted him profoundly, any doubt at Rosa's impossible transformation swept away beneath familiar touch. Belinda dropped to her knees, hands still knotted in Viktor's hair, and swayed toward him, hungry with the grasp of power.

"You could die for touching me," she whispered, her mouth nearly against his. She spoke Khazarian, but the witchpower in her blood raged and danced, working to play tricks on the man's memory even as memories were made. He would barely know she had spoken to him, but he would do her bidding with a need bordering on mania. She would be his object of desire, not because he had known Rosa but because she was a pure and genteel creature, so far above him as to be an angel. Such was her intent, and her experiments with Nina gave her no reason to doubt that Viktor, too, would bend to her will.

"I'll let you live, in exchange for your services." She knotted her hands in his hair more tightly, forbidding herself the impulse to loosen her fingers and drive them into his pants, to have him service her in more ways than one. Her pulse beat hot in her throat, desire unlike any she'd ever known for this man aching between her legs and rattling her thoughts. He was stronger than Marius, more delicious to dominate, harder to break, but he had gotten down on his knees to make a match with her and he could not, would not, deny her will. Belinda drew herself closer, putting her teeth over the heartbeat beneath his jaw, and bit hard enough to draw a strangled sound of mixed desire and resistance.

"Love me." The command sank into his skin with a golden

glow, stronger than the shields or witchlight she'd built as weapons. "Worship me." Viktor croaked agreement, shuddering beneath her mouth. "I am your queen," Belinda breathed. "You will serve me or you will die."

His acquiescing nod sent pleasure so strong it became weakness over her, and she sagged against him. His arms closed around her, solid and strong. For an instant intellect clawed through passion, leaving Belinda gasping and chilled. Stillness felt an impossible distance away, unreachable, untouchable, alien to her. In a moment of clarity she understood that it was using the witchpower that turned her into a creature of raw desire and rough lust, endangering everything that she was and everything that she worked for. *It cannot be found out.* Robert's concern made sense for a few burning seconds: if this was what she became when she touched the magic within her, she could not, should not, be trusted. Locking it behind a chypre-scented wall had been wise.

And arrogant. Fury shattered understanding. She was not a tool to be meddled with and played by the likes of Robert Drake. That was something he would come to understand; she would make certain of it. Belinda shoved back from Viktor's warm strength, lip curled in disdain as she studied the paroxysm of agonized need stretching his face. Less out of sympathy than the cold thrill of power, she slid her hand over the front of his breeches, felt his hardness through cloth and curled her fingers around him. One vicious jerk sent a spasm over him, heat seeping against her wrist.

Unkind delight curled her mouth again and she pushed him away, standing up in the same smooth motion. "Watch Akilina. Remember when she meets Sandalia and what they discuss. I'll come to you when I have need of you."

She stood outside Javier's door a long time, flanked by guards whose gazes looked politely through her. She did not look at them, not trusting the witchpower to lie dormant if she did. Not trusting it to not flare up and demand tribute from the unfortunate men who guarded the prince that night. They would die if she met their eyes; they would die because she would take them sexually, fully, and the noise of it would bring Javier to the door, and to hold her position in his bed she would cry rape and the guards would die.

The urge to use that power tickled the centre of her palms and itched at her until as little as she dared step into Javier's chambers so uncontrolled, she dared stay out even less.

Javier sprawled before the fire, linen nightdress falling around his knees, moon-pale legs stuck out in an ungainly fashion toward the fire. Belinda closed the door behind herself and locked it, hands tight on the bar as she leaned and stared at the casually bedecked prince. He looked up with a grin, wobbling a wine flask at her. "Akilina kept you longer than I expected. You did well, Beatrice. Even that crack about pigs fucking got a laugh. Here." He sat up, taking her in. "You look a bit disheveled. Did the Khazarian am-bassador have her way with you?" He gave her a raucous leer that was better suited to Sacha's face. "I miss all the fun."

"My lord, what do you feel when you use the witchpower?" Belinda's voice came beneath his, soft with something she was re-luctant to call fear, but could see no other name for. Javier's drunk faded with her question, his eyebrows drawing down.

"Feel? What do you mean? Did you feel something from Akilina?" He bounded to his feet, enthusiasm suddenly rampant. "Is she one of us?"

"No." Regret's thin edge slashed through her at the disappoint-ment in Javier's eyes, though he recovered instantly.

"No," he agreed. "It would be too much, for two women to come into my life so quickly, both bearing such power. Perhaps we're the only ones, Beatrice. But that's not so bad. At least we've found each other."

"Yes, my lord." Beatrice remained at the door, watching Javier as though he were an unfamiliar creature. "Do you feel anything?" she asked again, almost diffidently. "Do you feel . . . desire, the wish to . . . dominate?" She remembered, abruptly, the way he'd sculpted her body the first time they'd lain together, and thought that perhaps he did.

His expression, though, gave no hint of anything beyond bewilderment. "Do you?" Amusement cleared befuddlement away and he sauntered to her, deliberately leading with his hips. "Aah," he murmured. "A woman given power finds herself in the unfamiliar position of wishing to flex it, is that it? Does it excite you, Beatrice?" He crossed his wrists, laughter sparkling through his eyes. "Shall you be my cruel mistress?"

"Please." Belinda spoke the word carefully, turning her face away in order to make herself more vulnerable. She was too aware that the power running through her blood would make her words a command if she were not purposefully cautious. Javier's laughter would disappear into offense in an instant should she be that bold, and she couldn't afford to lose his attention now. Not with Viktor in the palace; not with Akilina and her unknown schedule to consider. "Please, do not mock me, my lord. This is not an easy thing to ask."

Javier uncrossed his wrists and touched Belinda's jaw, turning her face back toward his. "No," he said a few seconds later. "I can see that it isn't. I'm a man, and a prince," he added after a moment's thought. "It's natural that I should be in control, Bea. The witchpower helps to impress that on people, but . . . no. It doesn't waken in me a need to lord myself above others. But our stations are very different, and I think I can understand why you might chafe at the bounds of yours, when you and I both know what power you might command."

Belinda nodded, small motion, barely trusting herself to even that. Javier's fingertips felt cool against her face, as if her warmth might rise up and swallow him whole. She had let slip an opportunity to control his mother's court once this evening, shaping that chance into something new and, she hoped, something worth the risk of letting Viktor live. She could not afford to give in to hungry power and try to overwhelm Javier, not now. There would be other chances to wrest control in the court, but not if she pushed the prince so far as to fall out of his favour, even despite the witch-power.

A fleeting note of cool white slipped through golden magic, then spilled over it, the ordinary strength of her childhood stillness finally hers to command again. Witchpower faded beneath it and Belinda let it go gratefully, no longer hungry for the reading of emotions or the attempt to steal thoughts. It was a gift, for a precious few moments, to be unweighted by that power and its desires. Belinda let her head turn heavily against Javier's fingers, let herself sag against the door, and closed her eyes.

"What would you say," Javier asked in a low voice, "if I were to offer you the station that would allow you command?"

Belinda opened her eyes, bemused. Javier's hair flamed over his shoulders, firelight behind him lending it warmth that cast a golden glow to his skin. Shadows darkened his eyes to nearly black, devastating in the paleness of his face. His expression held cautious hope, so unexpected Belinda found a soft laugh to voice. "What, my lord?"

"I could offer you a duchy." Javier took a breath and held it, then exhaled. "I could offer you a crown."

Amusement burgeoned and Belinda straightened, a full smile on her lips. "Your mother would have a fit, Javier." Her smile edged its way toward a grin, a broad expression unfamiliar to her, but welcome as she reached for his wine flask. "She'd have apoplexy just at hearing you tease me with the idea. Give me that. Whatever you're drinking is fine stuff indeed. I want to try it."

Javier stepped back, holding the flask out of reach with what looked like a childish pout, though there was too much astonishment in his gaze for it to work. "I've already spoken to her, Beatrice."

"And I'm the queen of Cor . . ." Humour drained from her voice as surely as blood drained from her face as she took in Javier's growing insult. "Holy Maire, Mother of God. Javier, you're not— Javier?" Witchpower lay out of reach, dormant beneath the cloak of stillness that wrapped her mind. That habit had won over power was a relief now, for her untouchable core seemed shaken, doing nothing to slow her racing heart or the colour that reversed itself and began to climb her cheeks. Something was wrong with her hands: they trembled with cold emotion that strove to take her breath away. Tears stung at her throat and eyes, bewilderingly at odds with a fierce hope that burned her. Tears did not belong in the height of an emotion so extreme she was at a loss to name it. Neither excitement nor happiness went far enough; it harkened back to childhood and the moments of believing that Robert, in hosting Lorraine's court for a month, would introduce young Belinda to the queen. She had known the name of that emotion once; it had, perhaps, been joy. Surely tears didn't belong to joy, no more than such violent jubilation should belong to Belinda at all. Her heart's beat filled her chest too fully, taking her breath and threatening to knock itself out of her body. "Javier?"

"For all that Mother's the queen of the country, Lanyarchan lands are hard to offer you. They would be best, for it would spite the Red Bitch, but I could offer you grounds in Brittany," Javier whispered. "Enough to be landed gentry; enough to command a certain power yourself." He took a breath, still holding the wine flask out, away from his body, away from Belinda. "Enough to make coming to the crown more than a pauper's walk."

A smile found Belinda's mouth and turned it half up long before Javier finished his plea. "To spite the Titian Bitch," she echoed. Her heart hurt, sending spikes of pain through her arms and into her palms, down her belly and to the soles of her feet. The heart should not be able to make pain in such far reaches of the body, she thought, but it did, as surely as it had taken up all the room for air in her lungs. "A Lanyarchan lady strengthening Prince Javier's claim to that throne. Throwing Cordula's faith in Lorraine's teeth, a warning that we will stand together. It is—" She had to swallow to loosen the knot that her throat had become. "It is an excellent ploy, my lord prince."

"It is not," Javier said with great care, "only a gambit."

Pain lanced through Belinda's chest again, forcing a laugh. "Is it not? What would your queen mother say to that?"

"Nothing flattering." Javier dared a smile that looked to hurt as much as Belinda's breath did. "I would make you my wife, Beatrice." He cast the wine away, coming toward her to take her hands. "I may not be allowed to." The frankness there deepened his voice and made raw cuts of it. "But I will if I can. Yes, what I presented to my mother is a game, but she doesn't know about your power. Our power. I have no intention of putting aside a woman who could be the heart and centre of my reign in ways no one else could ever understand. Forgive me for the method of it, Beatrice, but I beg of you, will you play this game with me?"

For the second time in her life a man got down on his knees, as if he were to make a love match, and asked her to marry him. And for the second time Belinda put shaking fingers into his hair, and whispered, "Yes."

13

BELINDA PRIMROSE / BEATRICE IRVINE
13 November 1587 † Lutetia

"You wanted movement, my lord Asselin." Belinda spoke the words carefully, not out of respect for Sacha but out of respect for her own swollen jaw.

She had not come traipsing home to tell of Javier's proposal with a light heart, nor had she needed to. Eliza met her at the door with a fist balled so hard Belinda was certain she'd heard the other woman's knuckles crack when the hit landed. It had been Eliza's only comment; Belinda hadn't seen her in the two days since, nor did she expect to for some time yet. Belinda had opted to remain at home in the interim, as much to give the city time to spread gossip as to let the bruise fade. It had been, she ungrudgingly admitted, a magnificent hit. And she should have seen it coming. That she hadn't struck a note of discordant humour in her, and she spent entirely too much time studying the knuckle-shaped bruise along her jaw.

Sacha, the lag-behind—for Marius had visited as well, expression bleak and tempered only with the faint hope Belinda realised Javier must have given him, that she could not possibly be expected to actually *wed* the prince—Sacha had only come around after two days, and his outrage was as plain, if less physical in nature, as Eliza's had been. He, who had been quite free with laying his hands on Belinda's person, was a study in avoiding doing so now, although his fists clenched and opened as he stalked her parlour.

"I wanted movement, Irvine, not our friendship shattered! Have you seen Eliza?"

"She left." Belinda worked her jaw carefully, putting cool fingers against the bruise. "I assume she went to you or Marius until her temper passes. Her things are still here."

"She's *gone*, Irvine. No one has seen her. Not since Tuesday morning."

Belinda turned toward the stocky lord with genuine horror clenching her stomach. "Gone?"

"Marius is holed up sick as a dog, all the spirit kicked out of him, and Liz is gone. You call that movement, Irvine?"

"You didn't ask me to protect your friendship." Belinda turned away again, startled by the ache cutting through her body. "I'm Lanyarchan. Lorraine won't like this at all." She had taken her bruised jaw and retreated to her bedroom after Eliza stormed out, writing a hasty letter to her "dearest Jayne" that warned him of the Gallic prince's clever plan. Lorraine would be a fool to act on the empty threat presented by Belinda's unexpected engagement, but the act could be made, and a trap laid in which to catch a queen. "Surely Eliza could see it was a ploy. Doesn't she know Javier better than that?"

"Eliza's not looking with her eyes."

"Are you?" Belinda cast the question without expecting an answer. Sacha growled, so low and deep for a moment she thought an animal was indeed locked in the room with her.

"You're a nothing, Irvine. A backwater noble—"

"From a country Lorraine struggles to dominate, whose faith is backed by Cordula's power and therefore the possibility of Essandia and Gallin's armies. You wanted movement, my lord Asselin," Belinda repeated. "I am attempting to provide it."

"You've done nothing. This was Javier's idea."

"Are you sure?" Belinda asked, but shrugged. "Does it matter? Without me there would be no alliance to dream up. What," she asked more pointedly, "do you *want* of me, Asselin?"

"I want your word that you won't go through with this farce."

Belinda barked laughter, then winced, putting her hand against her jaw. "It is not the provenance of a minor noble from Northern Aulun to determine whether she will or will not marry the prince of Gallin, Sacha." She used his name deliberately, a reminder that in comparison to a prince's rank, he was barely more than she. "Would you have me standing at the altar and refusing my vows?"

"If necessary," Sacha snapped. "He can't marry you, Irvine."

"I think you and Her Majesty are in accord on that topic. Her objection I understand, but your motivations make me curious. I'd think I would make a less offensive choice than a carefully bred pureblood who could never accept Javier's casual friendship with Eliza or the importance of you and Marius in his life." She hadn't seen Akilina since the night Javier had proposed, and curiosity ate at her. It would be easy to learn from Viktor whether his mistress was infuriated over the development, but Belinda was reluctant to face the palace with Eliza's handiwork still visible on her face. Cosmetics could cover the bruise, but a keen eye would see it regardless, and it smacked of a weakness Belinda was unwilling to show.

"Perhaps I simply want him to marry Eliza, so our quartet isn't disrupted."

"Then you're far more of a fool than I'd thought," Belinda said. "He couldn't even if he wanted to, and not just for the station she was born to." Eliza's confession to Javier on the bridge hung in Belinda's ears, and the spasm of anger that crossed Asselin's face said he, too, remembered why their gutter-born friend could never aspire to the throne. That Belinda had reminded him of Eliza's flaw was clearly no kindness, and she moved to soften his temper with quiet words: "I hope she comes back soon, Lord Asselin. Does Javier know she's gone?"

Fresh irritation curled his lip, her sop a failure except in redirecting his anger. "Javier's been cloistered with his mother for two days. Haggling out the details of your wedding, I'm sure. He won't hear me, and he twists with guilt every time he looks at Marius. You've destroyed us, Irvine."

"You won't believe me when I say that was not my intent." Belinda gathered her skirts and lifted her chin, displaying the bruise to full effect. "Perhaps I can distract him from his mother for a little while. I'll tell him about Eliza, my lord. It's the best I can do."

"No." Sacha's gaze turned ugly. "It's the least you can do."

Belinda pulled stillness around herself, hiding in plain sight in the thin November sun. It would be easy—appropriate, perhaps—to enter the palace with fanfare and pomp, but she found herself shivering with distaste at the idea.

She wondered, too late now, what Robert would say to the hand she'd played. An engagement to a prince meant portraits, drawings, discussions of her face and figure across the breadth of Echon. It meant the ordinary prettiness she'd hidden in would no longer be a disguise, her anonymity gone. She might still move among the lower ranks without fear of discovery, but a placement in a household like Gregori's might be forever out of her reach again. It was a thought that should have come to her before she agreed to Javier's mad plan.

And yet. And yet, had she thought, she would have chosen the same path she now walked, separate and in shadows, because from within she could more closely monitor Javier and his mother. Could more closely direct them into dangerous waters, all to Aulun's benefit.

Besides, her complexion could be roughened, weight gained or lost, her hair darkened or lightened. Those things could lend her anonymity again, if such measures were even necessary. Belinda stood aside as a gaggle of court ladies passed in a rush of perfume and giggles. They looked through her, no more seeing her than they might see the air they breathed, and she watched as they disappeared down the hall in a flurry of bright colours and shining hair. Mundane disguises faltered and fell before the witchpower-granted ability to stand amidst a gathering and go unseen. The only danger there was in avoiding those who could see through her magic, and thus far, the only ones who could were on her side.

The thought slowed her as she approached Javier's chambers. Robert worked for the love of his queen, but Khazarian-born Dmitri—if indeed he were born of that northern country; his accent when he'd accosted her in the Count Kapnist's estates had been flawlessly Aulunian—had no such tie to Lorraine. Belinda stepped into an alcove, holding her breath as she conjured memory, the distant voices of her father and Dmitri as they climbed the stairs to Robert's sitting rooms. Dmitri's, low and marked with the Khazarian accent: *"—begun. The imperatrix is with child—"*

And amusement from her father: *"That was quickly done."*

"As it had to be," Dmitri agreed. *"With the imperator's wars, that Irina has even a chance of childbearing is—"*

"A blessing to us all," Robert's tone, sanctimonious, garnered a staccato laugh from Dmitri, one that cut through the stillness surrounding Belinda even now. She half-focused across the hall, understanding coming to the woman where the child had seen no meaning at all.

Ivanova Durova was no more the Imperator Fodor's daughter

than Belinda herself was. Dmitri had lain with Irina and gotten a child on her, and as much as Robert had, guided that child's growth to adulthood. Like herself, like Javier, Ivanova was witch-breed.

Sudden coolness poured down Belinda's insides, chilling the shadows that held her safe. Robert was her father, and Dmitri Ivanova's. Sandalia showed no signs of witchpower, and the king whose name Javier bore was long dead.

Belinda found that she did not, for an instant, believe that Louis IV of Gallin had carried the witchpower in his blood.

Who was Javier's father?

Laughter trilled in her throat, more desperation than humour. Belinda pressed herself against the walls, folded her hands against her mouth and winced as she found the bruise again. Its ache soothed her and she increased the pressure against it, ignoring pain until it faded. The impulse to flee the Lutetian palace, all the way back to Aulun, so she could put the question to Robert Drake in person filled her. It was not a question to be asked in a letter, even to dearest Jayne; those, while cryptic, could be discovered and de-coded. A hint, even the slightest hint, that Javier, like herself, was a queen's bastard, would send Gallin flying apart and shame both Sandalia and Cordula to no end.

Belinda's heart crashed once against her ribs and held there, emptiness in her chest that thrummed through her veins until it felt that she might erupt from negative pressure within her.

It would send Gallin flying apart and shame Sandalia and Cordula to no end.

Javier's ties to Lanyarch would be shattered. Sandalia was only heir by marriage, not blood, and for her son to have come from the wrong side of a marriage bed would break his claim to that long-empty throne. Likewise, his mother was regent in Gallin, holding the throne for her son.

Her son. Not Louis's son. Javier, as a bastard, had no right to

Gallin's throne. Only his heirship to Essandia would be legitimate, coming through his uncle to his mother to himself, and Rodrigo, for all his fondness toward Sandalia, might well not be able to see past a bastard child. Not when his faith in his church was so much to him that he himself had never wed and fathered an heir. His piety, Belinda thought, must have been a frustration to Robert and Dmitri, who now seemed to her intent on littering Echon's royal families with witchbreed bastards.

Yes. If it was their plot, then Dmitri had to be Javier's father, though the look of the ginger-haired prince held nothing in common with the hawk-faced man at all. Perhaps his pale skin and slim build, nothing more, certainly not the narrowness of his grey eyes or his long jaw.

Uncertainty washed through her. Javier looked far more like the washed-out blond king who was his father by law than like Dmitri or even his own mother. Maybe witchbreed magic was less rare than either she or Javier thought, and slept unnoticed through most generations, only sparking from time to time in certain families.

But then her own father should not have the power that he did, and perhaps then Ivanova, daugher of Irena of Khazar, had no power at all. But had Dmitri and Robert not been certain of that gift arising, then the circumstances of Ivanova's birth made little difference to anyone. Belinda quelled the urge to clutch her temples, as if she'd try to hold her thoughts together. No, witchbreed parents knew what they had when they made a child, and Robert would know, must know, who Javier's father was. Perhaps not Dmitri after all, his sharp features and darkness clearly not inherited by the witchbreed prince. Someone else, then, a user of witchpower outside of Belinda's realm of knowledge. Someone at court who could guide Javier in the development of his skills.

No.

Javier had told her she was the only one like himself. Belinda had recognized almost immediately that her father, too, was like them, but Javier had spoken freely of having no guidance, only his own sense of self to show him the way.

Robert didn't know. The thought came with startling clarity. Her father, who seemed to Belinda to be always in control, *did not know* that the prince of Gallin was witchbreed. Had he known, he would have influenced Sandalia through her son rather than insert Belinda into the realm. It was what Belinda herself would have done, and her father was far more calculating than she. Javier lay outside Robert's realm of influence, and that meant he, even more than Sandalia and her ambitions, stood as a threat to Aulun.

A chill of curiosity lifted bumps on Belinda's skin as she thought of other royal scions, and wondered how many of them were their father's children, and what purpose they served if they were not. *Her* purpose was clear: as the hidden daughter of Aulun, she was a secret weapon, trained to protect a throne that stood on the faith of a new religion. Ivanova, openly Irina's daughter, could hold no such position in her mother's court; she had been born in wedlock, if on the wrong side of the sheets, and no one would question her heirship. But that in itself could be a purpose, if Ivanova could be controlled and influenced through witchpower. An unbreachable Khazarian alliance would strengthen Aulun immeasurably.

Belinda shuddered in a breath through her fingers, then spread her hands wide, staring at her palms. Echon's fate lay in her hands more thoroughly than even Robert imagined.

Excitement darted through her, testing her external stillness like a hummingbird in search of life-giving nectar. She kept it locked within, golden witchpower cloaking her against all comers as she considered her needs. Foremost, always foremost, was to find proof of a plan against the Aulunian throne, but beneath that now lay the task of discovering who had fathered Javier de Castille. To learn, in short, what other players influenced Echon's royal families by way of the base side of a marriage bed. *It cannot be found out* thrummed in the back of her mind, her father's lifelong warning, and she thought that even if she had the means to ask, Robert might withhold that answer from her. She had often asked questions and rarely had them answered—that lesson had been learned early on. Better to discover what she could on her own and, armed with knowledge, come to her father with details that shone light on Sandalia's indiscretions and shattered Javier's claim to a trio of thrones.

To do otherwise was to question her own existence, focused and purposeful as it had been, and even with power growing inside her with its own ambition for dominance, Belinda did not doubt herself or her place in the world. And even if—alien thought, difficult to so much as endure, much less truly consider—even if she were somehow to be brought into the light as her mother's daughter, every step toward securing Aulun's future secured her own. The truth of Javier's heritage would inevitably help fashion that security.

It would take more than a hint. Belinda's head spun, glee rushing through her veins in sparks of golden light. The extraordinary potential of what lay before her threatened to burst her self-imposed calm, and she didn't care. It would take more than whispers to properly bring down the Gallic regent and her son. She would need proof of Sandalia's infidelities, and a wise queen would have done away with proof.

Belinda uncurled a slow smile at her palms. Sandalia had let one shred of proof go: Javier himself. Knowing what to look for, the rest could be done. Not by anyone, perhaps, but by Belinda, with her burgeoning gift for stealing thoughts and influencing emotion. It could be done, and when it was done, Ecumenic Echon would be in shambles, and Lorraine's Reformation throne safe for years to come.

Javier would never forgive her. Belinda swayed at the thought, letting her hands close into loose fists again. He, who had unleashed her witchpower and her heart, he who believed that above all Belinda wished to see him safely enstated on the Lanyarchan throne, he who was heir to half of Echon, would not forgive her if she so utterly destroyed his world. Nor should he. Belinda closed her eyes, regret lancing through delight until her heart hung in her chest again, aching with unfamiliar choice. Her duty was obvious.

And she would not shirk it. Nails dug into her palms and she let go a soft cry, deliberately forgoing stillness to revel in brief pain. To serve Aulun, to serve Lorraine, she would destroy Javier and with him the precious sense of belonging.

Unless she could convince him it was the only way. Dismissive laughter rose in her even as the idea formed. It was, perhaps, the only way for her, but she was a child of another realm, both in country and in heart. The few moments she would spend at Javier's side in the eyes of all Echon would fade and disappear beneath a lifetime of duty serving Aulun. Beatrice Irvine might briefly be remembered; Belinda Primrose would never exist.

Irritation surged through stillness, an unexpected rise of emotion. Belinda clamped it down, thoughts half bent to scolding the witchpower within her. Identifying the ambition that using power woke in her made it easier to draw back from it, though it rose more quickly each time she drew heavily on the gift Javier had teased to life. Its fire was only semi-welcome: Belinda craved the skills it brought, the ability to hide and influence, but shied from the raw sense of injustice it carried with it. She had accepted with open eyes and a clear mind her place in the world as Lorraine's natural child, and to find a part of herself boiling with resentment and striving for a place among the stars was uncomfortable and distressing. It made her wonder at her own beliefs, whether she was content with the lot she'd been handed, when a lifetime of knowing who and what she was had never troubled her before.

"It's still too early." Dmitri's voice, heard through a child's pretense at sleep. She had been nine then, truly no more than a child. Perhaps now, at twenty-two, she was still come too early to her

gifts; perhaps that was why Robert had never removed the barriers in her mind. But the witchpower that pooled in her mind told her otherwise: it had wakened her to Dmitri's arrival in Khazan, and overwhelmed her at the tavern in Aria Magli. Robert might yet believe that her magic should go untested and untrained, but that was a rare mistake on her father's part. True power would not be forever contained, and it had broken free outside of his influence and in its own time.

And so, too, Belinda thought, would she, if it were necessary in shaping Gallin's fall and Aulun's rise.

Skirts gathered, she finally stepped free of shadow and slipped down the hall to her lover's chambers.

AKILINA PANKEJEFF, DVORYANIN
14 November 1587 † *Lutetia*

There is something wrong with the guardsman.

Akilina chose him at random out of Gregori's ranks, once the death services were attended to. She chose him for his rough-hewn good-looks and a tendency toward cleanliness that most of his brethren didn't seem to share, and that, she realises now, is what's wrong. His thick hair looks greasy, his brown eyes bright with fever. Sweat stands against swarthy skin and trickles into his beard, and she thinks she can smell him, even from half a room away. It's not like him, and a combination of curiosity and disgust compels her to snap her fingers and gesture him toward her. "Lutetia doesn't agree with you . . . ?"

"Viktor, my lady," he supplies without resentment, though she's sure she's asked before. His gaze flickers to the side, unwilling to meet hers. That would be proper, except for the skittishness she sees in him.

"Look at me, Viktor." Command suits her voice well. Viktor draws his shoulders back, coming to full attention and bringing his eyes to hers. "Lutetia disagrees with you?" she asks again. "You've kept close to me since we've arrived, and you look ill." It's only as she says it that Akilina realises it's true. In the handful of days she's been at Sandalia's court, of all the guards, Viktor has never been far from her side. Even when weariness must have had him wanting his rest, he's been nearby. Delight curves her mouth and she considers him again, this time as a cat might a morsel. He needs bathing—God, he needs bathing!—but he's broad of shoulder and if there's a thickness to him through the hips, all the better; fragile men have never been to her taste.

That thought, inevitably, brings the pale, ginger-haired Javier to mind. He is beautifully shaped, though his slender body makes Akilina think of a boy not yet grown to a man's form. She has little doubt of his male assets, but now isn't the time to explore that road. Not with news of his engagement coming so quickly on the heels of Akilina's arrival that she might think it deliberate if she didn't know better. As it is, an alliance with the little Lanyarchan girl strikes Akilina as enormously funny, and she has every intention of remaining in the Gallic court long enough to watch the romance play out. There will, after all, be pieces to pick up afterward, and Akilina fancies herself something of an expert at puzzles.

Which brings her back to Viktor's attentiveness. It seems a simple puzzle, to be sure, but pleasing to unravel regardless. "Are you unwell?" Heartsick? she wants to ask, but it's far more entertaining to play it out and see if the man condemns himself with his own tongue. A guard ought not look so high as a noblewoman, though should her eye fall so low he dares not turn away. Such is the narrow path offered to the lower classes, and Akilina enjoys making a man walk its balance.

"Not ill, my lady," Viktor replies, but he sounds uncertain of himself. Akilina cocks an eyebrow and leans forward, arching her throat as she smiles up at him. His gaze falls to her breasts and then jerks away again, more caution in him than many a man bothers to show.

"Too little sleep, then." She traces a finger along her jaw, then down the line of her throat, watching Viktor struggle with where to put his eyes. "You've been near me my every waking hour, Viktor. Do you watch over me while I sleep, as well?"

"Yes, my lady." Viktor's voice has gone hoarse and he struggles not to watch as Akilina idly follows the curve of her own breast, mounded against corsets. The attempt is valiant, and she would admire him for it if it didn't amuse her so much.

"And why do you watch me so closely, guardsman?" Viktor's erection is plain to see against his pants. It's a shame he's so badly in need of a bath, or the afternoon might take a far more entertaining turn than Akilina had anticipated.

Viktor, thickly, says, "She told me to," and Akilina's hands grow chilly, ceasing their exploration of her body. The afternoon, it seems, will yet provide some entertainment.

"She?" That Sandalia would put a spy on her is to be expected. That she'd choose one of Akilina's own people is both audacious and foolish: the strain of surveillance is a thing to be worked up to, to be taught, not dropped into the lap of an amateur. It explains Viktor's failing health and his sharp scent; he is absolutely unprepared for this kind of work.

"Rosa," he answers, then draws his eyebrows down heavily and passes a hand over his face. "Rosa," he says again, but there's uncertainty in his voice. Akilina stands, moving closer to him even though doing so causes her to hold her breath.

"Who is Rosa, Viktor?" The command is gone from her voice, leaving gentleness. He seems close to breaking, this strong Khazarian guard, and it would be a shame for him to shatter before she understands the game he's been drawn into.

"Prince Javier's woman," he responds, and Akilina's astonishment blooms into laughter.

• C. E. MURPHY
"Javier's woman, as you so crudely put it, is Beatrice Irvine,
some ignoble gentry from Northern Aulun. *She* set you to spying
on me?"
"Rosa told me to," Viktor says stubbornly, and something in his
gaze clears, fever pitch fading as he turns a glower on Akilina. It's
a moment before he seems to realise whom he's scowling at, and
then he shakes himself and drops his gaze. "I'm sorry, my lady."
"Viktor." Akilina puts a fingertip beneath his chin and forces his
head up again. "Lady Irvine reminds you of a Rosa?" This is fine
stuff: a guardsman in lust with a lady. Better yet, the prince's woman.
Akilina could have his head for it, and make it a gift to Gallin.
Viktor, it seems, ceases to care that Akilina is his mistress, and
turns the full force of frustrated anger on her, black eyebrows
drawn low over dark eyes. There's desperation in him, a broken
understanding that bleeds from his gaze. The fever is back, burning
in him. "I've swivved the bitch, my lady," he snaps, and even as he
speaks it's clear he doesn't know how what he says can be, but that
he believes it with every fibre of his being. "She more than reminds
me. I'd swear on my own grave that she's the same bit that warmed
my bed and Count Gregori's in the days before he died."
Heat and cold slip over Akilina's body like a lover, raising queasi-
ness instead of passion. It fades in seconds, leaving heart-palpitating
excitement in its place. "Viktor, Viktor, Viktor." Akilina covers
his lips with her fingertip and steps closer still, risking staining her
gown with his sweat. "If you are not right, darling Viktor, it will indeed be your grave you swear on. Now tell me," she breathes. "Tell
me everything."
BELINDA PRIMROSE / BEATRICE IRVINE
14 November 1587 † *Lutetia*
"Eliza can't be gone." Javier's petulance astounded Belinda, his
hurt that of a child whose world had been so badly shaken he could

only stand and rail against it. "Where would she go? Why would she go?"

"Lord Asselin tells me she is, my lord," Belinda said unhappily. "And I haven't seen her since Tuesday morning." Javier hadn't noticed, or had not, at least, commented on, the bruise that marked Belinda's jaw. That was as well: she discovered that she genuinely preferred not to lay its blame at Eliza's feet—or fist—and she doubted Javier would accept clumsiness as an excuse. "Are there any childhood hideaways she might be able to make her way to?"

"Not without me." Casual arrogance filled the reply, making impossible the suggestion that Eliza had somewhere to go outside of Javier's personal haunts. Belinda held her tongue, waiting for a chance to propose the idea without insulting the prince. "Beatrice, she can't leave. I need her."

"Did you ever tell her that, my lord?" The part of the devil's advocate was an unfamiliar one, and Belinda took no relish in playing it. Javier alone was no doubt easier to manipulate than Javier surrounded by his lifetime friends, but the raw misery pulsing off him made Belinda want to throw her characteristic behavior away and gather him close in sympathy.

Javier made a noise of exasperation. "Why would I? We've been together all our lives." Again, the emotion that poured off him showed no indication that he could be in the wrong. It was a powerful thing, Belinda thought, supreme confidence in oneself. Powerful and dangerous, perhaps most especially to those who never had it challenged. Belinda believed in her own growing magic and in her skills, but not with Javier's royal conviction. Understanding how people might react was a survival trait for her; for the prince, it was something to be advised on by councilors and generals.

"You've been together all your lives, but still you've become engaged without warning her," Belinda pointed out. "You've been together all your lives, Javier, and she loves you. She's *in* love with you. Did it not strike you that such news might come most kindly from your own lips?"

"I told Marius!"

"Oh, God help me." Belinda let herself fall into Aulunian for the one phrase, endowing it with a Lanyarchan burr and all the impatience she could muster. "Yes, and that was well done, but those three are your *friends,* Javier. Marius isn't the only one who deserved to hear it from you. They all did, maybe Eliza most of all." Pride was as dangerous as Javier's boundless confidence, and even Javier had grasped the idea that the poor might be even more terribly proud than the wealthy.

"Well, then, I've got to get her back." Javier threw off his sulk in a fit of action, stalking across his chambers to fling open the wardrobe and root through it. Belinda watched, bemused.

"Shall you humiliate me by announcing an engagement and then riding after another woman, stopping to ask all the passersby if they've seen a beauty filled with rage come this way, my lord?"

Javier went still, so sudden and profound Belinda imagined for a moment that he had learned her trick of letting nothing touch him. She sighed and crossed to him, putting her fingers at the small of her back, where she herself wore a tiny dagger. "I want her gone no more than you do, Javier. If we're to find her, let's put a practical plan into place, rather than chasing hares across Echon. She's a woman alone, without money. She can't have gone terribly far in four days."

"She does have money," Javier said thickly. "I can't count how much she's stolen off me over the years. She . . ." He drew his hands from the wardrobe, rippling his knuckles as though a coin danced over them. "Practised," he murmured. "On me, I suppose, so she could steal from others without being caught. Oh, Liza, you fool."

It was not, Belinda thought, Eliza who was the fool. "Send men, my lord. Send them to wherever you can think she might be. Make it known that you're doing so, if you want. I can stand the embarrassment." She smiled faintly. "And Eliza will like that you've put up the fuss. It may bring her home."

Javier turned to look down at her, hope burning bright in his gaze. "Would it bring you home?"

"Yes," Belinda said gently, and smiled to seal the lie. Eliza would be found only if she wanted to be; Javier, Belinda suspected, simply had no understanding of where to seek the gutter-born woman. But relief turned the prince's eyes to slate and he nodded, drawing her close. Against her will she put her arms around him, feeling his sigh and brief tremble before he spoke against her hair.

"And what of Sacha? Is he as angry as all that, too?"

"Sacha has strictly forbidden me to marry you." Belinda made her voice light and tipped her chin up to give Javier another smile, this one intending to mask nothing but the truth. "I expect he'll denounce me as a harlot eager to spread my legs for anyone willing to move toward freeing Lanyarch from Reformation rule if I don't break it off with all due haste."

"Really?" A hint of welcome laughter warmed Javier's question. "And is that true, Beatrice?"

Belinda widened her eyes in a too-broad semblance of innocence. "Of course not, my lord. I'll only spread my legs for the prince's friends, and complain bitterly when they're coarse and inattentive lovers."

Javier's laughter turned full, a bark of sound over Belinda's head. She lowered her gaze, taking momentary satisfaction in the truth turned against Asselin, then looked back up to smile at Javier's teasing remark: "Splendid. I'll tell Sacha he's dreadful in bed when he comes to me with imprecations about your reputation." His humour faded. "And Marius?"

"Believes you'll put me aside, my lord." Belinda sighed, more genuine regret in the sound than she was comfortable owning to.

"The same story you told your mother. A mother might eventually forgive, but a friendship like Marius's is a precious thing to waste."

"He'll forgive me, in time." Javier's unflaggable confidence rang false. "It would help if I had a sister to marry him off to. Marius is inconsistent in love. You were—" Discomfort wrote itself over his face. "You were the first he bothered introducing to us."

"If I'd known about the witchbreed power," Belinda murmured, "I might have come straight to you, and we might have spared Marius's heart." Again, there was more truth in her words than she liked, and Javier drew her closer, sensing her melancholy.

"We two are alone," he said into her hair. "You couldn't know. Nor, I think, would you dare introduce yourself to a prince. You fail to watch your tongue often enough, Beatrice, but that boldness might have been beyond your ken." He chuckled without humour and moved away from her, tension in the lines of his body. "Or did you choose Marius so you might meet me?"

"What a horrible burden to always walk beneath," Belinda said after a moment, letting raw sorrow touch her voice. "It is lonely to be a prince, isn't it, my lord? Rumour said that Marius Poulin was your friend," she admitted cautiously. "I did not imagine he would bring me to meet you so readily." Truth lay in fine shards beneath her words, Javier seeming too delicate, in the moment, to ease with soothing falsehoods. "I could not have imagined what has happened." That, at least, was truth unvarnished, so much so that Belinda uttered an unnaturally rough laugh. "Who could?" she added, unable to help the question. To her relief Javier turned back with a wry smile.

"Not I. And I think that even if you had deliberately sought Marius out and used him to reach me, that I might forgive you for it, Beatrice. I have been alone with God and my power all my life, and whatever means brought you to me are means that I am thankful for."

"Then be thankful for a strong Lanyarchan oak, and the clever hands of shipwrights," Belinda quipped, and Javier smiled again. "Come, my lord," she said more quietly, and then amusement slid into her voice despite herself. "We have other things to think about, do we not? A wedding to plan, a throne to topple, and Lanyarch to frame for it."

14

ROBERT, LORD DRAKE
19 November 1587 † Alunaer

"We are unobserved?" The question is a matter of ritual, and that
is the *only* thing that brings it to Robert's lips tonight. He stands in
the queen's private meeting room with a letter clenched in his fist,
a letter that has made its way by ship from Lutetia to a miserable
hovel in Northern Aulun, then by horse, of which it smells, to his
estates to the west, and finally by his own harried courier to
Aulun's capital city, where it has come to end its days as a smear of
ink in Robert Drake's large fist.

"We are," Lorraine answers, and for a rarity she sounds amused
at the question. It's because of his own agitation, he knows, and yet
he finds himself too piqued to present even a semblance of calm.
"What on earth has happened, Robert?" Lorraine is in fine form,
indeed; perhaps he should remember that his distress improves her
humour. He is accustomed to being level-headed, and Lorraine has
always thrived on the temerity offered by her red-gold hair. It's
believed redheads are more prone to temper fits than others, and if
Lorraine is to be taken as an example, superstition is right.

"It's Belinda," he manages to grate, and for a startling moment
both of them cease all motion, the weight of that girl's name heavy

in the air between them. Robert refers to her as *Primrose* when he must discuss her at all with Lorraine, but their daughter is a topic he prefers to avoid. It's a matter of practicality, not sensitivity; a queen ought not know the details of those doing murder in her name.

"You have our attention, Robert," Lorraine says archly, when silence has gone on too long. "Pray, share your news with us."

"She has—She's—" Robert splutters and thrusts the bedraggled letter toward his queen. Her finely plucked eyebrows elevate and she takes it as if it were diseased, which may not be far from true. She unwrinkles it between long white fingers—even in her age, Lorraine's hands are lovely—and scans the travel-stained contents of the paper. Her eyebrows inch fractionally higher as she reads, until wrinkles appear in her forehead; she is not given to allowing herself such expressions, for they leave marks in skin that's no longer as resilient as it once was. When she looks up her expression is hugely amused, and that, Robert fears, is deadly.

"Congratulations, Robert. Your silent weapon is silent no longer." Lorraine hands him the letter and he crumples it again as she lounges in her chair, tapping a fingertip against scarlet-painted lips. A smile hovers behind her mouth, playing at the muscles of her face but not permitted to burst forth. "Has ambition proved too much for her? A queen's ba—"

Robert silences her with a slice of his hand through the air, abrupt motion that he would never dare in public. Lorraine's eyebrows shoot up again, more than enough commentary, but of all things, he will not permit her to say the words she nearly has, not even in the privacy of her unobserved meeting room. There are no ears to hear it, but it remains far better if there are no words to be heard. "A queen's bastard" is a condemning phrase, and not to the child, not in this age, not in this world. "If she were working from ambition," and this he believes, "she wouldn't have warned us of

Javier's plot. It's enough, Lorraine." He uses her name deliberately, something he doesn't often do; he hopes to sway her with its importance. "It's proof of movement against you. It's time to act."

He can see before she speaks that she'll reject his insistence. Lorraine's greatest weakness is her caution, though it may also be her greatest strength. That caution has let her hold a throne for nearly thirty years without losing it to a marriage bed or a battle. But it has also kept her from acting when she should, especially against Sandalia, who holds ambition like a flare against the night. The men of her court call it feminine sentiment, and still, after three decades, name it proof that Lorraine should not be permitted to rule alone. Robert knows that sentiment sways his queen less than a too-precise understanding: revolution and regicide are dangerous tools, and once broached, catch imagination far too easily.

Frustration rises, dark and hot within him as he's proven right with Lorraine's slight shake of her head. "An ambitious boy doesn't lay the grounds for action taken against another crowned head, Robert. Your Primrose says Sandalia approves, but words aren't proof. I will move." Her voice sharpens, as does her cool grey gaze, and for a moment Robert recalls that he is indeed in the presence of royalty. Lorraine expects her will to be obeyed, and in the end, he knows he won't go against her. To do so is not in his nature, no more than it is in Belinda's.

"I will move," Lorraine repeats, "when no other crowned head of Echon would hold it against me for doing so. We demand proof, Robert, unquestionable proof. We demand words written with treacherous intent and signed in Sandalia's name before we will call our sister-queen a pretender with ambitions to our throne and strike her down for it."

"My lady." Robert bows his head, unwilling to argue. Lorraine holds a hard gaze on him for long moments, establishing that her will is as supreme here, in her private chambers, as it is everywhere in Aulun. Only when he has held the submissive posture long enough does she relent with a quick gesture of her long fingers.

"We will, however, play your Primrose's game," she says more softly. "We will agitate and rumble and smell of fear, as if we are so uncertain of ourselves and our throne as to quaver at the idea of a Lanyarchan uprising. Perhaps we ourselves will lure young Javier into a trap, and hold his mother at bay that way."

She relaxes suddenly, regality fleeing from her stance and weariness greying her eyes. "Am I such a wicked queen? Robert," she says, and he's uncertain if she wishes him to answer. He thinks not, but Lorraine's lapses into ordinary humanity are as unpredictable as her temper, and she never questions herself, not in public, not in private. "My sister held the throne through a reign of bloodshed; my brother for so few days he is all but forgotten." She stands, crossing the room to where a window once was; now its only mark is stone of a lighter shade than the surrounding walls. She puts her hand against the seam, gaze turned outward, as though she sees things he can't. He is more certain now that she does not want an answer of him, only for his ears and silence.

"It's been a half century and more since my father split the Church and laid down Reformation law." Lorraine's voice holds a note of wryness: in confessing those years she confesses to her own age, for her mother was the woman Henry split from Cordula over. It's not an acknowledgment she cares to make; in fact, Robert often wonders if she quite realises how many years have passed. He knows she's too intelligent to deny the passage of time, and yet the determination with which she plays at youth and teases fresh marriage proposals on the proposition of child-bearing is so deep-set that it seems impossible she could maintain the facade without believing in it herself.

But now regret hollows Robert's heart to hear her admit to the years. It's an unexpected weakness to find inside himself, the hope and bizarre belief that Lorraine Walter can hold off age through denial, even when his eyes and intellect tell him it's a battle she, like everyone, must lose. "Lanyarch chafes under Reformation rule where Aulun has bowed its head to it. I don't want Constance's legacy, Robert. I don't want my name to be whispered as a butcher's—Oh, stop it," she says impatiently, and he startles, then curls an apologetic smile toward the floor. Her thoughts may be turned to things beyond the palace walls, but her attention is crisp enough inside the spy-hole room, and she saw his grimace that said she wasn't supposed to know the names laid at her dead sister's feet. "I'm neither deaf nor a fool, and Constance's name was drowned in blood long before I took the throne. A country does not easily sway between one faith and another. Surely it was right to hold with Father's religion, when a return to Cordula's brought such bitter bloodshed during Constance's years on the throne."

Now she hesitates, and Robert takes it as a cue to speak, though he keeps his voice quiet and diffident. "You have been right." There's no other answer he can give, but he also believes it's true: Aulun's tender new religion has drawn scars deeply across the whole of the island nation. But those that run deepest are the ones left from Constance's reign. Lorraine's older sister, daughter of Henry's first and only, in Ecumenic eyes, legitimate wife, Constance had been faithful to her mother's religion, and tried to turn the tide back to Cordula's church. Hundreds of Reformation believers had burned during her short reign, and in the end, she had paid for her faith with her life. For stability, for expansion, for practicality in moving forward, Lorraine chose wisely in choosing her father's religion.

And Robert wants nothing more than for Aulun to move forward. "You have been right," he says again. "I have no answers for contentious Lanyarch, save to cut them free and make them their own country, no longer subject to the Aulunian crown."

Lorraine turns a look so incredulous it borders on offense toward him, and Robert laughs. "Well, it's an idea," he protests, and Lorraine's expression becomes that much more appalled. Robert lifts his hands in apology and bows deeply at the same time, though he's still smiling as he rises again. "Forgive me, my queen. It was a terrible idea."

"Your humour sometimes bewilders us, Robert." Lorraine falls into formality, but there's a twitch in her voice that says she might give herself over to laughter as well, were she not a queen. But she is, and Robert wonders if she *can* laugh at such a jape, or if it's physically beyond her capability. He sighs, still smiling, and now turns his palms up.

"If I didn't occasionally befuddle you, my queen, you might grow bored of me and put me aside. My life would be meaning-less." It's meant as a quip, but his voice softens, betraying too much. Lorraine lowers her eyes as if she were still a girl and uncer-tain of how to respond to truth disguised as flattery. It was an em-barrassment, Robert thought, to actually fall in love with his queen. At least Dmitri would never know, and Seolfor; well, Seolfor.

"Let them play their game with Lanyarch," he says before si-lence grows too heavy. "Let Gallin think we tremble. We have Irina's treaty all but in hand, and with Khazarian troops we can quell that troublesome land if necessary. You must admit," he adds, suddenly thoughtful, "it's not a bad plot."

"Not if I were eighteen and uncertain of my throne," Lorraine says tartly, but she relents with a nod. "Better, perhaps, for stirring up Lanyarch than for threatening me, but even that can be trouble enough. Are you sure it's Javier's plot, Robert, and not your Primrose's? You taught her to be clever."

"No," he says, startling himself into another smile with the rec-ollection of Belinda's innocent gaze all the times she made the amused claim that he now offers for her: "Her nurse did."

Lorraine's eyes narrow and he shrugs it off, briefly and inordi-

330 · C. E. MURPHY

nately pleased with the child he fathered. "I believe she'll press it forward to the point of the hard proof that you require, but not that she would instigate a plot against you, Lorraine. She's loyal, and if she is not, there is someone there who watches her, and who will tell me if she should falter." Robert spreads one hand, admission of his own weakness. "I trust her, but I wouldn't be your spymaster if I didn't distrust my own certainty. She's watched."

"She's young," Lorraine says, "and he's a prince. Loyalty can be bought. We'll play her game, Robert, but we wish her to be extracted from the situation. Fetch her yourself, or send your man who watches her to do so." It's not a mother's concern behind the command, but a regent's self-interest.

Robert inclines his head, a promise, then lifts his eyes again to say, mildly, "It will be done, my lady." He cannot help himself, though: he believes in his daughter, and so adds, "If I'm wrong about her, my head for it."

It's careless, meant to show loyalty, but something cool comes into Lorraine's eyes again, and Robert is once more reminded that he stands in the presence of royalty. She doesn't need words to remind him that it could well be his head for it, nor that favouritism can fade. Well and truly scolded, Robert bows again, and in the hidden places of that obsequience rues the heart that loves a queen.

ANA DI MEO
22 November 1587 † *Lutetia*

Aulun is such a little distance away.

Ana di Meo fingers a letter sent to her only three days earlier, from Alunear across the channel, and imagines the journey it would continue on for days or even weeks yet, if it had to reach her in Aria Magli. There are mountain ranges in the way, a difficult enough journey in summer; in the winter it's easier to take a ship beyond Essandia's most westerly points and bring it back again into the Primorismare. There are storms to risk, of course, but there are always storms.

And one is brewing now, between Aulun and Gallin.

Ana climbs to her feet, letter held in her fingertips, and collects a warm fur to wrap around her shoulders as she crosses to a window that overlooks Lutetia. It's a grey city in the failing winter light, with the Sacrauna cutting a broad dark slash through it. She's not as close to the water as she'd like to be: after a lifetime of Aria Magli's canals, it surprises her how uncomfortable she is with cobbled streets and so little sound of running water. But she can see the river from her tower, and see the city besides. A cathedral rises up as the landscape's dominant feature, overwhelming even Sandalia de Costa's palace. God reigns here more surely than Man, and Ana supposes the church would have it so. For herself, she'd rather be back in decadent Aria Magli, where God and Man wrestle in the sheets every night and come morning bob and greet each other on the canals like distantly polite strangers. Lutetia thinks itself quite the centre of culture, but Ana finds it stifling.

Rue carves lines in her face and she taps the letter against the windowsill. If it's stifling, it's in part her own fault: she's chosen life in a tower, like a princess or worse, God forbid, a nun. Lovers and servants come to her full of gossip, and she rarely leaves her protected place. Not for her own sake, but because Belinda Primrose has made herself a fixture in the palace, and Ana di Meo, much as she would prefer to stand and watch the young woman weave her way through Lutetian politicians, can't risk Belinda seeing her. Ana knows herself to be striking; men remember her after only a glance, and she shared far more than that with Belinda.

And might have shared more yet, had the girl not drawn back, fever and distress blanching her features. Even now that expression stings Ana, though when Robert Drake had arrived to take Belinda away, much was explained. Ana had thought it revulsion; now she knows it for guilt, and that she can sympathize with.

Women of their nature are rarely allowed moments of freedom, and to be caught up when they're stolen . . .

Well. Ana paid the price for the path they'd looked at travelling, too, as damned by unfettered desire as Belinda had been. Robert had snatched away a chance for a few hours of joy without price, though to hold him accountable is both petty and pointless. She knows that as well as she knows her own name, and also knows her own character well enough to place blame comfortably, whether it was warranted or not. There is little in the way of bitterness in doing so, but everyone, queen or courtesan, counts coup.

Ana unfolds the letter onto the sill, reading over words she has no need to be reminded of. Robert's strong hand is undisguised in the pages, words of loyalty and love scrawled out as though passion had captured him in a fit and forced him to the pen.

He warms her with his promises, even when she reads the requests hidden by careful phrasing. It isn't her love he seeks, but news of Belinda's feelings for Gallin's crown prince. Not Ana's loyalty he wants, nor his own pledged to her, but details of Belinda's to her duty. It's a pity the world is not other than it is, for Ana can imagine one in which Robert's missives to her are nothing of coded questions, and all of the desire and fondness written on the surface.

But that is not this world, and so she calls for a servant to bring warm clothes not at all in the flowing new fashion set by the prince's cheapside friend, and not at all in the startling strong colours Ana prefers. She has her hair disguised beneath a hat, and dismisses the servant to do her own cosmetics, aging herself, and it is a different woman entirely who leaves the courtesan's tower. Gossip carried by lovers is all and well, but if she's to judge Belinda's emotions for Javier, she must see them together.

She joins a host of petitioners to see the queen, confident she won't be called upon: there are dozens of applicants, and she only one drab old woman among them. What matters is slipping through the palace doors and coming into the royal hall. She hasn't been this bold before; when she's taken it upon herself to watch Belinda with her own eyes, she's done it in church, or parks, or city streets, but that has been to watch the girl at play with the other men she's used to reach the prince. To tell Robert what he wants to know, Ana must stand among the privileged and observe without being observed.

And what she realises in moments is that something new has come over Belinda Primrose, a confidence that rivals her lover's. They do not stand together, prince and consort: he sits at his mother's side, a step or two below her while Sandalia listens patiently to a merchant complaining of ruined wares. Belinda stands well away, across the hall from Javier, but their connection is such that it takes Ana's breath. They have a sense of the forbidden about them, strange for a pair whose engagement has been announced. But Ana has no other way to describe the intensity that flows between them. If she didn't know better, she would think them thwarted lovers, ready to die for each other if they could not live together. Nor is she the only one who sees it: murmurs and smiles surround her, courtiers and commoners there to watch young lovers as much as pay attendance to the queen.

Of the two, Belinda is the more reserved: her gaze is cast downward, a picture of modesty in one of the new-fashioned gowns. It makes her look sweet and delectable, like a creature who should be thrown on the floor and tasted of, taking her innocence with tongue and fingers and shaming her modesty when gasps of unlooked-for delight come to her lips. And yet an undercurrent of strain seems to vibrate through her, telling Ana that despite her outward demeanor, Belinda listens, judges, plans. That's good; that's what Robert will want to hear.

But the other, the prince: he watches Belinda more often than he watches the queen or the people who will someday be his. It's his place, Ana supposes, to be the one who looks on her, being a man with no need for decorum. He looks like the one who *would* take Belinda on the floor, so much need burning in him that he would hardly bother sending courtiers away first. It's glorious to see, how passion warms his pale skin and how people glance toward Belinda with admiration, as though Javier's lust for her influences their own opinions. Javier is a natural leader, if he can pursuade men so easily that his passions are the ones they should follow.

Robert, Lord Drake, will be very pleased indeed if the prince of Gallin will follow Belinda Primrose to the ends of the earth and beyond.

Satisfied, Ana gathers her skirts and slips out of the palace hall to write a letter of reassurance. Oh, yes, she will write, there is love and lust and loyalty between them, but it runs deeper on Gallin's part than Aulun's, an opinion Robert ought to trust, for there's not a much better judge of character than a whore. And then she'll seal the letter and let a rider take it to a ship and the sea, for Aulun is such a little distance away, and Robert so very close.

BELINDA PRIMROSE / BEATRICE IRVINE
24 November 1587 † *Lutetia*

"Viktor." It had become too easy to use names in the weeks— months, now—that she'd been Beatrice Irvine. It would take re- training to fall out of the habit again, though at least a servant wasn't expected to be on personal terms with her mistress and mas- ter. Belinda whispered the guard's name again, almost singing it, and extended witchpower through the word, drifting magic through Sandalia's palace.

She felt him stiffen in more ways than one when her will touched his. Even from the distance his emotions surged, desire mixing with fear to make a potent cocktail. He stepped away from his posting, gaze lingering on Akilina for an instant, a moment in which Belinda thought she could *see* the raven-haired woman through his eyes. She was barely dressed for breakfast, wearing a shift of linen and an open robe thrown over it, and her gaze went briefly to her guard, then away again, dismissive as she turned her attention back to her meal. A thrill danced through Belinda at the possibility that another's eyes might be used to spy in such a way, but the images faded so quickly as to have been imagination, as Viktor walked blindly through the halls, drawing closer without seeming to know where his feet took him. Lust all but rolled ahead of him, strong enough that Belinda thought she could smell it, musky and warm in the cool stone hallways. It pricked her own interest, and for a fleeting instant the idea of risking taking her one-time lover anew appealed to her.

She cut off a sharp laugh at the back of her throat, making a fist at her side. That impulse was the witchpower, not her own intellect; she'd come to recognize its base desires quickly enough to route them. Anything else would be tantamount to suicide: the prince's soon-to-be wife could not, under any circumstances, be thought unfaithful. Even Sacha had ceased playing at that game, his obsession turned to searching for Eliza, though Belinda still waited for him to betray her to Javier. That she'd set up a defusal for his accusations was a start, but perhaps not enough, and the uncertainty rankled.

Witchpower whispered around the edges of her mind, golden and sultry, offering itself as a method of dealing with the stocky lord. Belinda set her jaw and put the temptation away: power was best used discreetly, and Asselin could be controlled through other means. She would not have wished Eliza to disappear, but it drew Asselin's attention elsewhere, and that was a gift not to be overlooked.

She had yet to confirm a meeting betwixt Asselin and the Khazarian countess, even with Viktor's help, nor had guarded inquiries into the young lord's finances turned up any hint of proof to back her theory of conspiracy between the two. That, too, rankled, though with more of a challenging itch than genuine irritation. Asselin was a surprisingly worthy adversary, his skill at dissembling nearly equal to her own—equal, perhaps, had she not borne the witchpower within her as an unseen weapon. Belinda liked him for his skill and loathed him for what knowledge about her he owned; that she fully intended to bring his life to an unexpected and violent ending seemed a reasonable recourse to the dichotomy of emotion.

A new spill of laughter, less sharp, washed through her at the silent admission. She was unaccustomed to finding herself wishing personal revenge, and wondered if that, too, was the witchpower, or if it was the noblewoman's trappings she'd worn the last few months. A serving girl manhandled by a lord had no path to reprisal, and in a decade of playing those roles Belinda could not, even with her haunting memory, recall a time when resentment had risen up against a man's greedy hands. It was the manner of the world, and nothing was to be done about it. Sacha Asselin had come into her life at the strangest time she could remember, and it would be to his own health's detriment.

Belinda shook herself, turning her gaze out a palace window to watch flakes of snow idle toward the earth. Asselin, half at Javier's request and mostly at his own demand, searched for Eliza, and kept himself out of Belinda's way. For the moment, that was enough. Until Viktor could confirm her suspicions with reports of a meeting, she would focus on tasks closer at hand.

Her thoughts conjured the guard, whose wave of lust rode her again just before he pushed aside heavy velvet curtains that protected Belinda's alcove from the hall, and the hall from winter's chill creeping in around the edges of lead-lined glass. Viktor let the curtain fall behind him, a questionable prudence that Belinda didn't comment on. She could neither afford to be seen with him nor be seen pretending *not* to be seen with him, but this floor of the palace was poorly travelled, and the wing she'd chosen even less so. All the better to flip her skirts up and have the man on his knees before her.

Viktor's gaze snapped up to hers as if the pulse of heady, dangerous desire she felt had leapt to him in turn. Belinda inhaled, deliberate and sharp through her nostrils, and cursed the very magic that
gave her sway over the Khazarian guard. "Well?" She spoke
Khazarian, keeping her voice low; the curtains would muffle anything they had to say, but Beatrice Irvine didn't speak Khazarian.

All the more reason to go unseen. A rough guard and a noblewoman from different countries have only one obvious language in
common, and Belinda doubted anyone would believe her protesta-
tions of innocence, should it come to that. Viktor takes another
step toward her as she speaks his tongue, and the question comes
into his voice again: "Rosa?"

"I'll be your Rosa." She smiled to hide irritation and walked her
fingertips up his chest, feeling witchpower flex and reach for him.
Marius and Nina were absurdly easy to manipulate, compared to
the stubborn Khazarian guard. Whether it was his familiarity with
her old self or something hewn out of dark nights and long winters, Belinda neither knew nor cared. "I'll be your Rosa," she
promised again, "if you'll tell me what Sandalia and Akilina discuss.
They seem to never see one another. Why is that?"

Consternation creased Viktor's brow. He folded his hand over
hers, enveloping it: his hands, like the rest of him, were large.
"Sandalia won't see her," he said heavily, then gave her a sly look
so open it might have been a child's. "Not during court, at least."

Belinda's heart caught and beat again more painfully, her breath
hanging empty in her chest. "When do they meet?"

"While you're spreading your legs for the count," Viktor said
nastily. "No, the prince. It's hard to remember, Ros—ah!" His
voice cracked as Belinda caught a hand between his legs, barely
stopping herself from making it a blow. It required trembling concentration to turn it into a caress, anger and power sparking
through her. Viktor's eyes glazed as she stroked him, her own pulse
rising and heat pooling between her thighs.

"Does it take the actual act? Is that why Marius and Nina were so easy, and you stand against me?" She whispered the questions in Aulunian as she rucked her dress up a palmful at a time. "Do you want to fuck me, Viktor?" That, she spoke in his own language, as if words were needed. He shuddered and dropped his breeches all in a single action, Belinda gasping with unexpected pleasure as he took her an instant later. Witchpower washed over her vision until she saw only gold, and with her mouth against his skin she whispered, "You do not know me, Viktor. I'm Beatrice Irvine, not your Rosa, and you must forget me and her when you walk away from this." She sent a trickle of stillness through the power, holding him away from climax. "But first tell me when Akilina and Sandalia meet, and why."

He groaned in protest, thrusting harder into her in search of his own pleasure. Belinda laughed, quiet liquid sound, and let her head fall back, riding his strength inside her for her own benefit. "Tell me, and I'll let you finish," she promised, and out of selfishness, murmured, "but keep doing that." A woman could separate out words from pleasure; surely a man could as well. Viktor's desperate grunts and fierce rutting seemed to belie that logic, and impatience took her. The witchpower stillness resided in him; she withdrew it and filled him instead with her own building desire. He cried out more loudly than he ought to have, strangled sound of release, and she forewent the urge for satisfaction to snap, "*Now*, Viktor, tell me of Sandalia and Akilina."

And finally, in gasping words, he did.

Aᴋɪʟɪɴᴀ Pᴀɴᴋᴇᴊᴇꜰꜰ, Dᴠᴏʀʏᴀɴɪɴ
24 November 1587 † *Lutetia*

Akilina watches Viktor slip out of the alcove, and taps a toe against the chilly floor. Her feet ache from the hard stone and her toenails are edged with blue from cold, but bare feet and the soft shift she wears made no sound as she followed her guardsman through the palace, unbeknownst to him and very clearly unbeknownst to Beatrice Irvine. Explaining her outfit will be unnecessary, should she come upon a courtier as she returns to her rooms: she is, after all, Khazarian, and can use that as an excuse for any oddities in behavior the palace hangers-on might observe.

She heard very little of the conversation from her hideaway; she heard much more clearly the sounds of passion. That alone would be enough to condemn Irvine on; Akilina is a countess and a noblewoman of repute, and Irvine is almost nothing. Even backed by her lover—by Javier, Akilina corrects her own thought, as it appears the term *lover* can be used generously when speaking of Beatrice Irvine—even backed by a prince's belief, Irvine's reputation would be shattered with Akilina's accusations of infidelity. Javier would have to put her aside.

But better still is the fact that what words Akilina did catch spoken between the lovers were spoken in Khazarian. That lends strength to Viktor's feverish insistence that he knew this woman on Gregori's estates in Khazar: at the very least, she has the tongue for it.

Ruining Javier's marriage is a delightful end in and of itself, but discovering the truth of who Beatrice Irvine is is the far more entertaining game. Akilina tucks her shift beneath her feet and stands watch, waiting for Beatrice to leave the alcove down the hall so that she might say she saw the assignation with her own eyes, both lovers identified.

In time, the curtains shift, but no one emerges. Akilina frowns and watches more closely, keeping her place until afternoon sun has crept around the palace to pour into her nook. Aching from sitting on stone and weary with the wait, Akilina rises and stalks down the hall to push back the velvet curtains.

No one at all is within the alcove.

It's only then that she remembers Viktor's flushed cheeks, the sickness that seems to ride him, and his mumbled accusation of witchcraft.

BELINDA PRIMROSE / BEATRICE IRVINE
25 November 1587 ✝ *Lutetia*

Belinda curtsied deeply enough to border on the absurd, keeping her eyes lowered and the deferential pose until Sandalia flickered her fingers, a gesture Javier had surely learned from her. And Eliza had learned it in turn, Belinda thought as she rose. The bruise on her jaw had faded—avoiding Javier's mother for the days it took to heal had been a challenge—and Belinda had taken care in dressing that morning, knowing Sandalia would insist on seeing her. Her gown was flattering, though not one of Eliza's new fashions; whether she chose to dress as Eliza had set fashion or not, it would remind the queen of her son's missing friend, and Belinda found she preferred the more familiar armour of an older style.

Sandalia, in contrast, wore one of Eliza's high-waisted gowns, and looked ravishing—or ravishable. She wore her nearly forty years well, but with the costume's soft lines and attention drawn to her bosom, she seemed some sort of Madonna, full of beauty and grace. Belinda curled the tiniest of smiles as she straightened, pleased beyond expectation that she'd been correct in the style suiting the Gallic regent. "Do we amuse you, Lady Irvine?" Sandalia's voice was cool; she knew as well as Belinda did that Belinda had been avoiding her, and a queen did not like to be treated thus.

"Not at all," Belinda said, then gambled on Beatrice's impetuosity and added, "It's just that Your Majesty is lovelier than I'd even imagined. Forgive me for being so bold, but the fashion suits you wonderfully."

Sandalia's mouth thinned momentarily, dry humour infusing her voice. "As you suggested it might. Will you now go to the Aulunian queen and mock her for the same dress?"

Belinda bobbed another curtsey and dared a brief, brilliant smile. "As Your Majesty commands. I would beg leave to bring a court artist with me, that he might sketch her expression when I do so."

Sandalia's mouth twitched again and she rose in a swirl of gossamer skirts. "We cannot decide if our son likes you for your tongue, Lady Beatrice, or if he likes you despite it. Walk with us." She stepped down from the throne dais to Belinda's side, startling the younger woman with her diminutive size. Even crowned—not heavily; the crowns of state were left for formal affairs, and Sandalia's daily tiara was a delicate thing of gold and jewels—even crowned, Belinda could easily see over the top of the regent's head, and heard herself ask, impertinently, "Was my lord's father a tall man, Your Majesty?"

Astonishing silence fled out around them, the courtiers who caught the question falling quiet so quickly it made others do the same, craning to see what they'd missed. Sandalia turned her head to look up the few inches at Belinda so slowly that for long seconds it barely seemed the queen moved. Her expression, when their eyes met, went beyond outrage into incredulity, and Belinda wished desperately for the ability to call a blush on command. "Forgive me, Your Majesty. I have no idea what came into me."

"You have no sense at all, girl," Sandalia said. "If Javier doesn't teach you to control that tongue he'd best cut it out. You cannot say such things."

"Your Majesty." Belinda put mortification into her voice, though that same impertinent part of her wanted to insist that she certainly could, though she clearly should not. God in Heaven, if this was what the witchpower brought out in her, Robert had been righter than he knew. A lifetime would be too soon to unleash the foolishness she found herself playing at.

And yet the question pricked her curiosity. Louis had not, from description, been an especially tall man, and paintings showed him as pale and aesthete, with none of Javier's height or colour. Belinda had no way to determine whether witchpower burned inside someone from a portrait, but looking on Louis's image, she would far more imagine his tiny, once-widowed bride to carry magic within her blood, and knew that Sandalia did not. It was far from proof, but it whet her appetite for the truth, and so she laid the question out and hoped, despite her appalling rudeness, that Sandalia might say something indiscreet in response.

"Louis was taller than I" was Sandalia's reply, after a frosty silence that brought them both out of the courtroom and toward Sandalia's more private meeting chambers. Surprise curdled in Belinda's stomach as she realised the queen had dropped formality; whether it was a sign of liking Belinda despite her unfortunate tendency to speak her mind, or whether she intended to appear soft until bitter hardness was necessary, Belinda was unsure. "As you so rudely implied, however, most people are. Perhaps Javier's length is from his uncle; Rodrigo, whom you have not met, is quite tall."

"And dark," Belinda said. "I've seen a portrait. He's extremely handsome."

Sandalia smiled unexpectedly. "He is. I would that he had wed and had children of his own. But there's always Lorraine," she added, dryness returning to her tone again. "Do you understand the political situation there, Beatrice? You give lip service to Lanyarch's freedom, but do you understand?"

For a moment Belinda imagined herself flanked by Sandalia on one side and her father on the other. It took effort to not glance to the side, looking for Robert, and she schooled her voice to show no amusement as she replied. "Henry of Aulun's first wife was sister to your father. There is no surviving Walter heir from that union; Constance, their one daughter, is dead these thirty-some years. Lorraine's a bastard child begotten through desperation that severed Aulun from Cordula and birthed the Reformation Church, and she, too, is without an heir." Belinda drew a breath.

"She's run Lanyarch's royal blood into the earth, leaving you the wedded queen to the throne, but without a child of Lanyarchan blood. Rodrigo woos Lorraine still, more in Cordula's name than his own, though if he should succeed, such a marriage might legitimize Javier's claim to any throne on the islands. In her eyes you and Javier, who are not of Aulunian blood, but who can trace line of descent to her throne, are pretenders to her crown, and dangerous."

"And it is your opinion . . . ?" Sandalia's voice was so steady she might have respected the opinion Belinda offered, though in contrast to her vocal quality, humour sparked around her to Belinda's witchpower senses.

"That with no legitimate Walter heirs, Aulun should be ruled by the royal family closest to it. There are those in Aulun who would make themselves kings," Belinda admitted with a shrug, "but the de Costas already bear God's seal of approval, and through Catherine you and Rodrigo are . . ." Too late, far, far too late, she recognized the injudiciousness of being so free with her opinions. She had, for a terrible moment, shared Beatrice's naive beliefs, that faith and rightness and God's will would protect her. That as a woman engaged to a prince, she might speak frankly to that prince's mother and have her opinions respected and considered. That Javier would protect her, even when she spoke sedition to a queen.

Her stomach knotted, knocking upward so hard as to make her teeth set with the impact; it took sudden and frantic control to not let that reaction complete itself. She spoke without swallowing down sickness, forcing herself to remain untouched visibly by raging alarm, and finished, "possibilities." If it was a trap, it was neatly set, and she was all the more a fool for stepping into it. If it was a trap, she richly deserved its jaws closing around her.

"You are a fool," Sandalia said. "Either a fool or so trusting as to be one, and I can afford neither. You're a political tool, Beatrice."

The tiny queen turned to face Belinda, eyes large and dark and utterly without mercy in her heart-shaped face. "You'll help us to see if Lorraine can be shaken loose from her throne, but you will not marry my son, even if he should insist on it."

"Your Majesty—" It took appallingly little effort to put the quaver in her voice, Belinda's hands cold with dismay. She knew better, had been trained better, and had still let herself be led. Witchpower danced golden and warm through her mind, uncaring of the danger she danced with. "Yes, Your Majesty, of course, but how—"

Sandalia offered a smile that laid her open to the bone. "You'll find a way to make him hate you, my dear."

"Oh . . . oh, no, I couldn't, I . . . I lo—" The words stuck in her throat, bringing warmth to her cheeks. Belinda clenched her hands in her skirts, allowing Beatrice's distress to override the coldness pounding within her. Denying the desperation with which she wished to wrap herself in stillness and forbid anything to touch her. The words that finished her protest were the emotions of a silly noblewoman, not of Belinda Primrose. Her heart fluttered and beat against her ribs, a wild thing trying to escape the sickness inside her. She was Belinda Primrose, the queen's bastard, an assassin and a spy, and she could not love a prince.

Sandalia's smile turned positively radiant, bringing a beautiful glow of youth and good health to the pretty queen. "You will," she said implacably. "You will, Lady Irvine, because our solution would be far less pleasant than that. We are finished with this discussion." She flickered her fingers, shared language of the body from queen to gutter rat, and said, pleasantly, "You're dismissed."

Belinda, uncaring of her dignity, of her lifetime of trained untouchability, uncaring of anything but the bewildering, consuming ache that rattled her bones and took her breath, gathered her skirts, dipped a clumsy curtsey, and fled.

SANDALIA, QUEEN AND REGENT
5 December 1587 † *Lutetia*

"That's her. That's the witch who did Lord Gregori to death." The girl standing in Sandalia's private chambers might be pretty, did hate not so contort her features. She is young, perhaps nineteen, with blond hair so thick and heavy she could be dangled from it. Her hands are clenched in her skirts, making wrinkles of plain working fabric, and she's terribly afraid of her surroundings. "I don't care that she's all tarted up and dressed as a lady. That's Rosa."

She speaks Khazarian; a tongue that Sandalia has only in smatterings. Sandalia looks to her translator, who repeats the girl's words back in Gallic. Sandalia nods slowly, and doesn't laugh: the wretched creature is using hate to push away fear, and Sandalia is not one inclined to believe accusations of witchcraft from the frightened. "Why do you think she's a witch?" She lets the translator do her work and keeps her focus on the girl whose face tightens with rage and, unless Sandalia is greatly mistaken, envy.

"Lord Gregori was strong and fit, my lady. A fever came on him too fast to be natural, not in the summer. Winter's the time for sicknesses like that. It came on him when *she* came—"

Sandalia lifts a hand as the translator speaks, and the girl breaks off. "When—Rosa—arrived in Gregori's household? That was when he became ill?"

The servant curls her lip reluctantly. "No, not till she went to his bed."

Sandalia once more refuses a smile, and nods for the girl to continue. "She went at him without stopping for three days, and on the fourth he was dead. Then she ran, like the craven devil's creature that she is. Why would she run, if she hadn't done him to death?"

Sandalia knows enough not to argue that question with the girl, either. Instead, she murmurs, "Why, indeed," which is translated to the serving girl's obvious delight. "You're certain it's the same woman," Sandalia says one final time, and the girl tosses her head with a sniff.

"Sure as the sky is blue." There's such a sparkle of laughter in the translator's voice that Sandalia suspects the servant said something far more crude, and that diplomacy has won out over accuracy.

"Thank you, Ilana. We shall—"

"Ilyana." The girl doesn't seem to realise she's correcting a queen, and Sandalia's elevated eyebrow has no effect. After a moment she amends herself, mostly because there's no sense in antagonizing the unpleasant young woman, and goes on: "Ilyana. We shall call on you again when we require your testimony, and in the interim you'll be expected to remain within the walls of the cottage we have provided for you."

Ilyana doesn't understand enough to know she's being placed under arrest. Her expression lights up as the translation is made, and she ducks a curtsey. The cottage is no doubt a far finer home than she's ever known, and as a guest, involuntary or not, of a queen, she will be waited on as if she were the lady and not the servant. It will be a rude shock to her to return to the life she once had, if she's lucky enough to be allowed to do so. She's allowed to go to the door unescorted, and beyond it, two guards, one Khazarian and one Gallic, will bring her to Sandalia's cottage. Only when the girl is gone does Sandalia turn to the translator, eyebrow lifted again in curiosity.

"Do you believe her, Lady Akilina?"

Akilina stands with animal grace, lithe even beneath the weight of petticoats. She wears a shade of coppery gold that should look terrible on her, but somehow enhances the angles of her beauty. "I believe she's a nasty little girl who wanted Gregori's bed for herself, but she's as certain as my guardsman that Your Majesty's

Beatrice and their Rosa are one and the same. Viktor," and the heaviness of a Khazarian accent weights the name, though her Gallic is usually exquisite, "tells me that Rosa wore a blade beneath her chemise, under her corsets. A small knife." She holds up a hand, giving the knife its length in demonstration. "Your Majesty could ask Javier . . ."

"No." Sandalia's reply is slow, thoughtful. "Better to see where his heart lies in the heat of the moment, I think. We'll discover the blade in another way. How," she adds absently, "did you get that little wretch here so quickly? It's a month's journey to Khazan even in summer."

"Viktor told me about her when he told me he was certain Beatrice and Rosa were the same woman. I sent a pigeon," Akilina says carelessly, "and the journey is a month if you travel in comfort. It can be made more quickly if you truly desire it to be done." She shrugs, coquettish thing, and throws a smile toward Sandalia. "And Ilyana's comfort wasn't my concern." Her smile fades, leaving her features beautiful but sharp; this is a woman honed to a blade, Sandalia thinks. "Did anyone come to you asking for Gregori's death?"

Sandalia finds caution stirring in her belly, cool and slow, at the question. She knows Akilina was Gregori's lover—that much gossip has spread to Gallic ears, especially with Akilina leading this Khazarian envoy into Lutetia. "Did you believe his death to be unnatural?" she asks slowly, not avoiding the question, but feeling it relevant. Akilina shakes her head in the negative and Sandalia nods, unsurprised. "No one that I know of asked Gallin for a Khazarian count's death. I'll ask my men," she says, meaning her spies and assassins, and Akilina nods her understanding as Sandalia finishes, "but I think I might have been told, if we were to play that particular sort of diplomacy. You knew him," she says delicately, playing on a different kind of diplomacy. "Who might have wanted him dead?"

Akilina laughs, not the sound of genuine cheer Sandalia's come to expect from her, but a bitter thing, edged. "Haven't you heard the stories about Baba Yaga, Your Majesty? Almost anyone would point to me first. Akilina Pankejeff, the witch who eats lives. But Gregori's death would only have served me if he'd married me first, and he was no more likely to do that than marry the imperatrix."

She jerks her eyes to Sandalia's as the words come down heavily between them, their portent unexpected and undeniable. Astonishment curls one corner of Sandalia's mouth. "Irina?"

"Widowed this past decade," Akilina gives back, thinking it out as she speaks. "Only a girl for an heir, but the child is strong and intelligent. Irina is as canny as Your Majesty or the Titian Bitch; she wouldn't have a suitor murdered unless . . ."

"Unless he thought he could pressure her into taking his hand," Sandalia murmurs. "Which he would only do . . ."

"If she had a secret." Sandalia speaks the final words as certainty; as only a woman with secrets of her own could do. She is a queen, and to speak so is not indiscreet; all men, and all women, too, have secret things hidden in their hearts. Akilina's gaze is forthright and almost sympathetic to that truth, and for a moment they are not queen and countess, but simply women standing against the tide of a world made by men, struggling with more difficulties because of their gender than even the men who try to tear them down could know. "Can you learn it?"

"Does it matter?" Akilina is aware, as Ilyana was not, when she takes a stance contrary to a regent's, but she doesn't back down from it. "Gregori's dead and Irina's secrets are a thousand miles away, but Beatrice Irvine's are here, under ou—Your Majesty's nose. Set me on her, your majesty, and we may find the answers to the Khazarian questions as well."

15

The coachman remembers Rosa, certainly, all lust and long legs and an eye for when to leave a bad situation. He rode her all the way to Khazan, Khazar's capital city, and he'd have done her longer if Gregori's son hadn't called him back to work. His eyes grow wary, though, and he lifts his hands in protest: if the whore's had a child, there'll be no pinning it on him; he was one of three he can guess in a matter of days.

An information-gatherer smiles and waves off the coachman's concerns. Wonders, casually, if Rosa said where she'd be going next, and the coachman snorts. He wouldn't know, but he pointed her toward a stagecoach business that a friend of his owns. That's his goal, he confides, to go into business himself and see more of Khazar, maybe leave it entirely and have a look at Echon. His friend has been as far as Gallin, and works with men from far-off Essandia. He's got more mundane routes, too, and where would somebody like Rosa go but back to her village? Ask his friend, maybe he'll know.

His friend took her south, all the way to Reussland, and of course he's sure it's the same woman. He was sure before he saw a drawing, and he's twice as sure now. What happened to her then, he's got no idea, nor any care, but a bit more gold might help him to remember.

It doesn't, which is a shame, and he's left coughing on his own blood and staring at his tongue, already stiffening from cold as it lies bright and red against the snow.

A pigeon makes its way to Hammabarg faster than a man can, three of them sent against the risk of hawks and frozen nights. A fat man who knows the countess's seal and trusts her for the money—he has ways of assuring that trust is met—begins to look for a woman who passed through half a year ago. He knows where she came from, what she looks like, and makes no suppositions about what direction she took. He knows she spreads her legs to pay for passage in preference to paying coin, but that she carried enough cash to travel from Khazan to Reussland when dour, now-tongueless Yuliy snorted at her sexual offerings.

It takes him seven days to find her. It should take fewer, but on the third day he finds a different woman, one no one is looking for, and takes his time with her, so that when he's finished, there's nothing left for anyone to find.

Three women meeting Rosa's description left Hammabarg alone in the right time frame. Two went west, ultimately toward Gallin; the third went south, riding on the back of a stagecoach with her skirts showing her ankles. That, the fat man wagers, is the one Akilina wants, and she's paying for his opinion as much as his tracking skills.

Akilina sets men on all three trails. The one who's forced to go through Swiss mountains in the dead of winter, following a trail seven months old, is bitter indeed, and all the more so when a pretty girl he met on a summer journey through the pass greets him on a village edge with a round belly and a fist for his nose. He finds himself in a church exchanging vows before his horse has cooled from its ride, and finds the horse sold to build another room on his bride's father's home for the new family to live in before the sun breaks noon.

He finds himself on foot in a mountain passage in the midst of a winter storm before the night is over, and his wife finds herself a widow when the morning comes.

Akilina finds herself beginning again when the fat man proves right and the other women are unquestionably not Beatrice Irvine. She is patient, and wealthy, and neither Gallin nor Irvine are going anywhere. She hires a man reputed to have no earthly vices, which means only that his vices are too dark to be shared, to send through the mountains this time, and he follows a trail now eight months old toward Parna.

He pauses conscientiously to report that the young widow gave birth to a girl, who has been christened in the church, thanks be to God that her parents were wed, and may God bless her father's lost and frozen soul. Akilina stares at that missive for a long time, finally laughing, even if a pigeon was wasted to tell her the news.

Perhaps because he is without vice, but more likely because Akilina is paying him very well, this hired tracker does not stop at the border of his own country. He follows Rosa's trail, travelling quickly and efficiently; Akilina's treasury will feel the weight of his haste. He comes, in time, to Aria Magli, and there comes to the very doorstep from which Rosa alighted on her afternoon of free-dom in the canal-ridden city.

The man without vices is a narrow blade of a man, his cheeks pocked with scars and his eyes deep-set and dark. The gondola boy who looks at him weighs his own small life, and the lives of his twelve, or eight, or fourteen brothers and sisters, and thinks of the pretty woman in blue who gave him coin for the day and a chicken to bring home to his family, and tells the man without vices the wrong bridge and the wrong time and nothing at all of the man who paid him to wait on Belinda Primrose outside her home.

It slows the tracker by a few hours, and when he realises the urchin lied to him, it brings a rare slash of a smile to his face. He returns to find the child, and because a gypsy man with a kind of calm readiness is watching, the boy's father still has nine, or fifteen, or thirteen children to his name when the man is done. He has what he needs now: the description of a man, and that of an unusually striking courtesan. *His* name, the tracker does not learn, but *hers* he buys off another courtesan, a woman with large breasts and little of the brains her kind are supposedly vaunted for.

A single morning later he sets loose the last pigeon, and with it the trail that Akilina wants finally, finally, finally comes to Gallin.

Belinda Primrose / Beatrice Irvine
4 January 1588 † Lutetia

Belinda chafed. As Beatrice Irvine, widowed wife to a depraved Lanyarchan lordling, she had become accustomed to a certain amount of freedom. It had been the limited freedom of a woman, unable to cross certain thresholds, reluctantly lent money to, wooed by those who might want a nobleman's title to add to their names, but it had been freedom.

Beatrice Irvine, fiancée to Javier de Castille, crown prince of Gallin, had no such freedom.

That the watching guards and constant eyes were bothersome came as a surprise to her. She would have imagined Beatrice's freedoms to be overwhelming—and they were, but in a different manner than she might have expected. Accustomed to a lifetime of hiding and going unnoticed, she had thought that playing an obvious role, one in the public eye, would alarm her; that a habit of circumspection would keep her from enjoying the part. Instead she'd taken to it, a truth that made her wonder, though only briefly, if Beatrice's easy laugh might have been her own, had circumstances been different. It was a speculation to be let go unpondered; her life was what it was, and imagining it otherwise sent a shudder of confused revulsion down her spine.

Still, those small freedoms that she'd known were now gone,

and she found herself resenting the fine life she lived. She picked at embroidery, surrounded by court ladies and under the watchful eyes of guards, until her fingers and her brain both seemed to bleed with weariness of it all. None of her discontent spilled outward; she kept it wrapped inside as thoroughly as she was caught under the guards' gazes. It was far more difficult, she'd discovered, to call the witchpower stillness and disappear from view when someone was actively watching her. That she'd done it with Javier and Sacha in the room suggested to her that intimacy was key there, as well; whatever connection a joining of flesh offered seemed to provide inroads to the minds of the men around her. The guards, patient, unobtrusive, watching, turned their focus on her more pointedly when she called witchpower and tried to hide herself in the shadows of plain sight. Ultimately more concerned with secrecy than proving, if only to herself, her ability to fade away and escape her polite jailers, she gave up trying and resigned herself to the boredom of stitching.

Weeks. It had been *weeks,* and for once Belinda shared Asselin's impatience. Her access to Javier had been whittled away, her ability to write freely to "dearest Jayne" compromised, and the thing that kept a stranglehold on her was that she could see no way to slip free the bonds that held her and escape into a different world for a while without threatening the position she now held.

For the first time in her life, Belinda thought she might understand, truly understand, the constraints that held Lorraine in place.

She, though, had advantages that Lorraine didn't share. It was possible, not even difficult, to surround herself with shadow and escape the palace, escape the guards and the narrow definition of what a court lady was, at least at night. Daytime belonged to dull interactions with women Belinda had nothing in common with, but nighttime, at least, was her own.

She had not, in weeks of plying Viktor and prowling the palace at night, found where it was that Sandalia and Akilina met, nor learned their subjects of discussion. The handful of times she touched skin against either woman, she'd stolen thoughts of open disregard from Sandalia; unlike Javier, the queen regarded Belinda as no more than a means to an end, and perhaps as a test of loyalty for her own son. It was not that Sandalia disliked her; on the contrary, she seemed to be more amused by Beatrice's inability to keep her tongue in her head than she let on, and she admitted to a personal weakness for Lanyarchans, whose king had been the first step on the path she now travelled.

Belinda closed her hand carefully around the edge of her embroidery hoop, turning the wood to more easily reach another set of stitches rather than flinging the whole mess away. Sandalia was as guarded in her thoughts as Belinda was, no more allowing herself active dreams of a pretender's crown than Belinda permitting herself remembrances of her true heritage. Even if Sandalia had, thoughts couldn't be proven, and Belinda required proof that was hard in the finding. That it would come through Akilina, she felt sure, but as yet there'd been no hint of it.

Nor was stealing thoughts from the Khazarian countess an easy task. Belinda had been raised to that tongue as much as any other, but her witchpower had been brought to life in Gallin. The precious instant lost in grasping understanding of one language over another clouded her ability to follow Akilina's unspoken ambitions, though her flawless memory helped to bring back those things she feared she'd missed. That she appeared to be missing, in large part, Akilina's vast amusement at a Lanyarchan provincial wedding a Gallic prince, only pricked her pride and made her that much more determined to pursue Akilina and Sandalia's hidden agenda.

Weeks of slipping through the palace at night, searching for the two women and their conspiracies, had largely left Belinda tired and snappish during the day, and none the wiser for her efforts. Viktor, voice thick with desire, insisted that they met in the queen's chambers, but even hidden by witchpower, Belinda had not dared those rooms, locked against visitors. She had learned passageways within the palace, searching for a back path to Sandalia's rooms that way, but had met with no success, found neither queen nor countess nor hidden, private places in the palace where they might meet. It was not, she told herself, Viktor's fault; he couldn't be expected to stand guard within Sandalia's chambers unless invited in, and no queen would lower herself, or grace an ordinary guardsman so.

She finished the last stitches on a rose and smoothed her thumb over the shining crimson thread. The delicacy of her position seemed absurd; she must push toward a battle for a crown without seeming to, without stepping over a nearly invisible line that made her treachery a gift worth handing over to another queen, and find proof of a plot that her own words were part of creating. It was a balancing act worthy of a theatrical troupe. Her latest missive from Robert—nearly a month old now—made it vividly clear that Lorraine wouldn't act without written proof, and since then Belinda's newly elevated place in the Gallic court had made corresponding with Aulun's secret spymaster too dangerous. She didn't know for certain that her letters home were opened and read, but there was no reason to suppose they weren't, and she preferred to err on caution's side.

Quiet rumblings had come out of Aulun at the news, officially carried, of Javier's engagement to a Lanyarchan noble. Better still, raw delight had driven a clan of drunken Lanyarch men over the wall that defined their southern border and into a cattle raid on Aulunian territory. A Lanyarchan banner had been planted in the midst of a field and an entire herd of beefstock driven north. The outraged, frightened landowner had sent to Alunaer for help, and rumour whispered that Aulunian troops were amassing near the island nation's northern border, though there weren't yet stories of skirmishes fought along the border.

Still, troops encroaching on close—to—Lanyarchan—territory was excuse enough, even in the dead of winter. Stories flooded into Gallin, new tales every day. They said the clans gathered in Javier's name, in Beatrice's name, putting aside their own differences to come together and face the Reformation threat. They said that Lorraine grew agitated on her throne, unwilling to commit to battle in the middle of winter, but less willing still to lose her contentious northern neighbor from her empire. Even now, when Belinda turned her ear to the chatter shared by the embroidering women, they spoke of almost nothing else. She kept her tongue firmly between her teeth, resisting the urge to point out the unlikelihood of fresh news arriving from Aulun each morning. It didn't matter: the point was to build confidence in the Gallic people and their monarchs that Lanyarch would stand up and fight for itself and Cordula given even a hint of support from the world across the channel. Gossip had its place in creating that confidence.

The worst danger of playing a Lanyarchan uprising was that someone might think to ask who Beatrice Irvine was, and wonder why no one remembered her. Belinda trusted that Robert would deal with that; that there would be a handful or more of men and women who remembered growing up with her, who remembered her marriage to some loyalist whose grounds were a gift from Lorraine. They would plant half-certain recollections in the minds of others, until Beatrice took on a life of her own, but it was still, always, a risk.

All the more reason, Belinda thought, to try to hurry the matter. The less time spent venerating a minor Lanyarchan noble who'd caught the eye of the Gallic prince, the better. She smoothed her embroidery out again and scowled faintly at it, reveling in the expression. Besides, never mind Beatrice's history, Belinda was like to find herself bored to the very death if she had to stitch roses onto a tapestry for much longer.

"My lady Beatrice." The voice was apologetic and unexpected; Belinda looked up to find Marius, elegant hat clenched in his hands, standing in the doorway. A titter arose from the women around her, sly looks exchanged as Marius bowed to all of them, perfunctory and polite, but left his gaze on Belinda. "May I speak with you, my lady?"

Genuine warmth lit Belinda's smile. "It would be my pleasure, m'sieur." She murmured an apology to the other women, leaving the room to a burst of laughter as the door closed. Marius, ever polite, offered his elbow, and Beatrice slipped her fingers through it. "It's been weeks, Marius." There was more question than reprimand in the statement, though Marius glanced at her to be certain of that. His dark eyes were mournful, as if he were an injured wild thing, not a man.

"I've been helping Sacha look for Eliza. It was . . . easier."

Belinda let the confession go a moment, tightening her fingers against his arm. "Have you had any luck?"

"Of course not." More realism coloured Marius's voice than had touched either Asselin's or Javier's when it came to the topic of Eliza's disappearance. "Liz won't be found unless she wants to be. If I were her, I'd have gone to Parna, or Essandia by now. Somewhere far away from all of this."

"Marius . . ." His name came to her lips again, too easily, and he shook his head in a preemptive denial.

"Maybe that's the advantage to her station. A prince and his friends may look for her, but she has no financial obligations or familial expectations to keep her in one place. Where would you go, Beatrice?"

"Aria Magli," Belinda answered, too much truth in the soft words. "If I were Eliza, as well-educated and as beautiful as she is, I would go to Aria Magli and become a courtesan or a rich man's mistress. I think I might make friends there."

"Liz isn't especially good at making friends." A guard opened a door for them and Belinda squinted against a sudden splatter of cold and rain.

"It's hardly the time of year for a stroll in the garden, Marius."

"There's a bower just down the walk. It'll keep the rain off, if not the cold. I won't keep you long." He quickened his pace as he spoke, moving against the rain and tugging Belinda with him. She groaned, half-laughing, and scurried to keep up.

"Please. Would you send me back to my stitches? I hadn't thought you a cruel master, my lord. I'll bear the cold a while, so long as I don't have to go back into that stifling apartment. At least the air is refreshing." She smiled at her feet, watching the path, then transferred the smile to Marius as he ducked beneath an arch of leaf-less branches and into a gazebo well-protected from the weather. He didn't so much as pretend a smile in return, and the expression fell away from Belinda's face as her forehead wrinkled. "Marius?"

"My mother," he said in clipped, precise tones, "has decided it's well past time I was married."

Belinda caught her breath, dismayed laughter riding it. "Who is she?" From the way he spoke, there had to be a bride already se-lected, a match made of good financial sense and, if Marius were lucky, a title to go with it. It ought not sting, that it did was dis-comfiting.

"Sarah Asselin," Marius said through his teeth. Belinda blinked at him, honest surprise warming her cheeks.

"Sacha's harpy-voiced sister? Marius, she's—" Belinda broke off, then said, helplessly and with perfect honesty, "She's a brilliant match, Marius. How—?"

"It seems Sacha was well-advised in sending me home to change clothes." Every word was spoken like a blade, cutting against Belinda's skin. "It seems I caught his sister's eye that day. Her mother has spoken with mine and the noose is all but tied. I do not want her, Beatrice. I do not love her and I do not desire her. I—"

"You," Belinda whispered, "are bound by financial and family ties where Eliza is not, and even if you and I had made promises of forever to one another, your parents have the strength to break those vows and send you where they will. She's a better match than I am, Marius. She's prettier, wealthier, and younger than I, and you've been friends with her family all your life."

"Javier could—"

"Could what?" Belinda asked gently. "Forbid you to marry her? What would you do? Go to him and ask him to release me now? Ask him to set this game he plays with Aulun on its ear for the sake of our happiness? He's a prince. Even if you could ask him, he couldn't agree." She stepped closer, curling her fingers against the merchant lad's chest. "This does not end happily for the likes of you and me, Marius. We've known that all along." His heart beat too hard beneath her touch; Belinda's met it in rate, pulse quick and uncomfortable in her stomach. "Do you like her at all?"

Dismay and outrage, suffused with guilt, surged through the young man, flushing his cheeks. "She's Sacha's sister, Beatrice. I've never *thought* about her—"

"—about her soft curves under your hands, or her mouth and body opening to accept you?" Belinda reached for his emotions with witchpower, striving for delicacy instead of heavy-handed overwhelming thought. An abstract fondness for the Asselin girl was there, no more thought of than a passing admiration for a fine horse or well-bred dog. She whispered encouragement to that, tying abstraction to the impulse of desire that made Marius blush more deeply. That want served to accentuate his guilt and dismay, but it could, would, tie the merchant's son to the lord's daughter, if he didn't fight it. Belinda wondered at the gentleness in herself, to try to soften Marius's pain. "This game with Javier may go on for months, even years, Marius. Waiting on a possibility is throwing your life away."

Marius's jaw clenched. "It's my life to throw away."

"It isn't." Belinda closed her eyes, almost swaying with unexpected regret. "We all have duties, Marius. We all have things we must answer to. Wishes don't make horses, my love, or beggars would ride. You must like her," she said. "Find it in yourself to love her."

"I only love you."

"You must learn to let it go." Words were half at odds with the tangle of emotion she wove, binding his want for Belinda to his unexplored desire for Sarah Asselin. That it was meant for his benefit was true; the young man would be better off out of love with Belinda Primrose. But the interweaving could benefit her as well, a cool calculation that seemed more like herself than the concern for his heartache. Should his love for Sarah be permanently bound to his desire for Belinda, she would never lose him as an asset. Whether true emotion, born on its own and growing in strength once the match was made, could undo what she put into place, Belinda didn't know. If so, using him again in the future might be lost to her, if unfettered emotion could scrape away the ties she wrought. But his loss would be no great matter in the longer term: she could not long anticipate staying in Lutetia or Gallin once Javier's plan to shake Lorraine on her throne was seen to fruition, unless the prince had his way and the promises he'd made were real.

"I only want you," Marius repeated stubbornly. Belinda turned an unkind smile and stepped a little closer, bringing her lips close enough to brush his ear.

"Only me?" she asked. "Shall I tell Nina that, then, or have you forgotten her already, my lord? You wanted her surely enough. Imagine now that it's Sarah's pale form beneath you, and tell me that you only want me." She dropped a hand, brushing her fingers over his groin, and chuckled at the hardness she found there. "Shall

I come to your chambers on your wedding night, Marius, and watch you take a virgin as you took Nina? You will be the husband, strong, indomitable, and only I'll know the weakness in you that wishes to submit."

Witchpower set her blood on fire, pushing off the winter cold until Belinda felt she could strip to the skin and go unscathed by wind and rain. She wet her lips, touching her tongue to Marius's earlobe, and he shuddered, a sound of desire strangled in his throat. Belinda's own rational mind warned her of danger, but the salty taste of Marius's skin and his too-fast pulse were a delight to her, making her smile against his throat. "Or would you risk it all for me? Your marriage, your stature, your friendship with the prince? Will you have me and damn all consequences, Marius? We mustn't, you know," she breathed, mocking with laughter. "We mustn't grunt and grasp and twist against one another, or seek pleasure in sharing bodies. Or would you break that commandment, my love? Would you fuck your brother's wife?"

Marius groaned again and knotted his hands in Belinda's hair, bringing his mouth to hers, savagery in the kiss. She laughed at his bruising strength, giving in for a few seconds before pushing away again, feeling her body flushed with desire and danger. "We mustn't," she said again.

And behind her, a woman's voice murmured, "Forgive me, my lord. I wish I had not been right."

Sickness curdled in Belinda's belly, birthing ice that burned the witchpower's heat from her blood. Marius flinched back, so much an admission of guilt that Belinda wanted to let fly a sharp cry of laughter. She turned away from him, faint curiosity cocking her eyebrow, no admission of guilt in her colour or expression. Her hands were not cold, despite the churning in her stomach and the shards of ice making their way through her body. She curtsied, brief perfunctory thing, then wrinkled her forehead as she looked from Javier to Akilina and back again. "Been right, my lady?"

"What are you doing, Beatrice?" Strain filled Javier's voice, shock sheeting off him as a precursor to the anger Belinda could sense growing in him. Akilina, at his side, stood as a bastion of smugness, though only severe disappointment and apology was visible in her demeanor. Belinda's witchpower remained chilled beneath the need to play out this scenario flawlessly, else she might give in to its impulse to step forward and slap the expression off Akilina's face. Javier, cheeks flushed with colour that did his complexion no favours, drew breath, and his voice cracked like a boy's when he spoke. "What are you doing with Marius?"

"Saying good-bye, my lord." Belinda dipped another brief curtsey, turning toward Marius as if in apology. "He's just come to tell me that he's to be wed."

"Marius?" Javier's voice cracked again, but this time with command. Marius blanched, then curled his hands into fists and let go a low laugh.

"Beatrice protects me from myself, my prince. I came here to beg her away from your side, rather than agree to the match my mother's made." He closed his eyes, his skin grey in the winter shadows. "More fool I, as she told me quite plainly that we were not meant to be. Forgive me, Jav, for my jealousy. Yes," he added dully. "It seems I'm to be wed. Sacha's sister, of all people, and by the ides of March, if my mother's will be done."

"Sacha's . . . ? And you . . . you came here to—?"

"To play the part of the fool. That's always been my role, hasn't it, Jav? You the prince, Liza the lover, Sacha the strong right arm. I'm the young one, whose passions and naïveté rise and fall so quickly as to make you all laugh. I believed you, Javier." He spoke bitterly, ignoring Akilina's presence, and Belinda's stomach clenched again, this time in warning. She lifted a hand to stay

Marius, and Javier lifted his to stay her. Fingers curled in reluctant acquiescence, she dropped her hand and watched Akilina from the corner of her eye. Smugness had left the countess as surely as it had filled her, and she cast her gaze from Marius to Javier, angry at losing control of a scenario she had clearly believed she owned.

"I thought you might find us a happy ending from all of this. Tell me, did you ever intend to give her up, or was it a story to make me hold on while you found a way to keep her close to you? I know as well as you do that she's like no other woman." Marius's eyes flickered to Belinda, poison in them instead of lust, then returned to Javier. "She wakens desires I never dreamed I had. I can only hope she has the same effect on you."

"But you would take her from me whether she does or not?" Softness filled Javier's voice, more dangerous than cutting words. Marius barked laughter, more derision in the sound than Belinda had imagined he could convey.

"If I could, my prince. If I could. It seems, though, that she's as much under your spell as any of us. We can't tell you no, Jav. We never could. And I'm not that much of a fool. A prince is a far better pairing than a merchant's son. I would have accepted it." He spoke quietly, eyes hard on Javier. "I would have hated it, but damn you, Jav, I would've accepted it if you'd said she was yours, and not thrown a bone. Am I worth so little as that?"

New softness, this time of pain, came into Javier's answer. "You're worth far more than I could ever give you. I told you that once, and its truth hasn't changed. You're better than I've ever deserved, and perhaps I thought . . . there could be a happy ending."

"It must be comforting to be a prince," Marius said with great precision, "for no one will tell you when you lie, even to yourself."

Javier, never swarthy to begin with, paled visibly. Belinda felt his will flex, injury strengthening his witchpower as he said, "Tell me, Marius, how badly I have lied to myself. Are you and Beatrice lovers?" The air seemed weighted with his question, so heavy that

Belinda herself wanted to blurt out an answer, any answer, to appease royal anger. She no more allowed herself to speak than she allowed her hands to curl in fear, or her colour to change as she anticipated Marius's response.

Marius laughed again, another sharp and ugly sound. "Would it be a relief to you if I said yes, Jav? Would that intimacy be enough to forgive my behavior? Would you then understand my rage and hurt at having her taken from me?" He turned his head, lip curled as if he might spit, then looked back at Javier, stood beneath the weight of Javier's will, and said, bitterly, "Beatrice and I have never shared physical love."

Bewilderment edging on disappointment shattered Javier's expression, even as Belinda held stillness close, refusing her stance a waver. She understood with vicious clarity the fine line Marius walked with his answer, understood his bitterness was not for losing her, or even pointed at Javier, but for what had passed between them in the name of passion. It had not been love. It had been something else, something darker and hungrier, lust and power marked by submission and domination.

She caught, for an instant, a glint of humour in Akilina's eyes, and knew that the Khazarian *dvoryanin* understood the game Marius played as well. Among them all, only Javier heard what he wished to hear, and Belinda thought how terribly right Marius was: no one would tell him when he lied, even to himself.

"I don't understand." Javier's whisper came though the busy silence of things unsaid. "I don't understand, Marius."

"It doesn't matter, does it, Jav? Whether you understand or not, Beatrice is yours. I'm a merchant, and you're a prince. It could never be any other way." Marius drew himself up, a startling amount of mocking in his sudden grace. He bowed first to Belinda, then to Akilina, murmuring, "Forgive us for airing such unpleasantries in front of you, my lady," and then turned to his prince.

"Duty calls me elsewhere, my lord. I hope you'll attend my wedding."

He bowed far more deeply than he had to the women, then stepped past Javier and Akilina to exit the garden bower, never looking back.

AKILINA PANKEJEFF, DVORYANIN
4 January 1588 † *Lutetia*

Akilina watches Marius go, then turns to Beatrice Irvine again, finding herself awash with admiration. Beatrice, or Rosa, or whatever her name truly is, is cooler than the winters in Akilina's homeland. The confrontation with Javier should have destroyed their relationship; instead it seems to have shattered a friendship much older and deeper than anything the young woman could possibly share with the prince. It suggests Sandalia was right not to bring Javier into the attempt to unmask Beatrice's true identity; if he can be swayed in the sight of one of his oldest friends, then mere words are unlikely to change his mind. It would be wrong to say Akilina is anticipating Beatrice's downfall with delight, but she would be telling herself false if she didn't admit to a certain enthusiasm for the project. Not for the hurt that it will bring Javier; despite what they say about her, Akilina takes no particular pleasure in causing others pain. She simply loves both puzzles and secrets, and understands that both have power.

Akilina Pankejeff is very fond of power.

Nearly all the pieces are in place to expose Beatrice. Akilina considers, briefly, sparing the prince his lover's exposé, but there's a part of her wedded to drama, if not cruelty. Her search for Viktor's Rosa has led her to fascinating discoveries; discoveries she has not yet shared with even Sandalia. Javier will regret, too late, being swayed by Beatrice's spell rather than standing at Marius's side. He's fortunate he's the prince; a lesser man would lose all status at the coup d'état that Akilina intends to present. If Javier is wise he'll accept that he has, indeed, been under a spell, and that Beatrice Irvine is a witch best meant for the burning.

Akilina meets Beatrice's eyes just briefly, and for a wonder, the young woman neither curtseys nor so much as inclines her head in acknowledgment. Her gaze is steady, cool hazel as she dares, at least for a moment, to hold herself equal to a countess.

Akilina likes this girl.

She'll like bringing her down even more.

A smile curving her lips, she graces Beatrice with one small nod, an admission of challenge, and then she gathers her skirts and slips away from the garden, eager to deepen the game.

BELINDA PRIMROSE / BEATRICE IRVINE
4 January 1588 † *Lutetia*

"You look at me as if you're no longer certain of me, my lord." Beatrice kept her voice soft, putting sorrow into it instead of accusation. Javier twitched, the first movement save breathing he'd made since Marius's departure. He hadn't so much as watched Akilina go, his gaze fixed wholly on Belinda.

"Marius has never spoken to me so," he said roughly, when another moment had passed. "How is it that you've lain a barrier between us all, Beatrice? Eliza is gone and Sacha will barely speak to me when he's not searching for her. Marius, my gentle Marius, has become brittle as ice. We four, who have been together since childhood, disrupted by one woman. How have you done this?"

"It was your own power that persuaded them to stay away from the opera." Belinda spoke carefully, wanting only reminder in the words, not blame. "Perhaps . . ." She hesitated, not for effect but out of genuine uncertainty, then exhaled a sigh. "Perhaps it was, or is, time for childhood to be left behind, my lord. They—"

"I will never give them up," Javier snapped. Belinda lifted her hands in apology, shaking her head.

"I meant no such thing. But friendships change, don't they? Nothing remains the same. I don't at all mean that you should lose them, Javier, but a reckoning, a redefining, may be at hand. It's inevitable, isn't it? You'll all marry, one way or another. You'll all have families and duties and responsibilities beyond those to one another. Perhaps I'm a harbinger." Belinda smiled faintly. "An ill omen."

"No." Javier sounded desperate as he stepped forward to take Belinda's hands, squeezing them until her bones ached from it. "You're the only one like me," he all but whispered. "You're not, you can't be, an ill omen. Marius is——" Desperation broke his words a second time and Belinda shifted his grip, so they held each other's hands.

"Marius fell in love with me, Javier, and you took me from him. His mother might have agreed to me marrying him, but she's neither privy to your plans nor a fool. I'm no longer a viable interest, and she thinks it's time he's wed, so Sarah Asselin it shall be. He's hurt and angry and I hope he'll forgive you. I hope you'll forgive him," she added more quietly. "I did not mean for any of this to happen."

That it had, and that it increased Javier's reliance on her, was a gift she hadn't looked for. Without his childhood friends at hand, Belinda thought the prince more likely to buck Sandalia's whim, and seek Belinda herself out when he was supposed to be otherwise occupied. It might lead him to share secrets that weren't his to share; Belinda would try to work that from him. Flat acknowledgment rose in her: she had been avoiding moving too abruptly within the court as much to keep eyes off her as to steal moments with Javier; it wouldn't be long before what time they had together came inevitably to an end. It was shocking sentiment to want to stretch that time out, and as well that neither Robert nor she dared communication while she was so publicly in the court's eye; Robert would be thoroughly displeased with her reticence, and Belinda would have no legitimate grounds on which to defend herself.

"I know you didn't." Forgiveness lightened Javier's voice, before reluctance deepened it again. "I should see Mother before the countess does. God knows what she'll tell her."

"That I'm a harlot not good enough for the royal house, so she should marry you herself," Belinda said drily. "Go. I'll take myself back to embroidering."

Javier quirked a brief, unhappy smile, then stepped closer to kiss her. "Don't abandon me, Beatrice," he murmured against her mouth. "I'm bereft on all sides. Without you, I lose hope."

"Never lose hope, my lord prince," Belinda replied. Javier broke from her, touching his knuckles to her cheek, then spun and strode away, sodden earth marking his passage through the garden.

Belinda exhaled, standing alone in the wind and chill, then made fists of her hands and called stillness to herself. Witchpower flared, golden light drawing shadows close until she felt the freedom of invisibility.

Thus wrapped, she threw caution to the side and went to seek out the secrets shared by Countess Akilina Pankejeff and Sandalia de Costa, queen and regent.

16

Anger propelled Belinda through the palace halls. Anger at herself for dallying with Javier, for luxuriating in the life of nobility; for allowing herself to lose focus. Anger, too, at Javier, for playing Marius so clumsily; as a prince he should have more ability with people than that, though perhaps inevitably royalty failed to understand its effect on the common man.

Anger, most exquisite anger, at Akilina Pankejeff. If her purpose were to split Belinda from Javier, she'd failed, but that she was willing to make such a blatant attempt at it rang caution through Belinda's soul. That very blatancy might have helped Belinda in defusing Javier's anger, though Marius's careful play with words had gone much further in doing that than anything Belinda had or hadn't said. Still Javier was no fool, and Akilina arranging for him to catch Belinda and Marius together smacked of a deliberation that the prince might have resented, had that card been necessary to play. Belinda didn't know the raven-haired countess well, but such an obvious hand seemed unlike her. And if it was, then she'd had a greater plan in bringing Javier to the young lovers in the bower, and not knowing that plan angered Belinda, too.

It was easy to stalk through the palace, hidden in plain sight, with anger to fuel the witchpower. It burned away the usual heady wash of sexual desire that using her magic carried; that, beyond anything else, was useful to know. If the impulsive, idiotic actions brought on by too much use of power could be headed off by focusing on rage instead of want, it was much the better for Belinda.

Tempestuous emotion allowed her to walk through Sandalia's audience chambers a few steps behind Javier, slipping through the doors before the guards closed them again without anyone being the wiser. It let her follow the prince, unseen, into the private dayrooms beyond the formal courtroom, where she had the presence of mind to stop just inside the doors, while Javier walked ahead. He didn't seem to share her gift for recognizing when witchpower was being used around him, unless it stood directly in conflict with what he wanted. But angry or not, there was no use in pushing the boundaries further than she had. A few feet of distance felt safer, even through the turmoil of frustration, and both prince and queen were well within viewing and hearing range.

Sandalia, in fact, lounged on a divan before a half-banked fire, her hair loose and informal; she clearly had no plans to be seen in public again that day. She quirked an eyebrow as Javier came to an abrupt halt and bowed without his customary grace, and a wave of amused curiosity splashed off her. "I won't like this, will I?"

"Only if you dislike me condemning your favourites," Javier snapped. Sandalia's eyebrows went higher and she sat up, making a small imperious gesture toward a chair opposite her. Javier flung himself into it, making its feet bump off a thrown rug and squeak dully against the cold tile beneath it. "Akilina is trying to destroy Beatrice, and she may well have already ruined my friendship with Marius."

Even consigned to shadows, Belinda put a hand over her mouth to hide the slightest hint of laughter from visible expression. Javier's easy arrogance appealed to her much of the time, but it could also be both appalling and amusing. Perhaps it was the near-godhood of princedom, but she had thought him able to accept his own failing when it came to the situation with Marius. To hear him place the blame elsewhere was a dreadful sort of delight. Hurt and anger pinged off him in sharp sparks, almost audible, like a rain of needles falling against a hard floor. In marked contrast, fresh humour rolled around his mother. "Do tell, Javier. What's happened?"

He sketched out the events in the garden, giving Belinda more innocence than she deserved and lingering over Marius's rejection and hurt. Sandalia listened silently, her laughter at first contained and then slipping away, until her response was as grave as Javier might wish it to be. "And you believe Akilina is at fault, for making more of their meeting than it was? What if she was right, Javier? What if your Beatrice and Marius were lovers?"

Javier snorted, derisive sound that barely touched the bleak disbelief Belinda could feel from him. "He said they weren't, and Marius couldn't tell a lie if his life depended on it. You know him, Mother. I'm not wrong."

Sandalia pursed her mouth, brief thoughtful expression. For an instant Belinda wrestled with the temptation to cross the room and touch the regent's smooth cheek, to steal her thoughts from her and understand what idea it was that held her for that moment. She held her ground, wisdom greater than curiosity: her experiments hadn't determined whether she could touch someone while hidden in shadow and still remain unnoticed. The queen's private chambers would be a disastrous place to discover the limits of her power did not stretch so far.

"It is true," Sandalia murmured after a few seconds. "Marius couldn't lie to save his own life." She watched Javier, who nodded agreement, and the corner of her mouth curled as her son read nothing further into her statement. Belinda breathed a silent exhalation, understanding quite clearly what Sandalia implied and Javier failed to read. Marius might not tell a convincing lie to save his own life, but his known inability to dissemble might well save another's. Javier, Belinda thought, would have to learn more about the way what was unspoken said as much as what was voiced aloud, or how careful truths could be infallible lies, before he would make a worthy king. She wouldn't have imagined Marius to have that double-speech within him, but then, he was a merchant's son. A reputation for honesty and a skill for using the truth to tell lies would do him very well, were he to follow his father's trade.

And unless Javier learned to not trust those around him to employ such tactics, he, unlike his merchant friend, would never follow well in his father's trade.

Belinda allowed herself a quick smile at the floor, expression hidden by habit even when shadows concealed her. Not in his reputed father's trade, at least; she was still curious as to his true heritage, but in the weeks she'd been half-imprisoned in the palace, she'd not yet found a way to direct Sandalia's thoughts to a lie told a lifetime ago when she could touch the queen's hand and steal the truth from her. It would come in time; truth always did.

"What would you have me do, Javier? Take Akilina aside and explain I can no longer listen to her counsel, because my son's jealous heart has taken a dislike to her?" Belinda heard teasing in Sandalia's voice, though Javier's tight expression said he was having none of it.

"You're the queen," he said petulantly. "You don't have to explain anything."

Sandalia laughed aloud, a thing rare enough that Belinda couldn't remember having heard her do so before. She had a much deeper laugh than expected, in contrast to her sweet soprano voice. It coloured Belinda's viewpoint of her, enriching her into sudden humanity as her smile carved lines around her mouth and bent her toward likability. It was a striking thought: Belinda had never conceived of queens as being likable or not; that was a thing reserved for ordinary human affairs. Lorraine was a creature for veneration, and Sandalia was her rival and therefore the enemy; that was all that mattered.

Unexpectedly, unpleasantly, Belinda wondered if she *wanted* Sandalia to die, and the idea rained chaos in her mind, breaking cold sweat on her skin. Within an instant she drew stillness to her, beyond the witchpower she used to hide herself from the room's other occupants. This was her childhood game, the one of not hurting and not fearing; it could be used as well to not think. Duty and desire lay on opposite sides of a vast divide; it was not her blessing or her curse to consider her own wishes as she served her queen. Duty made her the queen's secret blade; desire, as she lifted her eyes to look at Sandalia again, seemed a foreign conceit, and as quickly as she'd wondered whether she wanted the petite Gallic queen dead, she wondered why she would *not* want her dead.

Javier's sullenness had grown in the instant Belinda's thoughts were turned aside. He cared for being laughed at no more than anyone, and perhaps less: his royal mantle saved him from it often enough. "A queen," Sandalia told him, "can do far less as she likes than you might imagine. I will not put Akilina aside, Javier, so draw in your lip and cease your pouting. It ill becomes anyone over the age of three, especially a prince."

Javier did as he was told, though the emotions that pooled around him and crept toward Belinda were still black. "Why won't you rid us of her? We asked for no Khazarian contingent."

"Nor," Sandalia said after long moments, "did we ask for the support of Khazarian troops that Akilina and I have negotiated, to be ratified by Irina's own hand."

Javier's sulk fell away as abruptly as Belinda's interest piqued. Impulse again edged her forward, as though she might miss something if she remained more safely sequestered by the door, and she made her hands into fists, leaning toward the royal pair by the fire, but not moving further. "Mother?" Belinda could all but taste the leap of Javier's heart, excitement suddenly pounding through him where a breath earlier there had been a childish whinge. Sandalia regarded her son another long moment before standing and gesturing for him to follow. Belinda bit her lower lip and pursued them, matching her steps to Javier's and moving close enough to pass through the door Sandalia opened.

Sandalia paused, holding the door, forehead wrinkled at Javier as he passed in front of her and Belinda stepped to the side, holding her breath and keeping well out of the way. Javier turned back to his mother when he realised she was still at the door, curiosity tilting an eyebrow. "Perhaps you should consider rubbing up to Beatrice only at night, Javier," Sandalia said drily. "You smell of her perfume."

Red scalded Javier's cheeks and Belinda pressed a hand against her stomach, caught between horrified laughter and nausea. She had thought to trick the eye, but never to try fooling the nose. She would pour out her perfumes the instant she returned to her rooms. Javier mumbled an apology that Sandalia brushed off, closing the door behind her and locking it before crossing to a writing desk that dominated the private chamber. The rest of the room was equally businesslike, the windows too small to be looked through from the outside, the chairs arranged in such a fashion as to focus on the desk; here, Sandalia could hold court among counselors, herself sitting amidst the scribes as they scribbled and sketched out treaties as voiced by the men who advised a queen.

It took more than one key to open a heavy drawer within the desk. Sandalia tucked the keys back into her bodice, a location sufficiently secure that Belinda briefly despaired of acquiring them herself, and withdrew a stack of parchment, spreading the top pages out as Javier joined her behind the desk. Belinda held herself still again, heart crashing against her ribs while Javier traced a fingertip down one sheet of parchment, murmuring written words aloud: " ' . . . commitment of troops toward the administration of open water passages from Khazar's port town of Nvskya to the Essandian Straits.' 'Administration,' " he repeated. "A delicate word for indelicate intentions. This has your signature already,

THE QUEEN'S BASTARD · 375

Mother. Yours and Akilina's. Can you be certain you ally yourself
with Irina, and not her duchess?"

"Would you have me use seizure and control? We tread dangerous enough waters as it is," Sandalia said shortly. "The details of
ratification are at the top. Read carefully, Javier. Akilina acts in
Irina's name or not at all."

"Does my uncle Rodrigo know?"

A lance of guilt spiked from Sandalia, though her words didn't
betray it: "Irina still dances with him on a treaty. Their sexes suggest treaties should be made by marriage, and Irina wants that no
more than any of us." Belinda knew she spoke of the reigning
queens of Echon, an unusual sisterhood endlessly threatened by the
men around them. Javier allowed himself a brief laugh.

"Does something make the imperatrix think that Rodrigo's
eager for marriage? He's managed to avoid it for thirty years."

"My brother prefers to make his conquests peacefully," Sandalia
said. "It's why he still treats with Lorraine, and why Irina should be
cautious."

"Lorraine will die before she gives her hand and throne in marriage," Javier said. Sandalia lifted her eyes, pretty face carved with
an animal smile.

"Yes. She will."

The threat's weight settled over Belinda's skin like a cloak,
wrapping her tightly in it. Her fingers drifted to the small of her
back, where her tiny dagger lay hidden beneath clothes and corsets.
It would be very easy to end it now, to slip forward unseen and
drive the blade into Sandalia's throat. Javier would not be able to
save her, or raise an alarm quickly enough to save his own life.
There was no other choice, if she were to kill the queen now: it
must be both of them, so no one was left for a pretender's crown.
She could take the papers that Sandalia and Javier now gloated over
and return to Aulun; the treaty would prove her right to have acted

as she did. Lorraine's reluctance to put another regent to death would be mitigated by proof positive of plots against her, and with the witchpower helping her, no one would ever know Belinda had done the deed that saved her queen.

She found her skirts already gathered high, a hand twisted behind her back to snake its way beneath her corset in search of the blade she was never without.

"Akilina came as an ambassador in truth, then," Javier half-asked, still studying the treaty. "A woman."

Sandalia let a shoulder rise and fall. "Who better to trust than another woman, rather than the men who insist we are too weak to rule in our own right? There's a price, Javier." She turned a page, parchment whispering against itself. "This treaty has a price."

"They all do," Javier said mildly. His fingertips stopped their wandering, pressed against the sheet Sandalia had uncovered, and he read for a few seconds before breathing, "Ah. This cannot be what Akilina wanted, Mother. She came to Gallin in search of a throne." He chuckled, another soft sound, as Sandalia glanced at him in surprise. "I'm not that blind to reality, Mother, even with this match made to Beatrice."

"I'm glad to hear it." Steel crept into the queen's voice, then faded again as she touched the papers above Javier's hand. "And you're right, it isn't. But she cannot protest overmuch, or she'll lose her standing as an ambassador. And it benefits her, if not as thoroughly as she might like."

"She wants public adoration. But failing that, yes, standing behind the throne might do." Javier took a breath. "So you'll wed me to the Khazarian heir after all."

Cold sluiced through Belinda, chilling her fingers against the small of her back. Ivanova Durova, Irina's daughter. Dmitri's daughter. Belinda clenched her hand and let her skirts fall again, heart hammering once more. Neither Dmitri nor Robert would allow the engagement of Khazar to Gallin if they did not tacitly approve;

Belinda's hasty action in taking Javier's life along with his mother's could easily disrupt Robert's plans. She set her teeth together, a new flush of anger running over her. Hers had been a lifetime of servitude, never asking why, but this once, set loose in the Lutetian court, understanding her father's ultimate purpose might have been useful. Securing Lorraine's throne was the obvious end game, but allying the massive eastern country of Khazar to tiny Gallin had to go beyond that. Perhaps that alliance might end in a victory for Aulun that Belinda couldn't yet see. She would have to risk a letter to Robert, seek his guidance. Nothing else could clear her way.

"How will you secure the troops?" Javier asked softly. Sandalia dimpled at him, suddenly youthful.

"Your plot with Beatrice is proving to be the perfect foil. Troubles stir on Lanyarch's border. We need only push it far enough for Lorraine to risk invading, and then Lanyarch, under my banner, can call to Cordula for help in repelling the Reformation soldiers."

"Khazan is a long way from Cordula, Mother. We don't so much as share a religion with them."

"Irina treats with Cordula as well." Sandalia's voice was full of the same casual arrogance that her son's often carried. "The *Pappas* and his patriarchs see her overtures as a softening toward the Ecumenic faith, and intend, in time, to use them to convert Khazan. Until missionaries are sent, though, Cordula is happy to accept troops willing to fight where Cordula decrees."

"In Lanyarch and Aulun."

"And Alunaer," Sandalia finished, savage light of fanaticism suddenly bright in her voice. "We'll take the battle to the Titian Bitch's doorstep, Javier, and when it's done you'll sit on the island throne with a queen at your side."

"And what of Beatrice?" Javier's voice softened, deceptive in comparison to the resolve Belinda felt stiffening within him. "She and I have spoken of the need to put her aside, but we both believed there would be a match waiting for her. Marius is . . . no longer available. What of Beatrice?"

Sandalia touched his arm, a mother's reassuring gesture, and smiled. "She's come to mean a great deal to you, hasn't she, Javier? You spoke of giving her lands; I'll have papers drawn up for some small holding in Brittany. Marius may be consigned to another's wedding bed, but your Beatrice is young and pretty enough. Another man will come along. I promise to take care of her," she said, and Belinda could see in her eyes, and in Javier's, that once more, they both took what they wanted from her words. Sandalia felt of honey-coated steel, and Javier struggled with shards of hope and belief fighting against his determination to not release the witchbreed woman he'd found. It was he who acquiesced, though, lowering his gaze and his head to murmur, "Thank you, Mother," as a dutiful son should.

Belinda, slipping out behind them many long minutes later, wondered if such promises were what a noose tightening around a slender neck felt like.

BELINDA PRIMROSE / BEATRICE IRVINE
11 *January 1588* † *Lutetia*

Five long days of watching had not managed to provide Belinda with the opportunity to steal the keys that Sandalia kept on her person. She had, once, made her way back into Sandalia's private chambers with lock-picks in hand, only to narrowly avoid a tiny, vicious needle, its tip stained dark, popping out from the lock. Belinda had sworn under her breath, searching her skin for marks, and used a blotter to press the needle back into place. The lock required keys: they needed, it seemed, to be turned simultaneously, and two hands were simply not enough to hold in place two separate locks and turn them together. The witchlight couldn't be formed into something solid enough to manipulate the locks with her will, and after over an hour of attempting the job, she had reluctantly given up and let herself back out of Sandalia's rooms.

That had been one of the few times she'd successfully escaped watching eyes in the past several days. Much as she'd chafed at her guards in the previous month, they seemed ever-more ubiquitous now, perhaps the vestiges of Javier's uncertainty about her faithfulness. She saw no one and went nowhere without armed accompaniment unless she was with Javier in his chambers.

The morning previous, she'd been awakened by a dour-faced dressmaker, who stripped her to the skin—Belinda palmed her tiny knife frantically and threw it into the bedclothes as she was hauled toward the centre of the room—then stood her up and kept her there, corsets bound tight, while he built a dress on her, regardless of the pleas she made on her bladder's behalf.

He had none of Eliza's wild imagination when it came to fashion, but if his purpose was to turn Belinda from a provincial Lanyarchan into a Gallic noble to be reckoned with within thirty-six hours, he succeeded admirably. Belinda had been permitted two breaks from standing as a dressmaker's dummy to eat and relieve herself, and her peevish costumer had eventually deigned to let her sleep, warning he would be still earlier the next morning. Belinda shook off nobility's habits for the servant she was accustomed to playing, and at least managed to eat and use the necessary before he arrived again to sew her into a gown that rivaled not just Sandalia's wear, but even her own mother's.

His one concession to time was that he allowed her a long while to stand in front of a mirror, barely able to believe it was herself she saw there. Some of the sourness left his face as she stood, hardly breathing while she gazed at the woman reflected back at her.

Belinda Primrose did not look like her royal mother. She had none of Lorraine's dramatic colouring or, most especially, the widow's peak that all eyes were drawn to, whether they met Lorraine in person or saw her portraits. Belinda thought her own face rounder than Lorraine's, her eyes larger, her mouth more full; these were things she'd taken from Robert.

But bedecked royally, skin pale with powder and perhaps shaped more by maturity than she recalled it, looking at herself, she saw Lorraine in her for the first time. The gown was a shade the Titian Queen would wear: the green of young leaves, too bright for a winter day and yet utterly fitting for Belinda's youth and skin tones. Moreover, it brought forth the green in her eyes, making them far brighter and more challenging than she thought them to be. Lorraine's eyes were grey and narrow; cosmetics did something that hinted at her mother's eyes in Belinda's reflection. Even her hair, upswept and bejeweled with emeralds and rubies made, she trusted, of paste, looked lusher than usual, as if the firelight had taken up residence in it. She was by no means the redhead that Lorraine was, or even Javier, but there was golden warmth in what had always seemed to her an ordinary brown.

The gown itself was high-collared, stiff lace and gold threads itching furiously even through a wrap of soft old muslin. It thrust her chin high, making her neck long and elegantly slender. The shoulders were demure in their cut, sleeves coming to points over her hands. There was little of the puffed nonsense that could send a woman to walking through doors sideways in order to fit; that narrowness served to make her look delicate, a thought which Belinda might have laughed at, had she been able to catch breath to do so. She was a worker, strong and trained; to find herself looking fragile was all but beyond comprehension.

The bodice fit with appalling tightness, gold and white worked into the fabric to make a subtle pattern of roses. When the skirts finally flared at her hips, they, too, were far less extravagant than fashion dictated, but considerable enough to create a distinctively feminine shape to her form. Tall shoes lent her height, and only when Belinda finally turned from the mirror in astonishment did her chamber door open to allow Akilina Pankejeff entrance.

To Belinda's surprise, and even more to her gratitude, the Khazarian countess stopped a few feet from the door to look her over with admiration that bordered on amazement. "The queen told me Pierre was her best dressmaker, even above Javier's young friend and her radical designs. I believe it now. My lady Beatrice, you are exquisite."

"Thank you." Belinda's voice sounded faint to her own ears and she took a careful breath, straining against the corsets to Akilina's visible amusement.

"Let's hope you don't need to run anywhere today, my lady. I've brought you a gift." She stepped forward, offering Belinda a necklace that caught gold light in its pendant, a thumbnail-size piece of amber, carved as a rose. Belinda gaped at the jewel, heart seized as though she were still a child, offered not one, but two new gowns for the queen's visit. Akilina remained silent a few moments, long enough to let Belinda admire it, then asked, teasingly, "Do you like it?"

Belinda lifted her eyes, wide with unfeigned astonishment. "How could I not? My lady, I mean no disrespect, but *why*—?"

"It seems a suitable gift for a queen-to-be," Akilina replied, and dropped a wink that would better suit a lecherous old man. "And perhaps you'll recall someday who gave it to you. May I?" She took the jewel back and stepped behind Belinda, sending a thrill of nervous caution down Belinda's spine. Her touch was light as she fastened the necklace, the stone settling against the hollow of Belinda's throat, and both women turned to look at her in the mirror.

Amber flashed magnificent rich gold against the green of her gown, its chain so fine that it seemed to hover at her throat unsupported. The dressmaker—Pierre; he had never bothered to give Belinda his name—huffed a sound she took as approval, evidently satisfied that the jewel enhanced his creation.

"Thank you," Belinda said a second time, peculiarly aware that those were not words that often crossed her lips. "It's astonishing, and I shall indeed remember from whence it came."

Akilina smiled with more pleasure than necessary, as if hearing more in the words than was obviously there. "You're expected in the courtroom at the midday Angelus bells. I'd best go there myself; Her Majesty wants no one to distract from your arrival."

Colour built in Belinda's cheeks, less artifice than she might wish, and Akilina laughed as she excused herself, leaving Belinda alone with the dressmaker. "Thank you," she said to him as well, and his customary dour expression reasserted itself. Belinda fought back another laugh and turned to look at herself a final time before drawing a careful deep breath. "I suppose I should go. I'm to wait in the audience chambers."

"Wait here until the bells are closer to ringing," Pierre said abruptly. "Had the woman not been a countess and bearing a gift, I wouldn't have let her in. No one should see you, my lady. The effect is all the greater that way."

Belinda blinked at him, startled and then not, at his sudden opinion. He'd had them by the bucketload when it came to her gown, that he should have them in how to best show it off should be no surprise. "All right." She took another careful breath, dizziness spilling through her, and asked, "Could I perhaps have some wine, then? I'm light-headed."

He fetched some, and, unexpectedly, a croissant with jam, then stood by with a napkin dangling from his fingertips and a glower set onto his face. "I won't wipe my fingers on the dress," Belinda promised, and he looked increasingly dour that she'd even spoken the idea aloud.

Food, more than the drink, helped to steady her head, though with having done no more than stand and turn, Belinda knew she would be desperately glad to rid herself of the corsets when the time came. The idea of curtseying before Sandalia made her dizzy all over again, and she walked carefully to a chair, leaning awkwardly against its cushions; the corsets had far too little give to allow her to bend at hip or waist so she might sit properly. Still, the change of weight seemed to help for a few moments, even if Pierre scowled at the possibility of his creation being wrinkled by her carelessness.

He could not have made a better dress if his plan had been to forbid her any chance of stealing Sandalia's keys in the bare moments they would be that close to each other. Moving quickly enough, subtly enough, to pick the queen's pocket was unlikely even if she'd been graced with the chance to wear one of Eliza's gowns; doing it in the rigid contraption she now wore would be an impossibility.

She would have to risk the poisoned darts and damaging Sandalia's desk. It lacked any degree of delicacy, but perhaps there was someone she could hang for it, some servant who could be made out as a spy. An Aulunian spy, no less, though the idea brought on a laugh so breathless it could be called a giggle, escaped her. Pierre, disapproving of levity, turned a ferocious glare on her, and Belinda subsided, nibbling her croissant and sipping at the wine. Her heartbeat was too quick, and stillness kept slipping away from her, even when she ought to have held it close and let it help her forget the discomfort of too-tight corsets. It had seen her through a day and a half of Pierre's ministrations; to find it deserting her now was an irritation.

"The bells will ring the hour in some ten minutes." Pierre's voice cut through her reverie and Belinda shook herself, looking up. Her wine was finished, the croissant gone, and the napkin Pierre had offered was caught in her fingertips. She cast her thoughts back, recalling finishing the food and asking for the napkin, but it was a hazy memory, as if breathing shallowly had fogged her mind. She would be glad indeed to shed the dress, even if it made her regal.

"Thank you," she said yet again, and took the dressmaker's hand to let him help her rise; without it she feared she may well have been doomed to an afternoon of uncomfortable lounging, unable to rise or sit without some drastic change of state.

Breathing seemed to come more easily again once she stood; movement appeared to be the trigger, the changes of pressure tricking her into thinking she could draw more breath. She curtsied to Pierre, a small thing—the most she dared, and probably more than his station could ever aspire to—and left her chambers in a slow, stately glide that had far more to do with being unable to move more quickly than any particular need for the dramatically slow pace.

The corridors were empty, servants working to prepare a dinner feast and courtiers already in attendance in the audience hall. After five weeks of being watched, Belinda was finally alone in the palace, and completely unable to make use of that private time. Even if she dared slip through shadows to search Sandalia's chambers again, there was no way to do it in the dress she wore. Better to follow what plan she had, and make her careful way to the audience hall to accept the gift Sandalia had in mind for her.

It was as well she was a woman, and not a man come to be knighted. Bad enough to have the chamber hall doors swung open slowly in front of her, ponderously, with the rush of wind they made heralding her arrival even before a crier could shout out her name. Not since childhood, not since she'd bowed for the first time before the queen of Aulun, had Belinda felt the weight of so many gazes upon her.

Then, they had been tolerant, disinterested, amused. Now they judged, and not kindly: she was their prince's intended, she was backwater and without connections, and she was loathed by many for those things alone.

That she was also, this one day, beautiful, softened some hearts toward her and hardened others. Even uncalled for, the witch-power stretched out, tasting emotion and bringing it back to her in powerful waves. She was prepared for that, braced for it; the stillness held a cool calm centre against which admiration and dislike and envy broke and fell around her. Out of the cacophony she could pick out individuals whom she knew well: Marius, a bastion of regret, his pain a lonely note in the mass of broader sentiment. Sacha, full of smoldering rage tempered by a sense of intent that Belinda couldn't define.

Sandalia, nearly as cool as Belinda herself, as if she, too, had drawn stillness around her and did only what she must. Viktor, unexpectedly, his hunger and lust pounding through Belinda's control to bring the faintest heat to her cheeks. Akilina, whose easy laughter felt spiked, as if she had a delicious secret no one else shared. And Javier, whose pride in Belinda's appearance was softened by a heart-filling joy that Belinda could not, or dared not, name.

Below it all she felt a rumbling anger so thick and murky it seemed familiar; a human predilection toward violence, perhaps, the thin line that kept a group from being a mob near to being crossed over. She was not loved here, though with the thought her gaze skittered back to Javier. She was not loved here, save, perhaps, by one. Her slow footsteps measured the length of the hall with ear-shattering sound, no voices raised in murmurs to discuss her, even after she'd passed.

She curtsied before Sandalia, dropping straight down and inclining her head; there would be no forward bow from the waist to deepen her obsequiescence, not in that dress. For the second time she thought it was as well she wasn't a man coming to be knighted; the prospect of kneeling in the gown she'd been sewn into was absurd to the point of bringing a smile to her heart, though she didn't dare let one curve her mouth. She held the pose an achingly long time, the breath gone from her body before Sandalia finally murmured, "You may rise."

She *may*, Belinda thought, but whether she *could* was entirely another question. Concentrated effort pushed into her legs helped her to straighten, so slowly she knew others would call it grace, so long as they didn't see the tremble that suffused her body. She flickered her glance up once in thanks, then lowered it again, waiting for Sandalia's words.

They came, soaring over her head to reach the back of the audience hall; Belinda was merely a tool in a showcase; none of this was for her. "Today we have the pleasure of granting a noble title to one who has done this court great service. We have lands in Brittany to our north that are ripe and wooded, well-made for hunting and, we are told, for planting. We regret that there are no living quarters yet on these lands, but we have arranged for a generous allowance so suitable quarters might be built."

Delight sparked off Javier, boyish excitement at the prospect of overseeing the creation of a new retreat suitable for royalty. Sandalia, in marked contrast, remained wonderfully neutral; Belinda thought she herself could not do better. "We shall recommend artisans," the queen went on, "and perhaps it will be our honour to visit when building is complete.

"We shall provide a stipend for five years," she continued, "long enough that the fertile earth should begin to give its return, so our new friend might earn a living from her lands and provide to the crown some small measure of appreciation for the gifts we offer. All of these things and more we are delighted to give to one who has done us such service.

"But first," she said, and her attention finally came to focus directly on Belinda. "First, we must attend to the matter of Belinda Primrose."

17

The core of stillness within her turned to ice, utterly frozen, even as blood thundered in her ears, washing away all other sound. It brought back memory, memory so old that others said it couldn't be at all: a battlefield, red-tinged and rushing, but what had once been comforting now only emphasized the words that she had carried with her since her birth.

It cannot be found out.

It carried fear into her, intense and sharp, a part of her that could never be cut away. *It cannot be found out.* Somewhere, extraordinarily distant to where she now stood, Javier's voice tickled through the centre of her being, bewilderment lifting it high: "Mother?"

Outside herself, she could feel her expression turning to polite puzzlement, eyebrows crinkling as she glanced around herself, looking for the woman Sandalia had named. "Your Majesty?" The external performance would be flawless; that was the purpose of Belinda's very existence, of the lifetime's training in hard-won stillness that wouldn't allow her body or face to betray herself, even when turmoil shattered her insides. It was helped, unexpectedly, by the prison of a gown she wore: Beatrice Irvine, who laughed too easily and let emotion come too quickly, was hindered by the constricting corsets and high throat, but Belinda Primrose felt at home within such constraints: she had been born to a carefully stifled life, and knew well how to work within it.

"Forgive me, my lord prince." Akilina's voice, silky smooth, laden with such insolent smugness that a cat would envy it. Witchpower rage lit up Belinda's mind, golden ferocity that she thought must bleed from her eyes and nose and ears, so overwhelming was its heat. She did not, would not, let it fly free; her only hope lay in absolute innocence, and even a hint of anger now would be her undoing.

"There are things you must know about your intended."

"Beatrice?" Javier's voice cracked a second time and Belinda lifted her gaze to his, wide-eyed with incomprehension and a touch of fear.

"I do not know, my lord," she whispered. "I do not understand." Her pulse fluttered in her throat, such a gentle admission of girlish alarm and confusion that she almost regretted the gown's choking collar.

"Do you deny, then, that you are called Belinda Primrose?" Sandalia's question cracked out over the assembly, echoing against the chamber walls. No one within the hall spoke, their tension clawing at Belinda and telling her that to a man, they feared a word spoken would have them banished from the audience hall and they might miss the drama unfolding. A part of her wanted to laugh at the sheer eager hunger for theatrics; the larger part put away acknowledgment of the emotions that rose up behind her in favour of focusing on those immediately around her. Sacha had stepped forward, his fists clenched as he leaned toward Belinda, as though his very presence might crush her to the earth. Marius, too, had broken away from the crowd, making himself one of the little party surrounding Sandalia's dais and standing subtly closer to Belinda than to her accusers. Only Eliza's presence was marked in its absence. A sting of regret touched Belinda for that, though she had no idea what side the beautiful street woman might have come down on.

"I am Beatrice Irvine, Your Majesty," Belinda protested. "Born in Lanyarch in 1565, daughter of—"

Sandalia cut her off with a sharp movement of her hand, and Belinda caught her breath, staying her words even as she cast another frightened glance toward Javier.

"Mother, what is this jape?" The prince's voice was so low as to barely carry to Belinda, much less the breathless mass behind her. "Beatrice is—"

"A whore who'd do anything to get the Red Bitch off the Aulunian throne, Jav." Sacha grated the words out, vicious delight in them. "Know how I know that? I—"

"—fucked her?" Javier interrupted sharply. A whisper ran through the gathering and subsided again, even as Sacha gave his prince, then Belinda, a startled look. Javier's anger and his will rolled toward Sacha with undeniable power, demanding an answer; more, demanding the answer that Javier himself wanted. "Is that your tale, Sacha? You had the prince's woman and she was willing to take you for hopes of getting her voice heard in the name of war? It's an ugly ploy, brother," he said, voice dropping to a whisper. "Could you do no better than that?"

Quick triumph bloomed and faded in Belinda's breast as Javier stole the sting from Sacha's truth; even Asselin could see that he'd lost, that any protest he made claiming exactly that had happened would only make him look the part of a bitter fool. He turned a look of hate on Belinda, who lifted her chin to regard him coolly, as a woman insulted.

"Cleverly done, my lord prince," Akilina said without a hint of mocking. "If only Lord Asselin were the only one who knew of Lady Irvine's past. Viktor." Her voice thickened on the man's name, rich sounds of the Khazarian language filling that single word even when her Gallic was typically barely accented.

The stiff-bearded guard stepped out of the ranks, gaze torn between Akilina and Belinda. Frustrated laughter ripped a thread free of Belinda's internal control, witchpower striking through that weakness with only her half-formed intent behind it: he could not be allowed to speak. Javier's will had moments earlier dominated Sacha; now Belinda strove to do the same to Viktor, seeking the familiar lines of passion and desire to conquer him with. She was his queen; he ought not have been able to betray her. The newness of her powers, the training at Javier's hands instead of Robert's—fury at her father, for forbidding her the knowledge she needed to save her own life, shot through the ties she had to Viktor, strengthening them. She was not Rosa. She was his heart's desire, his loins' desire. He could not, would not, betray her. She sent hints of promises toward him, the rewards to be reaped from remaining silent, even as she cursed the frailty in her that had allowed him an avenue to tell Akilina what he knew. He clearly had; there could be no other reason for him to be called forward.

Belinda should have killed him when she'd had the chance. Frailty indeed, a woman's weakness, shared with her queen mother after all. She could let none of her anger show, only watch Viktor with wide eyes as she hammered loyalty into the sexual bond they shared.

"Beatrice?" Javier again, the strength of will that had sustained him now faltering. Belinda jerked her eyes to his, tearing her gaze from Viktor to the prince, and shook her head helplessly.

"I do not know this man, my lord." Whispered words, desperate with confusion; she could not afford to slip. Akilina laughed, a soft warm sound that ripped through the chamber's silent air.

"I watched them together, my lord. Watched Viktor go into an alcove and heard their sounds of passion. He called her Rosa, and she spoke Khazarian to him. Your pretense at mispronunciation was very good," she added lightly, and repeated "*Nyet*" the way Belinda had, shortening the vowels to an *i*. "Viktor," she said again, more heavily and in Khazarian, "tell them what you told me."

Do not, Belinda willed, and turned her frightened gaze back to the guardsman. He hesitated, hands balling into fists, then finally shook his head. "She is not my Rosa," he said thickly. "How could she be, so far from Khazar?"

Relief jabbed Belinda in the stomach and witchpower flared along the connection she had built to influence Viktor. Raw desire, pure delight, absolute pleasure: the guardsman made a deep sound at the back of his throat, shuddering as Belinda's unspoken thanks caught him on a primal level. Marius, closer to her, made a similar sound, his cheeks darkening as he realised the connection between himself and Viktor. Belinda felt the merchant man's heart spasm, the unwelcome pleasure found in submission suddenly making his pulse race. Belinda swallowed against a certain wicked mirth, seeing that the thing tying both men together was both having bent to her will. Javier, thank God, remained unaffected, the temptation she'd had to top the prince unacted upon and now a barrier to linking him into the domineering witchpower that ate at her veins.

White anger pooled around Akilina, though none of it reflected in her countenance. Admiration slipped through Belinda's control; the countess was as skilled at hiding emotion as Belinda herself. They might have been friends, if the world had been utterly other than what it was.

"He lies," a woman's voice said in Khazarian, and the white of Akilina's anger cooled. Belinda turned toward the new speaker as did the gathered throng, and among them she was the only one to know despair. Rationality gave way for an instant beneath a child's furious protest: this woman, this piece of nothing from a remote Khazarian estate, could not be there. Ilyana could not be in Lutetia, her thick blond hair dressed as a wealthy woman's might be, her clothes far finer than any servant might dream of wearing. She simply *could not be there.*

And yet she was, and all the anger and betrayed feelings in the world wouldn't undo that. Hate thickened the girl's voice, audible even if the words were foreign to most of the Lutetian court's ears: "She's probably got his cock locked in a box somewhere and will only give it back when he's cleared her name. Too bad for her she don't got the same hold on me. The bitch is a witch, Your Majesty. She did my lord to death and she's got Viktor under her spell. Probably your prince, too, the poor bastard. Her name's Rosa and I'll swear it on my grave."

Akilina translated, soft-spoken words loud enough for the first rows of courtiers to hear; ripples spread back through the congregation as the speech was handed from one listener to another. Belinda allowed growing horror and confusion to part her lips and wrinkle her eyebrows, tears stinging at her eyes as she turned away from Ilyana's accusations to listen to Akilina's translation of them. She took one tiny step forward, reaching toward Sandalia and Javier with shaking hands as she shook her head in denial. "I don't know this woman, your highnesses. My name is Beatrice Irvine, and I don't understand why this is being done. Surely I'm not a threat to a woman like her ladyship the countess." She let herself laugh, rough sound of distress. "Even I know I'm not the best match for his highness, and that if treaties required it I would easily be set aside in favour of someone like Countess Akilina. I can think of no other reason why—"

"Must we play this all the way to the end, Belinda?" Akilina interrupted so gently Belinda overrode her for several words. It was the use of her name that stopped her, chills creeping over her skin and making her grateful once more for the all-encompassing gown: barely more than her fingertips and face were visible to give away any changes in complexion that she might be unable to control. However Akilina had found her out, the thoroughness with which she had done so devastated everything that Belinda had ever been. Her name on the other woman's lips struck away her last chances at anonymity; even if she survived the next few minutes, Belinda

Primrose would be forever associated with Beatrice Irvine, and neither would ever be able to hide again.

But she drew herself up, dragging all the self-respect and command that poor Beatrice had left to her and met Akilina's eyes. "We must." The quaver in her voice belonged to Beatrice, whose fright and anger went nowhere near the depths of Belinda's fury. "I don't know who Belinda is, or why you seek to destroy my reputation, but if you insist on playing this farce I'll see it to the end, my lady. I see no other choice."

Marius cried out, a warning that came an instant too late. Belinda whirled, less grace or power in the movement than she might have wished, her clothing hampering her. Ilyana, forgotten as Belinda made her pleas to throne and countess, leapt forward with her hands clawed, scratching and scraping at Belinda's eyes. Belinda flung her hands up, green silk gown tearing with a shriek as dreadful as the sound that ripped from Ilyana's throat. They collapsed to the floor, Ilyana's weight bearing Belinda down, Belinda's arms crossed in front of her face. She could fight back, even constrained by the gown, but Beatrice didn't have Belinda's taught skills, and to cower was far better than to out herself by competence beyond that which she should have.

Another sound, terrible and pained, erupted from Ilyana's throat, and her body went rigid above Belinda's. Whimpering, half crying in the shock and fear that her persona felt, Belinda dared lower her arms a few inches, then screamed outright as Ilyana coughed blood and bile, blue gaze accusing even as it turned glassy. Her body jerked, then slumped heavily against Belinda's chest, blood drooling down her chin. Belinda screamed again, scrambling backward to get out from under Ilyana's weight, and knocked into Javier's shins. She looked up, gasping for breath, to see his unsheathed sword dripping blood on Sandalia's pristine carpets, and his gaze locked on Marius who stood on Ilyana's other side, his own blade still buried in the dead girl's back.

Marius let go his blade as if it burned him, lifting his hands against a sudden shuffle of guardsmen. "Forgive me, my prince. I forgot whose presence I was in."

"Away." Javier's abrupt word was to the guards, not his childhood friend. "I can hardly fault you, Marius, when your impulse was the same as my own." Each quiet word was infused with apology, the most a prince could offer, and the silence that rang between the two of them made Belinda's heart ache and pound and ache again, until spots of blackness came into her vision. Marius bowed finally, so deep it might have been mockery could she not, through waves of dizziness, feel profound sorrow and respect from the young man, and a lonesome forgiveness that would break the heart of the man he bowed to, could he but feel it.

"Beatrice." Javier's voice was gentle, as gentle as it had been to Marius. He offered her a hand, helping her to her feet; to her relief and embarrassment, the darkness faded from her vision as she was better able to catch a breath. "Are you all right?" He touched her cheek, making her aware of stinging where Ilyana's nails had caught flesh, but she nodded, carefully folding her arms across her torso as she tried to hold the bodice of her gown back together.

"I'm all right, my lord. I fear the same cannot be said for my dress." She offered a weak smile and cast her glance downward, not daring to look toward either Akilina or the queen. At her feet, though, lay Ilyana's body, and the part of her that was Beatrice shuddered and turned away, hiding her face against Javier's chest. His heart echoed loudly in her ears, and his voice came deep from her close quarters.

"Are you satisfied, Lady Akilina? What more would you have Beatrice go through? Your guardsman admits he's lying and this wretched creature is dead for your plotting." He rested one hand around Belinda's shoulders, lifting the other to snap and gesture for Ilyana's body to be taken away. His mother, still on her feet at his side, had not spoken or moved during the entirety of the display;

now she turned her attention to Akilina as well, cool curiosity in her voice.

"This was not the entertainment we were promised, my lady. Our gown is spattered with blood and our dais stained with it, all for the purpose of making us look a fool, it seems. Is this what your schemings have produced, and nothing more?" Her every word was beautifully precise, as though rehearsed, and for a faltering moment Belinda wondered if it were. Surely Ilyana's death had not been for show; Marius, for all his youth, would not agree to murder a woman for theatrical court.

That, Belinda thought with a ghost of inappropriate humour, was much more her sort of duty to carry out. But she had no sense of anything from Sandalia, for all that the queen stood very nearly touching distance away. Close enough to steal the desk keys from, but with no way to do it, not now, not at the heart of such a spectacle. The same horrid ghost of amusement came over her, squelching through her insides in search of a place to break free.

"I wish it were, Your Majesty." Another woman's voice, more painful in its faint familiarity than Ilyana's for all that Belinda had never heard it speak the Gallic language before. She lifted her head, the small motion denying all the stiffness that wanted to come into her body. The depth of shock that Ilyana's appearance had brought seemed to have faded: she felt no outrageous disbelief this time, only a sadness as deep as that which marked Marius.

The crowd of courtiers parted, allowing the woman to come forward. She wore, to Belinda's surprise and agonizing pleasure, one of Eliza's fashions, the loose flowing gown making the most of her height and her breasts, the vibrant lime fabric only wearable by a scant handful of women with her generous colouring. She dipped a curtsey, more perfunctory than polite, and kept her eyes on Belinda as she spoke. "I wish it were," she said again, more quietly this time, as if the words were an apology to Belinda, "and I wish that I had not been called to stand here before you."

"You are?" Sandalia asked crisply. She was cool and calm, unsurprised, unpredictable, unreadable. Satisfaction swept off Akilina, making Belinda's stomach tighten.

"I am called Ana di Meo, and I am a courtesan from Aria Magli. I knew this woman in Aria Magli, when she called herself Rosa, but moreover, I know her father. Through him I also know that she is called Belinda Primrose, and that her purpose here is to sow dissent and revolution in Gallin's heart, and if possible, to take the life of a queen."

Thunder crashed through the hall, voices rising in shouts of horror and excitement and dismay. Javier tightened his arm around Belinda's shoulders as if he could protect her from the surge of passion that swept the hall; indeed, the men and women gathered behind Ana stepped forward en masse, suddenly hungry for blood and information.

Belinda felt only silent astonishment, her soul emptied of anything else, even the witchpower rage. It would be her undoing to ask *why*, though she thought the question might be in her eyes, and that only the lush courtesan would read it as anything other than bewilderment. Indeed, Ana lifted a shoulder and let it fall in such a minute motion Belinda might have imagined it; it did not at all carry the answer she sought. Her gaze carried quiet regret but not guilt: whatever drove her, she would not lose sleep that night over betraying Belinda.

Belinda's mind danced back to the moment they'd shared at the Maglian pub, the injury she'd seen flicker through Ana's expression when the tavern's overwhelming emotional attack had made her draw back from the other woman rather than give in to the sweet, unbartered passion they'd both felt. To condemn Beatrice Irvine as a falsehood seemed an extraordinary retaliation for a fleeting moment's pain, but Belinda knew too well how desire dismissed could go astray, and had no other answer to consider.

Javier's voice, above her head, cut through the clamor, witchpower giving it strength: "Who is her father, that you make this outrageous claim and lend it his name as backing?"

Belinda thought, did not say, did not so much as breathe, *no,* and could not let herself close her eyes or flinch in dismay as Ana said, "Robert, Lord Drake, favoured of Lorraine in Aulun."

"Beatrice?" Javier whispered her name through the commotion rising in Sandalia's audience hall. Belinda allowed herself a laugh, a tiny shaking sound, and turned her eyes toward the prince, helplessness in them.

"What should I say, my prince? I can't end this farce by agreeing with them. I've never been beyond Lutetia, much less as far as Aria Magli. My father's name was Robert, it's true, but he was Robert Stewart, and held a plot of land in the highlands of Lanyarch. I don't know why they're doing this." She felt distressingly exposed, as if wearing Beatrice's too-raw emotions so openly stripped her to the skin. As if Ana had the power to undress her with words and show the Lutetian court the truth of the woman beneath Javier's consort. She could do nothing other than hold her ground and maintain her innocence, but doing so was draining the strength from her, and she didn't dare reach for the witchpower's uncontrollable fire to shore herself with.

"That is all you need say." Javier pressed his lips to her forehead, then lifted his voice. "We find this woman, these women," he said, including Akilina in his accusations, "to be troublesome and cruelhearted. Beatrice has done none of you any harm, and a woman's life has already been paid for your foolish, bitter games. I *know* this woman whom I hold in my arms." Passion deepened his voice and he tucked Beatrice against his chest more solidly. "She has given me more joy in the brief months I've courted her than a lifetime has known before. I had believed myself to be alone." His voice gentled again and he set Belinda back, his hands on her shoulders as he gazed down at her. The grey of his eyes was bright with passion, his fingers warm against her skin where her gown had torn. His thoughts whispered to her things he wouldn't say aloud to the gathered assembly: *She's like me, more than any of you can understand. She shares the power that I have. I will make this all right if I have to bend each and every one of you to my will, even you, Mother. I will not be left alone again.*

"She's shown me that I'm not alone," he said, almost for her ears only. "For that gift alone I would defend her to God Himself." He looked up again, anger darkening his face. "And I will hear no more of these accusations. We know where Beatrice Irvine is from. Ask yourselves instead what ends the Khazarian countess gains from this drama."

The crowd turned with his speech, grumblings twisting away from Belinda to focus on Akilina. Only the scant handful at the front of the throne room held steady in their stances: Marius, for whom Belinda could do no wrong; Asselin, for whom she could do no right. Akilina's confidence flagged not at all, and Sandalia held suspicion above any other conceit. Javier's steadfast trust was strongest, but the walls of dissonant, strident belief from each of them battered at her, threatening the still core she dared not release.

"I don't gain a throne from it." Akilina's reply was light. "You know that as well as I, Prince Javier. My aspirations reach beyond my grasp, I fear; I must learn to content myself with lesser objectives. This has nothing to do with me, my lord, and everything to do with the safety of your mother's realm. Of your realm, your Highness. How might I convince you of this?"

"Produce Drake," Javier spat. "Let me hear it from his own lips. Condemn Beatrice that way."

A serpent's smile slipped across Akilina's mouth and she curtsied so deeply as to border on ridicule. "Viktor."

The guard, whose eyes had never left Belinda, flinched at the sound of his name, coming to attention. Akilina nodded and he broke from formation, stomping down the cleared aisle through the courtiers. They drew back, watching him as if he were an alien thing, dangerous to them, and Belinda watched him go with a surety and a sickness rising in her. The doors at the end of the hall banged open to allow him exodus, and shut again with a final-sounding boom behind him.

Rage, underlying, too familiar, scented of chypre in the back of Belinda's mind.

"Do forgive me his condition, my prince," Akilina murmured to the silent hall. "He's been most reluctant to cooperate."

Belinda trembled in Javier's grip, not from fear but from fury. Akilina's smugness, her utter pleasure in the situation, was truth enough as to who would be dragged through the doors when they opened again. Belinda wanted, even without seeing Robert, to fall to her knees, to cry aloud and shriek her horror and dismay. She wanted her hard-learned stillness to desert her, to be allowed to be a child abandoned and forgotten but still seeking approval; to break away from what she and her father had made of her and be nothing more than an ordinary woman in a trying position.

Like everyone else, she flinched when the doors banged open again. The tiny reaction felt like her single nod to humanity, for she could not allow herself to fall into despair as Viktor and another man dragged Robert Drake's broken and bleeding form down the audience chamber aisle.

She did permit herself a cry of dismay, fingers pressed against her mouth, eyes round with horror. Beatrice Irvine was a gentle woman, and a man broken under torture was far from a sight she was prepared to see. She turned away, painful abrupt movement, to hide her face against Javier's chest, a plea shaking her voice: "My lord, I don't know this man. What have they done to him? Surely we're not such monsters . . . ?" Witchpower raged beneath her skin, searching for a weakness that would permit it to burst forth and act, though what form that action might take, Belinda didn't .

know. She only knew she wanted to lash out, and that she felt a marrow-deep resentment of the training that forbade it as powerfully as she felt reassurance at that training's strength.

Grimness filled Javier's response, more in feeling than in words. "I believe I would know the Aulunian queen's consort anywhere, even as badly treated as he has been. Akilina, you will explain this." Sandalia, at his side, sparked with a curious blend of resentment and relief that her son seemed finally willing to take a leading position. He was too much like his uncle, Belinda thought abruptly, and wondered once more at the father who'd gotten Javier on Sandalia. The distraction, however brief, was a welcome one, diverting some of the edged fury elsewhere. Sandalia, just within Belinda's line of sight, said nothing as she turned to the Khazarian countess, awaiting answers to Javier's demand.

"Viktor and Ilyana both spoke of this woman." Akilina gestured with her hands as she spoke, graceful motion encompassing first where Ilyana's blood patterned the rugs, giving the name to the dead girl, then including Belinda as a woman unworthy of naming. "They knew her as Rosa, on a Khazarian estate north of Khazan. My lover Gregori Kapnist died there and on that same day this woman fled." She all but wove a spell with her words, speaking softly enough that everyone leaned in to hear. "Tell me, Prince Javier, does your woman wear a knife at the small of her back?"

Javier's expression became nonplussed, turning from Akilina to Belinda and back again. "Not that I've seen." He offered a faint smile, suggesting, "If you like I could take her away from here and investigate in private."

A voice distorted with lust and envy came out of the crowd: "Strip the whore here and let us all see you're not bespelled, Red Prince."

Javier turned shocked eyes toward the courtiers, who tightened ranks rather than fall apart and expose the speaker. Belinda tried to call a blush and failed, anger at her inability bringing colour to her cheeks a moment later. Javier set his jaw and returned his attention to Akilina, whose unimpeachable confidence had faded a notch at his confession. "I had her journey traced," the countess said, voice lowered further. "To Aria Magli, where she met this woman and this man, whom I know myself. She was sent here from Parna, Your Highnesses, to bring down your throne."

"Drake has confirmed this?" Javier scraped the words out, earning Akilina's laugh.

"Not yet, my lord prince, but he will. Or perhaps Belinda could spare him the pain, and tell us all the truth."

"My name is Beatrice Irvine!" Belinda cried her reply with all the passion she could muster, frustration bringing tears to her eyes. Emotion leapt in Robert, sharp spike of pride that all but undid her, making tears more real than they had reason to be. "I do not know this man or this woman! They mean nothing to me, and I have no way to prove myself to you!"

"You do," Akilina said, full of liquid delight. Beatrice turned to her, hands spread beseechingly, and Akilina offered a razor smile. "Perhaps his highness would lend you an already-bloodied sword, and you might end Robert Drake's life to show your loyalty to your affianced and his kingdom."

Honest astonishment dropped Belinda's jaw, though it was Beatrice's horror that whispered, "You want me to . . . *kill* a man?"

"You're eager to bring down the Red Bitch's throne, aren't you?" Akilina asked gleefully. "Kill her favourite, prove your loyalty to Javier, and force Lorraine to overextend herself into an attack on Gallin in one smooth blow."

Sandalia stepped forward, exchanging a brief glance with Javier as Belinda turned to them, heartbeat high in her throat. "My lord, my lady, I . . . I can't—"

"It's a dangerous game you play, Akilina." Sandalia spoke thoughtfully, watching Drake and the Khazarian woman in equal parts. "You stand in our court and suggest a ploy that would have our country invaded by another. You must be very confident indeed of your resources."

Akilina, with wonderful precision, said, "As confident of the breath I draw, Your Majesty. There is no need to fear it will not come."

Sandalia turned her head, minute movement, to examine the raven-haired countess. "We are pleased to hear your sureness. We extend to you an invitation to remain safely within these walls until your confidence is borne out."

Muscle tightened in Akilina's jaw, the tension vanishing into a smile an instant later. "I'm honoured by your concern for my safety, Your Majesty, and delighted to accept."

"Very well." Sandalia turned her attention to Belinda with a familiar flickering of her fingers. "Proceed."

Thickness seized Belinda's throat, making her suddenly, itchingly aware of the gold-threaded lace scratching against the silk wrap. "What?" Her bluntness had charmed the queen in the past, but it was simple disbelief, not artifice, that forced the question.

"Marius's sword will serve," Sandalia said. "We do not care for the idea of Drake's blood staining our son's weapon."

"Your . . . Majesty . . . cannot expect me to . . ." Beatrice's faintness was Belinda's own, though the reasons were different. Sandalia arched an eyebrow sharply.

"Our Majesty can and does. Prove yourself, Irvine, or we will have you stripped and searched as threatened. Are you ours, or are you his?"

"Your Majesty, I cannot . . . I cannot . . . *kill* a man—"

"Do it!" Sandalia's command lashed out with a strength bordering on the witchpower's.

Golden rage swept Belinda's vision and she lurched forward a step, the "*No!*" that tore from her throat a memory before she heard herself speak it. Sandalia, only inches away, drew herself taut with fury—better fury than fear; so much as that, Belinda could still sense even in the midst of pounding, hungry power growing in her—and lifted a hand.

Belinda screamed, aborted sound of terror as guards closed around her, reaching for the torn places on her dress and shredding the fabric from her body even as she writhed and fought against them. A roaring cheer filled her ears, ugly thrills and delight from the courtiers, and she felt a dagger split the laces of her corset, bindings springing wide.

She caught it as it fell forward, clutching it to her chest and gasping for air, half astounded at the ease of breathing. Another pair of hands caught her underskirt, tearing its seam, and it fell away to expose her backside. A gasp of disappointment ran through those closest to her as it became clear no betraying knife pressed against her skin. She lifted her eyes as the guards parted, searching for Javier and trusting her fear and pathos to soften his heart.

There was kindness in his eyes. "You ought to have acted, Beatrice, but perhaps a woman's weakness is too much to overcome. Let me do it for you. You will respond, sir," Javier said with simple arrogance. "Confirm the duchess's accusations or refute them, but you will share with us your answers." He extended a hand, princely gesture, and with it Belinda felt inexorable willpower come forth from him.

She lifted her head, turning it toward Robert: a mistake, for it warned those eyes that knew to look that she had an expectation of what would happen. Only Javier himself might have those eyes, but of everyone in the courtroom, his were the ones she could least afford to betray herself to.

And his power bludgeoned into Robert's like a toy knight playing at siege against Lutetia's great walls. The scent of chypre filled Belinda's nose again, stinging her eyes to unplanned tears. Javier made no audible sound, but surprise lanced through him like a weapon itself, and he redoubled the effort, pouring a lifetime of easy command into the expectation that Robert would fold beneath his will.

Drake chuckled beneath his breath, the softest surprise in the sound, so muted that only one who knew him might recognize it. Agony lanced Belinda's heart, tearing her breath away as she saw, too clearly, the houses that would fall with her father's response. Deception upon deception, so tangled and twisted together she could no longer determine where to begin or end. Who, who, *who* was the Gallic prince's father, if not Dmitri, whose look was not at all stamped on him; if not Robert, whose surprise answered any doubt that might have lingered within Belinda. There had been secrets hidden in Javier's parentage, secrets revealed by his use of power; and now, unstoppable, came the last act of treachery that would undo her in his eyes forever.

Because her father had put a binding on her mind, and whispered *it is too soon, it cannot be found out,* and today, here, in this place, he had no idea that his daughter had come into her power, and that Javier de Castille had trained her in it, and that to fight the prince in the battleground of the mind was to condemn Belinda to death.

Knowing none of this, Robert lifted his gaze to Javier's, thin bloody smile cracking a mustache and beard that had grown too long under Akilina's tender care. He shook his head, clucked his tongue in disapproval, and pushed back, such a flexing of strength that it seemed the whole room moved beneath it. Javier staggered, his hand dropping, and then rage came into his face as he turned toward Belinda. Every aspect of his emotions were threaded with betrayal, truth brought to light by Robert's easy hand with the witchpower. Belinda knotted her hands in her corset, holding it against herself as if it made a shield, and wrapped stillness hard as iron around herself.

Javier's anger came down on her with the weight of anvils, fury lending its silver sheen more power than she'd ever felt in him before. It wasn't the playful jousts with witchlight; there was nothing visible in this attack, only wordless, silent will bearing down against Belinda's shields. Javier searched for weaknesses, believing her, as a woman, to inevitably have them. To her pride, he found none, his power rebuffed.

Pride lasted barely an instant. She might be his equal in raw strength, but the Gallic prince had a decade of training with his gifts that she did not share. A fresh onslaught rushed her, no longer searching for weakness, but simply crushing: that Belinda's power had been locked behind a wall in her mind was something not only she remembered, and with inexorable force, he squashed and contained that power again, pushing it back to where it had once been.

Belinda held a pinprick of light against him, struggling to keep it alive within her mind. They had practised shields and throwing blasts of power, but her gift was an internal one, safety from the outside world making an impenetrable cloak around her. It was not made to defend against a comer that pressed against it relentlessly from all sides; its instinct was to make itself smaller, hide in the shadows, go unseen.

Silence came, and the light winked into blackness.

18

Peculiarly, it was the gown's destruction that stung her first upon awakening.

A chill had already set in, making her aware of her bones in a distant, aching way long before consciousness was reached. It was dull discomfort, the sort of thing she had so long held herself against that it barely seemed worth considering; certainly it was unworthy of disturbing her rest. Later, when some of the blackness had retreated, she became equally aware of the temperature of her flesh: not so cold as to freeze, but far below what it should normally be, as though she'd kicked off covers as she slept and left a shoulder bared to the night air. She reached for the duvet and found nothing, its lack too removed to be meaningful to her. She drew in on herself, making herself a small curled thing against her hard bed without reaching awareness.

In time, sensibility began to creep back into her: the vague realization that her bed was made of stone; nothing else was so hard, nor pulled the heat from her body even when it felt warmer than the floor around her. Neither words nor clear thought conveyed that to her, merely a recognition of fact as deep as the cold in her bones. Sound encroached even more slowly: the drip of water broken by an occasional spill of the same, splashing against rock. Droplets spattered her body when that happened, bringing a shiver that she felt in her jaw and stomach but not on her skin's surface.

A dank scent came with the water, too-old straw grown soft with mold, and the stench of human offal gone uncleaned.

She knew where she was before consciousness came, and when she opened her eyes to darkness, all that was visible was a remembrance of Pierre's exquisite creation, shredded and torn and trampled beneath guards' feet. Courtiers would have surged forward to snatch up scraps, using a shimmer of gold or green to prove that they had been there the day Beatrice Irvine fell beneath the look of angry betrayal in Prince Javier's eyes.

Belinda sat up slowly, stiffness in every joint. Her hair fell around her shoulders, shockingly warm against the coldness of her skin, and brought a rash of gooseflesh to her. The dichotomy in temperature made her nipples tighten, absurd erotic thrill that activated genuine desire. She closed her eyes against the darkness, wet her lips, and whispered, "Javier," on that wash of longing, then folded her arms over her breasts, clutching her shoulders to contain what little heat her body had left.

She had not been left so much as her petticoats, all those things ripped away from her on the courtroom floor and left there when they took her away. That she had been given nothing at all to cover herself with suggested the remainder of her life could be counted in hours, not days: no queen would be fool enough to allow such a prize as Belinda was to die of exposure before she could be hanged in a public square, and the oubliette would ensure her death by cold within a few days.

Belinda found she was not at all afraid to die, and wondered if that was fatalistic acceptance or blind denial.

She got up because it was better to move than sit and wait for her fate to come. Better to force blood to flow through her body in hopes that doing so might warm her than to remain seated against the cold and feel life drain out of her one slow minute at a time. She found the walls of her prison: there was enough room, just, to open her arms and turn in a circle; stone brushed her fingertips when she did so. A few pieces of straw had enough strength to prickle her soles, barely felt through numbness, and the faintest crack of light came down from above. She stretched her arms up, searching for a ceiling, and found nothing. For an instant the darkness pressed on her, weighty, before she let go a raw laugh and cupped her hands together, calling witchlight.

A soft glow lit her palms and the confines of her prison. Above her, out of reach for even a tall man, a square of stone made most of the dungeon's ceiling. An oubliette, yes: simply a roofed pit to be dropped in and forgotten about, too wide to somehow scramble up its sides, too deep to reach its lip even if it were not closed up. There would be other cells elsewhere, but she—and Robert, she warranted—had earned special attention, a private dungeon such as this to prevent any other prisoners from falling on them and risking Sandalia's sport.

Her fingertips seemed warmer, the witchlight bathing them. Belinda spun it out, expanding the golden ball and stretching it until she literally wrapped herself in it as she so often imagined herself wrapped in stillness. Some of the ache faded from her bones, whether from actual warmth or an illusion of it she neither knew nor cared. It was a way to pass the time, building gowns of light from her power. When the warmth that spread over her body came from a different source, urging an exploration of her sex with her fingers, laughter broke through, unexpected in the cold stone prison. She'd learned to ward herself to some degree against the raging passion that built when she extended power to influence others; to find it equally demanding when she turned her magic on herself was disproportionately amusing. For a time she hoped with active enthusiasm that a guard might be sent to check on her; the prospect of being discovered locked in a black hole in the ground, writhing with passion, struck her as tremendously funny, an emotion Belinda was completely unaccustomed to experiencing or giving in to.

When stone finally scraped against stone and external light flooded her little prison, though, she had long since left witch-power desire behind, and instead lay shivering against the cold stone floor in darkness. Less stagnant air flooded her cell, bringing new chill with it, and she squinted toward the light.

Javier crouched above her prison at its lip, torchlight behind him to hide his face in shadow, though shadow did nothing to disguise the cold anger that rolled off him. He stretched out a hand, opening it; a dagger, no more than palm-length, fell to Belinda's floor with a clatter. "This was found in your bedclothes."

Belinda uncurled herself and reached for the blade, tucking it against her chest. She could thwart Sandalia's execution with that small knife, testing its sharpness in her own heart rather than Sacha Asselin's, as she'd once dreamed. "Perhaps the countess hid it there," she whispered. "Javier, I am so cold." She risked, as she had never risked before, a thread of power stretching toward the prince, seeking any hint of sympathy he might have for her.

"Not for long," he said implacably. "You die at dawn tomorrow. You and Robert Drake, for intent to kill a queen. Lorraine will have to deny you both to keep her throne, but it should go a long way toward destabilizing Aulun."

Fear, it seemed, had a place in her after all. Belinda's muscles contracted all over, urging a soft squeak of terror from her throat. "How can you believe the Khazarians over me?" The tremble in her voice was real, Belinda no longer able to tell her own emotions from Beatrice's. "I'm like you, Javier. Witchbreed," she breathed.

The slightest sense of hesitation broke Javier's surety. Belinda, waiting for the chance, whispered encouragement to that hesitation, sitting up on the dirty stone floor to lift her gaze toward the prince's. She made a pretty and pathetic picture, she knew, all wide eyes and tangled hair, dirt smeared across her naked body from lying on the ground. She kept her arms folded over her chest, a woman's frail modesty, and sent her own concept of her helplessness toward the man crouched above.

"Witchbreed like Robert Drake. Your father." Javier's words were relentlessly certain, but doubt fogged his emotions, hope sparking through in pulses he tried to quash. "I felt the power in him."

Belinda shook her head, sending curls over her shoulders. "If it's there, perhaps that explains how the Red Bitch has kept her throne so long. I don't doubt you, my lord." She shivered, half artifice and half genuine. "I don't doubt that he has the power, but your mother doesn't. Did your father? My mother died when I was born, and my father herded cattle. The power we share belongs to us alone, not our parents, Javier." The wish to be free of the oubliette was beginning to pound heavily in her veins, witchpower content to ride quietly until the possibility of escape was at hand. Now, with the stone ceiling removed, the urge to blast through delicacy and demand Javier bend to her will grew harder to fight, for all that Belinda knew it would be folly. She lacked the strength to stand against him with brute force; that had already been proven. She must be subtle, convince him from within of her innocence and of the rightness of her freedom. "I do not know him, Javier."

He made a fist of his right hand. "Then why did you spare his life?"

Incredulous, frightened laughter broke free. "My lord? Kill a man? *Me*? Perhaps it's easier for a man." Belinda's voice shivered with respect and not a little fear. "I am only a woman. I have no stomach for such things. That . . . that girl, the Khazarian girl . . . I had never seen a violent death so closely, my lord." She shuddered again, casting her eyes down as much to hide truth as to play at horror and a woman's gentleness. "I couldn't do that to any man. Forgive me for my weakness, please, my lord. I did not mean to betray you with it." She tightened her fingers around her dagger, against her chest, letting the action look like another shiver as she willed her captor to believe her. It was a reasonable argument, she whispered into the witchpower. A woman's flaw; Javier knew well she was a flawed creature, but she could never be the two-faced creature Akilina had made her out to be.

"Even if I believed you," Javier said slowly, "my mother never will. Robert Drake is a prize beyond imagining, and to take him from Lorraine far too great an opportunity to pass up. Innocent or not, your death is as much part of the pageantry as his will be."

"But he is the prize," Belinda echoed. "I might—" She caught her breath and cut the words away, letting Javier's hope and curiosity spike again. Making him ask, rather than putting the words into place for him.

"You might what, Beatrice?" He kept his voice low, as if someone might be close enough to overhear. Belinda shook her head, trembling.

"Nothing, my lord. Only a woman's fear. Only my fancy. Forgive me," she whispered again. "I couldn't ask it of you."

"It," he murmured. "To allow you to escape."

She cast her gaze up, full of desperation, and reached one hand toward him, fully aware of her nudity and of the affect cold air had on her body, her nipples tight as if in sexual arousal. Javier's focus slid from her face down to her throat, then to her breasts, where it lingered as she caught her breath. Desire pricked in him, fed back to her and heating the witchpower she stretched toward him; pink suffused her cheeks and spilled downward, unmistakable excitement to a man whose eyes wanted to see it. She looked to him as her savior, herself a helpless, dominable creature in a position of supplication; she had been his, was his, should be his and could be again through his choosing.

That she lifted only one hand, the other still holding and hiding her knife, was a detail she willed him to ignore. When he hesitated she let herself laugh, a sound of tears, and looked away, fingers curling in despair. "I am a fool."

"No." The word was strangled. "Beatrice—is it Beatrice?" Javier asked, half desperate himself. "Or are you Belinda, as they named you? It hardly matters," he added in a whisper. "How can I let the only woman like myself die?" He moved abruptly, stretching flat on his stomach to reach a hand into Belinda's prison. "Come. This will not be comfortable, but I can ask no one for help."

Belinda scrambled to her feet, shaking off cold as she grasped Javier's hand and almost cried out with its warmth. "Hold tight," he said. "Both hands."

She bit her lip and dropped her knife into the bits of straw. The blade struck stone at her feet, sharp metallic clang cutting into her heart: it may have betrayed her, but it was one of the few tangible things her father had ever given her. To lose it in the depths of a Lutetian prison was more bitter than she could imagine.

Less bitter than losing herself to those same depths. She clasped Javier's hand and wrist with both of hers with all the strength cold muscle could muster. Javier braced himself against the pit's edge with his free hand, eyes dark and serious on hers. "Are you ready?"

She only nodded, not trusting words. Javier surged upward, jaw clenched against strain. Belinda's feet left the ground and she cut off a shriek, caught somewhere between surprise and delight at his strength. It took effort not to kick, even realizing extra movement on her part would make her weight more difficult to manoeuver. He breathed hard, fingers white around her wrist, and she felt the determination of witchpower flare, as if it lent him the strength to draw her up. He went to hand and knees, the arm that held her still dropped with her weight, then opened his mouth in a silent roar as he dragged her halfway over the precipice's edge, falling backward as he did. She scraped over rough stone and swallowed pain, then pulled herself the rest of the way free, crawling forward to collapse against Javier's chest. Both heaved for air, Javier more than she, though he sat up within seconds, pushing her onto her heels with his hands hot on her shoulders. Questions fired in his gaze and she drew breath as if she might answer them before they were so much as spoken.

His eyes dropped to her breasts again, and desire, irrational and beyond thought, crashed through the hold he had on her. Belinda caught it with her own witchpower, stroking it and feeding it back to him hungrier than it came to her, then reached inside his grip to pull his shirt open. His warmth bled toward her, drawing her close, and she moved forward, hands dropping to loosen his breeches.

"Beatrice—" A dungeon floor was not Javier's idea of an idyllic romancing spot, that much was clear from his thoughts. Belinda stopped his mouth with a kiss, sliding cold fingers into his pants to curl her fingers about him, earning a quiet gasp and a thrust up into her hand. He said nothing else as she crawled atop him, wrapping her arms under his shirt and melding her body to his. His body was hot against hers, painful relief from the cold, and she rocked against him, letting herself whimper as the chill began to recede from her limbs. Witchpower responded to the heat, coursing through her and demanding satisfaction, but she held it off, burying her nose in the prince's throat as Marius's words haunted her: *we have not shared physical love.*

Love was too dangerous a word for one such as she, even before Akilina had moved to expose her. It left vulnerabilities that she couldn't afford; she had understood that since her childhood, watching Rodney du Roz fall to his death; watching her father so deliberately whittle away at the emotional structure he'd provided when she was very young. Belinda Primrose was not meant to know love, and she had not until lately felt its lack in the life that she'd led.

Javier slipped his arms around her, holding her as close as she held him. She could taste his thoughts, running free beneath the surface of passion, and shivered at them: they spoke too much of freedom and an escape from responsibility, ideas only whispered at in night's darkest hours; they were not daylight thoughts, no more for the prince than the assassin. It made commonality between them and flavoured Belinda's need with a kind of despair. All, *all* she could offer was what she did: her body, her mouth, her gentleness in place of coupling whose enthusiasm often touched on violence.

"Come away with me." She spoke against his mouth, knowing even as she said the words that even if he agreed she could never allow it to happen. Javier breathed laughter, breaking away far enough to look questioningly into her eyes. "Come away with me," she said again. Witchpower surged, rash agreement; whether it was her own or Javier's she couldn't tell. "Tonight. You and I are alike, Javier. Let us be together. Forget the rest of the world." She echoed the thoughts that he did not dare speak, could barely imagine speaking, and for the few seconds that they hung in the air she reveled in them, using them as her only way to offer in words what she hoped to say with shared bodies.

The thrill of the idea peaked and passed, reluctance flooding in its place, and her frustration rose, sudden and sharp. "Come away with me." She tore at his reluctance, weakening it, searching for a core that wanted to do as she proposed. "Do you not wish to? They could never find us, Javier, not if we didn't want them to. Perhaps you'd no more be a prince, but you would be free. Come away with me." She rolled her hips into his, offering physical gratification as pleasing at the dangerous thought she suggested, and Javier's resistance faded. It was a fairy tale, a dream for playing at, and for a few moments she lost herself in it as they came together in love.

He held her, gasping roughly against her shoulder, after, then drew a ragged breath. "If we're to go we should go now, Beatrice. Time must not be wasted."

"You have duties today, do you not?" she whispered. He hesitated, then nodded reluctantly, and she tightened her arms around him. "You must be seen attending them, Javier. I'll go to the docks and secure a ship to leave on the late tide. You'll leave the palace after supper—can you lose your guards?"

He laughed, low raw sound. "Sometimes. Yes, I will."

"Then meet me under moonlight." Belinda called witchlight to her fingertips, soft and golden, tracing it over his skin. He shuddered beneath the touch, eyes turning dark with desire, and a thrill of delight spasmed through Belinda's belly. Even a prince could be conquered, it seemed, if only she took the right path to it. "Come to the docks and I'll meet you there tonight, bring you to our ship, and we'll go away together."

She meant it. A jolt of astonishment cut through stillness imposed by habit. *She meant it.* Her heartbeat leapt, rabbit-quick, and she found an incredulous laugh bubbling deep inside herself. For those brief moments she meant her words with everything she had in her. If it were at all possible, she would make her promise of *We'll be together* real.

It was not in the least possible. Her spike of hope and excitement was already dying, larger purposes reminding her of her place and her duties. Desire twisted at her and faded beneath a curdling in her belly, a bone-deep revulsion of abandoning her mother's cause. It could be no other way, but she could never whisper that truth to Javier. Her life and freedom depended on his agreeing to her scheme; he must believe her, even when she herself could not.

She brushed her mouth against Javier's and rose from his lap, arms wrapped around herself again to ward off the chill. "Tonight, Javier."

He closed his breeches as he came to his feet, putting warm hands on her shoulders again. "And until then will you run around Lutetia naked?" he asked, a trace of wry concern in his voice. He released her to close a hand in his shirt and Belinda stopped him with a touch.

"I can get to the laundry and find clothing there without being seen, I think. The prince of the realm cannot be discovered walking the palace halls half naked, my lord. It would not go without comment."

"Prince no more after tonight," Javier said quietly. Steadfast emotion came through, no regret in it at all. He had never lived a life uncoddled by warmth and comfort; Belinda felt a bitter note that her lies would spare him learning regret for his decision. Eliza, she thought, would understand. "Are you certain, Beatrice? Your skin is still clammy."

She offered a weak smile. "Then perhaps we should leave the dungeons, my lord. If we can. The guards . . . ?"

"Dismissed." Javier's voice scraped low and raw. "Reluctantly, but dismissed. There is some good to being Sandalia's son. They aren't bold enough to forbid me a last while with my lover, even if I saw the laughter behind their eyes as they left. Help me put the lid back on the oubliette. No one will look for you until tomorrow dawn. You're to have no food, no water. Nothing until the priest comes to hear your confession, and then the axman."

"So that I'm weak and can't fight." Horror crept over Belinda's skin, chilling her more deeply, and she moved to the oubliette's far side, helping Javier to wrench the lid back into place. Stone boomed, and beneath the reverberations, Javier offered her his hand. Belinda shook her head, catching his fingers to kiss their tips, then whispered, "You can't be seen with me, my love. This cannot be found out. Go ahead, and I'll make my own way behind you. How long did you send the guards away for?"

"Until I seek them and send them back to duty. I'll give you a few minutes to slip away. Be careful, Beatrice." He hesitated, words caught in his gaze, then brushed his thumb over her bottom lip and left her knowing that things remained unspoken. Belinda watched until he was out of sight and his footsteps were faded before she drew shadows around herself, using her cloak of stillness to push away echoes of the things he hadn't said. Even so, they followed her as she slipped through the palace halls naked and unseen, until resolve faltered and she dropped into a corner, hands clutched over her head as she keened, all but silent, through her teeth.

Duty lay on her like weights, pressing down into the corners of her mind. Never in her life had it seemed onerous, never something to be shied from, and yet the heart of her wanted to keep the promise she'd made to the prince. Wanted to bolt from the palace and book passage on a ship to somewhere mad; on a ship to the Columbias, where no one could ever find them. Attending dreams had never been her station in life, was not now her station, and still the wish to follow them crashed through her with every heartbeat, pulling her body apart joint by joint, as the cold had done in the oubliette, sinking deeper and deeper into her. Her breath came raw in her throat, hurting, dry sobs accompanied burning eyes. Sickness roiled up, sharp and bitter, and she rolled onto her hands and knees to hack sour mouthfuls onto the floor.

Her fingertips found the seams of tightly placed flagstones. Belinda dug her nails down and inched forward, dragging herself from crack to crack. Duty lay ahead of her. Loyalty to her queen, to Aulun, to her mother, to the throne: all the things she had ever been. Somehow there was blood on her fingers, beneath the nails, but she crept onward, knees scraping, eyes dry, mind screaming protest and duty trumping all.

Steam bathed the laundry hall, comforting to muscles strained with the effort of continuing on. Teeth gritted with anger at her weakness, Belinda pulled herself into a pile of rough warm cloth, undisturbed by the sharp smell of sweat and work clinging to the unwashed clothing.

She was not meant to lose control like that: she ought to have been stronger than the cold that had invaded her core; ought to have been far stronger than the inexplicable war between loyalty and—even then she shied from the word, unwilling, perhaps unable, to name the emotion Javier had awakened in her. It was damnable, whatever it was: Belinda Primrose had spent a lifetime making herself stronger than the things around her; to find herself fallible now was an outrage. To find herself longing for a life other than the one she'd known was inconceivable. There was work to be done, and everything she was, everything she had ever been, everything she would ever be, was bound to that work.

And yet she could not stop *trembling*: her muscles ached with the tremors and her jaw locked from keeping her teeth from clattering together. Laundry maids hauled clothing from around her, cursing at the cloth's unaccountable weight. Desperate, she crawled further into the pile of fabric, burying herself in it and releasing witch-power for more conventional methods of hiding. She had slept in the oubliette, but rest had evaded her; that she could not afford to give into the fresh weakness of warmth and darkness was her last clear thought.

She didn't awaken until weight left her body and cold air brushed over her. She came out of the laundry before a maid's gasp became a scream, one hand slapped over the girl's mouth and her other arm wrapped around her neck, cutting off air. "Scream and you die. What time is it?" She loosened her fingers and the maid caught a tiny, terrified breath of air.

"S-supper, my lady." The appellation made Belinda want to laugh: such deference was so well-bred into the serving classes as to come through even under the most absurd of circumstances. Had she been caught as the poor girl in her arms was, she, too, would have been as polite.

Supper. The day was gone, then, and her chances to make right most everything were slipping away. Sleep had cleared her mind: there were so few things that truly needed doing, and all of them were to be done in the name of duty, not desire. "Has Robert Drake been executed yet?"

The girl shook her head, frantic little motion. Belinda exhaled in quiet relief, then brushed her lips against the girl's cheek. "Do you know who I am, girl?"

She nodded this time, and Belinda clucked her tongue, soft sound of dismay. "You ought to have said no."

Witchpower roared with satisfaction as Belinda cast the girl's naked body away minutes later, blood on her thighs staining the laundry, knotted fabric at her throat hiding any marks Belinda's small hands may have left. She smoothed the dress she'd taken from the girl—it fit well enough—and tucked her hair back, then slipped out of the laundry rooms as a faceless one of many.

AKILINA PANKEJEFF, DVORYANIN
12 January 1588 † *Lutetia*

Akilina descends into the dungeons with her mouth pursed distastefully; it isn't that she fails to understand the necessity of such places, or, indeed, that she's above making use of them. It's that the floors stain the hem of her gown, and the scent seems to linger in her skin for days, even when she bathes with perfumed soaps and has a woman to carefully wash her hair. Still, she believes it wiser to do her own bargaining, and she has an offer in hand that it seems Robert Drake cannot possibly refuse.

She is followed by two strong men, one her own guard, Viktor, and the other some broad-shouldered creature put in place by Sandalia, so that Akilina's polite house arrest might not be slipped. Viktor she does not object to, but the other man irritates her. It's all right; he won't for long.

There are four passageways in the dungeons. One leads deeper down, to where the ordinary dissonants and problem-makers are thrown—literally: the stairs simply stop some ten or fifteen feet below her, a gaping pit beneath them. It's crude, but extremely effective. Many are killed or broken simply by being tossed in, and those who survive turn on one another within a matter of hours. Such is the fate of petty men; it requires intelligence and planning to survive games of treason.

The other three passages lead to oubliettes, a particularly Gallic manner of isolation. Akilina snaps her fingers, sending Viktor and the other guard into the right-hand passage, where the scrape of stone on stone sounds, and then a crashing thud of heavy rock falling back into place. The floor beneath her feet vibrates, and she wonders if Robert Drake and Belinda Primrose can feel the shaking within their prisons.

Viktor exits with a shake of his head; Akilina nods toward the second passage. Moments later he calls, "Here," and she walks delicately into the passage.

Drake squints up at her from the bottom of his pit, and, unexpectedly, chuckles. It looks and sounds painful, though he manages a bow as well, and says, drolly, "Lady Akilina. To what do I owe the pleasure?" He cranes his head again, peering up at her, and she feels a surge of delight at how vulnerable he seems. It's an illusion built by their locations, but that makes it no less appealing.

"I have a proposal for you," she says in Khazarian. Viktor she trusts, but the Gallic guard will run to his queen with word of her intentions, if she lets him. Robert flicks an eyebrow upward and spreads his hands.

"I'm listening."

"You're to die at dawn," she says, which garners a nod from him. No surprise, no dismay, just agreement. She finds that she likes that in him; perhaps it's the same quality she finds delightful in his daughter. "I can save you."

"In exchange for?" His voice is steady; whatever he fears, it's not the threat of being left to die. Akilina crouches, though it means more of her skirt touches the filthy floor, and smiles down at him before murmuring secrets of state and treason into the dark.

BELINDA PRIMROSE
12 January 1588 † *Lutetia*

She had no poison of choice. Such things couldn't be kept in her bedchambers within the palace, and she had no time left to hurry into Lutetia and obtain arsenic or even something less subtle. It ate at her, being unable to leave that final gift in certainty; a healthy pinch would spell Sandalia's death, and leave Belinda free to tear herself from Gallic shores.

Slipping into Sandalia's private chambers was so easy as to bring frustrated tears to Belinda's eyes. She remembered too clearly hours spent watching, waiting, hiding in plain sight, hoping for the chance to steal into other dignitaries' quarters so she might fulfill her duties. A lifetime had been wasted in those petty behaviors, when she might have done what she now could, let shadow cloak her and force eyes to see through her even as she walked between armed guards and perfumed courtiers. She might have lived a life more like the one Javier had been born to, and been all the more secretive for it, as who could believe that a lady raised to the courts might have the skill or the will to thrust a dagger into a man's ribs?

Or a queen's. The thought whispered so softly Belinda barely let herself admit she'd thought it. Ten minutes earlier, while the queen and her courtiers ate supper, Belinda had stood at Sandalia's side, nimble fingers unfastening the catch on the Gallic regent's necklace, so she could slip away the keys that opened Sandalia's twice-locked office drawers. Once more so very *easy*, when she let desperation drive her. Too easy: had the court not expected Belinda Primrose to be buried in an oubliette until dawn, even the call of duty and the power riding her might not have pushed her into taking the risk. If anyone had dreamed she might be free, the shadows she cast around herself might have been breachable; it was only circumstance that allowed such tactics to be put to use. Still, the ease of it all made her burn with frustration and regret for a lifetime of harder choices.

She might so easily have ended it there, taken Sandalia's life in exchange for her own humiliation, but the tiny knife she carried no longer sat at the small of her back. For all its strength, Belinda doubted that witchpower would hide her through the process of strangling a woman with her bare hands. There were other ways to ensure Sandalia's death, and Belinda would be far from the palace by the time they were set in motion.

There was no light beyond frail moon shadows in Sandalia's office. Belinda moved almost blindly, using flawless memory to step around the chairs and find the desk locks in the darkness. The fall of tumblers sounded loud as waterfalls as she opened them, sliding free parchment that condemned the queen with her own hand. Not just one queen, but two: Irina would not emerge unscathed, either, even if she denied with all vehemence that Akilina spoke on her behalf. Belinda leafed through the papers in the dim light, watching for the royal seal, then set them on the desktop, satisfied as she closed the drawer again.

Another few minutes' work picked the first lock carefully, triggering the glistening needle. She used the hem of her dress to slip the poisoned dart free, bringing it to her nose to sniff and place the poison by its scent. It had none discernible; the glistening material was likely to carry the poison, rather than be it. Pleasure curved her mouth and she smeared the stuff on the fabric before reaching for the elegant glass that sat on Sandalia's desk. She wiped her hem around its edge, lacing it with poison, then tested the second lock to find another dart that she dropped into the nearest wine decanter. Sandalia's papers would be protected with something strong. A thief caught by poison and able to talk was more useful than a dead one, but a dead man was better than one who managed to escape. Sandalia would not dare lose state secrets to a chance at survival.

It was a pity Akilina couldn't be expected to share the queen's glass, but that was a dish best served cold; time would prove a chance to taste it. Belinda gathered up the parchment, a chill lifting hairs on her arms as if her very skin understood the import of what she touched, and she slipped toward the door, heart quick with triumph.

It opened before she touched it, sending her back into shadows with a smothered gasp that turned to a soft, incredulous laugh. "Robert?"

Her father, gratifyingly, flinched, then turned his head to gaze through darkness and find her unerringly. Belinda let witchpower go, feeling suddenly bright against the night, a beacon, and a smile turned one corner of Robert's mouth. "So this is where you've gotten to, Primrose. I checked the dungeons." His hand dipped into his vest—his clothes were still torn and stained, but he had straightened them on his body, made himself as presentable as a beaten man could be—and withdrew it again, silver glinting across his palm. "You seem to have lost something."

Another laugh broke from Belinda's throat as she took the dagger from Robert's hand. "Thank you. How did you . . . ?"

"I might ask you the same question, but neither is one to be addressed here. You have the treaties." He took in her bundled armload with a pleased glance. "How wonderful. My temporary employer will be so disappointed. Return to Aulun, Belinda. Show Lorraine what you carry, and know that your work here will force a war to change everything." He gave her a quick nod, turning away.

"Father." Belinda's voice broke as it followed him. He turned back, arching an eyebrow, and she took a step toward him, crushing the papers against her chest. It was not the time; he was right. There would be another chance to ask the questions only he could answer. She knew patience; it was the only virtue she might call her own. Despite that, the words scraped out.

"I *remember,* Robert. I remember Dmitri and the night you said it was too soon and came into my room to put a wall in my mind. I *remember.*" Surprise darkened Robert's eyes; surprise and something else: a hint of respect, perhaps, and a touch of dismay. Belinda's breath came short, need sparking off her so that she could nearly see it, golden fizzles of light born of her will alone. "All my life I've done Aulun's bidding. I'm my mother's creature; I'm yours. But what *am* I?"

A smile had begun to crease his beard. It fell away at her precise words, at mention of her mother, and Belinda fought down the urge to hawk and spit with frustration. "My mother," she repeated. "I know that, too. I always have, since the day du Roz died. I *remember,* Robert. Titian curls. Grey eyes, a pale face. *I remember my birth.* How can I? What am I?"

Now the smile returned, covering pride and astonishment, and her father touched her cheek, gentle paternal action. "You are my daughter." He nodded, still smiling, and she felt within him the same flex of will that Javier could command: a nearly unconscious expectation that no one would question him, or stand before his desires. She had once stood against Javier's whim, not cowering; it had been enough, then. It no longer was.

She stepped forward again, catching his arm with more strength than she knew she had, her fingers digging into his biceps. He dropped his gaze to her grasp, then lifted it again to meet her eyes with cool expectation.

Belinda's lip curled and she tightened her grip, rage and fear and witchpower boiling up in her. "*Father.*" Her throat ached from vehemence. "*What am I?*"

"You would not understand if I told you—"

Belinda let the parchment fall, clapping her freed hand to his face, almost a slap. Images, memories, words, all of them meaningless, shattered through her power: a creature vaster than any she'd ever imagined, sinuous and scaled, dangerous alien intelligence in its gaze. Respect beyond the profound for that monster; respect that was so inherent to her father that he literally could not live without it.

That respect, transferred in some peculiar fashion to Lorraine Walter, and wry amusement at human weakness.

A dragon in the stars, and a sleek silver thing that Robert's mind called a *ship*, though it could no more sail on the seas than Belinda herself could. It rode on the wind, and in the black spaces of the sky above.

Pain, so incredible it could only mean death, and then the mewling, horrible weakness of an infant's form.

A circle in the sky, like the moon, but blue and green and swirled with white. Ambition toward that sphere: clear focus, a deliberate plan.

Robert's will roared up, white and hard as a blow, no comforting scent of chypre in it, but only intent to break the drain of thought and memory. Belinda staggered back under the strength of his desire, head pounding, witchpower subdued. "I told you," he said gently, all the dominance and authority of his will disappeared, "that you would not understand. You have a purpose, Primrose. Let knowing that be enough for now."

"It will not always be enough." Belinda kept her voice low for fear rage would break through otherwise. Robert breathed a laugh, nodding.

"So I now see." He crouched, gathering papers, then offered them up to her from the subordinate position, curious smile still shaping his mouth. "Answers will come, my Primrose. You have time. And you must return to Aulun now. Lorraine will need you, and better for you both to be far away from Lutetia when Sandalia dies. I'll give you a week to be safely home before I act."

"I already have." Belinda looked toward Sandalia's desk, then took the parchment Robert had collected. "She'll sip from a poisoned cup soon enough, and Lorraine will see the papers that forgive her for condemning a sister-queen to death."

Startled admiration wrinkled Robert's forehead and he inclined his head after a moment, as much homage as she'd seen him pay any woman save a queen. "Then my journeys take me elsewhere, and you will learn to stand in my place at Lorraine's side for a time, Primrose." He straightened, then stepped forward to place a kiss on Belinda's brow, looking down at her with amusement and pride. "You'll do well," he promised, and his voice lightened with mirth: "After all, your nurse taught you to be clever. Now go," he murmured, and Belinda could not say if it was his will or her own that drew shadows around her, and propelled her toward escape.

ROBERT, LORD DRAKE
13 January 1588 † *Lutetia*

Only one thing remains to be done, and she is waiting for him. Composed, standing above the city in a sumptous tower, wearing one of the flowing new gowns in an off-shade of red, too much orange licking it to look well on most women. On her, it is magnificent, and even with her back to him, the gown's shape makes her look younger than she is. Robert knows why she's done it, and part of him even admires her for it, but as he lets himself in to her bower, it doesn't move him. Not enough.

She doesn't turn away from the city view. Her hair, lush and dark and falling free, makes a cloak over her shoulders that he imagines wards off some of winter's chill. If the circumstances were different, he might let himself bury his hands in it, inhale its scent, and be drowned in the pleasure of it all.

Instead, from the door, he says, "Why?" It's not important, but he's surprised at how badly he would like to know, surprised at how deeply these fragile, clever humans can touch him.

And she says, in a lighter voice than he's heard her use before, "They offered me something you couldn't."

"Your life." Oh, how he has fallen. He shouldn't have said even so much. Rue, or perhaps some closer cousin to distress, curves Robert's mouth, though he won't let himself look down. That would be too much; too weak, and that he cannot, or will not, allow himself.

She turns then, amusement and wonder in her eyes, and he holds in a flinch, knowing far too well that he should not have spoken. It's a long moment before she says, "That," as if it doesn't matter, and she's right, for it doesn't, and then lifts her left hand, where a heavy signet ring weights the third finger. "That, and this."

There's no guilt in the courtesan's gaze, and Robert is quiet a while as he takes in what the ring means to him, and what it means to Ana. "A friend to the crown of Gallin," he finally says, slowly. "What of Aulun, Ana?"

She shrugs, beautiful motion that ripples her hair and the light folds of her gown. "What of it? You've never really understood, Robert. I'm a courtesan, and a man came to me with an offer. Live like a duchess at Sandalia's bidding, or die at his hands a whore. There's no choice in that, my love. There's no choice at all."

Fog creeps over Robert's thoughts, making them thick and dull and slow. He cannot recall—and his memory is excellent—that Ana has ever used those words before. *My love.* Too much has changed too quickly, and for the first time he wonders if Dmitri was right, and he, Robert, is losing control.

He is *clearly* losing control, for there's the question of Javier, born to the power that Robert and Belinda and Dmitri all share, but born outside of Robert's awareness, raised outside of certain schools of thought and indoctrination. Oh, yes, he *is* losing control, but that, that is a thing to be dealt with later. Tonight there is only one thing left to do, and she stands before him, waiting on his silence.

Which he breaks with a confession that is unlike him: voice grating and low, he says, "I do not understand."

"Of course you do." Ana has a deep voice, but tonight, still, it's peculiarly light. Breathless, but not with ecstacy or laughter. More as though she dares not take too deep a breath, for fear it will cut her, and she does not want to spend her last hours in pain.

Then, suddenly, he *does* understand. Fog clears, his mind sharpening, and unexpected regret turns to a knife's edge within him. "Which is it, then? That you wished not to die a whore, or wished not to die at his hands?"

"Oh," Ana says, still lightly, "I wished neither, my love, but having had to choose, I chose not to die for him. It's a small thing," she says much more softly, and Robert suddenly realises they're speaking Parnan; that they have been since he entered the room. There should be the sounds of the canals around them; there should be voices lifted in laughter and anger and life from the waterways. That's how it should be, but it never will be, never again. "It's a small thing," Ana repeats, "but in the end, it seemed to be everything."

Robert's heart contracts. It's only a few steps across the room, long hard steps, but only a few, and he takes them swiftly, catching the striking beauty in his arms. She cries out, a quiet shocked sound, and he covers her mouth with his just briefly, before kneeling with her.

Off-orange fabric settles around them slowly, darker now in places, wet and sticky. She's silent, and he admires her for that even as she lifts fingertips to brush his lips, and then, strength spent, lets her hand fall again. He holds her, and at the last, breathes in the scent of her hair after all, and then rises, silently, to leave death behind.

JAVIER, PRINCE OF GALLIN
13 January 1588 † *Lutetia, the docks*

He has gone to some measure to disguise himself, his ginger hair darkened not with dye but with soot and ashes: it is a more temporary guise than he might like, but grey and black catch the light more naturally than pure black dye, and it only needs to work for a few hours. He has no especial skill at changing his weight with clever clothes, but he has packed both coin and food into a roll at his belt, thickening his slender hips. There is padding in the shoulders of his cloak, making him bulkier, and he can, at the least, take the street vowels he learned so well from Eliza and apply them to his voice. He remembers streaks of dirt on Beatrice's face as he drew her from the oubliette, and has mimicked them on his own, shadows changing the line of his jaw. It is not a perfect disguise, but it is enough to let him walk the docks late at night without notice.

There's a ship already on the horizon, black shape against the stars as it sails against the wind. That wind carries the scent of the sea, the heavy unpleasantness of rotten fish and saltwater, and Javier is certain that there is no hint of perfume, carried from the horizon, on that breeze. He is certain, and yet. And yet.

The tide has long since turned, and Beatrice has not come to him. *Beatrice,* he thinks; *no: Belinda.* It's an irrational conclusion, that Beatrice would have come to him but Belinda Primrose would not, and it is the only one he can bear.

Morning comes, and Beatrice does not. Head lowered, heart empty, Javier, prince of Gallin, climbs aboard a ship bound for Isidro in Essandia, there to seek his uncle's counsel, and sails with the dawn.

to be continued in
The Pretender's Crown

Acknowledgments

There are a handful of people from the RMFW who deserve particular and specific acknowledgments: Jessica Wulf, who ran the Colorado Gold writing contest for ten years, and during whose tenure I first placed in, then won, that contest; Monica Poole, who, at the beginning of my first Colorado Gold conference, gave me the most pointed and necessary critique my writing had ever received; Margie Lawson, whose incredible seminars helped me understand how to address Monica's critiques; and Karen Duvall, whose friendship and enthusiasm I never would have known without the RMFW.

It's an aphorism among writers that booksellers are your best friends, as they're the ones who give individual recommendations and get customers to actually buy our books. Duane Wilkins of the University Bookstore in Seattle, Washington, whether he knew it or not, went one step further and helped lay down the path that sold this book to the publisher. Now *that's* a friend!

Sarah Palmero and Stella Evans read and critiqued the first two hundred pages of *The Queen's Bastard,* and their response gave me hope that I could write in this wholly different style. Ted, as usual, was serenely confident of my ability to do so; it's good to have a husband who Believes. :) Not all of my usual suspects had time to finish the book, but Trent did, so my hat's off to you, too.

I do believe I may have made my agent, Jennifer Jackson, forget she was working and stay up too late reading this manuscript. That's pretty much the best compliment ever, and then on top of that she had insightful comments toward revision. Thanks, Jenn.

Finally, I'm still giddy over working with my editor, Betsy Mitchell. Betsy's a rock star, and the opportunity to write for her is the dream of a lifetime.

C. E. MURPHY lived for many years in Alaska before moving to Ireland. She is the author of the Walker Papers series and the Negotiator trilogy. Her hobbies include swimming, walking, traveling, and drawing.